TAKEN FROM HER HOME

A pulse-pounding Detective April Fisher crime thriller

C.J. GRAYSON

DS April Fisher Thrillers Book 2

Joffe Books, London
www.joffebooks.com

First published in Great Britain in 2024

© C.J. Grayson 2024

Cover art by Nick Castle

ISBN: 978-1-83526-355-6

CHAPTER 1

Just before 11 p.m., Mary Steadman sat patiently as the electronic double gates parted with a mechanical hum. Her delicate, manicured hands rested on the steering wheel of her brand-new Mercedes as she eyed the long winding driveway of her expensive home, partly lit up by the brilliant white headlights of the car she'd only bought last week.

When the gate fully opened and the mechanical sound faded into the night, she edged forward, maintaining a steady five miles an hour towards her extravagant, four-bedroom detached house. Behind her, the gates closed, and she guided the car down the narrow road lined with intelligent low-level lighting that brightened when they detected motion nearby. On either side of the road were freshly cut grass and exquisite gardens, bordered with wooden planters filled with every flower known to man.

It had been a long day for Mary, attending numerous meetings. For the last few hours, she'd sat at the head of the table in the conference room, listening to the board of directors explaining the lifetime benefits of an upcoming potential project. She was tired, glad to be home. She had to look over the plans for the charity event the company was planning next month.

The Merc reached the end of the winding drive, entering the vast open space of fine, compacted gravel near the house. She spotted the light on in her bedroom window and the gentle glow from the hallway lamp through the front door's glass. Arriving at a dark, empty house wasn't something she enjoyed doing, so she hoped to deter potential burglars by having those two lights on. It was coming up to almost two years since men had broken into her old home and attacked her, leaving her feeling violated and vulnerable ever since. The first thing she'd done the day she moved in was get a high-tech security company to install cameras around the house.

She stopped the car in her usual spot in front of the living room bay window, applied the handbrake and turned off the engine. A familiar silence enveloped her, and the food resting on the passenger seat smelled delicious. It was sometimes nice having quiet nights to herself when her husband, Gary, a business sales rep who travelled the country doing presentations to hi-tech businesses on improving their selling strategies, was away. He was due back early tomorrow and had suggested going out for a meal somewhere but said it was a surprise.

She shivered because of the December temperatures, and leaned over to the passenger seat, picking up the bag of food and a bottle of Diet Coke. Opening the door, she stepped out into the late, cool winter air. With one last glance down her driveway to make sure the gates had closed, she turned—

She froze, feeling an unsettling glowing inside. She focused, sure she'd seen something unusual that didn't quite fit.

'What . . . ?' Her voice was an uncertain whisper.

Squinting in the darkness at the gate, she watched intently with wide eyes, sure she'd seen the shape of something or someone lurking. After so long, seeing no movement, she smiled and shook her head, knowing she was letting her tired imagination run wild.

There was no one there, only immaculate lawns, sleeping flowers, and a closed gate. She was safe, Mary told herself.

Just before inserting the key into her door, her phone rang in her pocket. 'Jesus Christ!' she muttered, the sound disturbing the serenity around her. Pulling it out, she noticed the call was coming from a number she didn't recognise.

She accepted the call, raised it to her ear, trapping the phone between her head and shoulder, and opened the door with one hand while carrying the food and drink in the other. 'Hello?' she said into the phone, stepping into the warmth of the hallway.

The caller was silent.

'Hello?' she repeated, closing the door, and locking it. 'Hello?' Her tone became quieter, more reserved, the confidence fading as the caller remained silent.

Mary lowered her hand to see the screen to ensure she was still connected to the call.

'Hello, who's there?'

'. . . Nee for . . .'

She frowned. 'Sorry? Hello?'

'Ken . . . pore too.'

'Hello?' She pulled her phone away to check the call's signal. Four bars, so it had a full signal. She sighed heavily.

She hung up the phone, walked down the hall, entered her huge kitchen, and placed her things on the worktop to the right.

'Tim, turn on the lights, please,' she said.

'*Lights on,*' the automated voice known as Tim replied from a speaker above her. Within a flash, six dazzling spotlights illuminated her white marble kitchen. It looked so classy it was fit for a magazine. Clean white tiles made up the floor, reflecting the bright spots above, surrounding a colossal island where her sink and drainer were, along with two cookers and gas hobs. The right side of the kitchen consisted of a row of gloss-finished cupboards, both above and below. The end of the kitchen had a set of French doors leading to the rear of the property, where she'd stand to watch the world go by in the mornings, usually sipping her first coffee of the

3

day. The left side contained a side door and a large window with blinds that were custom-made to fit perfectly.

She'd named the male voice Tim after her father. He had died three years earlier; he never had the chance to see her become the managing director of such a prestigious company and move to such a house. He'd have been proud, she hoped. Saying his name daily was something to remember him by. The large circular clock fixed to the wall on the left between the door and the window informed her it was just after 11 p.m. She had hoped, after the conference meeting had finished at 10 p.m., she'd be home sooner, but she hadn't been able to resist the temptation of a burger and fries on the way back. One last treat before her diet started again tomorrow, something she'd heard in her head too many times.

Grabbing a plate from one of the top cupboards and a knife and fork from the drawer, she carried it all over to the huge table, then dropped into a seat and started eating. The circular wooden table could comfortably seat six and did so when friends were invited over for wine and gossip, but each time she ate alone, it reminded her of her solitude and long working hours.

When her phone rang again, she jolted forward, almost choking on the mouthful of burger she was chewing. She stood and darted over the tiles towards the worktop where the phone was, recognising it was the same caller as before.

Unsure what to do, she decided to answer it. 'What?'

Again the caller didn't say anything.

'Listen, it's past eleven at night. You can't—'

'I can . . .'

'You can . . . what?'

'I can . . .'

She was angry now, standing with a scowl on her face, the phone pressed against her ear. 'Who is this? What do you want?'

'I want you . . .' The voice was more precise now — a man's voice.

'Go away!' she screamed, ending the call, slamming her phone down on the worktop. Shaking, thinking about what happened nearly two years ago, she turned, noticing both kitchen window blinds still open. Unable to see anything but darkness, she was shaken up, thinking the worst.

'Tim, close the kitchen blinds. Now!'

'*Kitchen blinds closing,*' Tim's calm automated voice replied, then the blinds lowered simultaneously until they covered the whole of the windows. Feeling slightly relieved, she returned to the table and struggled through her meal, her fingers trembling as she picked at the fries and burger.

The man who had been watching her through the window for the past few minutes smiled. After the blinds lowered, he put the phone back into his pocket. He leaned forward and whispered, 'I want you.' His warm breath created a small circle of condensation on the surface of the glass.

CHAPTER 2

DS April Fisher glanced at her watch. Time to go. Not only was it late, but she'd also had a few glasses of wine.

'Please, stay a little longer,' her sister Freya pleaded, noticing her being conscious of the time.

'It's getting late, Freya . . . I need to be up in the morning for work.'

Her younger sister smiled, leaned across the sofa, and gently squeezed her hand. 'It's not late.' There was a short silence. 'Plus, I haven't seen you in ages, sis. You've been working so much recently. I've enjoyed spending time with you tonight. Do you like the tree? I put it up today.'

Fisher looked over at the Christmas tree. It was simple in decoration, but classy.

'It's very nice.'

'Yours up yet?'

Fisher smiled. 'You know I don't mess around with decorations. It's pointless. I'm never at home.'

'You're getting more miserable the older you become, April.'

They shared a smile.

Freya's living room and kitchen were in the same room, each claiming half the space. The living area had a small three-seater sofa that could fit two people comfortably, a round coffee table and a television fixed to the wall at the other end. The Christmas tree was at the middle of the longest wall opposite the door, with a large door to the right that opened onto a tiny balcony overlooking the car park two levels below. Although the kitchen area was compact, it had everything she needed, including a little circular dining table.

'So, you met anyone yet?' asked Freya.

It had been over three weeks since the sisters had spoken on the phone, maybe five weeks since they'd seen each other, and that occasion — the funeral of a distant aunt — hadn't been very intimate. Given they were so close, living less than four miles away, Fisher realised she needed to relax more and take a break, giving the people she cared for extra time and love. Fisher wasn't married. She was, however, in some ways, married to her job as a detective sergeant for the Greater Manchester Police force. The category of 'men' wasn't her expertise. Multiple bad experiences where the partners were cheating bastards or decent men carrying complicated baggage had been too much for Fisher, so she decided enough was enough. But what had sealed the deal for her current mentality was the miscarriage last year. She had been pregnant for six happy months until one day, she had started bleeding. Over a week, the bleeding became heavier, and the baby had sadly died. Her boyfriend at the time, a builder called Chris, in his late thirties, had told her from day one he had wanted children. He was over the moon when she had fallen pregnant and was excited about becoming a father. He had moved in with her after a year of them seeing each other, and things were going extremely well. But after the unfortunate miscarriage, he had become angry, blaming her for losing the baby. He decided to leave her in search of someone who wasn't at work all the time. Crushed, she had decided not to get too close to another man to prevent it from ever happening again.

Fisher shook her head. 'No time for a man. Anyway, how's your new bloke? Hope he's treating you right?'

Freya had finally saved enough money from working two jobs; she'd put a deposit down on a flat and moved out last month. At the age of twenty-nine, she knew, as well as their parents, it was time to stand on her own two feet and have her own space. The flat itself wasn't perfect. There was no denying it needed a little TLC, but being close to the city, it was ideal for Freya. She'd met a man online three weeks ago. They'd been on three dates, and so far he'd been a gentleman, according to Freya, not trying to get her in the sack within the first half hour of meeting. Fisher, being a police officer, was sceptical of everyone she met. Since joining the police when she was nineteen, Fisher, now thirty-five, had seen her fair share of what people were capable of.

Freya smiled widely. 'I think I'm in love, you know.'

Fisher edged forward, swatting her sister's forearm with a palm. 'Don't be ridiculous — you've known him less than two minutes, girl!'

'I know, I know . . .' she confessed with a shrug.

It was good to see Freya move out of their parents' house — God, it was about time. For years, Freya had had money given to her whenever she needed it, even when she was at uni studying to be a vet, which had turned out to be a waste of her time and their parents' money. Whereas Fisher had moved out in her early twenties, fending for herself and using her own money.

'I'll have to meet him soon, Freya. I can't have my sister seeing any old bloke.'

'He's not old — he's not even forty yet.'

Fisher raised her glass to finish the dark red liquid. She didn't usually drink red wine; she never usually drank any wine. If she were to have a drink, her choice would be vodka and Coke. 'You spoke to Mum?'

Before answering, Freya finished her wine, then lowered the glass. 'You want some more wine?'

Fisher shook her head, knowing Freya was avoiding the question.

'Have you spoken to Mum?'

Freya glanced away, focusing on her lap, breathing deeply. At the funeral they had all attended five weeks ago, Freya and their mother, Freda, had got into an argument about money. Naïve to the costs of moving out and paying solicitors and other such fees, it had left her short, unable to put down a deposit for a holiday with her friends next year. It was the first time their mum had said no to her demands, telling her she'd be there to help but not for unnecessary things like holidays. Freya was used to getting what she wanted, so she had claimed that their parents didn't love her anymore and been labelled ridiculous and childish before she had stormed out. It had been humiliating.

'I'm embarrassed about what happened at the funeral,' admitted Freya.

'Mum's owed an apology.' Fisher held her stare.

A half-hearted nod from Freya. 'I'll call her tomorrow.'

Fisher leaned forward and placed her glass on the coffee table. Freya's phone screen lit up on the arm of the chair. She picked it up to read the message, and Fisher watched as her eyes brightened. In a way, her sister reminded her much of herself. They were almost identical: slim, with dark hair down to their shoulders, and around five feet seven. The most significant distinguishing feature was that Fisher had big, alluring brown eyes, whereas Freya's eyes were blue.

'That the boyfriend again?'

Freya smiled knowingly, unlocking the phone, her attractive youthful face lighting up with a gentle blue haze. 'It is . . .'

'I'll leave you to it.' Fisher stood, bent over, and kissed the top of her sister's head while she focused on her phone. 'You look after yourself.' She pointed at the screen. 'Get to know this bloke more. I'm serious; you barely know him.'

'Don't worry about me.'

Before Fisher left the room, she went to the window and looked out onto the road below. She was wearing her usual work attire — dark blue jeans, a white blouse, and a dark blue jacket. From the double glass door leading to the small balcony, she could hear loud music playing from somewhere. Several windows in the opposite block were full of lights and dancing figures at a party of some kind.

One thing Fisher was usually good at — or perhaps it had become second nature thanks to her job— was being aware of her surroundings. A minute later, she walked down the apartment block stairs, smelling something musty in the air, possibly the trail of wet feet on the carpet from the earlier rain. She closed the main door to the building gently, respectful of residents, and stepped out into the cold, damp air. The sky above was so dark it was as if there was a thick, black sheet over Manchester. Not a single star was visible.

Passing her Volvo XC90 parked in one of the visitors' bays, she double-clicked her fob to ensure it was locked and placed her keys back into her pocket. Striding away from the apartments, she got out her phone and called DS Matthew Phillips.

'Ready?' he answered.

'Yeah, I'm walking to the end of the street now.'

She hung up the phone, and after reaching the end of the road, she stopped at the kerb, glanced both ways at the junction. A few cars passed but there was no one walking. Knowing DS Phillips would only be a few minutes, she decided to check her emails and catch up with her social media. Although under the influence of a few glasses of wine, she had noticed the two men sitting in the black Mondeo, watching her as she passed them. She then heard them get out of the car and follow her, with only one thing on their minds.

CHAPTER 3

Once she'd spoken to her friend about the random caller, Mary Steadman hung up, went upstairs, and placed her phone down on her bedside table. The spotlights in the bedroom were too bright, so she asked Tim to dull them while she sat on the edge of the queen-sized bed and tiredly undressed, placing her smart work attire in a tidy pile. In her underwear, she sighed heavily, exhausted from her day but feeling happier after speaking with Stacey — a friend she'd known nearly thirty years — who had told her not to worry about the prank call.

Mary had done well for herself, studying at night to get her degree in business studies, then working her way up to managing director of a multi-million-pound company.

She got up from the bed, went into the en suite, and turned on the shower. After removing her underwear, she stepped into the warmth of the falling water and sighed with relief. It was her favourite time of day. Indulging in the heavenly waterfall, washing her slim body with lavender-scented shower gel. She liked keeping to a routine; living in such a way kept her focused and motivated. Generally, by 9 p.m., once showered, she'd go downstairs, grab a paperback from her bookcase and sit down to read. She wasn't really into alcohol much these days.

She turned the water off, thinking about tomorrow—

The light in the en suite cut off, leaving her in total darkness. She looked over at the bedroom doorway. Darkness.

'Shit,' she muttered, trying to remember where the nearest towel was hanging and, more to the point, where her phone was so she could use the torch. She shuffled across the shower tray with her hands out in front of her, feeling herself about to hyperventilate. She stepped out onto the thick mat, grabbed the towel, and dried herself. She wrapped the towel around her and went into the bedroom. There was just enough light coming through the crack in the curtain at the far wall to see the large bed in front of her. She stopped near the bedside table and reached for her phone, running her fingertips across the surface of the wood.

'Where is it?' she whispered, unable to feel it.

In the middle of the carpet to her left, the sound of a text message beeped, startling her. The phone's screen lit up, dimly lighting the small space around it, lending a faint glow to her wardrobes, dressing table, and her coats on the hook near the corner.

She took a breath, trying to control her rising pulse. She knew she had put the phone on the table. Unless it had fallen off and somehow managed to roll across the carpet on its own while she was showering, but she was clutching at straws. Slowly and carefully, not wanting to make a sound, Mary made her way to the phone, bent down, and picked it up, the screen's glare dazzling her eyes as she unlocked it.

She read the message.

You're not alone in this room.

Her heart missed a beat, realising the meaning of the words. She looked around, trying to spot something, then her eyes eventually fell on the shape standing in front of the curtain.

Whoever it was, the figure was broad and tall, much bigger than she was.

She dropped her phone, which bounced off her toes and came to rest near her feet, but she was cemented to the spot, staring at the figure watching her, not daring to move, hoping the longer she watched it, the sooner it would go, like a figment of her weary imagination.

'Tim,' she whispered, the words almost getting clogged in her throat. 'Turn on the lights . . .'

'*Electronic voice activation is disabled,*' the voice calmly said from the speaker.

'Tim, turn—'

'Tim won't be helping you, Mary. It's just me and you now,' the deep voice said near the curtain, sending a chill down her spine.

Before she could react, the figure moved away from the curtain, disappearing into the darkness for a moment. Frozen, she felt the fear of adrenaline shoot through her. A second later, she felt pressure on the floor near her, but it was too late. Something snatched at her arm, then a cloth filled with an awful, foul smell was shoved into her face, covering her nose and mouth. After her legs gave way, her mind went black and she collapsed onto the carpet.

CHAPTER 4

The men from the Mondeo were both tall. One wore a matching black tracksuit and dark grey trainers and had a thin goatee. He walked with more of a swagger than the other, swinging his bony shoulders in the night breeze towards the end of the road. The other, who was slightly thicker in stature, glanced sideways at his friend to make sure he was ready for what was about to happen.

They both understood the task.

Grab her, put her in the car, and take her somewhere.

They'd been waiting a while in the Mondeo, knowing at some point, with the number of parties going on in nearby apartments, they'd get their chance with someone. It wasn't that the area was rough or known for its crime, but with many young couples and singletons occupying the flats, drinking too much and playing their music beyond what was considered neighbourly, there would no doubt be a vulnerable, lonely woman walking home.

On their approach, they eyed DS Fisher like two lions approaching a gazelle as she stood on the path's edge, gazing down at her phone. The thinner one slowly pushed his hand into his pocket and pulled out a penknife. With a thumb and finger from his other hand, he released the three-inch blade.

The other man watched him, then focused back on Fisher, seemingly unaware of them approaching.

They were close now.

'I'll grab her,' whispered the one without the knife.

The penknife man nodded once, keeping his dark eyes on Fisher's back.

It wasn't the first time they'd done this; they'd practised many times, had dozens of victims. They'd waited over two hours tonight for someone to walk out of the flats. When Fisher had walked by, it was their chance.

Light on their feet, almost a metre away, the man on the right raised his hand to grab Fisher's shoulder as the man with the knife readied himself to threaten her, make her go with them without a fuss. They'd take her back to the car, put her in, and drive somewhere secluded, where no one could see what went on. Afterwards, they'd drive away, leaving her feeling used and abused. They felt no shame doing it, nor did they care.

As the man's bony fingers reached for the fabric on Fisher's dark blue suit jacket, she spun around and with the pepper spray in her hand, she aimed it into his eyes and squeezed the trigger, covering most of his face. He jerked back a few steps, putting his hands to his face, immediately feeling the stinging, intense pain, temporarily blinded.

The man with the knife froze, unsure of what was happening.

Fisher turned to him, aimed for his face, and pressed down on the canister.

The man threw his arms up to defend himself, but it was too late; the liquid was already in his eyes, attacking the epithelial layers of his corneas.

'Fuck!' he cried, backing away from her, fighting the extreme agony.

Across the road, DS Matthew Phillips and PC Ashleigh Baan jumped out of their car and ran over, handcuffs ready. Parked further down, PC Adam Jackson and PC Joel Cairn leaped out of their unmarked car and bolted towards them.

Phillips and Baan wrestled the one without the knife to the ground, managing to turn him over and keep him still for long enough to get the cuffs on. Jackson and Cairn approached the one with the knife more cautiously, who had his hands up to his face but was potentially deadly with the knife still in his possession.

'You bitch!' he screamed as the effects of the pepper spray intensified. The nearby music had temporarily quietened; up in the windows of nearby apartments, curious silhouettes leaned from windows to see the commotion on the street.

He attempted to open his eyes but screamed doing so.

'You got him?' Fisher asked Jackson.

Jackson kept his focus on the thug and assured her he had.

'Careful,' she warned him.

The other man was held down to the floor, hands cuffed behind him, still moaning about the pepper spray. Phillips and Baan hauled him up as if he weighed nothing and marched him over to one of the cars.

It was obvious to Fisher that the man with the knife, although he couldn't see around him, wouldn't go down as easily. He started flaying his knifed hand wildly, swooping in huge arcs, hoping to slice something.

Jackson got Cairn's attention with a quick hand, signalling something to him. Cairn nodded in understanding, moving around to the left. Jackson moved to the right. By this time, Baan had returned, leaving Phillips near the car with the other one. The man with the knife was cornered against the fence of the end house; he wasn't going anywhere.

The area was now silent, the nearby residents seeming to realise what was happening, especially with the appearance of uniformed police and a maniac waving a knife through the air.

'Sir, we're going to need you to drop the knife,' Fisher said loud and clearly.

The man turned towards her voice. 'Piss off, bitch. My eyes! My eyes!' The figure lunged forward, obviously thinking Fisher was closer than she was, and swung the blade in another huge arc, slicing nothing but the cold winter air.

'If necessary,' said Fisher, 'we will use force against you.'

'Try it!' hissed the man, taking another wild swoop, again hitting nothing. 'Where are you?'

His eyes were red, puffy, and inflamed. Opening them caused more pain than keeping them shut. He wouldn't beat four officers in combat, certainly not being unable to see, but he'd do his best to hurt as many of them as possible.

Fisher took several steps towards him.

'Wait!' pleaded Baan, noticing her movement.

Hearing her footsteps, the man lashed again. He missed, but Fisher grew closer.

'No, don't!' screamed Jackson.

Fisher, who was only a few feet away, stamped on the ground near him, then lightly took a step back, moving to the left. The thug leaped forward, the knife sweeping through the air again. During his attempt to knife her, Fisher came in from the side and kicked him hard in the knee with the sole of her boot, causing him to cry out in pain, his knee buckling sideways until he was off balance and on the ground on one knee. The knife dropped from his hand, bouncing a few feet until it came to rest near the kerb. Within seconds, Jackson and Cairn were on top of him, turning him over and dragging his arms around to the base of his back.

'You bitch!' he shouted with his face against the concrete.

'Cuff him. Take him away,' Fisher said calmly, then moved away.

Once Jackson had him cuffed, they picked him up and took him to the other car.

'Well, that was stupid, April.'

Fisher turned to Phillips, who stood there staring at her in awe.

'What was that?' He shook his head.

She frowned and shrugged. 'What?'

'*What?*' He threw his hands out at her. 'You were unarmed, April. You had no uniform on, no vest, nothing. He could have killed you.'

She glared at him but said nothing.

'Have you been drinking?'

She didn't reply, instead looked away to where PC Jackson was putting the man inside the unmarked car.

'How much?'

Silently, she fell into a gaze, pulling her focus away from him.

'April?' He was louder this time, more persistent.

'A few glasses of wine, that's all. Been to see my sister.'

He raised a hand and put it on her shoulder, then moved closer so no one else could hear. 'This needs to stop, April.'

Without replying, she removed his hand from her shoulder, swivelled away from him, and started along the path.

'Where are you going?'

She turned to face him. 'Home.'

He glanced at his watch. 'April, don't be silly; it's late.'

'Don't worry about me. I'm a big girl. I'll see you in the morning.' She turned, walked off into the cool, late Manchester air in the direction of home, and never looked back.

CHAPTER 5

It was 8 a.m. Fisher was on her second coffee by the time DS Phillips walked in wearing his usual knee-length brown coat. The trademark that went everywhere with him, whatever the time of year. Luckily, with it being December, he didn't look as ridiculous as he did in July.

'Morning.' His voice was quiet. He removed his coat, hung it on the back of his desk chair, and sat down.

'Morning, Matthew.'

She drained her coffee and leaned forward, placing it on the desk.

He turned to her. 'Listen . . . I'm sorry about last night. I was harsh with you. I didn't mean how it came across. You weren't on duty. You had every right to have a drink.' She silently stared at him, waiting for more. 'I-I . . .'

She placed a hand on his arm. 'It's fine.' She removed it slowly and straightened her posture. 'I shouldn't have had anything to drink at my sister's. I know we had a plan. You're just looking out for me like you always are. I get it. And I'm sorry I walked off.'

'Make it home alright?'

'I was attacked by a gang of field mice but managed to keep them at bay.'

They shared a smile. Phillips, even in the chair, was much higher than Fisher. At six foot two, he was taller than most. His slim physique, pointy nose, and small glasses that shrank his light-blue eyes made him look even geekier than he was. He wasn't always a hit with the ladies but had charm that was, to an extent, quite charismatic. He'd worked with Fisher for years, starting around the same time as she did; although he was two years older, they'd followed the same path, starting as a constable, successfully patrolling the streets of Manchester before expressing an interest in CID. Their superior at the time, who knew they were made for something else, had approved the transfer without hesitation, wishing them the best in their careers. After four years as DCs, they had had been promoted to detective sergeants under the supervision of DI Thomas James, who'd been there longer than they had.

'The most important thing is that we got them,' Phillips noted. 'How many potential cases do we have against them?'

She picked up the file in front of her, opened it, and scanned the report. 'More than twenty victims who tell us the same thing.'

The two men, who they'd labelled as the Night Stalkers, had been kidnapping women for months now. It was the same scenario every time. A woman walking alone in a quiet street. One of the victims, who the men had taken to a field to rape, had remembered half of their registration plate when they had driven away. Traffic police put the details into the database with the car's make and model and set up cameras to alert them of any matches. Fisher had been at home when the call came, telling her that a potential match for the Mondeo had been seen driving along the A5067, taking a left onto Chorlton Road, before turning left onto Bold Street, then another left at Pickering Street. She knew the area well. Her sister had moved there, and it wasn't far.

She had jumped in her car, driven there, and quickly found the dark blue Mondeo parked with two men inside. Once parked, she had notified DS Phillips, who was back at the office finishing a report. He had swiftly collected a team of late-shift workers, including PC Baan and PC Jackson. She had then phoned her sister to see if she was in, as good an excuse to see her as any. On her way to her sister's apartment, she had gazed over, clocked them watching her, and, entering the front door, phoned Phillips to let him know there was a good chance it would be them. He had texted her soon after, letting her know they were in place and ready. The plan was for Fisher to walk past the car to see if the men would follow. They needed to catch them in the act. After Fisher had heard the car doors open and close, and while she was still standing at the kerb on Pickering Street, she had received a text from Phillips telling her to be ready with the pepper spray. She carried it around with her at all times.

'Hope they rot in there a while,' she said, closing the folder and placing it to one side.

'How's your sister?'

'She's okay — I'm glad she's standing on her own two feet now.'

'You should see more of her. You two get along well.'

'Yeah, maybe.' Fisher stood. 'You want coffee?'

'I wish I had a brother or sister. It was a lonely upbringing. Don't take it for granted.'

'Alright, *Dad*, thanks for the life advice. Coffee or not?'

He pointed at her empty mug. 'You're drinking too much of that stuff, April. You should be drinking more water.'

'Coffee counts towards your water intake anyway, so let me worry about that and answer the question.'

'Yeah, go on.' He tucked himself in while Fisher disappeared, heading down the aisle that separated the desks of the large office. Most of the desks were occupied by different ranks, some tapping away at keyboards, others leaning back in their chairs, talking into a phone.

She passed Baan to her right, who looked up and waved. 'Morning, boss.'

Fisher smiled and mouthed the word *coffee*, to which Baan nodded and beamed.

Through the glass office doors, Fisher headed straight down the brightly lit corridor. She glanced sideways as she walked, observing the hanging pictures of several officers at the station who'd received awards for their service or bravery. Fisher hadn't quite made the cut yet. Her superior, DI James, was on there, his tanned face all smiley with his slicked-back hair that always needed cutting. His award had been given for being in charge of the team that captured the Hand-Eye Killer.

After making three coffees, she placed the used teaspoon in the sink and positioned the drinks in a cardboard holder, utilising the spare slot for a handful of biscuits she found in the cupboard. On her way out, she almost collided with DI James as he marched through the door.

She swerved abruptly.

'Sorry, April.' He raised a hand. 'Spill any?'

'Not this time,' she joked, reminding him of the time he had walked into her, knocking a coffee from her hand and smashing the mug into what seemed like a million pieces, hence the use of disposable cups.

'I need to talk to you when you have a minute.' His tone was less playful as if the reason was something more serious than their near collision.

Her sigh didn't go unnoticed. 'Sure,' she said.

'My office, please.'

'I'll drop these coffees off and be straight down.'

She returned to the office, gave PC Baan hers, then placed the two remaining cups on the desk. Without a word, she turned and left.

'Where are you going?' DS Phillips said, reaching over and grabbing one of the coffees.

'DI James wants a word.'

Phillips's shoulders tensed. 'Good luck.'

Two minutes later, she knocked on his closed office door and opened it after she'd heard him beckon her in. 'Hey, Tom.' Feeling his stare, she sauntered over, pulled out the chair, and sat down. DI Thomas James was very good-looking. His large brown eyes, chiselled, bearded jaw-line, and tanned face turned the heads of most women, not to mention the long hair he obviously spent time brushing back and gelling every morning before leaving his house. Recently though, he'd gained weight, some of it noticeable around his middle where his shirts were getting tighter, and parts of his face too — but there was no denying he was handsome. He had yet to meet the right woman after his last relationship had fizzled out as a result of his excessive working hours and daily gym habits. He was still single despite being on some dating apps; while he went for casual drinks with random matches, none of them were too serious. The nature of his job meant he didn't have the time. Although he could be charming and looking into his eyes made you go weak at the knees, Fisher had never felt that way about him. She very much kept her work relationships professional and shut herself off from feelings that could jeopardise that, if there were any there in the first place.

She smiled at him. The scent of Jean Paul Gaultier hung in the air.

'Morning, April.' He edged forward. 'How are you doing today?'

'Just fine and dandy — you know me, Tom.' Forcing a smile, she knew what this was about, knew as soon as she'd walked in that morning he'd be wanting a word with her to discuss last night's events. She wasn't fretting, nor would she lose any sleep over it.

'So . . . last night,' he began.

She raised a palm and lowered it to her lap. 'Let's just cut to the chase, Tom.'

He glanced down at his desk, smiling, appreciating her eagerness to get whatever was on his mind out into the open. 'You know as well as I do it's not how things are done, April. I must say I commend you in one way for using your initiative. You got the call, gathered a team, and checked the place out first. You got the job done.' He paused, giving her a moment to chip in.

'So, what's the issue?' Her eyebrows furrowed to the point just above her nose.

'The issue is you engaged with a violent male flailing a knife around. Not to mention you didn't have a vest on. What were you thinking?'

The question lingered in the air, long enough for it to become awkward.

'Maybe it was a little rash. But in my assessment of what was happening, I felt I could manage it.'

Absorbing her words, he nodded and waited.

'And we have two men sitting in a cell right now. Two men who not only were going to attack me but have potentially attacked and raped over twenty women so far. And—' she raised a finger — 'no doubt would've continued to do so.'

He had little to say except, 'Just be more careful next time, April. You're one of our best.'

She winked, stood, and on her way out of his office, said, 'See you at the morning brief, boss.'

CHAPTER 6

Mary Steadman opened her eyes, feeling a pounding in her temple and the churning of nausea in the pit of her stomach. Her cheek was pressed against the cold, hard ground, and she lifted her head, the simple act causing dizziness as if she'd spent the last three hours on the waltzers.

'Jesus,' she muttered, lowering her face to the ground again, feeling the muscles in her neck aching. She was freezing, her skin covered with goose pimples.

Sudden thoughts returned to her.

Visions of her bedroom.

The lights going out while she was showering.

The silence in the house.

The figure in her room standing at the window.

Trying to lift her head again, she knew she wasn't at home. Where she lay was quite unwelcoming; it smelled musty, damp, and full of neglect. Judging by the light around her, it wasn't night-time anymore. Had she slept the whole night?

Wait, what was the smell she'd detected just before she passed out?

Struggling up, her body stiff and weak, she got to her knees, then wiped both her eyes to clear her vision. Her knees, thighs, and calves were in agony. She glanced down, immediately covering herself when she saw her clothes were missing. Why was she naked? She felt a wave of frost envelope her.

'What the . . . ?'

The space around her was a rough square, approximately seven metres by seven. The room had high stud walls, rising at least two metres above her head. The plasterboard on the walls had hundreds of screws visible, as if the room was missing the finishing coat of plaster to complete it.

There was no ceiling within the stud walls, instead an open void where she could see the roof of a much larger structure roughly fifteen metres above her. It looked like a warehouse or something industrial, the old, dirty black ceiling supported by a rusted metal structure just below it. The size of the place outside the small, studded area must have been huge, considering she couldn't see any walls from where she stood. On the roof of the warehouse there were dirty skylights, clear plastic squares spanning the room's length, offering a dim light similar to a dark forest at dusk.

She had no idea where or what this place was.

Still covering her breasts with trembling hands, she looked around. In front of her was a wooden door with a handle that looked electronic, the same type as on a hotel room door, but with a small hole for a key instead of a slot for a key card. The walls around her were bare, and the only exit was the closed door in front of her.

She sighed heavily, then took a step but stopped immediately after feeling a sudden, excruciating pain in her right thigh. Something wasn't right. She frowned, seeing a dark purple line, roughly three inches long, half an inch wide, on the outside of her thigh, extending vertically just above her knee, but it was too dark to see adequately.

'What on earth?'

She bent slightly, running several fingertips over the raised line, feeling tiny bits of fabric, sending a sheet of white heat through her body. Had her skin been stitched? She'd never had anything stitched before, but it was the only logical thing in her mind.

Focusing on the door, she struggled over and pressed down the handle. Locked.

'Fuck.'

Her trembling worsened with an unknown fear.

Why was she there?

Who was in her room last night?

Where had they taken her?

A flash of light startled her, the whole place erupting in a bright, blinding light.

'Hello?' she cried, pupils dilating. In the earlier dim conditions, she hadn't seen the narrow walkway a few metres above, fixed to a metal structure that seemed to span the length of the factory. Now there was light, she saw that the studded open-topped room wasn't empty as she had thought.

Over in the corner was a small box, roughly six inches by six, covered in a dark-coloured fabric. Just behind it, written on the wall, was a note saying *Open the box* in almost unreadable handwriting, scribbled in thick black marker.

Cautiously, she went over and knelt down, her right thigh shooting a wave of agony through her lower body. She winced at the pain, noticing blood oozing from the purple stitched line, which had cracked, the wound and skin tearing at the thin fabric used to keep it in place. The box had a small silver hook lock, so Mary flicked it to the side and lifted the lid.

Inside were two things.

An old, faded photograph of a young boy dressed in school uniform. The boy, roughly twelve or thirteen, was smiling at the camera. It looked like an annual school portrait photo. She studied the image, her frown deepening as the seconds ticked by, and then it dawned on her that it was a photo of someone familiar.

'What on earth?'

She felt the blood run down her leg onto the floor.

The other item inside the box was a pair of nail scissors, the tips sharp and deadly. Mary picked them up and frowned.

Around her, she heard a sudden shuffle of movement, but it wasn't inside the space she was in. It was coming from above, somewhere much higher. She lifted her gaze to see, her eyes frantically scanning the space.

A figure came into view on the narrow metal walkway above, followed by three more. The noises grew louder. Getting up and backing into the corner, a trail of blood followed her.

They stopped above where she stood, and the four figures looked down. They were all different sizes, all dressed in black. She couldn't tell if they were men or women, but they all wore black masks.

For half a minute, no one said anything. She glared up at them while they looked down at her, breathing heavily through their masks, eyeing her naked body.

'Who the hell are you?' she screamed, her focus shifting between them. Her echo gave a sense of the warehouse space, the sounds bouncing off the ceiling and walls, returning to her a second later.

The black figures just stared, saying nothing, not moving.

'Hello, Mary,' said a loud voice from somewhere close by. To her right, up in the corner of the square room, she spotted a speaker positioned on the wall. Beside it was a circular object, which looked like a camera, and a rectangular black box near it.

Someone was watching her.

'I bet you're wondering where you are and what's happened to you,' the voice said.

She dropped the photo and the nail scissors by her feet, deciding to cower into the corner, covering herself the best she could from the masks above.

'You have a choice to make, Mary. You have an item to use if you wish, an item that could get you out of that room. The door is locked, but there's a key somewhere in there.' The voice paused a beat to allow that to sink in. 'You will need to use the scissors to get the key. The key is inside your right thigh, if you haven't already guessed. You must cut the stitching, reach inside your leg, and get the key.'

Her eyes widened, her heart pulsing through her bare chest.

The figures gazed down at her.

'Be quick, though, because once you start cutting, you'll lose blood very quickly.'

She shook her head. 'I'm not doing it!'

'You will do it, otherwise you'll freeze to death in there.'

She shook her head from side to side. It was freezing, but it would take more than that to make her do such a thing.

'Mary, you must.'

'What is this!' Her scream reverberated through the space once more, and she started to cry.

'This, Mary, is your chance to live again.'

'What? What if I don't?'

'Then you'll never get out, and you'll die in there,' the calm voice replied.

Defiantly, she protested, 'I'm not doing that. There's no way I'm doing that.'

The figures on the walkway started to laugh at her.

She sobbed. 'I-I can't do it . . .'

'Mary, you have no other choice. If you look behind you on the wall behind you, you'll see a timer.'

She turned around slowly, frowning at the rectangular black plastic box near the camera, roughly half the size of a car's registration plate. Numbers appeared in red neon, indicating the digits 10:00. The numbers started to count down.

'I can't do this . . .' she sobbed.

'You have less than ten minutes to get the key,' the voice said. 'If the timer reaches zero, the door will never open. It's an electronic lock.'

Sighing, she thought about it, how much of this was true, then considered the box attached to the door lock. She bent over, picked up the scissors with shaking hands, and started cutting at the stitches with nine minutes remaining.

CHAPTER 7

They were seated in the meeting room when DI Thomas James marched in, dressed in dark blue jeans, brown shoes, and a white shirt, with a dark blue jacket that hugged his shape — clearly fitting him better before he'd put the weight on. His head was high, his shoulders back, the same way he entered each morning — a way to inspire others and get the day off to a good start. Your peers always respected you more and listened to what you said if you carried yourself well and had conviction in what you said, rather than slouching, looking tired and defeated.

In his hand was an A4-sized brown folder, which he placed on a desk at the front.

'Good morning.' His voice was firm, strong. Curious eyes focused on the folder.

He pulled a memory stick from his pocket, carefully placed it into the laptop, and picked up a small black remote. He looked down at the screen, used a finger to navigate to the file he needed, and double-clicked. He stood back from the whiteboard projected against the wall. The first slide was today's date, 9 December.

'Hope you all had a good sleep last night. Cold one, wasn't it?'

The heating at the station was on full, the room thermostat controlling the three radiators that were positioned just under each window on the right-hand side, the coldest part of the room.

'So, today, we're going to start with this.' DI James pointed the remote to the laptop and clicked, revealing a photo of a woman in her early forties on the second page. Her name was Debbie Johnson. Everyone in the room looked at the familiar picture. DC Arnold Peterson, a small but thickset gym-goer with a bald head, let out a sigh.

'Where are we with Mrs Johnson?' he asked, his voice loud enough to elicit an answer from someone.

PC Baan said, 'We've been knocking on doors in her neighbourhood. No one has seen her yet. Her next-door neighbour said it's usual for Mrs Johnson to disappear as she likes to get away with her friends every other weekend. But she did mention it's normally only for a couple of days.'

'Thanks, Ashleigh.' DI James nodded at her, then gazed at PC Cairn, a thin, bearded twenty-seven-year-old who had been in the force for over three years. 'Joel, you've missed some recent meetings. Would someone kindly inform PC Cairn about Mrs Johnson, please.'

DS Fisher smiled and turned to her left. 'Debbie Johnson, aged forty-one, went missing four days ago. She works from home full-time as a self-employed IT consultant, helping companies set up various computer programs to aid their businesses. According to neighbours, she isn't married and there's no sign of a boyfriend, nor does she have any children. A report came in two days ago from a Mrs Abi Witmore, who tells us she's one of her closest friends, saying she was worried and hasn't known a time in their twelve years of friendship they'd gone longer than a day or two without speaking. So after three days, she went to her house. After seeing no sign of Debbie and having made dozens of unanswered calls, she came into the station to file a missing person's report.'

Fisher turned back to face DI James, who thanked her with a smiling nod. He used this as an opportunity for his

31

colleagues to recap. He liked to see if they were all up to date and knew exactly what was going on.

James angled his attention to PC Amy Legg. 'Do we have her photo everywhere?'

'We do,' she said, her words getting clogged in her throat. She coughed. 'Sorry. Yes, sir, we do, across all our social media. I've spoken with Charlie from the *Manchester Evening News* and sent him some info along with her photo. He told me it'll be in tomorrow's paper.'

Amy Legg had been a part of Greater Manchester Police for under four years. She'd completed a degree in media studies after she left school, but although talented in that subject area, had struggled to get a job anywhere, even an entry-level role paying the minimum wage. A friend of hers knew someone in the force who'd mentioned Manchester was looking for PCs. Amy hadn't been keen at first, after hearing too many stories about attacks on police by the public. It had all seemed too dangerous. But she had also been pissed off being unemployed for so long, so she had applied, passed all the physical and mental tests, and was offered the role of a PC. Once out of her two-year training period, she had felt she wanted something else, something more. She'd always loved watching crime shows, particularly about forensics and murder. One of her colleagues had suggested enquiring about CID the previous month. It wasn't common practice to move over, but with her knowledge of the media, she thought she could help CID with their media platforms. DCI Andrew Baker had felt she would be an asset to their team.

'Thanks, Amy.' DI James strolled across the room to the window and peered out onto Chorley Road, watching the cars pass down below. Their meeting room was on the first floor, positioned almost in the corner of the building. Above, the sky was dark and grey, filled with thick black clouds that threatened rain. People walking on the path were dressed in coats, scarves, and hats. A woman wearing a red coat on the opposite side of the road carried an umbrella.

James pushed himself away from the windowsill and returned to where he'd been standing earlier. 'We need to start making more progress with this case. I haven't yet relayed the pressure I'm getting from DCI Baker on this one. He wants results and wants them sooner rather than later. We need to find Debbie Johnson.'

The door in the corner near him opened and in waddled PC Alan Ferry. He was big and overweight, with thinning hair. How he'd passed the fitness requirements, no one could fathom.

'Sorry to interrupt your meeting.'

DI James frowned, surprised to see him.

'Inspector Thorne sent me up to see you.'

'What is it, PC Ferry?'

'A body has been found at Chorlton Library on Longford Road.'

The DI frowned. 'Near the library?'

Ferry shook his head. '*Inside* the library.' He paused. 'They think it could be Debbie Johnson.'

DI James absorbed the news.

'I'll get Pamela Boone. She needs to head down ASAP,' Ferry informed him. 'Apparently, it's unlike anything anyone's ever seen.'

CHAPTER 8

The black masks glared down at Mary Steadman from the metal walkway above. The whole factory was eerie, silent. With trembling hands, still sobbing, Mary opened up the small nail scissors and attempted to make the first cut. Her quivering hands made it difficult to cut the close stitches on the side of her knee, the sharp point stabbing painfully into her flesh.

She yelped and put a hand over the wound to stop the sudden flow of blood, which streamed down her leg onto the floor. One of the masks laughed out loud, startling her.

A sudden thought came to her. What if this was a wind-up? How did she know the key to the locked door was in there?

Her head was pounding, shooting pains cascading through her whole body. She was so cold. The temperature must have been below freezing, although the morning sun shone through the building's murky skylights. She hesitated a moment, wondering what the time was. The board of directors expected her at the 9 a.m. office meeting, but going by the natural light above, it was past that time. Yesterday morning the sun hadn't shown until around 10 a.m., and today wasn't much brighter.

'What do you want from me?' she screamed in part frustration, part pain.

Naked, cold, and shaking, she had never felt so intimidated.

'It won't cut itself,' the voice on the speaker said.

Using her thumb and finger, she squeezed the area around the cut to see if she could feel anything hard that resembled a key. It was agonising, the stitching oozing with blood.

'Go on, cut it!' one of the figures shouted. It was a male voice, rough, filled with anger.

Who were these people?

'Cut it out, Mary,' said another. The voice belonged to a woman with a much higher pitch but with the same serious tone.

Mary knew she had to get through the locked door. There was no other way out. Focusing, she placed her left hand around her right wrist to steady herself as she tried again. Halfway through the four-inch stitching, she stopped and gasped, the pain almost unbearable. She prodded with a finger for anything that resembled a key. Howling in agony, the tip of her finger probed through layers of flesh and soft tissue.

'Yes, that's it!' a voice said from above. 'Poke yourself.'

She wanted to scream at them and stab them with the instrument in her possession. But she needed to get out of the room. Removing her bloody finger, she wiped it on her thigh and took careful hold of the scissors again.

'Focus,' she whispered to herself. 'You can do it, Mary.'

Slowly, she cut away the fibre stitching a tiny bit at a time, each cut forcing the wound to open more. She winced. Once she cut it away, she dropped the scissors, making a metallic ping that echoed around her.

'Get the key!' one of the figures above her shouted. 'Get it!'

Ignoring their teasing, she took a breath to block out the sickening pain and severe cold she felt, her body now almost vibrating against the December temperatures and blood loss around her feet.

'You're running out of time, Mary Steadman.'

She looked up at the speaker where the voice had come from and stared into the camera next to it, scowling hard.

With her thumb and two fingers, she gingerly pushed them inside the wound, fighting the will to scream, going further. She shuddered, yanking her hand back quickly when she felt the bone inside.

'Jesus!' she cried, placing a palm to her mouth for a moment, fighting the urge to be sick.

'Time is running out,' informed the voice on the speaker. 'Tick-tock.'

Taking another steadying breath, she forced her fingers deep inside, her stomach roiling at the pain and the realisation of what she was doing. To her surprise, she could feel something hard, an object that felt different compared to when she'd touched her bone.

She leaned over further, trying to see what the object was. It appeared to be the tip of a solid, cold key. She frowned. The key was much further down than the cut had been made. Whoever had cut her leg and put the key in there must have pushed it so far down that it was almost unreachable.

Unless she cut further.

'You guessed it, Mary.'

She stared up towards the speaker, tears streaming down her face.

'The key is deep in there. You'll have to cut into your skin another few inches to get to it.'

Squeezing her eyes shut, she pushed hard on the wound, slowing the blood flow. She could not endure that pain, cutting into her skin like that. She wasn't a doctor. But did she have a choice? Determined, she opened the scissors as wide as possible, positioned them so the blades reached the bottom of the gaping red hole, and, clamping her eyes closed, she squeezed, the layers of skin slowly slicing under the pivotal force of the tiny blades.

'Fuck!'

She dropped the scissors and pushed both hands onto the cut to suppress the agony. It momentarily relieved it, but it wouldn't last long and certainly wouldn't get her out of that room.

'When I get out of here, I'm gonna kill you all!' Her voice ripped through the cold, stagnant air above her.

Behind the masks, the faces smiled at the empty threat.

'Come on, you can do this,' she said, reminding herself she was a powerful woman; she could do anything.

Mentally, she counted to three and forced the tips of her fingers deep inside, the end of the key between her thumb and forefinger. She squeezed and pulled upwards, the metal object sliding until eventually it was high enough to pop out. The relief she felt was indescribable as she held on to the soaking red key, seeing it through streams of tears.

She limped over to the door, half her body smeared in blood, and tried to place the key into the slot, the end of the key stabbing the metal around it until she managed to keep her hand steady enough to insert it. Using the last of her remaining energy she turned the lock, pushed down on the handle, pulled the door towards her, then entered the next room.

CHAPTER 9

DS Matthew Phillips jumped into Fisher's white XC90, closed the door, and put on his seat belt. Fisher did the same, started the engine, then reached over to turn the window demisters on, the sounds of the heater purring away. A faint scent of cherry lingered in the car, the air freshener hanging from the rear-view mirror the obvious culprit.

'Wish my car was this tidy, April.'

She offered him a smile. 'I don't have a kid, though.'

'That's true.'

To their right, they watched DI James get into his Range Rover. Moments after, the sound of the 3.8L engine rumbled in the cold.

The temperature on the dash told them it was only two degrees. Recent weather reports suggested it would hit sub-zero at some point.

'Come on,' said Fisher, sighing. They couldn't see a thing through the windscreen.

Phillips sat forward, wiping the inside of the glass with the back of his palm to help, but soon enough, the warm air started to clear it.

'Unlike anything we've ever seen, eh?' Fisher repeated the earlier words of PC Ferry when he had interrupted the meeting.

'I was just glad to end the meeting early, to be honest, April.'

She turned her head and scowled at him while the condensation faded. 'I thought you loved meetings. Highlight of your day, I think.'

'Absolutely,' he said, grinning. The radio volume was low, beating gently from the car's surround sound, a classic from the past, one of the Spice Girls' songs.

'Must be serious if he's requesting Pamela Boone straight away.'

'Guess we'll soon see, April.'

As soon as DI James had thanked PC Ferry for the message, he had ended the meeting and asked Fisher and Phillips to head straight over to the library. Phillips had grabbed his long brown coat and a scarf. Fisher was already wearing her signature outfit: the dark blue blazer, white blouse, and dark jeans; she grabbed a scarf and gloves too. PC Baan rode with DI James. He didn't want them all there, not knowing what the day ahead had in store for his team. Every day was different in this job; they all knew that. Chorley Road wasn't the closest police station to the library where the body was found, so other police officers would attend to secure the scene and keep people out. He could always request his team if needed. They'd got the message because officers already thought the victim resembled Debbie Johnson, whose face they knew from a recent photo.

Once the windows had fully cleared, Fisher turned the heating vents to blow in their direction, the welcoming warmth rushing into their faces, then edged the gear into first, carefully pulling out behind DI James's Range Rover. The car park had been gritted first thing that morning, but Charlie, the handyman, had missed a few areas. Fisher knew this because she had almost hit the corner of a parked vehicle an hour earlier, taking the corner a fraction too fast.

'Can I change this shit?' asked Phillips, light-heartedly.

Fisher slowed at the car park's opening and glanced at him to figure out what he meant. He was referring to the radio.

'I thought you'd like the Spice Girls.'

'I'd rather dip my balls in a pan of boiling water, to be honest.'

Fisher looked right and pulled straight into the empty road, shaking her head as she tried to block out the mental image of him crouched over a pan of boiling water. 'Put whatever you want on, Matt.'

Around fifteen minutes later, they pulled up outside Chorlton Library. Fisher wasn't much of a reader, but she did know — from God knows where — that this library was the second busiest in Manchester and had been around for over a hundred years. It appeared to be a single-story building, but externally it was tall, with four grand sandstone-coloured pillars supporting a traditional overhanging dome-like entrance foyer. Above the door it read: *Public Library*.

On their way over, Fisher and Phillips enjoyed the music Fisher had in the CD player.

'You know, I haven't listened to Billy Joel in years,' said Phillips. 'My dad used to listen to him.'

She smiled. 'I pronounce it like the name Joel, not Jo-el.'

'Same thing. What's your favourite song?'

'Tough one, that. "Piano Man" or "The Longest Time", depends how I feel.'

'Do you still see your mam and dad?'

'Yeah, sometimes. I see my sister more, though.'

Phillips knew she needed to let herself go a little and enjoy her personal life — it was important. He'd mentioned it to her only last week but, judging by her reply of '*This* is fun' referring to the overwhelming mountain of paperwork on her desk, it was obvious she didn't want to talk about it as he left to go home to his fiancée Janice and three-year-old son Dominic.

The scene at the library was already hectic: three police cars, an ambulance, and a small white van which Fisher knew belonged to their senior forensic officer, Pamela Boone.

'She got here fast,' noted Phillips, pointing at the white van Fisher stopped behind. Turning the key, the sound of the engine faded along with the rasp of Chad Kroeger's voice still singing the lyrics to one of Nickleback's early hits. She stepped out into the freezing winter's day, where the air smelled fresh, a faint scent of coffee coming from somewhere, reminding Fisher she'd left half a mug in the meeting room which she'd never get the chance to finish.

DI James somehow squeezed his mammoth car into a gap beyond the forensic van. Fisher and Phillips stood on the kerb, waiting for him to take the lead. After all, the discovery had been brought to his attention directly.

'Ready for this?' James murmured as he approached them.

Fisher and Phillips nodded at him. They followed him across to the tape strategically placed to stop people accessing the path in front of the library. Already a small crowd had formed, standing just beyond it, but a young, twenty-something PC with good posture stood guard, ensuring no one got through. Fisher noticed an elderly lady in a motorised wheelchair waiting at the tape, appearing less than impressed, unsure how to get around now that the path was closed.

At the library's door, a female PC with dark hair and a scowl watched them duck under the sagging tape and approach her. She could tell they were CID not only by their clothes but how they moved, with that almost arrogant swag.

'Morning,' she said, in a voice deeper than Fisher had expected. After inspecting their ID badges, she held out a small bag of plastic disposable overshoes which they all took and put on, Fisher almost losing her balance and having to lean a shoulder against the wall. The PC pulled the door open for them and closed it once they were inside.

The air within the library was noticeably warmer; there was a hum from a nearby heater somewhere. Fisher couldn't spot it, nor did she care; anything to take the December chill from her bones. If you were to judge the inside of the building, you wouldn't think it belonged to the outside; it appeared to have been renovated and modernised very recently whilst externally, it had kept the original, historical facade. A faint smell of fresh paint lingered somewhere amid compressed paperbacks and aging hardbacks.

A man dressed similar to DS Phillips — wearing a long black coat instead of brown — was mid-conversation near the small reception desk. He noticed them and excused himself away from the elderly lady he was talking to, presumably someone who worked at the library, judging by her intelligent appearance, gentle manner, and red badge hanging from a lanyard around her neck.

He put out a big, strong hand. 'DI Alex Tunsten.' He was tall and broad, and his voice was deep, clearly from Scotland, but Fisher couldn't be sure where. James had seen him at previous meetings he'd attended but wasn't sure of his name.

DI James shook it, introduced himself, then motioned to Fisher, Phillips, and finally Baan. DI Tunsten held his attention on Baan for a noticeable second too long, a shade of pink colouring her cheeks.

'Please, come this way,' Tunsten said, turning. They trailed him towards the right, passing shelves of books until they reached an open doorway, above it a sign for the toilets. Before he entered, he turned to them. 'Oh, before we go in. Put these on.' In turn, he handed them a pair of nitrile gloves.

Fisher smiled. 'Don't worry, we have our own. Thanks, though.' She plucked two pairs from her suit jacket pocket and snapped them on. Phillips did the same.

'Your forensic tech is in there,' he added.

They put the gloves on, DS Phillips clumsily taking longer than the others. 'Take your time in there. Don't touch anything.' DI Tunsten paused. 'I hope whatever you've had for breakfast this morning doesn't come back up.'

Fisher gave a tight-lipped smile.

'Follow me,' Tunsten said, leading the way.

CHAPTER 10

Mary Steadman entered the next room, hoping this nightmare would soon end. Was this all a dream? Had the lights really gone out while she was showering? Perhaps she'd seen that dark figure in her room just after she went to sleep. Was the key in her leg a figment of the same dream, moments before she was to wake up?

It all felt too real.

The pain in her leg was borderline excruciating and too real to be just a dream. She started to feel dizzy thanks to the blood loss, her balance threatening to go at any second.

If freedom was what she had hoped for, then the room she now found herself in wouldn't offer that. It was similar to the first room, but something was different; there was a large, cubed object located in the centre of the room. She frowned at it, unable to work out what it was.

As she dragged herself closer, she heard a shuffle of noises from above. The figures moved along the narrow, metal walkway above, with the perfect view of what would happen next.

'Do you think this is some kind of game?' she spat at them, then screamed, 'Sick bastards!'

One of the figures laughed deeply, the others remained quiet, dark eyes watching and waiting.

Like the previous one, this room had a camera and a speaker high up in the corner.

She sighed heavily, spittle leaving her mouth and collecting on her chin. If she hadn't pressed a hand on her leg to slow the blood loss, she would have wiped it off, but she was past caring now.

The box in front of her was comprised of two parts. The top part was a glass cube. On the side facing her was a small hole about the size of a tennis ball at roughly chest height. Inside the box was something she couldn't work out. Was it a bar of soap with some kind of metal tube connected to it? The rear side of the box seemed dark from where she was standing, leaving only three sides of the box with transparent glass panes.

Her frown encouraged a voice to come through on the speaker in the corner. 'Go on, Mary. Don't go all shy on us now.'

Through gritted teeth, she powered through, peeling her attention away from them as she pulled her bleeding leg along with her. She stopped at the glass box and studied it, trying to keep her weight off her injured leg.

'What on earth?'

Was it wax?

Whatever it was, a cylindrical metal bar was fixed to it and ran to the rear inside wall of the glass box. She paused, trying to work it out. A small red button roughly the size of a ten-pence piece could be seen where the metal rod was fixed to the back of the box.

Squinting, she gazed around the box, her eyes falling to the base of it.

'What is that?' she muttered quietly enough, reaching only her own ears. Most of it was flat but, in the centre, directly below the ball of wax, was some form of nozzle pointing upwards.

'Mary,' the calm voice said through the speaker.

She snapped her neck in the direction of it.

'You did well in the last room. You surprised me. I tried to put the key nice and deep. So, well done.'

She grimaced at the exaggerated praise, fighting the urge to scream again, knowing it would only give them satisfaction to see her struggle.

'This room contains, as you can see, a glass box. If you haven't worked out the object in the middle, it's a lump of wax with something inside. You must put your arm in and press the little red button at the back.'

She frowned in hesitation, knowing this task wouldn't be pleasant if it was anything like the last.

'What happens when I push the button?' she asked, pulling her attention away from the box and eyeing the rest of the room in search for alternatives. It was empty, same as the last. Except without a photograph of the boy dressed in school uniform and the small pair of scissors. Instead, a large glass box taller than her.

'There's only one way to find out,' the voice replied.

Up on the narrow metal walkway one of the masked people laughed. The sound was deep, evil.

Considering the words and lack of choices, she shuffled closer to the box, turning to the side. She kept her right hand against her knee to stop the blood loss and cautiously placed her left hand through the small hole which had been cut out, sanded in the shape of a perfect circle, leaving the edges smooth against her skin as she pushed inside until her fingers were an inch from the button. She stopped, doubting herself, unsure about going any further.

'Do it!' one of them shouted. 'Push it!'

She took a deep breath and touched the button with a fingertip. There was a ticking sound, followed by a low *whoosh*, before a massive flame expelled from the nozzle at the bottom of the box, the whole box becoming an orange glow.

'Fuck!' she shrieked, pulling away quickly, retrieving her hand from the box. 'Jesus Christ!' The hairs on her arms had singed; her whole arm was tingling in agony, a putrid whiff of burning filling the space around her. She glared at her arm, inspecting it closely. Luckily, she'd escaped any severe harm to her skin.

While rubbing her arm, she took shallow breaths, wishing this whole thing was over. Inside the box, she noticed the waxy object had a shine to it; the heat that filled the box had begun to melt the wax away.

'Come on, Mary.' The plea came from the speaker.

'What do you want from me?' she cried, clamping her eyes shut in defeat.

Three of the masked figures laughed, their evil echoing around the stale air of the warehouse.

'If you haven't worked it out, you need to melt the wax to get the object. The object is a key. A key to get through the next door.'

CHAPTER 11

DI Alex Tunsten had entered the male toilet at Chorlton Library
first. Now, he wanted James, Fisher, Phillips, and Baan to take
their time, to absorb the scene before them. He knew from
what he'd felt when he first entered that it would hit them hard.
The smell was unusual and unlike what they would expect.
The scent of bleach, air freshener, toilet cleaner, and hand soap
was missing, instead the aromas of gone-off meat with fruity
undertones lingered in the air, circulating in the radiator's heat.

'God, what *is* that?' Baan said, covering her mouth as she
stepped through the threshold.

The toilets were rectangular. In front of them, as they
entered, were two cubicles, both their doors closed. Turning
left, DI James, who was directly behind Tunsten, eager to
see the scene, could see two sinks fixed to the wall with various types of copper and plastic pipework underneath, going
off in different directions. Above the sinks, a long mirror
spanned the width of the wall. He caught his reflection,
and behind, he noticed Fisher trailing him. Their overshoes
lightly scraped off the tiled floor as they strolled in.

'Please, keep well clear. I'm still working,' Pamela Boone
said, just out of sight.

Reaching the sink, Tunsten whispered, 'Brace yourself.'

'Just stay near the wall,' Boone reminded them.

DI James raised a palm in understanding and stopped a few metres back.

Tunsten took a step to the side, his back now to the sinks and mirror. Fisher drew level with James, and both of them, with wide eyes, focused on the urinal next to Boone, who was down on her knees looking at something below it.

Fisher raised a hand to her mouth, lost for words. DI James just stared, his mouth gaping open. They'd been told it was unlike anything they'd ever seen, but they weren't expecting this. Phillips and Baan were behind them, leaning across to have a look.

'Jesus . . .' DI James sighed and turned away, making way for Baan and Phillips to get a closer peek.

Tunsten watched DI James move over to the wall to the right, turn away, and raise a tight fist against his lips.

'Different, isn't it?' DI Tunsten said to James.

'You could say that.'

'Who found this?' asked Fisher, unable to pull her attention from the urinal.

'John, the library's cleaner. First thing this morning, when he opened up and did his rounds. He normally starts with the toilet, then does the rest of the library.'

Fisher nodded.

Resting inside the urinal to the left was something the detectives hadn't seen in a long time. It was the first time PC Baan had seen one in person, not just from a photograph.

A human head severed at the neck.

The longer they studied the head, the more unbearable the scents became.

Baan leaned forward, placing a hand on Fisher's right shoulder to steady herself.

Fisher angled her way. 'You okay, Ash?'

'Think I'm gonna throw up.'

'Please don't, Ash.'

Baan gave a thin smile.

As they couldn't see the neck, it wasn't clear how the head had been detached from the body it belonged to.

Pamela Boone would move it when she was ready and had analysed the scene.

The colour of this woman's face was a purply-blue, evidently due to the lack of circulation that the heart would have supplied if the body had been connected to the head. Fisher was no forensic technician and, if it was Debbie, she couldn't be sure just from looking if she'd been dead for the four days she'd been missing. The whites in the eyes showed retinal blood vessels. She was showing signs of putrefaction, but the removal of the head and the heat from the radiator might have sped the process up. When coroners and forensics preserved bodies or parts of them, they knew to reduce the temperature, slowing down the decomposition rate.

The dead eyes were still, almost staring directly at Fisher, but it was a stare-out Fisher knew she'd never win. The shoulder-length blonde hair appeared dyed pink, but a closer look showed the clumps of hair matted to her scalp in dried blood. Some strands were tucked under the head, and the rest hung over the edge of the urinal.

'Can we turn the heating down?' asked Phillips, knowing the heat would only speed up the body's decomposition and certainly wasn't helping them focus.

'I've already asked that, Matthew,' said Boone.

'What're your thoughts — think it's Debbie?' asked DI Tunsten, the question aimed mainly at DI James. Fisher chirped in when he failed to reply.

'Maybe. It certainly looks like her from the photo we have. Hair colour matches. The shape of her nose.' She leaned forward a little, the others watching, wondering what she was doing. Boone tilted her head, watching her for a moment. 'Eye colour is similar too. Yeah, it could be her.'

Debbie Johnson had been missing for four days now.

Fisher backed away slightly, turning to Baan, giving her a half-smile, understanding how she felt. She knew her well, and although she was a highly experienced police constable, she hadn't dealt with many scenes similar to this one.

'We'll give you some space, Pamela,' Fisher said to Boone. 'We'll be outside if you need us.'

CHAPTER 12

Mary Steadman was almost hyperventilating now, under-standing the task she had to complete — push the button at the far side of the glass box to ignite the flame long enough for the wax to melt so she could get the key.

The concept was easy, but the reality of the task was hid-eous: to place her arm into a confined space she knew would cause horrific pain to get a key to let her out of the room she was trapped in.

How long would she need to hold the button?

How hot was the flame?

Based on the length of time she'd pressed it moments earlier, it was scorching and surely wouldn't take long to warm the wax until it was soft enough to get the key she needed. God, she'd do anything to be in her 9 a.m. meet-ing. The thought washed over her: sitting at the head of the long table in the conference room, surrounded by men and women in suits trying to buy her approval, the room lined with glass walls that cost more than most of them made in a year.

There must be another way to do this.

She paused with her hand on the edge of the box, fingers trembling, poking through the hole a few inches.

'It won't melt itself,' one of the masked figures told her from the walkway above.

Ignoring the voice, she took a deep breath, knowing she could do this. But instead of pressing the red button she tried to scratch away at the hard wax to see if it would break, but it had hardened and was as solid as a rock. Disregarding the wound on her leg, which was now seeping heavily with blood, making her feel light-headed and unbalanced, she accepted there were no other alternatives.

She placed her hand inside, braced herself, and pressed the button.

The colossal flame roared upwards, filling the box in an orange flash. She screamed something inhumane, a terrifying sound that made your blood curdle. The fire attacked the lump of wax, its coating becoming shiny before it started dripping onto the base of the glass box. The pain was unbearable. Her skin was bright red and started to blister; the blood rushed to the surface to repair the damage.

She gasped loudly, releasing the button.

The flame went out.

She ripped her arm from the box and fell to her knees, holding her burnt, blistered arm close to her body. Tears rolled down her face.

One of the masked strangers above laughed at her, but all she could hear was the thumping of the blood rushing through her ears.

'Please, just let me out!' Her plea was so high-pitched and desperate that it was almost inaudible.

'Keep going, Mary,' encouraged the voice of the speaker. 'You're nearly there.'

Her feet were so saturated in blood from the wound, she almost slipped getting back up. This time she used her other arm, knowing she couldn't take any more damage to her left arm. She inserted her right hand, grabbed the warm, melted wax attached to the metal rod, and tried to push some of it away, but it wasn't quite warm enough and had cooled and hardened again.

Taking a lungful of air to steady herself, the stench of burnt flesh hitting her nose, she pushed the button again and held her breath. The fire ignited, filling the box once again. The wax started to melt, along with the skin of her right arm.

She wailed again, this time louder, her pain echoing around the warehouse. Through streaming eyes, she watched the wax inside the box melting.

'Come on!' she shrieked, her whole body jolting in waves at the indescribable agony.

Her skin was red and bubbling, then it dried, the moisture in the layers evaporating under the intense heat.

The key was visible.

She gasped, letting go of the button and attempting to grab the key. But the flame didn't stop this time. It kept filling the hot box, kept burning her skin. The hole where she'd put her arm, which was up to her bicep, had become tighter because her own arm had melted to it.

She panicked and tried to yank it out, but it wouldn't budge. It was as if the hole were becoming smaller, biting into her skin, not allowing her to free herself.

The skin started blistering heavily now, followed by the grotesque sound of crackling skin and sizzling blood, which oozed into the base of the box. The smell was horrific as the skin started turning black, becoming charcoal over the heat of the fire.

'Help me!' she pleaded. 'Help!' Her arm wouldn't budge.

She watched blackened chunks of flesh fall away to the base of the glass cube and then she passed out, her body becoming limp but her trapped arm holding her dead weight up.

The masked figures stared silently from the walkway above, breathing heavily, absorbing the scene below them. They could smell not only Mary's burning skin but the smell of her fear and their own satisfaction.

They enjoyed every gratifying second of it.

CHAPTER 13

After Fisher and Phillips left Pamela Boone in the toilet, they located the woman DI Tunsten had spoken to when they arrived, standing nervously at the reception desk with her arms down by her side, her fingers interlocked as if she were unsure what to do. She appeared to be in her mid-sixties, although nowadays it was almost impossible to tell the ages of people.

'Hey,' Fisher said softly. 'Can we have a word?'

She nodded twice, keen to help.

'I'm DS April Fisher.' Fisher held out a hand.

The woman shook it. 'I'm Alison. Welcome to Chorlton Library.' Her voice was shaky and forced, almost getting blocked in her throat. She was short and had to tilt her head back to look at Fisher. Phillips, at six foot two, absolutely dwarfed her.

'I'm aware you spoke with DI Tunsten a little earlier, but are you okay answering some more questions?'

Alison nodded. 'Of course.'

'So, what happened this morning?'

The librarian took a breath big enough to fill her small lungs. 'We open at eight. John, our cleaner, came in at half past seven. He walked through the main doors and hung his coat over there.' She pointed to a coat stand against the wall behind her, a few metres beyond the reception desk. 'He told me he went to put the heating on — like he does every morning — but it was already on full.'

'Is the heating normally on?'

She nodded. 'We keep it low, so the library doesn't freeze, but turn it to full when needed.' DS Phillips wandered off to look around. Fisher noticed him go but kept her focus on the older woman.

'Then what happened?'

'John grabbed a box of cleaning stuff from the room out back; he normally starts with the toilets. He can't stand dirty toilets. He used to work at a different library where teenagers would hang out nearby, come in to use the toilets and not give a toss about the books. They always left a mess; urine and tissue all over the floor.'

'Is John still here?'

'Yes, he's out the back in the staff area. He'd usually be home now but I asked him to stay in case you needed to speak with him. I'll get him.' She disappeared for a few moments and returned with a small, thin man. 'This is John.'

He smiled, showing a glimpse of some missing teeth.

Fisher nodded. 'Thank you for staying to speak with us. Can I ask you what happened?'

'I went in the toilet and screamed. I was the only one here at the time. I found the . . . the . . .' He trailed off, unable to say *head*. 'I dropped the box of cleaning products and left, immediately phoning Alison. I didn't know what to do. She told me to ring the police.'

'Okay, thanks.' Fisher paused in thought. 'Who has access to the library — who has a key?'

'John and I for starters,' answered Alison. 'Another woman who works here, Elaine, has one too. But that's just a spare in case I ever lose mine.'

'Is Elaine here today?'

She shook her head. 'Elaine only works Monday to Thursday. She has Fridays off, goes out with her husband or something.' There was a sour tone in her words. Fisher assumed Alison wasn't married, or she didn't do much with her husband if she was.

Fisher pushed her tongue to the side of her mouth. 'What time did you close up last night?'

'I locked up at six. Stood at the bus stop across the road and waited for the bus to come. Then I got home about half six.'

'Where do you live?'

'In an apartment near the centre. Greengate.'

'What did you do when you got home?'

'Made something to eat, washed up, did the laundry. Watched TV. My husband died only last year, leaving us with debt I wasn't aware we had. They took everything from me.'

'Okay. So other than you two and Elaine, has anyone else got access?'

'Not as far as I know.' She offered a small shrug.

'Have you got CCTV set up in here?'

Alison turned and pointed to several cameras in various areas. Fisher caught one behind the reception desk, high up on the wall.

'I know there won't be a camera inside the toilet, but have you got one that covers the entrance?'

Her brows furrowed to the centre of her forehead. 'I'm not sure. We've never needed them for anything since I've been here. I can check?'

'Where is the footage stored?'

She turned and moved away from the desk. 'The staff room. Follow me.'

Moments later, they entered through a doorway into the small corridor behind the desk, where Fisher noticed four doors. The nearest to the left was closed — a unisex toilet for the staff, according to the sign. The room beyond that was used for storage. The door in front of them looked tougher than the others, presumably a rear entrance and exit for staff. They took the open door on the right, which led to a small square room with a table in the centre. A sink and a small counter with a toaster and microwave were on the far wall. Next to it, a cupboard and a wall full of posters about books, health and safety legislation, and Manchester City Council. There was a small chipboard with Post-it notes and useful numbers like takeaways and local taxi firms.

Alison led Fisher to the nearest corner on the left, where a small desk supported an electrical box. Sitting atop was a monitor showing six cameras dotted around the library. Two screens showed the building's exterior. The camera at the front of the library indicated police clearing the scene; the other camera exhibited the side of the library, where Fisher saw a small crowd gathering at the tape, wondering what the hell was going on.

'How many entrances are there?'

'Two. There's the main entrance you came through when you arrived . . .'

'The other?' Fisher pressed.

Alison sighed, annoyed at Fisher's impatience. She left the desk and stood at the threshold to the room, pointing to the door at the end of the tiny corridor Fisher had noticed moments earlier. 'Just there.'

'Can we look at the footage from last night, please?'

Alison sighed again, this time not hiding it. 'I don't know how to — as I said, I've never had to. I wouldn't know what to press.'

Fisher pulled one of the chairs around the table and placed it near the monitor. She grabbed hold of the mouse, clicked on various icons, managing to find a folder named 'CCTV'.

'Have you found something?' Alison shuffled forward, squeezing close to Fisher, who could smell her sweet perfume. 'I've never touched it before,' the librarian added.

In the folder Fisher had clicked, there were a further twelve folders with the names of the months on. She clicked December, which brought up another series of folders, each representing a day of the month. She clicked on yesterday's date, Thursday 8 December, but the folder was empty.

Fisher stared silently.

'What is it?'

'There's no file.' Fisher shrugged, then tried today's date, Friday 9 December, and clicked again.

'Damn,' she whispered, seeing no file in there either.

Fisher looked at the electrical box below the monitor more closely, eyeing the small slots and wires. Using her finger, she pointed to something. 'Should there be something inserted in that slot? A memory stick of some sort?'

'What do you mean, Detective?'

'I don't think this device can store data. Knowing what I know, I'm sure a memory stick should be inserted here.' She pointed at the small rectangular slot. 'If there was one here before, there isn't one now. It's been removed by someone. There's no footage saved anywhere.'

CHAPTER 14

Mary Steadman had been dead for a few minutes when the flame inside the box stopped. The idea behind the box was that she wasn't getting out whether she obtained the key or not. Mary had seen the hole she'd put her arm through as something basic, but the mechanism inside was much more complicated than it seemed. Through the flick of a switch, the hardened ring nipped and eventually closed, trapping her there while she suffered one of the worst deaths imaginable.

The masked figures up on the walkway, who had seen enough, started making their way back to the access stairs they had come up from, and entered a room where a man was sitting at a computer, wearing the same mask.

The person behind the desk pulled his attention away from the computer screen, where he had watched the whole thing via the cameras positioned high in the corners of each room, and looked their way.

'Are you satisfied?'

The first one, a male, tall and wide, nodded but said nothing. The next figure was smaller and thinner, more likely a female.

'I personally enjoyed it,' said the thin figure.

'Good. I'm glad.'

An awkward silence filled the space. The four figures stood in the middle of the room, staring at him. Heat came from an electric fan, slowly spinning in an arc next to the desk, warming the office. A faint smell of coffee lingered somewhere, but there was no evidence of any half-filled or empty mugs.

'But I want more,' countered the figure behind the probable woman. 'I want more . . .'

The man sitting at the desk smiled behind his mask and nodded in compliance. 'Don't worry, there'll be more. Plenty more. I'm just getting warmed up.' He slowly stood, knocking his chair back with the back of his knees.

'Thanks, that's good to know,' replied the stocky figure.

'One by one, if you could go into that room, remove your mask, and leave the building, that would be great. I'd like to thank you all for coming.'

'It was our pleasure. Until next time.'

They left the room one at a time and waited a little until the next one left. Every few minutes, there was a sound of an engine, then the faint crunch of tyres as they disappeared into the city away from the warehouse.

The remaining mask looked at the man behind the desk. 'Should we contact you, or—'

He raised a hand. 'I'll be in touch.' He grinned behind the mask. 'Don't worry. It won't be long.'

CHAPTER 15

Frustrated with the CCTV footage, Fisher left Alison near the library's main desk and caught up with Phillips, who'd been wandering slowly around with his notepad.

'Find anything?'

Phillips offered a smile. 'Just all these books.' He wasn't much of a reader either. 'There're a couple of cameras positioned around. Any joy with anything back there?'

Fisher's shoulders dropped an inch. 'There's no memory stick in the recorder. There's no footage from yesterday or last night.'

Phillips frowned. 'Think it's been removed?'

She shrugged again, then turned her focus to where the toilets were. She spotted DI James speaking with DI Alex Tunsten, who nodded and smiled about something. Probably from one of their annual dinners, a private joke between them.

'I'm going to speak to Pamela and see how she's getting on.'

'I'll stay to have another look around, see what I can find,' he said.

Inside the toilet, the smell hadn't improved, and if anything, had become worse. The radiator, although it had been turned off, was still giving off some heat. Fisher thought about putting a hand over her nose and mouth but decided not to. Instead, she curled a few strands of loose hair behind her ear.

'Hey, Pam.'

Boone turned her head towards her and smiled. 'Hey, you.'

Pamela Boone was the senior forensic tech for the Greater Manchester Police based on Chorlton Road. Several other forensic techs worked under her at the station, some of whom were partway through their degree. Most of their time was spent in the lab, their learning focused more on analysis than field work, but Boone was always in the thick of it, getting stuck in. She had recently turned fifty, and it had to be said, with her slim and petite figure, looked good for her age. With short blonde hair, she was once described as a pixie, but had been called worse over the years. The wrinkles around her mouth and crow's feet at the edges of her eyes had worsened from a trademark smoking habit in recent years. Many times Fisher had turned up to a crime scene to find Boone outside the cordon with a cigarette hanging from her mouth. A few sergeants and inspectors had expressed their opinions about it being unprofessional, to which she'd responded that she couldn't care less. They'd nod and walk on, knowing she was the best in the business.

Boone turned to Fisher. 'Do me a favour, April. Turn off the light.'

Fisher backed away, went to the door, and flicked the switch. Due to the lack of windows and natural light, the room went pitch black. To her left, Boone lowered her hand to her forensic kit, felt for her UV lamp, and switched it on. Around the urinal, they could see the same blood they noticed with the light on, only a different colour. Below it was evidence of a spill that looked like it had been cleaned up, roughly a foot in size in between the cracks in the tiles.

'See that?' Boone said, crouching.

Fisher nodded. 'Yeah. Blood?'

'Looks like it.' Boone stared in thought. 'Under UV light, blood is easily identifiable. It has a certain tone to it. Appears as though whoever put it here had a little spill. They did an okay job but couldn't remove all of it.'

Fisher took a step back and gazed around the room, seeing if she could spot anything else.

'What's this?' She frowned at the mark just behind her heel. She moved to the side as Boone swivelled, still crouched. The mark certainly piqued her interest. It looked different from the blood marks.

Fisher made way for Boone, who shuffled a few steps over and lowered herself with her UV lamp.

'That more blood?'

It was the same as before; the tile's surface was clean, but whatever it was had pooled in the grout lines that dipped just a fraction under them.

Boone exhaled and shook her head. 'No. It's not blood.'

Fisher picked up on her confidence, knowing it wasn't blood, so her next question was obvious.

'What is it?' Fisher racked her brain, wondering about the possibilities.

Before Boone answered the question, Peter Sterling, the crime scene manager, entered. Fisher looked his way, offering a thin smile.

'Morning,' he said sternly. 'We having a UV disco in here?'

Fisher smiled thinly.

'I hope you're keeping clear?' His question was directed at Fisher, standing a few feet from Boone and the head in the urinal.

Fisher nodded. 'Of course.'

Fisher didn't like Peter Sterling at all. He was an arrogant, self-centred arsehole who thought he was above everyone and everything. Two years ago, he had been promoted to CSM after being a senior tech for as long as Fisher could remember. It wasn't that he didn't suit the role, he had masses of experience and was undoubtedly the right candidate at the time, but after his promotion, he had changed.

'How are we doing, Pam?' he asked Boone, towering over her. He was six foot two, and as slim as a chip. He'd lost any traces of hair a decade ago and shaved his head once a week. Last week Fisher had seen a photo on his desk of him and his wife from way back, sporting a full head of hair, and had smiled to herself.

'Good, boss,' she replied, focusing on what Fisher had noticed. 'We've found something, I think.'

Sterling frowned, his thick bushy eyebrows furrowing to the centre of his tanned, wrinkly forehead.

'In my opinion, it could be semen.'

Neither Fisher nor Sterling were sure what to say. Boone reached over to her pack, grabbing a swab from a pack of a dozen. She held out her light for Fisher to hold, then gently scraped it across the surface of the tiles through the substance.

'Semen?' Fisher finally asked.

Boone nodded. 'Semen.' She picked an empty bag, dropped the swab into it, ran her thumb and finger across the top to seal it, then placed it into her pack.

'How did semen get here?'

Boone raised her eyebrows for a moment but said nothing.

Fisher stood straight, investigating the remainder of the floor. No more visual evidence could be seen anywhere under the power of the UV light. The thought still remained in her mind. She couldn't shake it.

'Semen?' she said again.

'Semen,' Sterling repeated.

'I'll get it tested,' assured Boone, 'but from my experience, yes.'

Fisher stood still, thinking in the darkness, watching Boone's shadow delicately angle the UV light across the floor to ensure there were no signs of anything else.

'Can you tell how old the semen is?' asked Fisher.

'Yes, we'll be able to,' answered Sterling, although the question was for Boone.

Boone, who had also seen the change in Sterling's personality, kept her focus on the tiles and sighed lightly, frustrated at him. It wasn't too long ago they had worked as a pair, helping each other out, solving cases together. But as soon as there was news of the old CSM, Andy Jacobs, possibly retiring, Sterling had spent much of his time with him doing his best to learn exactly what work was involved in the role, not failing to mention they had started going out together. They had become drinking buddies. Boone couldn't care less about the promotion and felt sorry for him and how hard he desperately tried. He was welcome to it.

'Pam?' Fisher pressed, almost disregarding Sterling's response.

'Less than twelve hours, I'd say, but we'll get a better idea soon.'

They knew, from where the sample of semen was, it was possible that whoever put the head there was a male, narrowing the list of potential suspects in half. It was also very likely that this particular male had placed the head in the urinal, taken several steps back, and sexually pleased himself until he ejaculated on the tiles. In an attempt to clean it up, he'd probably spread the semen into the grout line and missed it. The thought of someone doing that sent a shiver down her neck.

'Can you turn the light back on, please, April?'

Fisher moved around Sterling, who deemed himself too important to move out of her way, went over and hit the switch, the light almost blinding them for a moment. Boone placed the lamp back into her kit and used the rear of a gloved hand to wipe her damp forehead.

A moment later, they heard footsteps at the door. Phillips appeared, still wearing his long brown coat.

'You not hot in that?' said Fisher, eyeing him up and down.

'Maybe a little,' he conceded, but they both knew he wouldn't remove it out of stubbornness.

'What have I missed?'

'Just forensic stuff,' replied Sterling, as if it would go over his head.

Phillips ignored his sarcasm and looked to where Fisher was pointing near the base of the urinal. 'Signs of blood there.' She moved her extended arm towards herself, stopping at the area near her feet. 'Another substance here. Pamela is confident it could be semen.'

They all continued to watch Boone work, as she placed both hands on the side of the head and carefully lifted it a few inches upwards. The dried, matted blood on the hair clung to the porcelain surface until it reluctantly peeled away. Boone lifted the head high enough to see underneath where it had been cut; she was curious to see how it had been removed from the body.

'What are you thinking?' asked Fisher, lowering herself, but she couldn't see much.

'It's a clean cut, nice and straight. Although—' Boone brought the head a few inches closer to see the edge of the skin — 'it may be a saw of some sort. An electric saw, maybe.'

She tipped the head back, exploring the inside of the throat and neck area, suddenly frowning. Between the cluster of blood, tendons, and a small, sheared bone which she knew was the spine, there was something unusual.

'Ahh, what's this?' She turned to Fisher.

'What do you need me to do?'

'I need you to hold the head a second.'

Fisher took a deep breath. She'd seen a human head in the past but never had the pleasure of holding one.

'Okay.' She shifted her feet to steady herself. 'Just want me to hold it?'

'Yeah, exactly like I am. I see something that doesn't belong.'

That got both Phillips and the CSM intrigued.

Boone slowly handed the head to Fisher, who was almost taken aback by the weight of it, although she shouldn't have been. She'd read somewhere once that an average human head weighed around eleven pounds, which wasn't far off a stone.

'Tip it back, please.'

Fisher turned her wrists, allowing Boone to see the underside of the head. 'That enough?'

'Yeah, hold it there,' whispered Boone, then reached down to her left, grabbing a small Maglite, and pointed it at what had caught her eye.

'What is it, Pam?' asked Phillips.

Ignoring him, she grabbed a pair of tweezers from her kit and very carefully nipped the object's edge, which was almost paper thin. She pulled gently, the object sliding out a tiny bit at a time. Fisher could feel Boone pulling a little, so she kept a good hold on the head. Phillips scowled at the tweezers, watching the object being pulled from inside.

'There it is.' Boone kept the tweezers nipped tightly. The object was thin, flat, roughly two inches by six, covered in blood clots and a brown-yellow fluid. It was solid, folded along one length, and the other had two parts. Was it folded paper?

'What's that?' Fisher said, curiously leaning to one side to see around the head.

'I have no idea.' Boone took the folded paper in her left hand, placed the tweezers back in her kit, and used a finger from another hand to separate the two edges until it was flat. Phillips and Fisher leaned closer.

'Who's that?' probed Sterling, also leaning over, his gangly figure like a drooping tree.

Neither detective could see what he meant. When Boone turned the photo around, they saw an image of a teenage boy around thirteen, dressed in a school uniform.

'Why on earth is that photo inside the head?' Phillips shook his head in disbelief.

'I think the more pressing question is who the boy in the photo is,' replied Fisher.

CHAPTER 16

Fisher and Phillips left Boone in the toilet to work. Alison was spotted at the reception desk, sitting at the computer, a dim glare on her face. She held a phone to her ear and spoke quietly. Fisher heard the word 'sorry' before Alison disconnected. Perhaps a customer was ringing to ask about a book or wondering when the library would be opening again.

As Fisher headed towards the desk, she noticed PC Baan approaching her from the left.

'April, there's been a call at the station. A missing person's report. Thorne wants us to go check it out. I told him I'd ask you first.'

Fisher smiled. 'Thorne is your inspector, so if that's what he wants you to do, then you'll have to.'

Baan nodded and turned away.

'Who made the missing person's report?' probed Fisher before she left.

'Guy called Gary Steadman. Said his wife's missing.'

'How long has she been missing?'

'Dispatch noted he returned home from a business trip early this morning and said she wasn't there. Her phone was there, and so was her car. The bedroom is a bit of a mess. It's unusual for her.'

'Okay. Let me know what he says.'

Baan smiled at Fisher. 'I need to pick Adam up from the station. He's just clocked on now.'

'I thought PC Jackson was away for a few days?'

'He was. Just got back this morning.'

'Straight back at it, eh?'

'You know what it's like working for this department.'

Fisher smiled knowingly. 'Keep me updated.'

'Sure will.'

* * *

PC Baan swung by the station on Chorlton Road to pick up PC Adam Jackson. He was waiting at the station's rear entrance with a grin on his face as she approached in the marked Astra.

He opened the door and lowered himself in. 'Morning.' His tone was chirpy and upbeat. He looked good, his hair was neatly combed, and his face, judging by a noticeable rash under his chin, was freshly shaven. A whiff of something woody pulsated from him, one of the many aftershaves he was obsessed with.

'Someone happy to be back at work?' Baan turned up the heating inside the car, edged the gear into first, and slowly navigated around to the car park exit.

'I'm exhausted, to be honest, Ash. Must have covered fifty thousand steps over the last few days.' He took a deep breath of air, exhaling slowly.

Baan screwed her face up at the thought of how his legs must be aching and how cold it must have been to be camping in this weather. He'd been up to the Lakes with a few friends. He'd finished his shift on Tuesday, then driven straight up, meeting them there. They had tackled their first task Wednesday morning, walking up Helvellyn, which took them the best part of the day. Thursday's activities included climbing Scafell Pike and Skiddaw, which had almost broken them, although they were all fit and of a similar age. They'd packed their tent away earlier that morning and driven back home, his friends heading back to the North East.

'What's with the whole climbing thing anyway, Adam?'

Baan moved through the gears, heading west towards Gary Steadman's house.

'I don't know. I watched the film *Everest*, and ever since, I've got into it. Been talking to some friends I know. They said they were walking. Thought I'd put a few holidays in, join them.'

She raised her brows and glanced his way. 'Think you'll ever do that?'

'Huh?'

'Everest?' she prompted.

'I'll see how long it takes me to recover from the Lakes first.'

They shared a laugh. It wasn't long before they slowed at a set of double gates. Baan stopped the Astra and pressed her window down, and a rush of cold air seeped in. It was just above freezing this morning, set to reach a high of only four degrees. Baan was dressed in her uniform with an additional fleece to cover the arms she'd have on show in the warmer months. Johnson was dressed in the same attire.

She leaned out and pressed the button on the device attached to the metal pole, causing a sudden high-pitched drone. A few seconds later, she heard a voice.

'Hello?'

'Hi, I'm PC Ashleigh Baan, with my partner, PC Adam Jackson. We're here in response to a call you made regarding a missing person?'

'Yeah. Wait a second. I'll open the gate.'

After a loud beep, then a mechanical hum, the gates slowly opened away from them to reveal a long winding driveway that led to a large cube-shaped house surrounded by neatly trimmed laws and colourful flowers.

'Someone's doing all right,' noted Jackson.

Baan stopped the car beside a brand-new Mercedes, the tyres crunching gently on the gravel. On the other side of the Merc was a large Ford, though Baan was unsure of the model. They got out, the fresh December air flooding into their lungs as they breathed. Baan knocked on the door, took a step back, and waited.

'Hey, thanks for coming,' Gary Steadman said as he opened it. He was short but stocky with thick shoulders. His face was hardened not only by age but with an impressive tan he had got from either a recent holiday or frequent use of sunbeds. He eyed them both. 'Please come in.' He stepped aside to give them plenty of space, his muscular chest protruding from a tight-fitting T-shirt. They entered through the impressive-looking threshold into a wide, spacious hallway with plenty of floor space. Steadman closed the door and headed for the kitchen.

'Follow me, please.'

He flicked on the kettle. 'Coffee?'

'I'll take a tea, please,' replied Baan, 'if you have any?'

'Of course.' He picked a teabag from a wooden container, dropped it into an empty mug, then addressed Jackson. 'Tea, coffee?'

'I'm fine, thanks.' He raised a thankful palm, went over to the table, and pulled out a chair.

Moments later, they were sitting at the table, discussing how he'd arrived home at 8 a.m. that morning, surprised to see Mary's car there as she'd usually be at work by then.

'She's the managing director, so her days are very long,' he explained.

Both PCs nodded. Jackson pulled a small notepad from his vest pocket and started making notes.

'I thought maybe she was starting late, but I couldn't find her in the house. In the bedroom, her phone was on the bedside table, and the bed covers were ruffled. There was also a towel creased on the floor. She always hangs them up over the towel rail in the bathroom. She has OCD about that, let me tell you.'

'Any idea where she could be?'

Steadman shook his head. 'At this time, like I said, usually at work.'

'Where does she work?' Baan asked, edging forward a little, comfortable in the warm kitchen.

'They have an office at the boat shed in Salford Quays.'

Baan knew the area, aware the rent of the place must cost an arm and a leg.

'Is it possible she found a different way into work this morning? Maybe got a lift in?'

'It takes over half an hour to drive it, so she normally goes earlier to avoid the rush hour, although it's always busy in the city. No one at the office lives near here, so I can't see it.' He shrugged.

'A train, perhaps?'

He quickly shook his head. 'She hates them. Plus, she wouldn't have left without her phone. It's stuck to her hand most of the time.'

'Does she exercise?'

He nodded. 'She runs, but not on the roads. She sometimes goes to a gym on her way home from work.' His eyes dropped to the table. 'I just don't understand where she is.'

'Can we look at the bedroom — you say there's a towel on the floor?'

'There was. I picked it up and hung it on the door.' He stood. 'But you're more than welcome to have a look up there.'

After they removed their shoes, they followed Steadman upstairs onto a wide landing. The walls were lined with expensive-looking photos with extravagant frames along the way to the bedroom, images of mountain ranges and still lakes with the sun setting in the background. Baan took a brief moment to inspect them as they passed, thinking it was almost like a moment of inspiration each time they left the bedroom, something to build them up, get them ready for the day.

'Nice photos,' commented Baan. Steadman, as if he didn't have time for chit-chat, ignored her, stepping into their huge bedroom. He pointed to the floor.

'The towel was there.'

Baan and Jackson looked down. 'Anything else that's unusual?'

'Yeah. One of the board members had got my number and rang me, asking if I'd seen Mary this morning. She was late for a meeting and he couldn't get hold of her — a building firm were interested in tendering for an upcoming project.'

'What's the nature of her business?'

'Construction. They design everything, right down to the last nook and cranny. But they hire contractors in to bid for their services. These smaller companies know if they can win Mary round, they'll have work for months, possibly years.'

PC Jackson slowly wandered around, scanning the room. He hadn't ever stepped inside a bedroom so big. It spanned the full width of the house. He spotted something.

'What's this?' he asked Steadman, pointing to an area of carpet beside the bed, closest to the window.

Steadman, who was on the opposite side, frowned before making his way around the queen-size bed. 'What?' He sounded annoyed, as if whatever Jackson had found, he should have noticed it.

'Here.'

Baan followed him around the bed to have a look.

On the cream carpet, there was a darker patch between the bed and the window, the shape of a circle, roughly a foot.

'What is it?' Steadman asked, his face developing into a scowl.

'Do you or your wife wear your shoes up here?'

He shook his head almost before Jackson had finished the question. 'Absolutely not; the carpets are fairly new. We like to keep them that way.'

'You noticed that mark before?' Baan said.

For a moment, Steadman didn't answer. He stared at the darker area, which was now obvious, clearly feeling stupid for not noticing it before they had arrived. 'I can't say that I have.'

'There's more here.' Jackson shuffled to the right, turning his body to see the rest of the carpet. 'And there.'

Baan looked at the area he was pointing to.

'Mr Steadman, do—?'

'Please, call me Gary,' he countered.

'Gary,' Baan said, 'do you know of anyone who may want to cause your wife harm?'

'You think someone's been in our house?' Steadman placed a hand on his hip and tilted his head. 'You think someone broke in and took her?'

'At the moment, we don't know anything, Gary. We hope to gather as much information as possible to determine where your wife is.'

He nodded and thought for a moment. 'Off the top of my head, no, I can't think of anyone who'd want to harm Mary. But . . .' Both PCs looked his way, waiting. 'Maybe people in her industry; contractors she let go or didn't pick for the bigger jobs. I don't know.' He shrugged hopelessly. 'She doesn't talk about her work much when she's home. She likes to unwind and . . . have a glass of wine. Switch off, you know.'

Judging by the empty glass on her dressing table, Baan could believe that.

'Do you have cameras?'

Steadman looked at Jackson. 'We have one at the gate and one at the rear of the property, looking out at the garden. We had more, but we're upgrading, so the company who is doing it disconnected the other three.'

'Can we see them?'

He nodded at Jackson. 'Follow me.'

Less than a minute later, they were downstairs in the dining room. The PCs followed Steadman through another door that led into a rectangular room about half the size of it. It had a window overlooking the side of the house. Baan gazed out and noticed the garden below in the near distance. To the left was a small desk with a monitor on, sitting atop a black box that looked similar to a Sky box.

Steadman pulled out the chair and took a seat, wiggling the mouse to awaken the screen. There were two squares at the top, both showing a visual, one of the front gates, the other of the rear garden. There were three boxes underneath, each with the same 'undetected signal' message in the top-right corners.

Baan and Jackson stood behind him, watching the screen.

'Could you take it back to last night?' asked Baan.

Steadman let out a small sigh as if to say *give me a chance*. He clicked a button at the bottom corner of the screen, opening a folder with more folders and files.

'What time did she get home?'

Steadman frowned in thought and turned to Jackson. 'I spoke with her just after nine last night. She told me she was in a meeting and would be there a little longer. I'm assuming she came straight home.'

'Just start it from there, then,' suggested Baan. She leaned, pointing to the footage of the front gate. The camera was just outside the property, fixed to one of the columns that supported the metal gate, focusing on the area before it. 'Make that screen bigger, please.'

They watched silently until the time in the corner was 10.54 p.m., and a haze of light followed by Mary's Mercedes filled the screen. Steadman shuffled a little, happy to see she'd got home. A moment later, the car vanished, and the gates closed.

'Which other cameras will pick her up now?'

He turned and shrugged at Baan. 'The one at the front of the house usually, but it's turned off. It's one of the disconnected ones.'

Baan sighed lightly. 'Okay. I know this may sound like a stupid question, but are you one hundred per cent sure she isn't here?'

Steadman glared at her as if she had three heads. 'Don't you think I've already checked every room before I called you guys?'

Baan ignored his sarcasm; he was frustrated. It was understandable. She'd dealt with all sorts of people during her career, seeing the finest of what Manchester had to offer. 'Can we go back to the front camera again, please?'

It appeared Steadman was going to ask why but he said nothing, doing as she requested. From 11 p.m., he fast-forwarded the recording until around 12.30 a.m., when the gate opened again.

'Wow, stop it there!' Baan snapped, stabbing a finger at the screen.

'Okay, okay.' Steadman paused it and took it back a minute, starting with a closed gate. He pressed play. The gate opened slowly then the Mercedes crawled by. The window was up, so they couldn't see her face in the driver's seat. He noticed the time in the corner. 'Where on earth is she going at that time?'

'Did you speak with her after the text around nine o'clock?'

'She texted me at half eleven saying she was getting a shower and going to bed. So when I found the towel this morning, I assumed that's what she'd done.'

'Well, the car's here now, so she must have come back. Fast-forward it, please.'

He did, and they all watched carefully, seeing if a sudden flash of light came from the right. At 1.32 a.m., the light appeared. He stopped the recording to let it play. There was the Mercedes. After the gate opened again, the Mercedes moved forward, the driver's window down a few inches.

'Hold up,' said Jackson, shuddering a little. 'What's that?'

'What?' Steadman glared at him. 'What's what?'

'Leave it paused.' Jackson leaned over his shoulder, pointing at something. 'Who's that?'

They both followed Jackson's finger, which almost touched the screen.

He highlighted a shape in the driver's seat, visible through the open window. The car's brilliant white lights reflected off the gates, bouncing back and hitting the car, allowing Jackson to see the figure.

'See it?'

Baan and Steadman both squinted and agreed.

'Does that look like your wife?'

'It looks too big for Mary,' he admitted. 'She has blonde hair, not short dark hair.' He brought a finger up to scratch the side of his head.

'My thoughts exactly,' agreed Jackson. 'It looks like it could be a man.'

'So if that's a man driving my wife's car, where the hell is Mary — is she in the passenger seat?'

Although it wasn't the clearest of images, if there had been someone sitting beside the man, they would be visible.

'What the hell's going on?' asked Steadman.

CHAPTER 17

There were two sounds in the small room. One belonged to a computer sitting atop a desk against one wall, the internal fan in the CPU unit whirring, the other belonged to the flow of water travelling through the radiators below the desk, inches away from the man's feet. He could feel its warmth radiate through his bones.

It had been an eventful morning for him, which in hindsight had gone exactly as he'd planned. Watching the police arrive to secure the scene fascinated him. The way the public gathered at the crime scene tape to see all the commotion, the look of confusion and wonder on their faces. The desperation to know why Forensics were there.

He leaned back in his chair, remembering the scene unfolding in his head. The white Volvo slowing, pulling over to the curb. The door opening, a female detective stepping down from her car, confidently making her way across the road with her head held high, readying herself for whatever he had left for her and her team inside the library.

Sitting at the desk, hoping the police were enjoying themselves, the man took a lungful of warm air and held it for a while before releasing it into the warm, stuffy room. The window had been closed to block out the late morning chill.

The faint sun was shining against the glass, but it offered no warmth.

He glared back at the computer screen, focusing on the research he'd conducted over the past few months. Then his eyes fell on the photos in the space in front of him. Six pictures were lined up from left to right, all A4 sized and in colour, photos he'd pulled from either their social media profiles or ones he'd taken himself. It felt more accurate, more personal, knowing he'd taken those photos, that he'd been so close to them without them being aware.

He reached over, grabbed a black marker from a selection of pens, removed the lid, and brought it to his nose. He sniffed loudly, sucking the intoxicating fumes up inside his head. He lowered the pen, smiling, feeling a moment of giddiness, and marked the photo furthest left with a huge black cross from corner to corner.

'I'd apologise to you, Debbie Johnson, but you only have yourself to blame,' he said, staring at her picture.

The photo had been taken two months ago, in a bustling bar in the city. It had been around 10 p.m. The place had been loud and energetic, hustling with keen drinkers and teenagers who used a fake ID and eye-catching cleavages to gain entry. He missed that age, going out like that, carefree, not giving a shit about anything but where the next bar was. Debbie had been at the bar in conversation with a friend, occasionally laughing at each other's jokes. The man had to admit she'd been attractive. There was no way she had looked forty-one; her figure should have been on the cover of a magazine. It was hard to believe what she'd done, what hurt she'd caused to others.

He picked up the photo and stared at her face for a moment. 'Rest in peace, Debbie.' From a drawer under the desk, he pulled out an A4 folder, opened the flap, and placed the photo gently inside.

He closed the drawer and picked up the following photo of Mary Steadman. This one he'd pulled from her business website. The image was professional, the quality of the lens enhancing the fabric of her clean, crisp suit and the whites of her perfectly formed teeth. It was evident from the photo she was an assured individual with plenty of money. She hadn't been so confident earlier that morning at the factory, he thought to himself.

He picked up the pen and lowered it to the photo, then stopped and stared, deciding not to. He'd put the cross on her face later, when the police eventually found her. His second masterpiece. Until then, he'd bide his time and, when the time was right, move on to his third victim. He'd done enough research to know what he was doing. After gathering the remaining photos, he gently placed them into the drawer.

He stood up, put his chair in, and gazed out the window. The park opposite was empty, which wasn't uncommon for this time of the day because most children were at school. Above the trees, a bright sun was breaking through a heavy blanket of clouds. Turning to the closed door, he smiled at the mask hanging on the back of it.

CHAPTER 18

A few hours had passed. After conducting interviews with some locals who, unfortunately, hadn't seen anything helpful, and the fact that the recording device in the office had been removed, giving them nothing to go on, the detectives' moods had worsened. Fisher and Phillips had grabbed something to eat on the way back to the station. Phillips had almost finished, but Fisher hadn't touched hers yet.

'Are you not eating that?' He nodded at the unopened tuna sandwich on her lap.

She sighed heavily, looked his way, and gave a thin smile. 'Not in the mood for food, Matthew. I'll have it later.'

He smiled thinly. 'Is everything okay, April?'

She brought a hand up and used her thumb and forefinger to squeeze her nose before sniffing. 'It's just not every day you see a woman's head resting in a urinal.'

He nodded in understanding. 'You're right. It isn't.' He looked back across the station's car park, which was only half full. DI James's Range Rover was there, the glossy paintwork reflecting the low, dazzling sun.

'We'll catch the bastard, whoever did this to her.'

He nodded again, feeling her frustration. 'We always do.' He then patted her arm. 'Right, come on, DI James wants us in the meeting as soon as we get back.'

They grabbed a quick coffee from the canteen and were the last ones in the room. DI James, who stood at the front with the black fob in his hand, gave them a disapproving stare as they made their way to a seat. PC Baan and PC Jackson were there, along with DC Peterson, PC Amy Legg, and Inspector Eric Thorne, seated close to Baan and Jackson on the window side, no doubt catching some of the heat from the warm radiators.

'Right, guys,' DI James began. 'It's now December. It's coming up to Christmas. It's a time to be spending with loved ones, in the pub with friends, or at home with family, sitting by the fire with hot chocolates to warm our hands.'

Fisher frowned at him.

'But if we don't make any progress we won't be doing any of that. It sounds harsh, but that's the reality here. We'll be working every hour we can to keep our city a safe place for the people in it.'

Everyone in the room sighed.

'April, would you mind coming to the front and sharing what you have so far?'

She nodded, putting his last comment to the back of her mind. 'No worries.' She stood, went to the front, and turned to face everyone. 'This morning at Chorlton Library, a janitor opened up just before seven o'clock. During his cleaning routine, he discovered the head of an, as yet, unidentified female resting in one of the urinals in the library toilet.'

'A head? A human head?' asked PC Legg. She gazed around at her colleagues before looking back to Fisher, who was staring at her.

Fisher nodded. 'Yes. The library is still secure. Pamela is down there with a few PCs from another department.'

'Jesus,' Legg replied, slowly running her hand through her hair.

'I was there with Pamela when she carefully lifted the head from the urinal. Tucked up inside the throat was a photo of a schoolboy who looks to be around the age of twelve or thirteen.'

'Do we know who the boy is?' DI James asked from her left.

'Not yet. The photo is being analysed for prints. Once we've done that, we'll cross-reference the image in our database, but I'm not holding any hope that a photo of a schoolboy will bring us much luck. The female victim we found has blonde hair and, from the photo of Debbie Johnson, there's a good chance it could be her. Pamela has extracted some DNA from the head and has bagged it for testing.' She paused, taking a deep breath. 'At the scene, close to where we found the head, Pamela said there were traces of semen on the tiled floor.'

'Fresh semen?' enquired Inspector Thorne, his eyebrows meeting just above his thick nose.

'Yes.'

She let that sink in across the room; a few faces understood the possibility that the person responsible placed the head in the urinal and stood back, pleasuring themselves at the scene in front of them. PC Legg winced and looked away for a moment.

'So, we have the suspect's DNA?' Thorne said, edging forward a little to adjust himself on the seat. Fisher nodded again. 'Well, that's something,' he added.

'What about cameras?' DC Peterson this time.

Fisher turned to him, taken aback by his question. Peterson was often quiet and rarely spoke up in the daily meetings. One to one, you couldn't keep him quiet, but he usually allowed others to talk in a crowd. He didn't like the focus of others.

'There are a few cameras outside the library. One out the front covered Manchester Road, and another at the back of the library covered an access door mainly used for deliveries and maintenance. I checked the footage from last night and found nothing. The recording device is old and seems to be missing a memory stick or a plug-in hard drive of some sort. The footage isn't there.'

Collected sighs swept the room.

'I'm going to speak with Liam Harper at the control room to see if he can see anything in the nearby streets.'

Most of them nodded in agreement.

'So,' DI James said, moving forward, holding out a thumb, 'we have the DNA of the victim.' He then extended his index finger. 'We have the DNA of a potential suspect.' A third finger. 'We have a photo of an unidentified schoolboy who we assume is important to this unfortunate event.'

'Do we have Debbie Johnson's DNA yet?' asked DS Phillips.

Fisher pointed at him, grinning. 'I was just going to mention that. Thank you, Matthew. No, we currently do not. I'm going to send—' she looked towards Inspector Eric Thorne for his approval — 'PC Baan and PC Jackson to Debbie Johnson's house to collect anything we can extract her DNA from, if that's okay?'

Thorne nodded firmly. 'Absolutely. We're here to assist you guys in any way possible.' He nodded at Baan and Jackson, who replied to the gesture and focused on Fisher again.

'Good.' DI James clapped his hands and rubbed them together quickly as if he was trying to warm himself up. 'We're making progress. DCI Baker wants a word about what's gone on this morning, so I'll be happy to tell him our positive actions moving forward to get the results we need.' He ran a palm through his long, slick hair. 'Right, team, let's get some results. Dress up out there. There's a storm coming.'

CHAPTER 19

They had wiped Chorlton Library completely clean. The head found in the urinal was bagged and tagged, and the photo carefully placed into a clear plastic bag. Any other potential traces of anything were swabbed and labelled. Before Boone left the library, she and several other PCs, meticulously searched the library for anything else important. Over an hour and a half later, they concluded that, other than what they had found in the toilet, there was nothing of interest they deemed crucial to this horrific case. Boone dabbed the entrance and exit door handles for prints but knew more than likely the suspect was intelligent enough to wear gloves, but they had to check. They'd also taken the library assistant's fingerprints too, so she could add them to the database for when the results came back.

Located on the ground floor of the police station, she walked through the door into the rectangular-shaped forensics lab. Bright lights shone down from four long, modern ceiling lamps, illuminating the room. There were two empty worktables in the centre, with a workbench to the right containing equipment such as analytical balances, moisture analysers, and microscopes. Over to the left, another bench housed a heating and drying oven and an incubator.

A storage cupboard to her immediate right contained bottles and various tubes.

It was just after 2 p.m. The trainee forensic techs, Stacy Coors and Jasper Allan, were over to the right, occupying the space between a microscope and one of the analysers, collecting fingerprints off the photo of the schoolboy that Boone had removed from inside the head. They were both wearing gloves, leaning over the image on the table, carefully sprinkling the thin powder onto the surface of the photo. Boone noticed Stacy's red hair reflect the vivid light directly above her. If there was a physical fingerprint on the picture, they'd usually photograph it for analysis. Boone stood back, watching them closely. After the powder had peppered the photo, Stacy tore off a strip of clear lifting tape from a nearby roll and slowly positioned it onto the image. Jasper leaned in to see.

Boone smiled at them. She'd had them for nearly two months; both had almost completed a degree in forensic science at Manchester University. They were doing a placement year before going back to finish their degrees. Stacy was twenty-four, tall and thin. She liked to wear plain clothes that didn't stand out in a crowd — although her red hair contradicted that — and was generally, so far, quiet and reserved. Jasper was almost thirty. He was more outgoing, flamboyant, and louder, wearing a bright-coloured top with his usual blue jeans. He had the best moustache that Boone had ever seen, so long it curled at the ends, something Daniel Day-Lewis would be proud of, along with dark hair he gelled and brushed back. He was always asking Boone questions and doing activities first, so to see Stacy applying the lifting tape pleased Boone.

'We found anything?' asked Boone, behind them.

'Jeez, Pam!' Jasper placed a hand on his chest. 'You scared me there.'

'Sorry.' She leaned over their shoulders. 'What have you got?'

Stacy tilted her head a little as she carefully removed the tape from the photo and held it up against a bright fluorescent light on the wall. 'Looks like a partial. Got it from the corner.'

Boone grinned, patting her on the back. 'Good work, you two. Store the print. We'll do some database searching very soon.' Boone left them and went over to her desk at the end of the lab. She had hoped they'd find something because the print was her own. While the trainees were busy doing something else, she couldn't find any marks on the picture of the boy, even using the lab's high-tech LED devices and developers. She knew the suspect had worn gloves and had been careful, so for training purposes, she had applied her own print for the trainees to find.

Desperate for a cigarette, she decided to wait until 3 p.m. and sat down at her desk, pulling herself in. She shook the mouse to awaken the computer and logged on to the system. She'd stored the DNA of the victim and would wait for PC Baan and PC Jackson to bring an item from Debbie Johnson's apartment to see if there was a match later this afternoon.

Until then, she glanced to her left at the large plastic box on the closest table. Inside the box was the head belonging to the library victim. She had to look more closely as to how the head had been removed from the body it had been attached to. She was aware the trainees hadn't seen a head before, not in their first two months anyway, and pondered the idea for a moment, wondering if it would be too much for their fragile minds. Finally, she settled on the assumption that if they were to make it in forensics, the best way to start would be at the deep end.

'Stacy, Jasper,' she said.

They both turned her way, peeling their attention off the photo.

'Please come over here. I'd like you two to have a look at something.'

CHAPTER 20

DS Fisher let out a shiver at her desk and rubbed the out-side of her arms, seriously considering removing the jacket from the back of her chair and putting it on. Something had happened with the heating just after lunchtime which had knocked it off. The maintenance man mentioned something to do with the gas supply to DI James, and that they were getting someone to fix it. The earlier heating had warmed the office nicely during the morning, but it was amazing how quickly the office lost its warmth, inviting the freezing December temperature through the building's walls.

'Sod this.' Fisher pushed her chair out, grabbed the jacket, and put it on quickly. 'Freezing in here.'

DS Phillips laughed. 'I'm alright.'

'You're wearing your big daft coat though,' she replied, reaching over and playfully hitting his shoulder. 'Look like a clown in that thing.'

'Don't be jealous, April,' he said, focusing on the report he was typing on his screen. 'Only a certain type of coolness can pull this look off.'

Fisher sat back down and pulled herself in to carry on the report she had almost finished. DI James had asked them to do their morning reports to cover what went on at the library, while Boone was doing forensics. They often did them at the end of the day but didn't see the harm in complying with James's wishes. At least it would be one less thing to do later.

'Jesus,' a voice said behind them.

They turned to see PC Baan rubbing her palms together. 'It's like an igloo in here — it's actually warmer outside. Why isn't the heating on? Are we cutting back costs on energy usage as well?' She made a small 'O' with her mouth.

'Something to do with the gas supply, maintenance said. They're calling someone in to fix it.'

Baan nodded at Phillips and looked back to Fisher.

'April, I'm just letting you know that Adam and I have been to Debbie's apartment. We contacted one of her friends, Abi Witmore, who let us in to get whatever we needed.'

'Was she okay with you doing that?'

A nod from Baan. 'She was. We took a toothbrush, hairbrush, and an electronic cigarette — one of those vape things.'

Fisher nodded.

'She wouldn't stop asking questions, though,' Baan added.

'Understandable.'

'Obviously, I didn't tell her that Debbie's head was possibly found in a library toilet.'

'Appreciate that,' Fisher replied. 'Thank you.'

'I've handed the items to Boone. Said she'd get straight on with it.'

Fisher reached for Baan's hand. 'Thanks, Ashleigh.'

'Only doing my job.' They shared a smile. 'Right, I'll go see Inspector Thorne. Let me know of any developments and if you need us, okay?'

They released hands, and Fisher watched Baan walk down the aisle and through the double doors into the corridor.

'You two are good friends, eh?' noted Phillips, seeing Fisher's gaze.

'We are, Matthew.' Fisher smiled briefly, then swivelled back to her desk. 'She's been there for me over the years. A good person to have around.'

Just as Fisher had finished her report, her mobile rang in her pocket. 'Hello?' she answered.

'Hey, April, it's Liam from City Hall.'

'Hey, Liam. Thanks for getting back to me.'

'Sorry it wasn't sooner. I received your message and have been looking into it.' He sounded upbeat, which excited Fisher.

'Great, thanks.' Fisher sat straighter in her chair. 'What do you have?'

To her left, out of the corner of her eye, she spotted someone walking past her. She turned, seeing the back of a man, wearing workwear, carrying a toolbox that looked heavy thanks to the way his right side tipped as he moved. Keeping the phone to her ear, she frowned, sure she'd seen him before. Maybe he was here about the heating?

'We have a camera on Manchester Road and . . . DS Fisher, you there?'

She focused back on the call, looking back at her screen. 'Sorry, I was just looking at something. Say that again.'

'A camera on Manchester Road picked up a small blue van next to the library just after two in the morning. Unfortunately, it came from behind, so there was no view of the driver.'

'What happened?'

'Well, to be honest, not much. It stayed there for an hour. No one got out of the vehicle or got in. I've watched it three times over. But it's the only thing I have in that area. We have blind spots, which we are trying to rectify. That's what our campaign was about last month.'

'You got a registration for the van?'

'Only a partial, unfortunately, but I'm not one hundred per cent. The last three letters could be S, C, and T.'

'Okay. I'll check it out. Thanks for getting back to me. If there's anything else, don't hesitate to call. Thanks, Liam.'

She ended the call and placed her phone on the desk.

The man who had passed her put his toolbox down out of sight and checked the wall at the back, just behind the last row of desks. Fisher stood and watched as he bent forward a little, focusing on the floor. It looked like the heating pipes ran along the back wall.

Then the man turned slightly and turned his attention to Fisher. When she met his gaze, he quickly turned back, focusing on the pipes again.

Initially, Fisher had thought the man was a stranger, but when they made that very brief eye contact, something was familiar; Fisher was sure she'd seen him somewhere before.

CHAPTER 21

After Fisher had arrived home just after 7 p.m., she switched the engine off. She sat for a moment in silence, resting her head against the headrest, and closed her eyes. The sound of muffled talking grabbed her attention. Two teenage boys walked past, chatting with each other and playing music on their phones. So much for headphones, she thought.

With what seemed an effort, she opened her door and stepped onto the path with her laptop case. It was freezing now, well below zero. She promised herself she would wear something more suitable to work on Monday, something over the top of her usual white blouse and dark blue suit jacket.

Luckily tonight, there was a spot right outside her house on St Nicholas Road, meaning she didn't have to park outside Raymond's house several doors along. At least the Volvo would be out of harm's way for the night. The previous week, Raymond, a mid-sixties single guy with the thinnest goatee she'd ever seen, had thrown a party and invited what seemed like the whole of Manchester to it. The noise of the music was not only loud, but the choice of playlist was horrific. Fisher wasn't the only neighbour to think that either.

Penny, who lived two doors along from Fisher, the house next to Raymond's, had knocked on Fisher's door to ask if she could go and have a word with them. The last thing she had wanted to do was cause an issue, but it was approaching 11 p.m., and it was the courteous thing to do. Fisher had told Penny she would sort it, and once it reached 11 p.m., she had stepped outside into her garden to listen. It seemed Raymond played loud music purposely to annoy people. Inconsiderate and vile conversations could be heard by most of the street and the row of houses behind, and Fisher knew she had to intervene, so she had knocked on his door. He'd opened it, almost struggling to remain balanced through his alcohol consumption, and stared at her with half-shut, glassy eyes.

'Mrs April, how very, very nice to see you,' he slurred, his words just audible to Fisher.

'Raymond, it's late. Would it be possible to turn down the music a little for our neighbours' sanity?'

He scowled and toppled forward, heading towards Fisher, who stepped back quickly, but he grabbed the door surround to prevent his fall. 'I am so . . . I'm sorry about this. I'll turn it down pronto.' He stood straight, making his best impression of an army soldier, and saluted her with a flat hand against his forehead, almost hitting himself in the eye. 'Aye-aye, captain.'

'Thank you,' she said before leaving and noticed a reduction in the noise, so she went to bed feeling like her words had at least given the neighbours a chance to sleep. When she went out the following morning, her car door had several scratches. The car next to it, belonging to another neighbour, had also suffered some alterations. She questioned Raymond immediately, who, judging by how he looked, was suffering a horrific hangover and couldn't be arsed with her. She made sure to go back later and ask but he said he knew nothing about the scratches and shrugged it off.

Happy to now be home after the day she'd had, Fisher walked through her gate, closed it, and opened her front door. The lamp she had on a timer was on, lighting up the hallway and most of the kitchen. She kicked off her shoes, placed her laptop on the floor against the wall, and turned on the heating before removing her jacket. While the house warmed, she had a long soak in the bath. Usually, she was more of a shower girl, but she needed the soak today.

Leaning over the edge of the bath, worried about dropping her phone in the water, she scrolled through social media for a short while before settling on watching Netflix. After a brief browse through the crime category, she chose an American programme she'd heard good things about and clicked on episode one.

After it had finished and the water had become tepid, she rose from it and used her toes to remove the plug. Once dried, she hung the damp towel on the towel rail and went downstairs in her thick dressing gown, noticing the time on the clock was almost 9 p.m. The house had warmed considerably, judging by the condensation on the kitchen window. Beyond the glass, she noticed a guy in the house opposite, upstairs in the window, with his top off. He seemed to be still, focusing on something, and judging by his tanned skin and athletic physique, it was probably a mirror. There was no harm in taking pride in one's appearance, but when the man started flexing his muscles, she knew it was time to reach up and lower the roller blind.

Wanting to relax, she opened the fridge and stared at the bottle of Coke. She grabbed it, placing it on the worktop. She took a bottle of vodka from one of the lower cupboards and positioned it next to the Coke, pondering to herself, and decided she'd rather have coffee, not wanting to get too carried away, what with having work tomorrow.

'Another night,' she decided.

In the living room, she sat and grabbed the TV remote. There wasn't much on, so she opted for the second episode of the series she'd just started. As it wasn't yet half nine, she leaned forward, placing her mug on the coffee table in front of her, found her mum's number, and pressed CALL as she sank back into the comfort of the sofa.

Freda picked up. 'April, what's up? What's happened?'

Fisher frowned. 'Nothing, Mum. I'm just calling to say hi, that's all.'

There was an unsettling silence on the other end.

'Mum?'

'I'm sorry, April. The last time you called me at this time, you gave me some bad news.'

Fisher thought about her words and realised she was right. It had been a Friday night when she'd miscarried all those months ago. A lot had happened in that time, and they'd spoken dozens and dozens of times, but thinking back, she usually called her parents during the day.

'I'm sorry, Mum.' She smiled. 'Fortunately, no bad news tonight. Not from me anyway.'

'Good. That's good.' Her mother's tone softened. 'You see the news about the missing woman?'

Fisher sighed, but it was light enough not to reach the phone. 'I did, Mum. I saw it.' The last thing she wanted to do tonight was think about work, especially after how today had gone. 'Hopefully we'll find her,' she countered positively, despite knowing the woman was almost certainly the victim they'd found at the library.

'How are you both doing, then?' Fisher asked, moving the conversation away from anything work-related.

'Me and your dad are fine, April. You know. Still here.'

Fisher could hear the dull tone in her voice. Last year, Freda had had a cancer scare. Found a few lumps in her right breast and feared the worst. Through quick and efficient treatments and highly skilled doctors, the lumps were removed without any complications. She was rechecked several months ago and was in remission, but Fisher knew she lived in fear it would return at any moment. Fisher was fed up with telling her she needed to stop thinking about it and enjoy what was left of their lives.

'Good.'

'Your father and I are going to London tomorrow. Got a few nights booked in a Premier Inn near the London Eye.' Her tone had noticeably chirped up.

'You didn't mention this!'

'We've only just booked it. Got a last-minute deal on the rooms and going down on the train. The station is literally around the corner from the hotel, so it should be pretty simple.'

Fisher sighed.

'What, April?'

Fisher frowned, then realised her sigh was louder than intended. 'What?'

'You sighed into the phone. I heard it. You do that often, just to let you know.'

'I do?'

'Yeah,' Freda replied. 'So, what is it? Why did you sigh?'

'I-I never sighed, I . . .' She trailed off, not wanting to lie. 'Just be careful in London. There are dozens of pickpockets doing the rounds. The area around the Eye is the fourth worst spot for people's phones and handbags being snatched.'

'April, have you forgotten your father was in the police for most of his life?'

'No, Mother, I haven't. I'm fully aware of that. But the world has changed, and it isn't for the better. It's easy pickings for these thugs nowadays. Young kids driving around on scooters, grabbing people's phones from their hands when they're taking snaps of Westminster and Big Ben — these are everyday occurrences.'

It was Freda's turn to sigh, and she didn't hide it either.

'All I'm saying is, be careful,' Fisher pleaded.

'We'll be fine. We went there last year. No issues. We have a few things planned too. Going to see a show tomorrow night.'

'You did well booking it all in the time you have. Normally things are sold out.'

'I'm not the crazy, old, useless bat you think I am, you know.'

That made Fisher smile. She reached forward, took a sip of coffee, then placed the mug on the table again. 'Have you spoken to Freya yet?'

'Not yet,' Freda said. 'She hasn't even called me.'

Fisher thought for a moment, remembering that Freya had said she would call her before she'd left the other night.

'Give her time, Mum. I know how she acted at the funeral was a little embarrassing, but she means well.'

'Just a little?' her mum countered. 'She caused a scene, April. I wanted the ground to swallow me whole. It was ridiculous her going on like that.'

'She's never been subjected to real life. You've always given her everything she's ever wanted, and now she's struggling to pay her own way, frustrated she couldn't go on holiday with her friends. It might be petty, but that's all it boils down to.'

'We've given her enough.' The tone was dull again, with a touch of anger.

'And I totally agree. She's taken the piss for far too long, but she's working two jobs now. Yes, they're not career-defining jobs, but at least she's trying to stand on her own two feet. She misses you.'

Freda didn't respond for a moment. 'She said that? She misses us?'

Fisher knew she hadn't but lied anyway for the sake of her family. 'She did, yes.'

'I'll call her tomorrow,' Freda said. 'Anyway, it's been nice speaking to you, April. But we're about to start . . . *what is it, Mark?* Hold on, April.' The phone went quiet for a few moments. 'Sorry, your dad was asking how you were and if you're working the missing woman case, Debbie Johnson?'

'Tell Dad I'm okay, and yes, I'm involved in the case.'

Freda moved the phone away from her mouth and relayed the message to her husband.

'Any leads yet?' Fisher heard her father ask, assuming he was sitting close by.

'Tell him not yet.'

'Okay, April. Speak soon, love. Oh, are you still coming over for Christmas?'

'Yeah, of course.'

'Watch how you go.'

'I'll pop over before then to see you both.'

The call ended, and Fisher took a lungful of warm air filled with lavender coming from a candle on the table.

Exhausted after the call, she picked up the remote and took the time bar back to the beginning of the episode, knowing she'd missed the first twenty minutes. Just as she pressed play, her mobile rang.

'God, who's—?'

She saw Freya's name on the screen and answered it quickly. 'Freya, you alright?'

'Yup, I'm good. Hey, listen, I'm going out tonight with Alan. Just wondered if you want to tag along. You could meet him for the first time.'

Fisher frowned and looked at the clock on the opposite wall. 'Freya, it's nearly ten o'clock. The last thing I'll be doing is going out in the city. Is that where you're going? The city?'

'Yeah, we're heading out soon. You meeting us out?'

'The only thing I'll be meeting is my pillow, and it won't be long until that happens, either. Sorry, Freya, not tonight, okay? Maybe next weekend or the next time you fancy it, just let me know.'

'You sure I can't tempt you? Alan did say he was bringing a friend out with him. I've been showing Alan photos of you online. He showed his friend and said he was interested in meeting you. Said he likes your hair.'

'Well, tonight, my pillow will have the pleasure of my hair.'

'Okay, fair enough,' replied her sister, finally accepting that Fisher wouldn't be persuaded.

'You didn't say I worked for the police, did you?'

'Of course not. I wouldn't do that. God, you've reminded me more than enough times about the security of your job.'

'Okay, good. By the way, you need to ring Mum. You said you would the other night and haven't, so please ring her.'

'Yeah . . . okay. I'll call tomorrow, depending on my hangover.'

'Go steady in town, be aware of what you're drinking.'

'April, I'm not twelve years old. I need to go. Speak soon.'

Before Fisher responded, the line went dead. Sighing, she put the phone back onto the table and slumped back into the sofa again, grabbing the remote and pressing PLAY. The first episode of the American crime drama had been good so far. A female corpse was found under a bridge in a park in New York, wearing only underwear and with cuts to her arm. The most exciting part was when they found her clothes hanging from the underside of the bridge, like in some cult scene. The fictional detective, a mid-fifties guy with a beard, seemed interesting, meticulously moving around and talking with the forensic team.

Just as the second episode ended, something tripped the motion detector on the doorbell, the sound coming through her phone to notify her.

Fisher jolted upright and snapped her neck to the clock on the wall.

10.30 p.m. Who on earth was at her door at this time?

She struggled up from the sofa, back and legs aching, and grabbed her phone from the table. She unlocked it and opened up the app that showed the camera fixed to her door looking outwards on the world, where she could see her path, an open gate that she knew was closed after she came in, and her Volvo parked out front.

But there was no one on the screen.

Frowning in confusion, she clicked on 'live' mode and watched for a moment, waiting for someone to appear. The last thing she wanted to do was open the door late on a cold December night.

Clicking the 'unmute' button, she said, 'Hello, who's there?'

After no reply, she assumed the motion detector had been set off by someone walking by, reminding her to alter the sensitivity of the camera tomorrow. There was an option to view a clip showing where the motion was picked up, but her exhaustion got the better of her, and she returned her phone to the pocket of her dressing gown.

The night was still young, so she left the living room, took a right, and headed for the kitchen. Then she heard it.

Tiny taps at the front door.

She spun around and stared down the hall.

'Hello?'

She took her phone out, opened the app again, and went into 'live' mode. Nothing. No sign of anyone.

Maybe it was an animal pecking at the door, perhaps some kind of bird looking for food. After a minute of staring at the door, the sounds faded into nothing. Had she imagined it?

Could the sound be coming from the heating pipes that ran down the wall near the door? They had the tendency to expand when the heating was on, often causing a knocking sound. In the past, she'd been worried about mice and rats, and had called someone to investigate. Because of how frequently it happened, the pest control guy had asked her to put her heating on, and after they heard the sounds, he explained it was that. Turning, she went into the kitchen and flicked on the kettle.

Then there was a bang at the door.

This time, she knew it wasn't an animal. She cautiously padded down the hall, her socks almost silent on the wooden floor. She closed one eye and looked through the peephole. Nothing. She picked up her key from the stand on her right, slowly turned the lock, and opened the door.

'Jesus Christ,' she said, raising a hand to her mouth. She recognised the woman on her doorstep, curled into a ball-like shape. 'Penny? Penny, is that you?'

The woman she recognised as her neighbour groaned a little. 'Help me, April.'

'What . . . what happened?' Fisher lowered to her knees and took hold of her, turning her over to see her frail face. There was a cut to her cheek, and blood streaming down her throat and T-shirt. She shivered in the winter cold.

'Penny, let's get you inside.'

Managing to help her to her feet, Penny winced a few times, signalling even Fisher's grip was causing the pensioner some discomfort. In the living room, she carefully set her down on the sofa.

'You wait here, Penny, I'm—'

'Please, don't go, April!'

'Okay, okay. I'll stay right here.'

Fisher plucked her phone out and dialled for an ambulance.

CHAPTER 22

Once the paramedics arrived at Fisher's house, she waited in the living room while they aided Penny. Despite being a neighbour and knowing Penny considerably well, she was unable to answer the questions they were asking, because so far, Penny hadn't said much. Fisher explained to them she was a detective and that Penny lived two doors down.

'You found her at your front door?'

Fisher nodded, watching the two young women assisting Penny, handling the situation well with experience and competence, making Penny feel comfortable and safe very quickly.

'Has she said what's happened?'

'No, not yet,' replied Fisher, concerned.

The larger, blonde-haired woman unzipped her medical bag and grabbed a few items, then explained they were going to give her something for the pain, while the other, dark-haired medic gently pressed on various places on her body to see where the location of the pain was.

'There?' she asked, very tenderly pressing her ribs. Penny winced and leaned over as if protecting herself. 'Okay, sorry, Penny.' She turned to the blonde one. 'Severe pain in her ribs.'

The blonde nodded, leaned in, and inserted a needle into her arm. 'We'll take her to hospital to get her checked out. The doctors will give us a better idea of the full extent of her injuries.'

Fisher nodded in understanding.

'Are you going with her?' the dark-haired paramedic asked Fisher.

The only thing Fisher needed was her bed, but if being with Penny brought her comfort, if someone simply being there to hold her hand made her feel at ease, it was the least she could do. 'I can if Penny would like me to?'

'Penny,' the medic said, 'would you like April to come to the hospital with you?'

She was in too much pain to speak, but judging by the expression on her face it appeared the morphine was kicking in, and she slowly bobbed her head to indicate she would.

The medic looked up at Fisher. 'Is that okay?'

'Sure. Let me get changed.' Fisher left the room and took the stairs two at a time. She threw some jeans on, a long-sleeved T-shirt, and a jumper, then opened the door under the stairs and grabbed a thick coat.

Back in the room, the paramedics were gently helping her from the sofa.

'Does she have any close family? Anyone, you know of?'

Fisher thought. 'She has a daughter called Lydia who lives about an hour away, and a son called Jake who lives in London.'

'Are you able to contact them to inform them she's injured and that we're taking her to the hospital?'

Fisher pulled out her phone, checked through her contacts. 'I have Lydia's number.'

While the paramedics put Penny into the back of the ambulance on a trolley, Fisher made a call to Lydia, informing her about what happened.

'Has she been attacked?' asked Lydia.

'I don't honestly know.' She explained the cut on her face and the tenderness in her ribs. 'The doctors are going to have a closer look. It might be a good idea for you to come up and watch over her.'

'Yes, absolutely. Bless her. I'll set off and ring you when I'm there.'

Fisher hung up, went outside, and locked her front door. 'I'll take my car and meet you there.'

The medic turned and smiled. 'Thanks for this.'

Fisher got into her Volvo, turned the heating on, and followed the ambulance to the hospital.

* * *

It was almost 2 a.m. by the time Fisher returned home. At this point the world felt like something out of Narnia; everything in the street was covered in a thin layer of fresh snow that sparkled under the nearby streetlights. The sky was a dull black; not a single star could be seen.

She locked the car, went into her house, and cleared the living room table of the empty mug and tidied the cushions. When she went to bed, she still had to leave the house in an orderly fashion — no empty cups or plates left, no cushions out of place. Shoes needed to be placed together neatly at the door, coats hung up, and clothes put away. She didn't so much have OCD, but items needed their place. She couldn't cope otherwise. Probably another reason why she was happy and content on her own.

* * *

She woke before her alarm clock went off just before 7 a.m. Sitting up, surprised she wasn't tired after only five hours of sleep, she pulled the covers back, swung her legs out, and padded over the soft cream carpet to her en suite. The house was cold; the thought of going outside sent a chill down her back.

She turned on the shower, put her underwear in the wash basket and stepped in, closing the sliding door, immersing herself in the glorious hot water. Without a care for the recent energy price increases, she spent nearly twenty minutes in there, thinking of multiple things. One: how Penny was doing. It turned out, once she was in less pain and able to explain what had happened, she had been in the kitchen and had turned, lost her balance, and fallen awkwardly, hitting her face on a corner of the worktop. On her way down, her ribs had collided into the cupboard, severely bruising them, but thankfully nothing was broken.

The second thing on her mind was the image of the head in the urinal they found yesterday. The woman's eyes staring up at her. Still and lifeless.

The third thing was wondering where the missing Mary Steadman was. It was strange that someone in her position would just go missing, unless something bad had happened.

The last thing on her mind was whether her sister had phoned their mother yet to apologise.

She was always thinking about things; she never switched off.

Dried and dressed, April went downstairs and made coffee. She noticed a text from her best friend Kim asking her if she was up for going out next weekend, along with a photo of the dress she had bought, which she must have received while in the shower.

She decided it would be quicker to call Kim, so with a fresh coffee in one hand, her phone in the other, pressed against her head, she wandered into the living room and sunk into the sofa. They chatted for a while about all sorts; they hadn't seen each other in almost two weeks, which was a record for them, so had plenty to catch up on.

'I've been busy, Kim — you know, with work,' explained Fisher.

'I know, April. I just can't wait to see you, that's all. Please promise me we'll go out next weekend. A new bar's opened.'

Fisher had no idea about a new bar opening or where it was, but said, 'Yeah, sounds good.' She knew herself she needed a little time away from work, time to let her hair down and relax a little.

'Hey, you might even meet someone.' Kim giggled down the phone.

'I don't have time for men,' Fisher countered, laughing too, secretly hoping this new bar wasn't filled with teenagers or creepy old men on the prowl for meaningless one-night stands.

She heard a buzz on her phone, and pulled away, looking at the screen. An incoming call. 'Listen, Kim. I need to go. Someone's calling — it's important. I'll ring you tomorrow, okay?'

She hung up without a response and answered the call. 'Hey, Pam.'

'Morning, sorry it's early,' said Boone. Her breathing was heavy, and she could hear the wind in the background. Fisher imagined her outside somewhere having a cigarette.

Fisher glanced up at the clock in her living room, seeing it had just gone 9 a.m. 'It's okay. I'm surprised you're calling so soon.'

'I pushed the results through the lab sooner than usual. Came into the office this morning.'

'Good work — what do you have, Pam?'

'The DNA from the items we collected in Debbie Johnson's flat matches the head.' She paused a moment, allowing it to sink in. 'I can confirm the head belongs to Debbie, DS Fisher.'

Fisher remained silent, but it only confirmed their thoughts yesterday. If it hadn't belonged to Debbie Johnson, they'd have had a whole different issue. 'Okay, Pam. Thanks for getting back to me. I'll inform DI James.'

'I've emailed him the report, but I thought I'd let you know personally. Hope you didn't mind.'

'Not at all. I appreciate any progress we make. Thank you.' Fisher smiled.

'Enjoy the rest of your day.' When Boone ended the call, Fisher stood, leaving her phone on the sofa, and went to the window. The street was quiet; most of the cars parked overnight were gone. Across the road, she could see the park through the metal railings, where a couple of dog walkers carefully made their way, no doubt to avoid slipping on the icy paths, courteously nodding as they passed each other. Although it was cold today, the bare, frost-covered trees were a silhouette against the bright morning sky.

She looked down at her watch. Although it was Saturday, a couple of things were on her agenda today. Despite seldom using it, she wanted a new table for the dining room to eat her meals at and use her laptop on, to sit with a better posture; sitting hunched over the sofa was doing her back no good. There were a few places on her mind, Sofology and Furniture Village being two of them, plus they were pretty much next door to each other and were only five minutes away in the car. She remembered buying a table from Sofology last year, strangely recalling the assistant, an attractive guy in his early forties called Marcus, as being charming, something she had put down to her pregnancy hormones at the time.

After putting some washing on, April put on her shoes and slipped into the knee-length duffle coat she grabbed from under the stairs, then opened her front door, stepping down onto the damp ground, immediately feeling the cold on her skin.

She opened her car, and just as she was climbing inside, heard something behind her.

'Good morning.'

She stopped halfway into the car and turned towards the voice on the path. Behind her stood her inconsiderate neighbour Raymond, smiling as he sauntered towards her.

'Morning, Raymond.' She wondered what he wanted. They rarely spoke; if they did, it was only in passing. Fisher's complaint about the noise the other night had been the first time they had engaged in any conversation. He stopped a metre away and looked down at her.

'How's Penny doing?'

Fisher frowned, curious how he knew about what happened to Penny. 'How do you mean?'

'I heard she picked up a nasty injury last night. I saw the ambulance here.'

'Did you?'

He nodded twice. 'It's a shame when these things happen to the older generation, isn't it?' Grinning, he walked back to his house, but as he went through his gate, he turned to Fisher and smirked.

Seething inside, Fisher scowled at him until he opened his door and disappeared into his house.

CHAPTER 23

Chorlton High School
Twenty-seven years ago

After the boy had finished his maths lesson, he looked down at the watch his father had given him, noticing it was almost lunchtime. The watch wasn't new, nor was it anything special. It was one that his father no longer used because he'd bought a shiny, flashy new one with the bonus he'd received from work, the same bonus the boy hoped his father would use to buy him a new football kit.

He walked down the corridor, took a left, and slowly made his way through another corridor with doors either side, leading to geography or history classrooms. He hated history. No, he despised it. It wasn't that he didn't understand it or found it too easy, but why look back at what's happened in the world when we should be looking forward to the future? He'd once expressed this opinion to Mrs Cairn, and she'd nearly throttled him, stating passionately, 'History is the most important subject. Everything we do,' she'd explained, 'goes down in history.' He had rolled his eyes and didn't mention it again.

It was lunchtime. He joined the back of a queue that stood forty deep. In front of him were Jack and Phil, two of the school thugs in the year above. He swallowed hard and kept his eyes down on the floor, avoiding any potential eye contact if they turned around and spotted him. Sure enough, they did.

'Hey, fat boy,' Phil said.

He focused on the ground, his face warming at the possible confrontation.

'I said, hey, fat boy.'

In front of Phil and Jack, a girl told them to behave and leave him alone. Fortunately for him, they listened to her and turned back to face the front.

It was daily comments such as this that made him hate his life. He had no friends. No one voluntarily sat next to him in class unless the teacher made them. And working in groups made him severely anxious because everyone mocked him every time he spoke, so he made it a habit to stay silent.

After collecting his food, he made his way over to the tables. There were two spaces at the nearest six-seater table, four of the seats occupied by two girls and two boys in his year. On his approach, carrying his tray of food, the closest boy caught his eye and shook his head, indicating he didn't want him to sit beside him.

The boy sighed, moved along, and placed his food tray on the next table, pulling an arm free from his rucksack, and positioned it near his feet. Once seated, he unzipped his bag and picked out a book. His mother always encouraged him to make friends and socialise, but it didn't come easy to him. He was more interested in reading books. Every time he got in from school, he'd go to his room and sit on the floor, a book resting on his lap and eyes glued to the words inside. At first, his mother and father were proud of their son for reading. He loved thrillers but also read non-fiction books about anything. Politics, economics, business practise. He'd even read a book on medical procedures he'd got from the library.

But as time went on and his bedroom reading habits became a daily occurrence while other school children were out playing football and hanging around with each other, he continued to sit in isolation, his eyes fixed on the pages. Sometimes, he'd sit on his bed so he could look out of the window down the street, where he could see kids younger than him, laughing and joking with each other, and wondered where it had all gone wrong for him. Then he remembered when Tim had come to his house after school when they were twelve. They had had their tea and went up to his room. Tim was cool, much cooler than he was, and wanted a little excitement, asking if his parents had any dirty magazines under their bed. He said he didn't understand what he meant, so Tim explained, but it didn't ring any bells. He didn't understand the words *sex* or *porn*. Tim felt a little sorry for him, so he clarified things a little, expressing that he hadn't yet lost his virginity but had kissed a girl and was planning to. He then pulled his trousers down from nowhere and revealed his penis to Tim. It was safe to say Tim didn't go back to his house for tea or speak to him anymore at school.

'This isn't healthy,' his mother once said.

He'd replied with so many silent stares that his parents had given up trying with him. As far as they knew, he had no friends and no girlfriend.

At the table, where he sat alone, he took a mouthful of mashed potato, opened his book where he'd put his leather bookmark, and started to read. Every now and again, he gathered a forkful of food and put it in his mouth, but his eyes never left the pages.

He felt something hard hit his back, causing him to jolt forward.

'What you reading, fat boy?'

He knew the voice belonged to Debbie Johnson and decided to ignore it — he'd become very good at deflecting the negativity that came his way. Then she pushed him in the back. 'I bet you can't even read. You're thick and fat.'

Yes, he was overweight, but definitely not thick. He always got top grades in every subject and had several certificates lining the walls in his bedroom.

'Are you deaf?' He felt another shove in the back, this time from Mary Steadman. 'Fatty!' They sat down opposite, smiling at him.

'Leave me alone,' he whispered without looking up, his eyes still on his book.

Mary leaned forward, tilting her face, putting a palm to her ear. 'What was that?'

'I said leave me alone,' he repeated, this time a little louder, but it was barely audible.

'You're pathetic, you know that?'

He didn't reply or do anything, just continued to read his book — *Of Mice and Men* by John Steinbeck. His lack of response angered Debbie, who leaned forward, grabbed the book, and threw it across the canteen. It landed on the dull red tiles and bounced off the wall on the other side. Most of the canteen filled with laughter.

Without a word, he simply stood, walked over to the book, picked it up, then returned to the table unfazed by what had happened. He sat back on his seat, placed his book out in front of him, and, remembering the page number, opened it where he was.

Debbie pointed at him, her finger inches from his face. 'You're just one big fat loser.'

Then Mary and Debbie disappeared through the doors, laughing.

A tear escaped the corner of his eye and trailed down his cheek.

CHAPTER 24

Present day

Fisher had woken several times during the night, mainly from the unexpected heavy rainfall in Manchester, causing the continual tapping on her window ledge that came from broken guttering above her bedroom window. It had been on her to-do list, but last night had reminded her to push it up and get it sorted out sooner rather than later. At four in the morning, the third time she woke, she spent ten minutes searching for local plumbers, settling on Waterfixit, who did guttering, and made a note in her phone to contact them first thing.

At 7 a.m., she opened her eyes. The room was still dark. The streetlight near her window shone dimly against her closed curtains. Unsure whether to drift back off to sleep and make the most of her Sunday morning, she sat up, rubbing her tired eyes.

'Right, let's go,' she whispered, swinging her legs off the bed onto the floor. She shivered immediately because the room felt like an igloo; she was sick of the winter. She thought back to all those hot, clammy summer days when she wished it was colder, and kicked herself. It was true with most things; you didn't truly appreciate them until they were gone.

Fisher didn't have much planned for today. Her mother had texted her asking if she'd like to join them for Sunday dinner, which had taken her by surprise. Since moving out to live on her own, which she had done at the age of twenty-one, she couldn't be bothered by the faff of making a roast dinner just for herself. The amount of washing up afterwards wasn't worth it, even when she covered the dinner in mint sauce, a condiment she adored. She still opted for something quick that could warm in the microwave. She told her mother she would love to and she'd be there just after midday.

Her parents lived in a large semi-detached house on Seymour Grove, a long road that started from Talbot Road and ran south until it changed to Manchester Road. The house looked very different from when they had moved in all those years ago, with a two-story extension to the side of the house offering two extra bedrooms and the garage below that Mark used for his tools and a home gym. Then they'd got a low-level extension at the rear of the property which they used as a sitting room with a sixty-five-inch flat-screen fixed to the wall and a four-seater sofa. Mark complained that their back garden was too big, so getting the extension and decreasing the garden size wasn't something that really bothered him. It just meant he'd finish cutting the grass quicker and enjoy his retirement watching TV.

Seven minutes after she set off, Fisher slowed her Volvo on Seymour Grove near the junction of Ayres Road, indicated left, and with only two cars waiting at the traffic lights, had adequate space to pull onto her parents' spacious driveway. They used to park the cars on the kerb, but with the traffic it often caused a blockage.

She parked the car next to the red, four-year-old Ford Fiesta their parents had bought for Freya. It had been a steady, reliable car so far, going against popular beliefs in the online car communities that Fiestas had certain issues — or was that the manufacturer Ford in general? Fisher couldn't recall. It had done Freya well for the four years she'd had it, so no complaints from her. Any car was good until it broke, which everyone knew, they all did sooner or later.

She turned the engine off, opened the door, and approached the house, wearing a thick coat to keep the cold at bay. She tried the door but it was locked, so she placed her key inside but it wouldn't turn. Frowning, she knocked instead, then took a step back, looking out at the traffic on the road.

'April,' she heard her mother say from the step. 'Next time, just walk in. We don't bite.'

Fisher smiled and stepped up, kissing Freda on the cheek. 'I would have done if it was open.'

'That'll be your dad, you know how he is. He always leaves the key in.'

Freda extended a hand and gently rubbed her back. 'Come on in; it's freezing out here.' Once inside the warmth of the hallway, she said, 'I've missed you. Your sister is already here.'

Fisher was going to say she'd already noticed her car but smiled instead. 'I'm looking forward to catching up with her.'

After removing her coat, she hung it on the old-fashioned coat stand by the door and slipped out of her shoes, placing them on the rack near the base of the stairs. A scent of lavender floated around from the plug-in near the radiator. Her mother started towards the kitchen but stopped, turning to Fisher, halting her in her tracks. She whispered, 'Just to let you know, Freya and I have spoken about what happened at the funeral. She apologised for embarrassing us like that.'

Fisher nodded in understanding but smiled inside, proud her sister had done what she said she would, despite her stubborn reluctance.

Freya was in the living room with their dad, both sitting on the sofa a few feet apart, focusing on the TV.

'Is there anything from this century we can watch?' Fisher said as she sat down on the single-seater chair near the window.

Her mother asked if she'd like a coffee, to which she said yes. Mark and Freya picked up their empty mugs and held them in the air.

'I'm not your skivvy, you know,' Freda reminded them, but took the mugs anyway. 'Same again?' Mark and Freya nodded. Her mother looked at Fisher. 'You don't take sugar, do you?'

Fisher sighed and patted her lap. 'Mother, how many times? No, I don't.'

'She's getting forgetful, she is,' said Mark when she'd gone. After Fisher settled into her chair, her dad asked, 'So, caught any bad guys recently?'

'Not as many as we'd like.'

They laughed. Fisher tilted her focus to the TV fixed to the chimney breast, wondering how they watched it so high on the wall.

'What about that missing woman?' persisted Mark.

Fisher sighed lightly. The last thing she wanted to do when she was away from work was to talk about it.

'Leave her be, Mark.' Freda entered the room, clearly overhearing what he'd asked. 'She has enough on her plate with what's going on in Manchester at the moment. Let her have a day off.'

Mark gave a closed-lip smirk, holding up an apologetic palm, and said no more on the matter. He, of all people, knew what it felt like to be bombarded with question after question when he got home after a hard day.

Freda had brought in the drinks on a tray, along with several biscuits. Fisher leaned over, grabbed her mug and a chocolate hobnob, then sunk into the sofa. Soon enough, Freda disappeared into the kitchen, where the smell of food lingered, letting them know that dinner was coming soon. When the food was ready and served, they all took a seat in the dining room and clinked glasses.

'We should do this more often, girls,' said Mark, before tucking into his food. Bellies full, they washed and dried the dishes and settled back in the living room, this time Fisher sitting between her mother and sister, her dad on the single chair. They spoke about Freya's new boyfriend, Alan, who she'd barely known five minutes, but for some reason, for

Freda, the idea of one of her daughters finding love melted her heart.

'You should find a man,' she told Fisher, who sighed, sick of the repetitive conversation, and explained she didn't have time for that. 'But you do, April. You used to have a man. If you had someone, you could . . . you know, try for another baby.'

Fisher sighed again, not wanting to be reminded of the miscarriage.

Freda then looked at Freya. 'You two thinking of children?'

'Jesus, Mother.' Fisher frowned. 'They've only just met — give her a chance. Are you that desperate for grandchildren?'

Her mother's face hardened a little. 'Yes, we'd like grandchildren at some point. What parent wouldn't?'

Fisher could sense the conversation taking a negative turn and focused back to the western film, which, judging by the scene on the screen, was coming to an end. She looked down at her watch.

'Somewhere to be?'

She looked at her mother. 'No, just curious about the time. Chill, Mother.'

'I am chilled, April. Thank you.'

Fisher frowned in her direction.

'What, April?'

Fisher shook her head, not wanting to get into a debate. 'Nothing, Mum.'

'What is it?'

'I feel like you wanted a grandchild, and I failed you.'

Mark edged forward. 'Now come on, April. Your mother isn't saying that; she's just saying—'

'Well, maybe it was for the best,' added Fisher.

'April, don't you ever say that again.' Freda shook her head, disappointed. 'Your time will come, I'm sure of it.'

'I can't be bothered with men. They're too much hassle.'

'You'll find someone one day, I'm sure of it.'

Fisher looked away, feeling a headache coming on. The conversation had upset her and she wanted to leave. 'I don't feel well. I'm going to go home.'

116

'April, I'm so . . . sorry. I-I shouldn't have mentioned anything.'

Fisher stood and left the room.

'April, please!' begged Freda, trailing her into the hall-way. Ignoring her mother, Fisher put on her coat and shoes, left the house, got into her car, and headed for home.

CHAPTER 25

It had gone 8 p.m. when Callum McCauley arrived home, pulling his brand-new silver Audi A4 onto his driveway. The street was dark and quiet; there wasn't a soul in sight, not even a dog walker doing one last lap before going home and locking up for the night. He opened his car door and slowly climbed out, careful not to drop the pizza balanced in his hand. His twelve-year-old son Jacob got out of the other side, slammed his door too hard — a habit he'd picked up despite his father consistently reminding him — and dashed around the front of the car.

'Hurry, Dad, I'm starving,' he claimed, rushing to the front door.

'You had a cheeseburger three hours ago.'

'I'm still hungry.'

Jacob opened the door and Callum followed him inside, then locked it, before making his way to the kitchen, smelling the delights of the food inside the box tucked under his arm.

'Pizza's here!' he bellowed, his voice reaching every room in the house.

'Coming,' his wife said from somewhere upstairs.

In the kitchen, he placed the massive box on the table and opened the lid from the nearest flap, revealing the monstrous sixteen-inch pizza inside, topped with all kinds of meats and an abundance of cheese.

Jacob moved his hand forward to grab a pre-cut slice.

'Wow, just wait, young man,' Callum told him with his hand out. 'See what others want first. You've had a cheese-burger already.'

'But that was like a week ago. I'm hungry, fam.'

He smiled at the extraordinary range of vocabulary his son had picked up from YouTube. 'See what your sister and mam want first.'

Accepting his dad's words, he waited until they arrived, and judging by the patter of footsteps descending the stairs, it wouldn't be long.

'How was the game?' his wife Linda asked, leaning in to kiss him. She grabbed one of the plates Callum had got from the cupboard and grabbed the two closest slices to her.

'It was awesome, fam!' yelled Jacob. 'Fernandes scored a hat trick. He's unreal.'

Smiling, Callum placed a hand on his son's thick mop of brown hair. 'See, Jacob, I said you'd like it.'

Jacob had never really been into football all that much. Most of his friends played at school and for teams outside, but Jacob didn't hold much interest. His activities included more rugby, and cricket in the summer. Callum had played a little cricket when he was younger, but if he had to choose, it would be football over any other sport.

Linda raised a palm and patted his head. 'Glad you liked it.'

'He's talking about getting a Manchester United top now,' said Callum, smirking Jacob's way.

'Hey, I didn't say that,' protested Jacob with wide eyes, then laughed, realising his dad was winding him up.

After plating their food, they made their way into the living room. Priya attempted to sly off upstairs, but Linda told her to come into the living room so they could eat as a family, something they'd always done. Despite her claims, it didn't matter if it was a takeaway and not a 'proper meal'; they'd still eat it together.

The choice of TV wasn't great, and it didn't come as a surprise when Priya disappeared off to her room after she finished, and Jacob was sent upstairs to get a shower and get settled for bed. They both had school the next day.

Callum and Linda chatted for a while. She told him about her girl's day with Priya and what they'd done, heading into the city to do some shopping being the highlight. He told her about his jobs planned for the week. He had a boiler to fit on the outskirts of Manchester and moaned about the travelling time to get there.

'Work is work though, love. You're not going to turn it down,' she countered.

He knew she was right. The plumbing business he had started only last year had been promising, with an influx of work from the get-go, but as time passed, work dropped due to other people doing fast-track plumbing courses and setting up for themselves, which had really pissed him off. He'd done his time, serving four years of training, the way it should be.

'Also, Geoff might need a hand in the morning, so might leave earlier than usual.'

'What's he doing?' she asked, wondering what his friend was up to.

'He's getting a delivery to the yard, but the usual lad isn't there. Said I would give him a hand.'

They chatted more, enjoying hearing about each other's day. When the time approached 9.30 p.m. and his food had settled, Callum rose from the sofa, gathering the empty plates his children had forgotten to clear away and went to the kitchen. Linda told him she was heading up to run a bath, meaning she didn't want to be disturbed for at least half an hour. Before he started doing the dishes, he switched on the TV fixed to the wall on his right; he enjoyed the sound even if he wasn't watching it.

After he placed the first washed glass on the drainer, the sound of a knock froze him. Frowning, he looked up, turned, and focused on the kitchen window, realising the blinds were still up. All he could see was the darkness in the garden. He turned off the tap, sauntered over, and leaned on the wooden unit to have a look out. It would undoubtedly be Derek next door messing about in his garage, something he often did, no matter what the time.

He couldn't see anything. It was pitch black — so dark, in fact, he couldn't even see the figure standing a few feet from the window, staring at him.

CHAPTER 26

Fisher was nervous, standing ready at the open door, listening to the wave of noise coming from inside the large conference room on the first floor of the police station. She'd planned to run a bubble bath and stay there until her skin went wrinkly, watching the series on Netflix she'd started.

But it wasn't to be.

DI James had called her, asking her to do a press conference about the police discovering the body of Debbie Johnson, which was the last place she imagined to be at 10 p.m. on a Sunday night. She asked him why he wasn't doing it — he was the more senior detective — but he explained he couldn't make it and didn't feel well. She knew, in her heart, it was because he'd put on a little weight, and it was, strangely enough, affecting his confidence. It was something they kept between themselves.

Inside the busy room, standing near the front, a woman dressed in a blue suit jacket and a matching pencil skirt looked at Fisher through the door and nodded firmly, indicating they were ready for her. Fisher took a breath and entered, feeling the glares of the reporters and cameras as she made her way to the podium in the middle of the closest wall.

Fisher had changed into her usual workwear. She didn't feel professional wearing anything else.

She stopped behind the stand, turned, and looked out at the watchful eyes, feeling her cheeks warming in anticipation of what was to come. She smiled, appearing confident on the outside, but inside, her heart was pounding. Public speaking had never been her strong point. All those eyes watching. Judging. Waiting to pick up on a wrong word or something that offended someone, which was becoming more frequent nowadays. Gone were the days of good old-fashioned honesty.

The room fell into silence, the last of the whispers fading away.

'Hello, everyone,' she started, her voice clogging in her throat. 'My name is Detective Sergeant April Fisher. I stand before you because I need to make the public aware of a discovery.' She paused a few seconds. 'The discovery of a head that we believe belongs to missing forty-one-year-old Debbie Johnson. The disappearance of Mrs Johnson is perhaps something many of you are aware of, thanks to our social media teams. But we discovered her this morning at Chorlton Library.'

'What did you find?' one reporter shouted. A male voice, stern, straight to the point.

Fisher swallowed her saliva before she answered. 'A woman's head was found in the library toilets. From photos of Mrs Johnson, we surmised it was her. Following DNA matches between the head and items found at Mrs Johnson's apartment, I can confirm on behalf of the police that the identity of the deceased female is Debbie Johnson.'

Whispers swept the room.

'So, you just found the head?' another voice asked, coming from the right.

Fisher turned in their direction and nodded. 'Yes, so far.'

'Where's the rest of her, then?' the same person asked.

'At this moment in time, we aren't sure.'

Another collection of sighs and disheartened murmurs filled the space.

'How long was Mrs Johnson missing for?' The question came from the same man who'd asked the first.

'Almost five days.'

'So, in five days, what have the police done to find her — maybe you could have prevented this awful thing?'

Fisher felt the sweat building up on her back. She desperately wanted to remove her suit jacket but knew by doing so she would appear flustered under the pressure of the media. Her last press conference had been several months ago, and she hadn't missed doing it, that's for sure.

'Her disappearance was brought to our attention two days ago by one of her friends, who said it was unusual to go so long without speaking to her. We filed the missing person's report and followed up by doing a background check on her, primarily going to her apartment to see if she was okay. Her car was there, but she didn't answer.'

'Did you go into the apartment?'

Fisher shook her head. 'We didn't go into the apartment. We didn't have cause to break her door down.'

'Even though you were concerned for her safety?'

'At the time, without fully knowing Mrs Johnson's day-to-day life and routines, there was nothing suspect in her behaviour.'

Fisher's response got several approving, understanding nods.

'Although her friend had informed you she was worried about her?'

God, she thought, *this is a tough crowd.* She promised to tell DI James he'd be attending the next conference. As it went on, she felt her face cool down and became more confident in answering the questions.

'So,' said a woman at the front with a raised hand, wearing a red scarf that matched the colour of her hair. 'What happens now?'

'We do whatever we can to find the person responsible. Rest assured, there might be someone dangerous walking the streets, but we'll get them. We always do.'

'You didn't catch Phil Haddon,' another reporter noted, rolling their eyes.

Fisher sighed. Phil Haddon, a suspect who had killed three teenage girls over five years ago, was still missing.

'We aren't here to speak about Phil Haddon,' stated Fisher loudly, her stare sweeping the audience to ensure they were all aware of that. 'Now, are there any more questions related to the current case?'

CHAPTER 27

After finishing the washing up, Callum McCauley had settled down to watch the news in the living room. Linda was
still in the bath, and the kids were showered and up in their
rooms.

He enjoyed this quiet time by himself. No demanding
children. When the kids were younger, he had found it difficult being a father, mainly due to the demands of his job,
going out early in the morning and getting back late at night.
All the kids had wanted was a slice of his time. It wasn't
that he was a lousy father. It was hard when he'd been out
for more than twelve hours a day, and when he got home,
he believed he was entitled to his own time to relax and do
what he pleased, which led to countless arguments between
him and Linda over the years. Fortunately for his sanity, the
kids were old enough now to keep themselves company and
didn't even bother to ask him if he'd like to play Connect 4
with them or watch a film. It might have something to do
with him saying no too many times, but he didn't dwell on it.

There was a special press conference on the news. A
smartly dressed, attractive woman — DS Fisher, according
to the information bar at the bottom — was speaking at
one of the police stations in Manchester, letting the public

know that the body of missing Debbie Johnson had been found. Although he didn't have much respect for the police and enjoyed the reporters grilling DS Fisher on what their intentions were next, he frowned in thought.

Debbie Johnson.

'Debbie . . .' he whispered. 'Debbie Johnson.'

Callum pulled out his phone and searched the name on Facebook.

'See you when you come up,' Linda shouted from upstairs. 'I'm going to bed.'

'Okay. I won't be long,' Callum replied, tilting his head so his voice would project towards the hallway and up the stairs.

'You are coming up tonight aren't you?' she shouted.

He often fell asleep on the sofa while he was watching something and sometimes didn't make it to bed. 'I'll be up soon.'

He heard Linda's footsteps above until she presumably climbed into bed, leaving the sound of only the TV.

Slowly he scrolled through the profiles that had come up, looking for any familiarity in the small profile pics on the left-hand side, but none of the fake smiles belonged to anyone he recognised.

The clock on the wall told him it was approaching 11 p.m. He was usually asleep by this time. Knowing he had an early start in the morning, he pulled himself up, slipped his phone into his pocket, and switched off the TV. The whole house fell into an eerie silence. He left the living room, switched off the lamp near the door, and started climbing the stairs, when something caught his eye.

A light.

He shifted his weight onto his left foot, peering over the banister, noticing a light coming from the kitchen. By the colour and brightness, it was the strip light under the cupboard near the sink, which he was confident he'd turned off before he left. He patted his thigh, annoyed he'd wasted the electricity while in the living room. Due to the rising energy prices, he kept tabs on their energy usage, switching lights off when they weren't needed and only using the heating when they were cold, wearing their thickest jumpers.

He turned on the lamp in the hall so he could see and headed for the kitchen, still mulling over the unit cost of electricity in his head to calculate the month's usage. He jumped and froze when he heard the bang near him.

'What was that?' he muttered quickly, staring at the door under the stairs.

He pulled open the cupboard and flicked on the light. A broom had somehow fallen, and the handle must have banged off a wooden shelf where he kept a selection of tools and various-sized boxes with junk he'd repeatedly told Linda would come in useful one day. He frowned, wondering how it had happened.

After lifting it back and watching it for a moment in case it did it again, he closed the cupboard and went into the kitchen towards the light near the sink, remembering how angry he was about the wastage.

Then it clicked, the name Debbie Johnson. He did know her from years ago. She'd gone to school with him. Yes, that was it. 'Chorlton High School,' he muttered, nodding to himself as he leaned forward for the motion-detected switch.

As the kitchen fell into the darkness, he heard a sound from above, a dull thud of some kind, probably Linda going to the bathroom before settling into bed. At least he'd be able to tell her the news, about the woman found, that he knew her from years ago.

When he turned to head for the hallway, he stopped and stared with wide eyes, stunned at what he saw.

The prominent silhouette of a figure standing a few feet from him, still as a stone.

Callum wanted to say something, but he couldn't speak. A thousand thoughts swam through his head, attempting to figure out who the shape was.

'Shit . . .'

Fight or flight.

'What . . . who are you?' he whispered, barely managing to project his voice. He realised he was shaking now.

The figure remained terrifyingly silent, breathing slowly, the slight rise and fall in his shoulders visible against the light from the lamp in the hallway behind him.

Callum squinted but couldn't see their face, just a black shadow with no features, no expressions; he had no idea who was standing in his kitchen. Knowing he didn't possess the same physical attributes as whoever this was, he weighed up the possibility of something physical happening in the following seconds. His heart thumped loudly, beating strongly against his chest. A stranger standing in your home, lurking in the shadows, was never a good sign.

'I said, who are you?' he begged, keeping his voice low, the thought of his family upstairs coming to his mind. He didn't want them to know what was happening, didn't want them to feel terrified like he did right now.

Desperate to move, Callum realised his feet were stuck to the tiles, and his body was rigid, as if his flesh and bones had turned to concrete, a statue with constant fear in its wide eyes.

Come on, think, he demanded of himself. *You're the man of this house. Your house. Think.*

Needing a light to see who it was, he dashed to the left, leaning over, and swept his left hand under the motion detector to turn on the cupboard light. The light flashed on, illuminating the sink and worktop, but he didn't have a chance to turn and see the figure because an arm came around his neck, squeezing his windpipe, followed by a fabric cloth forced over his nose and mouth.

It smelled disgusting.

Before he knew it, the smell faded, and his world went black.

* * *

The figure slowly lowered him to the floor and waited, listening for any sounds in the house. Any sudden footsteps on the landing or intrigued family members coming down the stairs.

Nothing. Bending down, he grabbed an arm and the waistband of Callum's jeans, and, in one fluid motion, hauled him up onto his shoulder like he weighed nothing more than a bag of sugar. The stranger then made his way silently across the kitchen, his black boots light on the tiles, and opened the back door with his free hand, and after stepping out, quietly closed the door behind him, carrying Callum McCauley away from the house.

CHAPTER 28

The only positive thing about it being a Monday morning, despite the fact they had to wait until the weekend for a day off, was the weather. Yes, it was cold, but they expected it; it was December. It was a few degrees up from yesterday, the sun hovering on the horizon as DS Fisher pulled her Volvo into the police station on Chorley Road, forcing her to pull down the sun visor to aid her in finding a space.

She parked up just before 8 a.m., applied the handbrake, and switched off the engine. To her right, she could see DS Phillips's red Mondeo, a car he'd purchased a few weeks earlier, the windows with condensation halfway up the front windscreen, indicating he'd been in a while already.

To the left, she spotted DI James's Range Rover, and judging by the windows, he'd just pulled up, but he was nowhere to be seen in the car park. She stepped down from the car and made her way to the entrance door at the back of the building. Inside, PC Baan loitered as if she was waiting for her.

'Morning, Ash.' Fisher greeted her with a tired smile. 'Monday again, eh?'

Ignoring Fisher, Baan said, 'DI James is in with DCI Baker.' Fisher nodded, waiting for her to elaborate as it wasn't unusual for James to be in a meeting with the DCI, especially on a Monday morning, to catch up on any weekend developments that Baker wasn't aware of. Baan noticed the vacant look on Fisher's face, the lack of concern. 'It seemed serious,' she added.

'Serious how?' Fisher frowned.

'I don't know.' Baan pointed at the door. 'I walked in with DI James, then DCI Baker came out of nowhere as if he was waiting for him and told him to get in his office now.'

'What did James say?'

'He nodded at Baker, followed him, then turned back and told me to wait for you and ask if you'd do the morning brief.'

'Did DCI Baker say what it was about?' Fisher thought back to anything that might have happened over the weekend. The only thing she could think of was the press conference last night, wondering if she'd done something wrong or said something offensive to upset some sensitive soul somewhere in the world. Fisher nodded and glanced down at her watch. It had gone just past 8 a.m. 'Okay, no worries. Right, let's get to it, then; we have a lot to discuss with the team. Are you joining us?'

'Yeah. PC Jackson is waiting up there, keeping my seat warm.'

'Inspector Thorne okay with that?'

Baan nodded. 'He advised it. He wants us to keep up to date with you guys.'

Baan and Fisher left the reception and went down the corridor. Baan took a right after Fisher had said yes to a coffee and told her she'd be straight up with it, while Fisher continued, taking a left and ascending the stairs to the first floor, totally unprepared for the meeting but confident she knew enough to get her through regarding the current cases the team were facing.

Before she reached the room, Fisher could hear the conversations inside. She entered, noticing DS Phillips sitting over near the radiator, stealing its warmth, a luxury they hadn't had for most of Friday.

'Morning,' she almost shouted, stopping in the centre of the wall near the door.

DS Phillips frowned her way, curious about her greeting everyone.

'DI James is in a meeting with DCI Baker and has asked if I'd step in for him.'

Her words were met with several nods, and people readjusted their positions to face her. PC Baan entered the room carrying two coffees and handed Fisher one.

'Thanks, Ashleigh.'

Baan smiled and sat next to PC Jackson.

Along with the usual crowd of CID members, Pamela Boone, the forensic tech, was there; DI James had requested her presence beforehand to provide updates on the discovery of Debbie Johnson's head at Chorlton Library. Sitting on the desk behind Boone were Stacy and Jasper, the trainee techs, who wanted to be involved in the meeting too. Jasper wore a lime-green T-shirt and red jeans, and Stacy was smartly dressed, appearing to take her job a little more seriously. DI James usually liked to keep the meetings 'in-house', but Pamela had vouched for them, saying it would do them good to understand how their work affects CID and how policing progress is measured.

'So,' Fisher started, attracting the attention of everyone, 'I'd like to first speak about the so-called Night Stalkers.' She focused on Baan, who knew she'd spoken with Inspector Thorne about their interviews and sentencing. 'What's the latest with them, please, Ash?'

Baan cleared her throat, the question surprising her. 'Erm, after their DNA was found inside one of the rape victims — yes, semen — they've confessed to fourteen rape charges in total, so as you can imagine, we're happy, along with the women of Manchester, that these animals are behind bars.'

'Good.' Fisher offered a tight smile, glad to get the meeting off to a positive start but knew it wouldn't last. 'Just to recap the events of Friday, we received a call from the cleaner at Chorlton Library, who discovered the head of Debbie Johnson in the library's toilet. After further testing, we can confirm the head did belong to Debbie. For those who aren't aware, we also found a sample of semen on the tiled floor in the toilet. It appears to have been cleaned, but there was evidence in the grout lines which the suspect had missed.'

The two forensic techs, Stacy and Jasper, frowned at each other, not following. Jasper raised a hand.

'Yes, Jasper?'

He tilted his head, narrowed his eyes. 'I was just wondering, by semen, what . . . how did it get there?'

'At this point, we don't know for sure. When Pamela discovered it, she made us aware the sample was fresh.' Fisher shrugged. 'Our only explanation is that the suspect had stood back, watching the head inside the urinal, and sexually pleased himself until he'd ejaculated.'

Jasper winced at the thought of someone doing that, but it didn't bother Stacy, who found her colleague's reaction somewhat amusing.

'So, we know it's Debbie Johnson.' Fisher nodded and started taking small steps around the front of the room. Everyone kept their focus on her. 'Why her? What do we know about Debbie Johnson?'

When the silence seemed to be the only answer, Fisher said, 'Well?'

'We know that Debbie Johnson was forty-one and lived alone,' Phillips said. 'She had no boyfriend or partner. She worked from home as an IT consultant in some form, and her life was quite straightforward up until she went missing a few days ago, as reported by her friend Abi Witmore.'

Fisher acknowledged DS Phillips's answer. 'Thank you, Matthew.'

'What else do we know?' she probed, this time louder, ensuring everyone knew the question was open.

Quietness swept the room. Phillips seemed to be thinking of something to add but came up short.

'Exactly. We don't know enough. But I know something: we need to know Debbie Johnson as well as she knew herself. We need to know why someone chose her and, more importantly, why she was a target. From the kill, it's clear to us it wasn't a random attack or an impulsive act of violence. Whoever was involved had thought this out.'

'What makes you say that?'

Fisher frowned at PC Jackson. 'Say what?'

'That it wasn't an impulsive attack?'

She tilted her head in disbelief at his statement. PC Baan turned her head in his direction too.

'Tell me why you believe it wasn't?'

PC Jackson appeared lost for words, unable to back his statement up.

'Well?' Fisher didn't like being put on the spot like that, and his question — especially the way he'd asked it — surprised her. 'To answer your question, Adam, I believe it wasn't an impulsive act of violence because if it was, it would have been in a bar or a shop, a random encounter between two people. Not someone cutting someone else's head off, placing it inside a urinal in a Manchester library, standing there and masturbating over it, then cleaning the scene up afterwards. The person wasn't seen by any cameras, nor did they trip any alarms. It's likely the person had access, so maybe had a key.'

Her answer seemed to silence Jackson, who offered the slightest of nods and looked down.

'If you wouldn't mind staying behind, please, Adam,' she said. 'I'd like a quick word with you. Thanks,' she added without a response. 'So, we need to find out everything we can about Mrs Johnson. I mean everything. Past boyfriends, previous jobs, friends, and even the school she went to. Pieces of random information might be nothing but could mean everything. Right, let's get to work.'

* * *

'You handled yourself well in there,' DS Phillips said, placing a hand on Fisher's shoulder as he leaned over her.

She tucked a few strands of hair behind her ear. 'Thanks.'

'What did you say to PC Jackson after we left?'

'It doesn't matter. He's just young.'

'He's old enough to know not to be clever, though,' countered Phillips, sitting at his desk next to hers.

Fisher waved it away and logged into her emails, seeing almost a dozen new ones appear. A few were from Forensics, one from the pathologist Jack Wilson, who'd personally examined the head. The subject of his email was *Where's the rest of her?* followed by a couple more from DI James with information on slight changes to policing laws.

'Why are they changing things?' muttered Fisher to herself.

Phillips read the same email, picked up his coffee to have a sip, and shook his head. 'God knows.'

Fisher's phone rang. It was Susan from the reception desk at the front of the station. She answered.

'DS Fisher, we've had a call come in from a Linda McCauley, saying her husband went missing last night.'

'Go on . . .'

'Said he was at home last night but this morning wasn't there. She thought he'd gone to help a friend with something but noticed his phone was still downstairs in the kitchen and his van was still outside the house.'

'Did she say if there were any signs of anything unusual?'

'Nothing other than her husband not being at the house or reachable.'

'Okay, you got an address?'

Susan told her.

'Okay, thanks. I'll check it out.' Fisher hung up.

Behind them, quick footsteps distracted them both away from their computer screens. Turning, they saw DI James charging across the office towards them, his hand quickly brushing back his hair, something he often did when he felt stressed. However the meeting had gone with DCI Baker, clearly it wasn't very positive.

'April, Matthew,' DI James spat, stopping near them. They both frowned at him.

'We've had a call about an hour ago from a librarian.'

'If it's Alison from Chorlton Library, I said I'd ring her—'

He gave them a thin, defeated smile. 'No. It's someone else, from a different library. Another body's been found.'

CHAPTER 29

It had just gone midday as he pulled his sleeves over his freezing hands, feeling happy it hadn't taken too long for the small crowd to gather behind the tape, fixed from a handrail to the nearest tree, which sagged in the gentle wind. The tape then continued to the next bare tree, wrapped around once, then on to the next. The trees were situated around the library like guards protecting a queen, covering most of the grass between the single-storey building and the pavement, where the crowd had been kept to give the police enough space to work the scene.

The presence of the police and crime scene tape always attracted a crowd, no matter where it was. It was the snowball effect — a gathering attracted more interest, and so forth. The cordoned-off area marked a space the public couldn't access, only filling their imaginations with what they couldn't see.

Was it another body?

A woman?

A child this time?

What was so crucial inside the small library that they couldn't see it?

Most of them had seen the press conference on Sunday night, where the dark-haired DS Fisher had stood answering questions from the Manchester media about the woman who was found at the library.

Had it happened again?

'Hey!' a man nearby shouted, catching the attention of the PC. The constable he was talking to did well to ignore the man's question. 'Hey, I'm talking to you, pig. What's going on?'

The PC didn't rise to the insult and remained professional, focusing on the gathering crowd to ensure no one attempted to duck under the tape, especially local reporters who were known to bend the rules or media enthusiasts searching for their next viral video.

You'll soon see, the man next to him wanted to say but kept his thoughts to himself. He was aware of the traffic behind him coming and going, slowing to a crawl, obviously interested in the commotion, then moving on to wherever they were heading.

He shuffled back from the tape, wriggled through the crowd, and once near the road, made his way around the back of the group to the turn-in, a small road with a U-bend mainly used by buses dropping and picking passengers up. He noticed more police around the other side standing by the tape to prevent access from that side.

Smiling, he waited.

* * *

Fisher spotted the tall sign for Lidl up ahead on the right, the logo against the faint winter sun behind it, rising into the clear, crisp blue sky, starving the day of the remaining morning darkness. She didn't know exactly where the library was, but Phillips knew it was opposite Lidl. Judging by the crowd gathered up on the left, he wasn't wrong.

'This must be it, just up here,' she said.

Phillips raised a hand from the passenger seat, pointing. 'Past the crowd. There's a turning into the car park.'

Fisher nodded, kept her focus on the crawling car in front, then peered at the people on the left and the tape fixed to the surrounding trees, acting like a barrier to keep the scene in one piece.

The car park was long but narrow. Fisher found a space next to Boone's forensic van. Occupying the closer spots were police cars, three of them Vauxhall Astras, one of them a Peugeot, and a dark blue Ford Mondeo.

Fisher sighed as she switched off the engine. Phillips glanced over, feeling her exhaustion and the pressure and weight of another body being discovered. Would it be the same — a human head inside a urinal? Or would it be something else? She knew one thing: a headache was forming in her temples, which she put down to probably too much coffee. Pointing to the glove box in front of Phillips's legs, she said, 'Open that please and grab me some paracetamol.'

He frowned but didn't comment. 'Here you go.'

Once she'd knocked some back and drained a bottle of water, she climbed down from the high seats of the Volvo and took her time looking around the grounds of the library, specifically for cameras that might have captured anything of interest. Unfortunately, she couldn't see anything obvious. Then she focused on the crowd standing by the tape watching her. Fisher was astounded how much time some people had.

'DI James coming down?' Phillips asked.

'He's aware of the situation. Messaged to say he'll be down when he can.'

On their approach, Fisher noticed a canal behind the library. A red-and-blue barge drifted behind the library building, down the river towards the right. There were benches at the edge of the water, empty because the area had been cordoned off, but if people were to sit and watch the barges go by, or stare at the resident wildlife, that would be the perfect spot.

The nearest PC watched Fisher and Phillips approach with a cautious frown. He hadn't seen either of them before and raised a palm to halt them in their tracks. 'You with us?'

Without saying a word, Fisher picked her badge from her suit jacket and flashed it to him.

He nodded and lifted the tape over their heads as they passed through. The library was much less grand than the previous one they'd been to, almost appearing like a luxury portacabin of the type office workers used for temporary office space overlooking building projects. But instead of looking flimsy, it looked solid, with walls painted a dull green that blended with the surrounding grass and nearby trees.

A woman stood at the entrance door facing away from them. Fisher knew it was Boone. Not only did her white coveralls give her away, but the plumes of smoke rising and wisping off in the gentle breeze were an indication. Boone turned with a frown upon hearing footsteps.

'Hey, April.' Her face softened, and she gave a thin smile, not showing any teeth. 'Another one to keep us entertained for a few days, eh?' It was as if crime scenes like this didn't bother her anymore; as time passed, they became routine. She took the final drag on her cigarette, dropped it on the ground, and stubbed it out with a heel. She then grabbed two fresh blue plastic overshoes from her pocket and, one by one, slid them over her shoes.

'You want any?'

Fisher nodded. 'Please.'

'Where's Super Sterling at?' asked Phillips, raising his brows.

'Super Sterling — I like that.'

They all smiled.

Once the detectives had put them on, Boone said, 'You ready for this?'

'Not at all.' Fisher sighed, then glanced at Phillips, who shook his head.

Boone's smile went from ear to ear. 'Follow me, you two.'

CHAPTER 30

Chorlton High School
Twenty-seven years ago

Just after English literature class, the boy headed for his locker at the end of the corridor. He hated it, knowing he'd have to pass the other lockers to get to his, which was located next to the caretaker's cupboard that was usually locked — it didn't used to be, but the naughtier ones used to open it and play stupid games with the chemicals.

He didn't mind that it was locked now, because of what had happened last year; Steve Adams had waited at his locker with no other intention than to grab him and throw him in, then see how long he could hold the handle to keep him inside before a teacher came along to spoil the fun. That eight minutes inside the pitch-black cupboard had been one of the worst times of his life. Once Steve had thrown him inside, the boy had screamed, feeling all sorts around him: sweeping brushes, mop heads hanging on the wall near him, plastic containers, rags, blankets, old waterproof coats the caretaker would use when it was raining outside. At one point, he was sure an enormous spider had crawled across his hand, but he couldn't be sure — he was petrified of spiders. He tried to find a light, but little did he know the switch was outside the door.

But that wasn't the worst part of it.

As the students laughed from the other side, they were unaware that the teenager trapped inside had knocked over a tin of special cleaner containing acid. It had splashed on his arm, causing an awful burning sensation. When the history teacher Mr Eckles spotted Steve with both hands holding the door handle, he yelled, scattering nearby students. Frozen, Steve immediately let go of the handle and cowered into the corner, unsure what Eckles would do. He was big and tall, sported a thick beard, and had the blackest eyes you'd ever seen; students were petrified of him.

When the teacher turned on the light and opened the door, he found the boy crying on the floor, holding his arm, which was red and blistering. The smell of cleaning fluid escaped into the corridor. The school put Steve in isolation for a month for that, and luckily the boy had a month off from him, time to battle the other bullies who roamed the corridors, making his school life even more miserable.

The boy was happy this morning. The English class had gone well. His teacher, Miss Palmer, a twenty-something blonde-haired woman who others in the class had teased him for fancying, had marked his work with an A, saying he was top of the class. It made him feel good about himself because, other than his reading, school subjects were the only good thing he had in his life.

He opened his locker with the key he kept on a fraying lanyard around his neck and put some of the books he wouldn't need inside, then locked it, slipping the key down the neck of his school shirt.

'Well, if it isn't the teacher's favourite pet,' said a voice.

He knew the voice. Steve Adams, who was in his English class.

The boy sighed, closing his eyes, and turned sheepishly towards him. 'Listen, Steve . . .'

With Steve was Callum McCauley, and a couple more, all wearing mischievous smiles on their smug faces.

'I'm listening,' Steve replied loudly, getting in his face and preventing him from leaving his locker area.

'Please just leave me alone. I've . . . I've done nothing wrong,' the boy pleaded quietly, not looking Steve in the eyes, who stared at him.

'*I've done nothing wrong*,' Steve said in a mocking high-pitch voice.

'Go on, then,' Callum said to Steve, standing beside him.

The boy's eyes got teary, keeping his focus on an area near their feet, desperate for the moment to pass, but he knew it wouldn't.

'Look at me,' Steve demanded.

When the boy self-consciously raised his eyes, Steve rocked his head forward quickly, landing a headbutt on the bridge of the boy's nose. Immediately, the force of the blow knocked him back into the lockers with an almighty clatter, then he slipped to the ground, clutching at his erupted bloody nose with both hands. The crimson liquid fell through the boy's shaking hands onto his white T-shirt, then down onto the linoleum floor.

As the other boys all laughed and high-fived each other, the boy bawled his eyes out and curled up on the floor.

CHAPTER 31

Present day

Fisher was surprised at how hot the library was.

'Don't worry,' Boone said, knowing they'd feel the sudden heat. 'I've asked them to turn off the heating.'

Fisher nodded her approval.

The ceiling was much lower than Fisher or Phillips had assumed, judging from the outside. Spotlights were strategically positioned to illuminate the space effectively. To the left, by a long narrow window, were a cluster of beanbags, gaudy matting, and small bookshelves filled with thin, colourful books with cartoon-like characters filling the front covers. An open area for smaller children, the detectives presumed. Over to the right was a low, wide desk with a computer screen, a printer, an array of paperwork, and a small metal box containing bookmarks. A vacant black swivel chair was behind it, and beyond that, on the wall, several notices with opening times and upcoming events, one of which a local author was attending.

Beyond what they assumed was the children's area was a half-closed studded partition with several worktops lined with computer screens, keyboards, and mice. All the screens were black and in sleep mode. On the walls of this small section were posters on career advice and adult classes to aid them with their maths and English.

They followed Boone to the reception desk, where a woman was talking to a man they didn't recognise wearing a dark grey suit and brown shoes. Judging by his posture — straight back and chest out — not only was he a gym-goer but someone who considered himself important. He gazed at them on their approach with his large brown searing eyes and maintained a serious look in wonder at who the approaching strangers were.

'Sir,' Boone said to the suited man, then indicated to Fisher and Phillips with her hand. 'These are Detective Sergeants April Fisher and Matthew Phillips.'

The man excused himself from the woman he was talking to and leaned forward with a stern face. He looked to be around fifty, judging by the crow's feet lining his eyes. 'Pleasure to meet you. I'm Detective Inspector Allen. I don't believe we've met.'

'No, sir,' said Fisher, shaking his hand firmly. 'DS April Fisher.'

He then shook Phillips's hand, who squeezed that little bit harder to match Allen's tough persona and his vice-like grip. Allen then explained he worked at Manchester Police Headquarters, which was close to the library.

'You work for DI Thomas James?'

'We do,' replied Fisher.

'Where is he?'

'Said he'll come here shortly. He's held up with something.'

Allen nodded but said nothing.

'I've read your reports on what you found at Chorlton Library, the head in the urinal?'

The detectives nodded.

'Interesting crime scene.'

'What are we looking at this morning?' asked Fisher.

'I like that — straight to the point.' He turned slightly, turning his focus on the bookshelves towards the back, which made up most of the library's space on the right, beside the room of computers. Unlike that space, the shelving ran twenty or thirty metres until it hit the wall. Fisher looked down, seeing several rows of shelving all packed with books. Down one row, she saw a tall, narrow window, where another barge, this time a yellow one, floated by.

'Follow me.'

Fisher and Phillips followed DI Allen past the reception desk and down one of two aisles. Phillips's face was flushed, the library's heat finally getting to him. He contemplated removing his long coat but didn't. Fisher noted DI Allen's walk, how he seemed to carry a slight limp, maybe his right knee.

Allen turned his head slightly so they could hear him. 'The call came from Dorothy, the lady I was just speaking to. She's the receptionist here. After opening up and doing a quick sweep of the building, she noticed the smell and tried to find the source. That's when she found it.'

Instead of asking what was found, Fisher and Phillips kept listening and trailing his footsteps, scanning the books ahead to see if they could spot anything before he revealed the exact location.

'Here we go.' Allen stopped and pointed to the left.

At head height, in the space above the books and the shelf above, was a human head facing outward to the aisle. The eyes were bloodshot and wide open, staring right at them. Tiny blood vessels covered the eyes' whites like the tiny roots of a tree. Long, dark matted hair filled much of the space on either side and rested on the books beside them, covered with dried crimson blood.

Fisher stared at the woman's eyes, matching her stare until she turned away, spotting Phillips take a lungful of air and let out a heavy sigh.

'You alright?' she asked Phillips, the colour visibly draining from his face. Without a word, he managed a nod.

'You think it's your missing girl?' Allen asked her.

She thought about it for a moment, reflecting on the photograph they had of Mary Steadman. There were definite resemblances, that's for sure.

'Yeah, I think so.'

Footsteps came from the left. Pamela Boone approached with the crime scene manager Peter Sterling, who had just arrived. Boone had already been in and seen the head before even Fisher and Phillips had pulled up and ran through the scene briefly with DI Allen. Before doing anything else, Sterling had told Boone to wait for him as he wanted to get in on the action. *Why not get here on time, then?* A question on the tip of Boone's tongue, but she kept that one to herself. It was easier to play nice.

DI Allen held out a hand to the approaching CSM, who took it firmly. 'Peter Sterling, crime scene manager.'

'Detective Inspector Allen, based out of HQ.'

'Pleasure to meet you.'

Sterling nodded, then looked away from the DI and focused on Boone, who moved a few steps down the aisle and pointed up at the head. Sterling wandered down and peered at the face of the woman staring out.

'What do we know?' he asked Boone.

'We know as much as you're seeing. I haven't touched it yet.'

Fisher pointed. 'Do you think there's another photo tucked up inside there?'

'There could be,' Boone replied. 'But I'd like to show you all something else first.'

Fisher and Phillips traded a quick glance and frowned, following Boone almost ten metres along the bookshelf until she stopped and pointed. This time, whatever it was, she was indicating it was located on the opposite side, roughly knee height.

'What is it?' asked Phillips.

'Have a peek. Don't be shy.'

Phillips and Fisher lowered, smelling it before seeing it. Phillips threw a hand over his nose, but Fisher took in the stench of burnt flesh.

'Jesus.' Fisher scowled up at Boone. 'Is that someone's arm?' Everything about the shape of the object indicated it was a human arm. It was severed just past the elbow, roughly where the bicep started, but the skin didn't suggest it was human because it was melted in various parts, burnt and brittle in others, the worst being just before the elbow joint, which was jet black and hardened. Fisher finally gave in and covered her nose.

'That smell is horrific, Pamela.'

Boone gave a thin smile. 'It isn't pleasant, no.'

Peter Sterling was standing behind Fisher, keeping his distance based on the detectives' reactions to the smell. He'd smelt enough burnt flesh in his time not to want to relive all those moments again, and no matter how many times you experienced it, it wasn't something you got used to.

Standing, Fisher took a step back so she could breathe better. 'Pam, is there anything else here besides the head and the arm?'

'Follow me.' Boone took several paces further down the aisle, and on the same side, at head height, she stopped, turned, and pointed. 'Look.'

Fisher visibly sighed, preparing herself for what Boone was going to show them. The detectives stopped by her side, observing the object in the space above multiple books and the shelf above. Fisher frowned and tilted her head in an attempt to work it out.

'What . . . what is that?'

It was obviously human flesh, approximately a foot long and ten to twelve inches thick. There was a nasty cut at least five inches long, nearly an inch wide. Blood had congealed around it, and muscles, tendons, and a bone were visible inside the wound. After a moment, she asked, 'Is that a leg, or a thigh, maybe?'

'I think it's someone's thigh, judging by the size and length of it,' Boone noted.

Fisher lifted her hands and dropped her face into her palms. 'This just gets better.'

DI Allen said, 'Interesting scene, huh?'

'You could say that,' Phillips commented. 'I wonder if they all belong to the same victim?'

'I guess we'll know when we send off the DNA samples.'

'What are you starting with?' Sterling asked Boone, standing with her hands on her hips, ready to crack on with her work.

'I'll start with the head, I think, if you're happy with that, boss?'

Sterling's ego was visibly filled. 'Sure, Pam. Might as well get the fun stuff out of the way.'

'*Do* you think there's a photo inside there?' Fisher asked for the second time.

'There's only one way to find out, April.'

Boone took a deep breath and reached up, placing a hand on either side of the female head. Sterling held up a hand.

'Hold on. Have you taken photographs and a short video of the scene first?'

Boone stood for a moment, her hands still touching the head, amazed at his question. Leaving her hands where they were, she slowly turned to him, tilting her head. 'I'm not a bloody trainee, Peter. Of course I have.'

He backed away with an apologetic palm up. 'Okay, just checking. You do your thing.'

Fisher and Phillips exchanged a knowing look, then watched Boone carefully pick up the head, lifting it high enough to bring it forward so she could lower it gradually to the ground on the plastic sheeting she'd already laid out.

'April, pass me that torch, please.'

Fisher went to the forensic kit, grabbed the torch, and handed it to her, trying to ignore the not-so-wonderful smell the head was giving off.

'Thanks.'

Boone then angled the bright light to the base of the bloody head, checking inside the flesh, blood, and tendons for any sign of the same thing they'd found at the previous scene. Sure enough, a small straight edge was folded in half among the mess of soft tissue. Fisher knew it was another photo.

Boone pulled it free and gingerly opened it. It was the same photo as the last, the image of the young boy dressed in his school uniform.

Everyone leaned in.

Fisher's shoulders dipped half an inch. 'Who on earth is this boy?'

CHAPTER 32

While Fisher was at the library, PC Baan and PC Jackson were asked to head over to Callum McCauley's house, following up on the report that he'd vanished the night before. It was a well-presented house, the paintwork on the windows and door done recently.

Baan knocked on the door.

'Hello,' said the woman as she opened it. The uniformed Baan and Jackson seemed to lessen the scowl on her face, but there was concern in her eyes. 'Come in, come in.' She moved aside, motioning them in.

Once inside, she said, 'I'm Linda. Thank you for coming. I wasn't sure how long it would take for you to get here.' She moved past them. 'Please, we'll sit in the kitchen.'

Baan and Jackson followed her, absorbing the house's decor and the photos on the wall in the hallway. They sat down at the kitchen table, the aroma of something sweet coming from a burning wax melt on the windowsill.

'You have children?' Jackson asked, remembering the photo of a girl and a young boy they'd passed a moment earlier.

'Yeah. Jacob and Priya. Both at school.'

'Nice names,' noted PC Baan.

Linda smiled briefly.

They knew the nature of the visit; Baan wasted no time getting straight to it. 'So, Linda, when was the last time you saw your husband—' she referred to her notes — 'Callum McCauley?'

'Last night. Callum and Jacob had been to the Manchester United game and got home around eight.' She frowned. 'We ordered a takeaway, sat down to eat it, then the kids went upstairs to get sorted for bed. Callum and I spoke a little, then I went up for a bath.'

'What does your husband do, workwise?'

'He's a self-employed plumber.' She sighed, focusing on the table for a moment. 'Long hours sometimes.'

'I can imagine. Bet he works all over?' Jackson this time.

She nodded at him. 'Yes, he covers some miles.'

'So, when you went up for a bath, what time was that?'

'Maybe half nine, ten o'clock, I'm not sure exactly.'

'Then what happened?'

'I was about half an hour in the bath, then got into bed, watched the television, and must have fallen asleep. I woke up around three in the morning, switched off the TV with the remote, and turned over.'

'You didn't notice he wasn't in bed at that point?'

She pressed her lips together. 'I can't say for certain. I often fall asleep watching the TV and then wake up and turn it off. I didn't notice if he was there or not. He often falls asleep downstairs and sometimes doesn't make it to bed before the next day.' She offered a slight shrug.

The PCs waited, wondering if their relationship was facing struggles, but knew it was none of their business.

'Then I woke up at seven and he wasn't in the bed. I checked downstairs and found it strange that Callum wasn't there. But he did mention last night that he might be helping a friend of his with a delivery.'

'Does this friend have a name?'

'Yeah. Erm, he's called Geoff. He has a builder's merchants just a few miles away. I don't have his number or remember the name of the merchants.'

Baan nodded, waiting.

'So, I texted him to say, *Have a nice day*, and then around eight o'clock, I opened the living room blinds and noticed his van was still here. And that's when I was confused.'

Baan took a deep breath. 'Is it possible that Geoff picked him up?'

Linda pondered the idea, scratching the tip of her nose, but shook her head. 'He would have been going straight to his job afterwards, so I can't see it, really.'

'Okay.' Jackson jotted a few notes down on a small notepad.

'Are there any signs of a break-in?'

'I don't think so. I heard him when I was in the bath. I think he took the bins out. One thing I did notice was that the door had been left unlocked, but assumed he'd been out before we got up and forgot to lock it. You know how forgetful men can be.'

The PCs smiled at her attempt to lighten the grim situation.

'Have you got a photo of Callum?' Baan asked. 'We can pass it to our media team and get it out on the news.'

'Is it something I should be worried about?'

'Within the first twenty-four hours of absence, we don't classify anyone as missing; we simply don't have the resources to allocate our media team to it, but as soon as we pass that time, we'll do it.'

Linda understood with a nod but clearly disagreed in her own head. She knew her husband and his behaviour, and that he'd been stressed with work recently, but it wasn't like him. She stood up. 'I'll get you a photo.'

'Thanks.'

PC Jackson stood from the table, closed his notepad, and slipped it back into his jacket pocket. He slowly wandered around the kitchen, admiring the cupboards and worktops.

It was apparent it was pretty new. He went over to the door and meticulously looked around but couldn't see anything out of the ordinary.

Linda returned with a photo and handed it to PC Jackson. 'There you go.' She smiled. 'I'm sure he'll be fine.'

From the table, PC Baan smiled thinly back at her, thinking something different.

CHAPTER 33

Once Boone had visually inspected the head at the library with Peter Sterling, she meticulously wrapped it in thin plastic, then placed it inside a black flexible bag, saving the nearby crowd from seeing it being carried to the forensics van. It was safe to say they didn't need a coroner to visually inspect the body at the crime scene. It went without saying that a head required a body to function, so a simple photo of the head alone would satisfy Norma Eggleston, one of the local coroners at Manchester City Council. With just the image of the likely Mary Steadman, along with DNA proving it was her, the coroner would be happy for the Manchester Police to get a doctor to issue a death certificate on behalf of Mrs Steadman.

Boone then did the same with the arm, and the part of the body she was confident was the thigh.

Away from the forensics team, Fisher stood with Phillips and the receptionist, who told them her name was Dorothy. She was barely five feet tall and plump. DI Allen had spoken with her and didn't need to be a part of the conversation, so he spent some time with his local PCs, who were doing a grand job securing the perimeter.

'Sorry, I know you've already done this,' Fisher said, 'but can you run us through what happened?'

Dorothy relayed the story of opening up this morning at 8 a.m. They used to open at 10 a.m. but last October the library's opening times had changed. Fisher and Phillips got the feeling by her tone it had inconvenienced her morning routine, then listened to how the morning buses caused further issues.

Fisher nodded in understanding, encouraging her to get to the point quicker. After all, there was a murderer out there somewhere.

'So, I walked in, as usual, and went through to the staff room. It's only small. I hung my coat up, put my bag there, and switched all the lights on. We used to leave the lights on to deter people trying to break in since we installed all the computers, but the bigwigs in the council told us it was unnecessary and a waste of electricity.' She shrugged. 'Anyway, I don't know, I thought I could smell something strange, you know, something burning. I went to the computers to see if there was a loose wire or something. Nothing.' She went on to explain why they had the computers, that the library was now doing coding classes for all ages and that people used them to improve their maths and English skills. 'As I moved further down, the smell got stronger. And that's when I saw the head. I screamed, ran back up, phoned the police immediately.'

'Were you alone at this point?' Phillips asked, holding a small notepad and pen.

She nodded. 'Yes. Jack turned up around five minutes after. He helps me with things here. I used to do it alone, but we have people coming and going all the time.'

'Where is Jack?'

She pointed behind her, towards the staff room. 'He's in there. He's pretty shaken up.'

'Did he see the head?'

She nodded, taking a deep breath as if reliving the point where she first laid eyes on it. 'Who . . . who is it?'

'We don't know for sure yet. We'll let Forensics deal with that.'

Dorothy raised a hand to her mouth, gently shaking her head. 'It's just awful. Never in my life have I seen such a thing. I mean, why here? Why our library?' Her eyes suddenly widened, and she pointed at Fisher. 'Wait! Wasn't there something found at another library a few days ago?'

Fisher offered a thin smile and nodded, explaining the other discoveries.

'So, first Chorlton Library, now Newton Heath? Jesus. What's going on in Manchester?'

'That's what we're going to find out. Can we speak to Jack?'

She waved her hand. 'This way, follow me. He's kind of shy — very sensitive — and, like I say, really shaken up, so you may have to be careful with him.'

CHAPTER 34

In the staff room, a rectangular room with a table in the middle and an area at the back filled with cupboards, a sink, and a worktop, the air was warm and thick, presumably coming from an electric heater plugged in near the window.

Sitting at the table, not too far from the heat source, Jack rocked back and forth. It was barely visible, but Fisher noticed. He had very short blonde hair and was clean-shaven and seemed to be around the age of thirty. He wore a thick coat that he hadn't yet taken off, which made both detectives feel hot.

'Jack,' Dorothy said gently, 'would you like me to turn that heater off? You must be melting in here.' Without a response, she went around the back of him, leaned over, and flicked the switch, the gentle hum fading into silence. 'Jack, these are police detectives. Can they ask a few questions?'

He kept his focus on the table but nodded his head.

Dorothy also cracked the window open, allowing some cold winter air to creep in. She turned to Fisher and Phillips. 'Ask away . . .'

Fisher thanked her and stopped a few metres from Jack, slowly pulling out a chair a couple along from him, careful not to invade his space. She introduced herself and Phillips. 'How long have you worked here, Jack?'

'Nearly a year.'

'You enjoy it?'

He nodded. 'I love books.'

'Yes, he does,' agreed Dorothy, 'he loves reading. That's all he does at home.'

'That's great. I love books too.' Fisher smiled at him. 'So, when you turned up this morning, can you tell me what happened?'

'Well, he came in, and then we saw the head,' replied Dorothy.

Ignoring the receptionist, Fisher asked him the question again, wanting Jack to answer.

He flicked his focus from the table to Fisher, holding her gaze. 'I love books. This was like something from out of the books I read.' His eyes widened as if he found a certain excitement from it. 'The head on the books. The head on the books.'

Phillips, standing near the door, frowned at him.

'That's right. The head on the books. Did you see it?'

He nodded. 'Yes. The eyes. They were big.'

Behind Phillips, a collection of voices came from outside the room, followed by frantic footsteps. 'Please, let me in.'

'You can't go in there . . .'

Through the doorway came a woman in her fifties dressed in a green duffle coat and woollen hat. 'Jack. Oh God, Jack. There you are.' She passed Phillips, then rounded the rear of Fisher, who swivelled, trailing her movements as she threw her arms around Jack, hugging him tightly.

'He's okay, he's fine,' Dorothy calmly reassured her. 'He's just a little shaken.'

'I'm not bloody surprised. What kind of sick place is this?'

Dorothy frowned. 'I'm sorry?'

'You heard me! My son has been given an opportunity to do something with his life, and you let him see this?'

'Hold on, please,' protested Fisher. 'Everyone needs to calm down and speak like adults.'

'Calm down?' the woman said. 'Jack texted me telling me there's a human head in the library and that he's terrified.'

'I know, that's why I called you, Jean,' explained Dorothy.

'Come on, Jack.' Jean helped her son up. 'We're going home. We need to get you out of here.'

'You can't, not yet,' replied Fisher. 'We need to speak to Jack before he goes. He's a witness.'

Jean sighed heavily and sat down next to Jack, accepting what Fisher had told her.

'Is that okay, Jack?' asked Fisher, more out of politeness than giving him an option.

He nodded shyly, knowing the sooner he told them what happened, the sooner he could go.

'So, you saw the head?'

Jean's eyes widened as she stared at Fisher. 'Detective, is this really necessary?'

'It really is, yes.' Fisher focused back to Jack. 'So, what happened?'

'Well, the head was on the top of books. The eyes were . . . big. The blood, it-it had soaked into the books, changing their colour.' He turned to his mother. 'I don't think people will be able to read those books anymore.'

She half smiled at him, waiting for him to go on.

'And that's it.'

'You didn't touch anything, did you?'

He shivered and edged back into the chair, the thought of doing so apparently making him sick. 'Graham Totto would have touched it.'

'Who?' asked Fisher, frowning.

Jean smiled, tilting her head. 'It's a character in a book series he's reading. It's nothing to worry about.'

Phillips eyed Jack curiously and scribbled more on the small notepad in his hand.

'That's all I know,' he said, offering them no more than a light shrug.

'Okay, Jack. Thank you for answering. You're free to go.'

Jean stood first and helped Jack to his feet, not that he needed it, but she was being overprotective.

Fisher, Phillips, and Dorothy watched them leave the room, and eventually the room fell into silence.

'I'm sorry about that,' Dorothy explained. 'We've had a hard time with Jack.'

Fisher waited for her to expand on that.

'We got a call from the job centre last year about him. He's been let go from previous roles, and they were wondering if we'd give him a chance here. He came for the initial interview with Jean — his mum, the woman you've just met — and explained it would do him good to have some focus in his life. He works part-time here, Monday to Wednesday.'

The detectives nodded.

'Who else works here, other than yourself and Jack?'

'Well, there's Luke — works Wednesday to Friday, sometimes on Saturday, depending what he's doing. We also have a cleaner who comes in three mornings a week, usually on Monday, Wednesday, and Friday.'

'Who's the cleaner?'

'Oh, she's lovely. I feel quite sorry for her, to be honest. She's quiet. Doesn't seem to do much outside of work, judging by our conversations.'

'Her name?'

'Patricia.'

'Patricia . . . ?'

'Oh, sorry.' Dorothy smiled, shaking her head. 'Patricia Hawthorn.'

'Was Mrs Hawthorn working this morning?'

'She phoned earlier, left a message saying she'd picked up a bug from her daughter. Been sick all night with it. She sounded terrible.'

Phillips noted that and focused back on Dorothy, who stood awkwardly staring at them. 'What about CCTV — does the library have that?'

'Of course.' She squinted as if stating the obvious. 'During our revamp last year, everything was updated. The

162

computers, the wiring, the lighting, all the works. Manchester City Council paid for everything. At least the taxpayer's money went to good use and not the politician's pockets.'

Fisher silently agreed with the librarian's opinion. Over the years, Fisher had found that the generation before weren't shy about giving their views or saying how they really felt. It was a shame the world had changed, giving more people the right to become offended at the slightest comment. Fisher felt for the generations to come in more ways than one.

'It's just through here.' Dorothy wasted no time leaving the room, at which point the detectives rose from their chairs and followed her to the computer in the library's main room. To their right, they noticed Boone and Sterling down the aisle, Boone carefully wrapping one of the body parts and placing it into a dark-coloured bag. Sterling looked up at Fisher but was too important to acknowledge her and focused back on Boone.

The librarian sat down on a chair and pulled herself in, her padded stomach pressing hard against the edge of the low table. She took hold of the mouse, gave it a shake, and entered her password.

'How many cameras are inside the library?'

Dorothy scowled in thought, tapping her fingers, then she looked up at Fisher, standing to her right. 'I think there are five.'

'What about outside? Do they cover the entrance and exit doors?'

She nodded. 'We have the entrance and exit door over there.' She pointed to where they'd walked through when they first arrived, then swivelled half a turn, stabbing a finger towards a small corridor behind them. 'There's a back door through there. When I lock up, I sometimes use that door to leave. There's a camera just above that door too.'

It sounded positive this time, unlike at Chorlton Library.

Dorothy turned back to the screen. 'Okay, so what am I doing?'

The detectives watched her closely.

'Who's your favourite author?'

Fisher frowned at her. 'Sorry?'

Dorothy spun round. 'Your favourite author?'

She didn't understand how this was relevant to looking at the CCTV. 'I don't read,' she simply answered, trying to push this along. 'I only said that to Jack to build a rapport with him.'

'Shame.' Dorothy focused back on the screen, and the detectives exchanged a frown. 'Books are the keys to our souls,' she added. 'I read that once somewhere.'

Fisher didn't comment because she didn't want to stop her looking for the camera system, and really thought it was absurd there were body parts less than twenty metres away from them and the librarian was reciting quotes.

'Here we are, oh . . .'

'What's up?' Fisher leaned over her.

'Hold on.' The librarian returned to the previous folder and stared for a moment, making sure it was definitely the right one. 'Strange.' She then double-clicked the folder, but it was blank. 'I don't understand. There should be at least five files here. One for each camera.'

Fisher mentally noted that the folder name was today's date and heaved a sigh. 'Can you go back to yesterday's folder — is that an option?'

'I can, but the files won't be in there.'

Fisher knew today's files wouldn't be in there but didn't bother explaining her train of thought. She wanted to see if the cameras had picked up anything unusual the previous day or night. The first folder had shown the seven folders Dorothy had mentioned that should have been in today's folder, covering the two cameras outside, one above the entrance door and another at the rear of the building. The other five clips covered the five cameras inside. After nearly thirty minutes of scanning them, they didn't spot anything unusual, apart from mid-morning when a man walked in, shortly followed by a man wearing dark blue overalls, looking around the age of sixty, carrying a toolbox, a pack of drain rods, and a rucksack that appeared too heavy for him.

'Who's that?'

Dorothy leaned in, getting a better look, signs that her eyesight was fading with age. 'Oh, that's Luke. We were closed yesterday, but there was an issue with one of the toilets. Blocked. Something to do with the pipes being old. He called a plumber.'

Fisher nodded, surmising the man carrying the tools was the plumber. They continued to watch. The camera positioned above the entrance door of the toilet, between the hours of ten to half past twelve, didn't show the plumber leaving the toilet. Luke milled around, passing the desk and going into the staff room now and again, occasionally checking on the plumber. Once, he made a cup of tea from the staff room and carried it over for him. They continued to watch until the plumber and Luke had gone. The last three hours of the clips featured the inside of the library sitting in total darkness.

'So, that takes us up to midnight?' checked Fisher.

'That's right.' Dorothy shrugged. 'I don't understand where the rest've gone. I'm sorry.'

The detectives stared at the blank folder for a few moments, thinking hard, sinking deeper into a hole they were struggling to get out of.

'Does the plumber look familiar to you?'

Dorothy nodded. 'Tim Wadkins. Nice bloke. Luke arranged it, although he's quite handy himself, so I'm surprised he never gave it a go.'

'So, other than Luke and this plumber, no one else entered the library yesterday?'

'Judging by the cameras, no. There are no blind spots either.'

'Would you mind phoning Luke and getting a name and number for the plumber, please?'

'No problem.' Dorothy picked up the phone from the receiver and pulled a notepad from one of the drawers built into the desk, containing a list of useful numbers. Once dialled, she pressed CALL and put it to her ear.

'Yes, Luke, it's Dorothy . . .' They spoke for a few minutes while both Fisher and Phillips stared intently. 'Okay, thank you.'

'What did he say?'

She put the phone back into the slot, which caused a beep. 'He said he came here around ten, then left around half twelve, which we can see by the cameras.'

'Okay. Do you know Tim Wadkins?'

'Yeah, he's a local guy. We've used him before. Has a few lads working for him. His number is in the back on a business card he once gave us. Hang on, I'll get it for you.'

Once Fisher noted the plumber's number, she decided she needed some air. They'd been inside the library for almost two hours, the air thick and stagnant. The combined smell of burnt flesh and old books started to turn her stomach. 'I need some air, Matthew,' she said before disappearing outside.

She moved a few paces from the entrance door, over to the wall to the left, feeling exhausted. A headache was forming. She took a breath and looked out at the crowd. She phoned Tim Wadkins and spoke with him. He confirmed what Luke had said and told Fisher he'd left an invoice for the completed work. She thanked him and hung up, placing her phone into her pocket. Within a minute, Phillips came to her side.

'You alright, April? You don't look too good.'

She turned to him and smiled. 'I just needed some air, that's all.'

He returned the grin. 'Okay.'

She noticed the crowd had thinned a little, but still, a healthy number of people were watching from the cordon. These people were relentless.

'Matthew?'

Phillips turned her way. 'Yeah?'

'Another murder in a library, and we don't have anything to go on. What are we going to do?'

'I'll be honest, I have no idea.' He focused back on the people watching. 'We need to do something, though.'

166

To their left, they heard a familiar car engine. It was DI James.

'This is all we need right now.'

* * *

He'd waited for a while before she appeared at the door of the library, looking tired, miserable, and fed up. 'Aww, you don't look very good, Detective,' he whispered, his voice fading into the cold wind. A woman nearby wearing a bobble hat frowned his way, unsure if he was talking to her or not, but he concentrated on DS Fisher, who'd wearily moved away from the entrance door over to the wall to lean on for support. A moment later, he saw DS Phillips come out of the library and take a few steps towards her. They spoke about something.

'You think this is rough. It's only going to get worse.'

The woman next to him frowned his way. 'I'm sorry, are you talking to me?'

The man pulled his attention away from Fisher and Phillips and smiled at her. 'A jolly good day, isn't it?' Then he disappeared into the crowd.

CHAPTER 35

At 3.30 p.m., DI James called for an emergency meeting. Everyone was there, including Peter Sterling and Pamela Boone, who were seated over near the window, quietly discussing something on her iPad between them. Boone had just arrived at the lab when Fisher turned up, telling her that DI James wanted her; although she was busy, she had reluctantly agreed. Often it was easier to play along and get these things over with. After all, she knew it wouldn't last long. James wanted her there because she'd help things move forward.

'Thank you all for coming on short notice. I know at the end of the day we all have shit to be doing, so I appreciate the time you're taking by just being here.' The DI's forehead was covered in a sticky film and sweat saturated the back of his shirt. Not looking too good, he quickly loosened his top button and stretched out his collar for a bit of air. 'I'll start with the bad news.'

He took a deep, long breath and exhaled. Everyone watched him, anticipating what he was going to say next.

'I've spent most of the day with DCI Andrew Baker. He's been reviewing how we fare up against other local departments.' His shoulders noticeably dipped. 'I need to be honest; it isn't good. It's far from fucking good.'

Seldom did DI James lose his professionalism and resort to swearing.

'In what way, sir?' asked Fisher.

'He's been comparing our stats with other departments, and it's taking us too long to get results. He actually wanted to run this meeting himself, but I told him I'd do it. I told him I'll get the results he needs.' He shook his head. 'I'm sorry if it feels like I'm taking it out on you guys. Believe me, I'm not — really, I'm not.' He moved from the front of the room and strolled to the window, then looked out on the road that ran parallel with the building, seeing the bumper-to-bumper traffic, headlights shining impatiently against the rear of the next car. On the horizon, the sun faded quickly. Manchester was falling into darkness.

'For those who are not up to date with what's been happening, I'd like to invite DS Fisher or DS Phillips up here to give us all a quick recap.' He held up a hand to explain further. 'They have been at both crime scenes and know what's going on as well as anyone. Either one of you is fine.'

Fisher looked to the right towards Phillips, who didn't seem keen. She knew him well enough to know he wasn't the most gifted public speaker.

'I'll do it.' She stood up, went to the front of the room, and turned to face everyone. She knew the room was full, but looking out, literally everyone was there: PC Jackson, PC Baan, DC Peterson, PC Amy Legg, PC Joel Cairn, Inspector Eric Thorne, and Sterling and Boone.

'Okay . . .' She took a deep breath and briefly ran her palms through her hair, as if collecting her thoughts. DI James took a seat next to DS Phillips and smiled at her.

Talk about leaving me on my own, she thought. *Unless you're testing me? Focus, April.*

'Earlier today, we found a human head, a burnt arm, and a part of what we think is a thigh at Newton Heath Library.' She looked over at Boone near the window. 'Are we any clearer on that yet, Pam?'

'Yes,' Boone said, nodding. 'I can confirm it's a thigh.'

PC Jackson raised a hand. 'Did Liam from the library spot a van parked outside of Chorlton?'

'Yes, but we couldn't get a full visual on the plate.'

'Brilliant,' DI James said, not hiding his sarcasm.

'What about outside Newton Heath Library? On the road. The council cameras?' asked PC Baan.

'Do we have an ID on the second vic?' asked DC Peterson, frowning at her.

'We're confident it's Mary Steadman, but we're checking DNA with items we collected from her home.' She gazed over to Boone, who agreed with a nod.

'We'll know soon, April,' added Boone.

'If the victim is confirmed to be Mary Steadman, then we know both victims are forty-one. I think that's too much of a coincidence to be overlooked.'

'Was there another photo?' DI James asked.

'There was. It was the same photo that Boone pulled from inside the head of Debbie Johnson. The same photograph of the schoolboy.'

'Who is he — do we know yet?' PC Legg asked.

'Not yet, Amy.'

Silence filled the room, waiting for Fisher to go on. She thought hard about what to say next.

'We need to find out if Mary Steadman and Debbie Johnson knew each other, and if so, how? Were they in the same social circle? Are other people in that circle at risk? Did they work together?' She focused on PC Baan and PC Jackson. 'Can you two do some digging on that, please?'

Baan nodded. 'Sure.'

Fisher then said to Inspector Thorne, 'Sorry, sir, I should have asked.'

He threw up his hands in surrender. 'Not at all, anything to help you guys move this forward. We have plenty of PCs, so Ashleigh can do some digging this afternoon. I might need Adam, though. I have to go to an estate to speak to someone, and if I'm being honest, I could do with the backup.'

PC Jackson smiled at him, feeling wanted for a change.

'I'll speak to Liam about the local CCTV around Newton and see what we can find.'

DI James stood. 'Thank you, April. Okay, people, get to work. Let's not give DCI Baker any reason to sack us all.'

CHAPTER 36

Callum opened his eyes almost twenty-four hours after he found the stranger standing in his kitchen, staring at him. His head felt thick and foggy with a dull, thumping pain. He remembered the figure before he switched the light on, then nothing. Why couldn't he remember?

Immediately he felt cold and used his hands to pat down his body; first his stomach, then lower towards his penis and thighs. He found it odd that he had no clothes on — where the hell had they gone?

His body felt numb, pressed against the freezing concrete floor. In addition to the numbness, his right hamstring felt tight as if he'd pulled it again, mentally and physically taking him back to an early agonising rugby accident when he was in his teens.

'What the fuck?' he whispered.

Above him, as his eyes adjusted, he saw a high ceiling, realising wherever he was, it was huge. He moved his hands, feeling the whole of his body aching as he did so, placing them on the ground to aid himself into an awkward sitting position.

'Hello?' he said, his voice echoing and bouncing back to him. 'Where am I?' This time anger and frustration crept into his voice.

Who'd done this to him? Removed his clothes, put him here. At this moment, the man in the kitchen was the only logical answer. He sniffed, smelling a faint scent of burning coming from somewhere, but it wasn't like a wood-burning smell you'd associate with fire; it was different. The kind of smell that made you unsure of yourself, knowing something wasn't quite right. Something was burning that shouldn't be.

He clamped his eyes shut and physically shook when the lights flashed on. He threw a hand up to protect his eyes, and as he lowered it, he became aware of the space he was in. A studded room, roughly twenty feet by twenty, with walls so high they seemed to go on endlessly. On one wall was a closed door, but the other walls were solid, covered in plasterboard. Behind him in the corner, he spotted a camera.

Immediately, Callum jumped to his feet, shivering as he did so, wrapping himself with his own arms to fight the freezing air around him. 'Where the hell am I?'

Silence lingered in the air for what seemed like for ever until there were multiple sounds above. Footsteps. Clattering off something metal, echoing in the ample space. Bang, bang, bang. Now the lights were on, it was clear to see he was in some kind of factory or warehouse.

When he noticed the first figure stepping into view on the walkway above, he glared in amazement. 'What the . . . ?'

A further three figures made their way out, stopped, and turned to face him, joining the first one. They all wore masks to hide their faces and didn't say a word. He was terrified.

Feeling conscious of his naked body and downright pissed off, he screamed, 'Who are you freaks? What the hell is going on here?'

Needing to escape, he frantically glared at each wall, weighing up the odds of climbing them. Maybe if he had a good run-up, he could reach up and grab the top of the wall, then pull himself over and get the hell out of there. With nothing to lose, he turned and ran at the wall behind him. The sole of his right foot slapped the plaster as he tried to get enough friction to propel himself high enough to grab the top, but he fell several feet short.

'Ahhh!' he cried, falling to the floor and cracking his right knee.

He tried again, this time with a longer run-up but failed miserably, missing the top of the wall by almost two feet.

He growled in anger and stared at the masks. 'What the hell do you want from me? Where are my wife and kids?'

There was a crackle to his right from the speaker he'd spotted moments earlier.

'Don't worry yourself, Callum McCauley. Your wife and children are safe. I can assure you of that.'

'Who are you?'

'That, at this moment, does not matter,' the voice replied evenly. 'What does matter is who *you* are.'

'What does that mean?' Callum frowned, still scanning the space, trying to muster a way out.

'Do you remember the boy in that photograph near the door?'

He scowled, noticing something he'd somehow missed on the floor. It was a photo. He went over, bent down, and picked it up.

'Where . . . where did you get this?'

'Again, that does not matter — do you know that child in the photo?'

Callum nodded, recognising the boy in the school uniform.

'As you may have seen, there is a pair of scissors near you on the floor.'

Callum moved the photo to the side, seeing the nail scissors down by his bare feet. He bent down and picked them up.

'Now, you'll be putting it down to your rugby accident from when you were eighteen, but the feeling in the back of your thigh isn't your hamstring.'

He turned, moving his leg back to gain a better view of the stitched wound. 'I don't understand.'

174

'This is only the first round. It's simple. You need to use the scissors to cut the stitches and get the key I've hidden inside your leg. Then you can access the next room.'

'Wait, what? Are . . . are you serious? This isn't a game!'

'I haven't been more serious in my life, Callum McCauley. And yes, that's exactly what it is. A game. My good friends up on the walkway will watch you to make sure you're getting on okay.'

Callum gazed up at them, feeling the heat of their stares. One of the figures started to laugh. A deep, baritone laugh which made him feel so insecure and small.

'Which of you took me?'

Ignoring his question, the voice said, 'Get to work. We're watching . . .'

'There's no way I'm doing it.'

More laughter from the masked figures watching them.

'Mr McCauley, if you turn around, you'll see a timer on the wall.' He turned around, examining the ten-minute timer appear in red neon digits. 'That is how long you have until that door locks for ever. Once it reaches zero, you're stuck. And how long do you think you'll last down there?'

Callum didn't answer.

'I'm afraid you're out of options. The time starts now.'

Pondering what he'd been told, the realisation of what the task entailed horrified him. Tears welled in his eyes, but he decided to stay strong and determined. Could he really cut something out of his leg? The thought sickened him to the core. *Get to the next room. Get the hell out of here and find the man responsible. The one who had taken him.*

He hesitated, holding the scissors in his shaking hand.

'Time is running out, Mr McCauley,' the voice on the speaker told him.

The neon digits informed him he had just over nine minutes.

He started cutting the stitches. As they broke away, the wound split open, and small bursts of blood seeped down his calf and onto the floor. Wincing in agony, he cut the last stitch, then dropped the scissors. He was in so much pain but hid it from his face. That amazed the figures watching over him as he pushed a finger inside the cut.

'Jesus Christ . . .' he muffled through gritted teeth, fighting not to look at it. He hadn't ever felt pain like it, and it wasn't just the pain making him feel nauseous but the act of doing something no one should ever do unless they were a doctor. Whatever he could feel with his fingertip was warm and wet, but there was no key or metal.

'Shit! Come on . . .'

'Time is ticking, Mr McCauley,' said the voice on the speaker. 'You're losing blood quickly.'

A couple of the figures watching from above started laughing.

He glared at them with so much hatred and disgust and, most of all, fear; what else would happen to him if this was only room one?

There, he thought, feeling something hard. Frowning, he stared down at his leg, seeing his index finger almost knuckle deep into the wound.

Then it dawned on him. Whoever had put the key in there had purposefully put it too far out of reach, knowing there would be only one way to get to it: cut more skin.

'Fuck,' he whispered, trying to compress his frustration, not wanting them to know how much they were winning. Not that being trapped in a room, his penis shrivelled to almost nothing, a massive gouge in his leg with a pool of his own blood below his feet, was anything close to winning.

He paused a beat, clamping his eyes shut. *Come on, Callum*, he told himself. *You can do this*. With a deep breath, he positioned the scissors at the bottom of the cut, his grip on them loose and not very convincing. After another breath, he pressed the scissor handles together, the razor-sharp blades slicing through the flesh, and tried to suppress the scream coming from his mouth with his left hand.

'Jesus!' he screamed, dropping the scissors after cutting another inch of skin, causing more blood to escape his leg, adding to the crimson mess on the floor. He pushed his fingers inside, screaming as he did so, and managed to nip the top of the key with his index and middle finger.

'Oh, God.'

He whimpered and physically shook, on the verge of passing out. His body was red hot one second, then freezing cold the next. He couldn't control his heart or his trembling body.

'Think he'll pass out?' one of the masked figures said up on the walkway. 'He's shaking.'

'Oh, I hope he doesn't. The next room will be fun for him,' the closest replied. They both smiled behind the mask towards each other, then continued to watch Callum get the key.

Finally, he pulled the key high enough to actually see it and then kept it as still as possible, using his thumb and index finger to get a better grip and release it from his body. He exhaled in relief, dropping to his knees, his leg in agony. He stared at the bloody key in his hand.

'Well done, Callum,' the condescending voice said on the speaker, then, as if he was hosting a game show, added, 'You may proceed to the next room.'

Shaking, Callum struggled to his feet and limped to the door, blood seeping down his leg. He inserted the key after missing it a few times, turned the lock, pulled it open, and saw what was inside.

'Oh, God . . .' he whispered.

CHAPTER 37

When Fisher arrived home, it was dark and miserable, the streets' drains overloaded with thick, deep streams from the sudden downpour. The forecast had mentioned it might rain, but on her way home, looking up at the intense black clouds, even in the darkness she could see the downpour was inevitable.

She pulled up, managing to get a space directly in front of her house, and turned off the engine, listening to the water cascade off the windscreen and roof of her car, sounding like marbles being dropped on a sheet of metal.

With the daunting thought of getting from the car to the house in the rain, she leaned over, grabbed the fabric handle of her laptop bag from the passenger seat, and opened the door quickly, then jumped down, wincing at the pounding rain as she darted for her front door. Once inside, she removed her coat, hung it over the radiator, and kicked off her shoes. The lamp in the hallway, which she'd programmed for half past four, the time it got dark, was already on. Down the hall, she noticed a light in the kitchen. 'Huh?' Had she forgotten to turn it off before she left that morning?

'What a day,' she muttered, entering the kitchen, flicking on the kettle, and grabbing an empty mug from the cupboard above the worktop.

'Hey, April,' the voice said behind her.

She dropped the mug onto the worktop and was lucky it didn't smash. She swivelled around to find her sister Freya sitting at the circular table, smiling at her. Fisher placed a hand on her own chest.

'Jesus, Freya, for God's sake.' She panted heavily and doubled over but eventually managed a smile. 'What on earth are you doing here?'

'Sorry,' her sister said, holding her hands up, then she laughed. They used to try and scare each other when they were younger, often waiting upstairs and jumping out when the other was least expecting it, but Fisher soon became wise to it. So this small victory for Freya was something she'd waited decades for. 'Did *I* just scare *you*?'

Fisher pressed her lips together. 'That wasn't fair, though.'

'Yes.' Freya made a fist and shook it several times in celebration.

'Seriously, though, what are you doing here? You could have let me know you were coming.'

'I was passing by, thought I'd come and say hi.'

'But I wasn't in.' Fisher frowned.

'I know, but I knew you wouldn't be long, so I thought I'd wait.'

Absorbing her sister's words, she turned and poured boiling water into a mug and stirred her coffee, knowing her sister's visit wasn't random. 'I see you've helped yourself to a drink. Want another?'

Fisher went over, grabbed her empty mug, and filled it again. 'There you go.' She placed it down in front of her. On her way home, she had planned to get a quick shower, then open her laptop to do some digging on Debbie Johnson and Mary Steadman. It would have to wait. Fisher knew from previous relationships, when Freya was upset, she'd turn up at hers unannounced, needing a shoulder to cry on.

'So, what's up, Freya?' Fisher took a sip, lowered it back down. 'I know there's a reason you're here.'

Freya gave a thin smile. 'You know me too well . . .'

'Better than you know yourself. What's up?'

She scratched her forehead and looked down at the table in thought. 'Just men.'

Fisher smiled, taking another sip of hot coffee. Seeing her sister's face right now was a reminder that being alone was easier than being in a relationship; it was another way to fail, another reason to be upset if things never went right. Life was simpler.

'I looked at his phone and saw texts from someone else.'

Fisher leaned over, took her soft hand in hers.

'I understand why you don't want a man — life's easier, isn't it?'

'Did you confront him?'

Freya nodded. 'Yeah, then we argued. He told me I shouldn't have been looking at his phone in the first place, and it isn't what it seemed.'

'I was going to ask . . . why were you looking through his phone?'

Freya leaned back, breaking Fisher's hold, feeling embarrassed. 'I-I don't know, I . . .' Fisher waited, watching her closely. 'I guess I had a feeling that something was off.'

'What did the messages say?'

'That she couldn't wait to see him and so on. There was a photo of her with her tits out.'

Fisher smiled sadly. 'They're all bastards, Freya, one way or another. Better off without them.'

'Yeah, you're right. His loss, then.'

'That's my girl.'

Fisher hugged her little sister until she was able to smile again.

'Have you eaten?'

Freya shook her head. 'Not yet, no.'

'Fancy a pizza?' asked Fisher, knowing she was meant to be eating more healthily, but one more day wouldn't do any harm. Freya smiled, so Fisher opened the takeout app on her phone.

Then they moved to the living room and put the television on, although Fisher was mainly listening to Freya talk about how upset by men she was. The lamp was on in the corner, creating a relaxing atmosphere. Fisher had poured them both a glass of red while they waited for the food and she could feel her cheeks warming despite only having half a glass. She knew that when she was tired and stressed, it didn't usually take long for the alcohol to affect her.

By 10 p.m., they'd eaten and cleared away, and even though Freya gave her the impression she was settled for the night, Fisher apologised and said she needed time to work on something before sleep.

'It always comes first, doesn't it?' Freya said, putting her shoes on at the door, lightly shaking her head.

Fisher shrugged and hugged her. 'We'll sort something with Mam and Dad soon?'

After seeing her out, Fisher had a quick shower and with in ten minutes was downstairs in her dressing gown, sitting on the sofa with the laptop on her knee.

First, she opened her emails to catch any she'd missed during the day, remembering she'd seen the notifications on her phone but hadn't much time to read them earlier. There was one from DCI Baker to the whole team regarding a monthly statistic; some of the information on it related to what DI James was relaying to them all earlier. She sighed. Management was coming down on them hard. She knew they needed to find out who was responsible for the library murders.

She opened her internet browser and paused when her phone beeped with a text message. She picked it up, seeing it was from Boone, the senior forensic.

April, the DNA from today coincides with the items from Mrs Steadman's house, so I can confirm it was Mary Steadman we found.

Thanks, Pam, she replied, and hit send, placing her phone back on the coffee table. She had massive respect for Pamela

Boone, had known her for as long as she'd been on the force. Boone wasn't interested in impressing people, probably less so now that Peter Sterling was her boss, but she loved helping people and worked relentlessly. Some might have received such info and waited till the morning to pass it on, but Pam never did; as soon as she knew, she would tell the relevant people to help the case move along.

Fisher picked up her personal notes on Debbie Johnson, including her previous addresses and previous jobs. On a separate sheet of paper, she had similar information on Mary Steadman. The only real similarity was that both women were the same age. Looking at their social media accounts, she then figured out that both of them were born in Manchester. Taking that with a pinch of salt, which she often did with most things on social media, she knew she'd have to locate their birth certificates to really know for sure. But assuming that they were both born in Manchester and were the same age, was there a chance they had gone to the same school or college? Manchester was a big place, but maybe their paths had crossed somewhere else.

She sat thinking for a moment. Her focus slipped from the laptop screen down to her notes and the photograph of the schoolboy found in both of the victims' heads.

'Why is he so important to you two?' she asked.

The house remained silent while she thought about it. Frowning, she leaned over, noticing something she hadn't seen before: the boy in the photo wore a dark blue blazer, and she could see the top half of a badge at the bottom of the photo.

'Where's that from?'

She brought the image closer to make out the details. It looked like the top of a green triangle with a thin blue loop next to it. Without seeing the full badge, it was difficult to identify. Sighing, she typed in *schools in Manchester* in the search engine, pressed enter. She then scrolled through the list of primary schools, and, one by one, located their individual crests. Nothing was similar to the one on the boy's blazer. She then searched for secondary schools and did the same, scrolling through the list, surprised by how many schools there were in Manchester and the surrounding area.

Then she found something similar but not exact. Chorlton High School. She clicked on their website, and it showed an enlarged version of the logo at the top of the page. Perhaps the logo had been altered from when the photo was taken, but she was confident Chorlton High School was the one she was looking for.

CHAPTER 38

Callum limped further into the second room. The pain in his leg was close to excruciating and he didn't know how much longer he could stand.

The figures had shuffled down the metal walkway and watched him from above. Doing his best to ignore them and the pain in his leg, he focused on the A3-sized photo pinned to an easel of the boy in the school uniform. The moment he saw the boy's face, memories from his school years flooded back. Beside the photo was a black box around two feet tall by two feet wide, the same in depth. The box rested on a wooden stand, so the top of the box was around the height of Callum's chest.

He stopped at the box and stared at the photo next to it. The boy's innocent blue eyes glared back at him with no judgement, but Callum felt judged by his actions; he felt terrible, disgusted with himself.

He placed his hand on the top of the box for support, seeing something on top of it.

'Put your hand inside. Push the rubber seal down,' one of the voices said. A male voice, rough and direct.

He angled his gaze up to the walkway. 'What's inside?'

'The key for the next room . . .' the same one replied.

'What else?' Callum knew it wasn't going to be that simple. The figure just shrugged, offering no more.

With a deep breath and desperate to get out, he edged closer to the box, his bare stomach pressed against the hard wood, and cautiously placed his bloody, trembling hand inside, piercing through the small, sealed hole. He knew from the lock on the door the kind of key he was looking for; the usual yale lock. First, he didn't feel anything, not knowing what he might find. If this room was anything like the last, he expected the worst. Frowning, he lowered his hand further, wondering how deep the box went.

'Ahh,' he muttered, feeling something moving. Tiny little things. Hundreds of them. 'What the fuck?'

He yanked his hand out of the box and noticed dozens of ants crawling over his skin. Shaking profusely, he swatted them away with his other hand, but before clearing them, he felt a pinch, then another — sharp little nips. The ants were biting him.

The figures were laughing from the walkway now, physically rocking back and forth, chuckling to themselves.

'Bite him,' one of them said, then proceeded with a chant: 'Bite him, bite him, bite him.'

'The key is in there somewhere, Callum. Try again,' encouraged the voice from the speaker.

Smacking his hand until all the ants were off, he built up the courage to do it again. Getting the key was the only way out. Judging by how much blood he was losing, it wouldn't be long before actually getting out alive was an option he wouldn't have.

'Come on, Callum, for God's sake. The key. Get the key . . .'

He pushed his hand in quickly and frantically felt around the base of the box, feeling the thousands of tiny ants crawling all over him. It was seconds before he felt the first bite, then another, and eventually just a constant stinging sensation.

'There!' he shouted. 'Got you!'

He plucked the key out, but his hand got caught on the hole's edge, and he dropped it.

'Fuck!' he bellowed, slapping the side of the box with his other palm. Then he had a brainwave. He picked up the box with both hands to feel the weight of it. By this time, the ants were all over his body. His legs, arms, and stomach were all covered. Relentless nipping at his skin. He turned the box upside down and let thousands of ants fall out the hole along with the key, which made a dull, pinging sound. Luckily for him, the metal caught the reflection of the lights fixed to the stud walls of the enclosure to help him locate it.

'Clever little bastard,' one of the masks commented.

He rustled through the sea of moving insects, running his hands across the concrete floor until he managed to pick it up, then dashed over to the nearest wall, swatting at his skin, removing himself from the biting ants.

'Get the fuck off me!' he begged, his arms swaying hysterically.

About a minute later, free of them, he stared at the ants on the hard floor with hatred. There were so many of them he didn't dare move, the base of the room was practically black with the God-awful insects looking for food or something to bite again. Where the ants had bitten him, he realised the bites were burning and stinging, becoming intensely itchy, so much so he started scraping at his own skin to relieve it, but it only worsened. Moments later, he began to feel dizzy and couldn't control his breathing, his heart pumping quicker than it ever had.

'Quick, get to the next room!' one of the masked figures encouraged.

He nodded, desperate to get out of that room, and dashed to the door, not caring about standing on the ants on the ground, and inserted the key, opening the door. He slammed it shut to stop them from following him, but dozens crept under the door.

'Piss off!' he screamed at them.

The figures once again moved down, readying themselves for the next room.

In the centre of the space, there was a bottle with a press handle, similar to a lotion found in a chemist.

'Callum,' the voice on the speaker said. 'Use the lotion to soothe the ant bites. It'll make the burning pain go away.'

Without a second thought, he quickly pushed down on the handle, catching a handful of white lotion, and began smearing it onto his body, starting with his arms. It smelled weird and very sweet, almost sickly, like honey mixed with something else. He then got some more, covering his legs, careful not to rub any into his wound. The lotion did seem to help momentarily as he applied more to his stomach, neck, and face, and he continued to do so until his whole body was covered in white cream. He looked utterly ridiculous.

'Ow, you fuc—'

He looked down, amazed to see hundreds of ants by his feet. He jumped back and noticed an army of ants coming through the door from the last room, all moving directly for him.

'I'm sorry, Callum,' the voice said slowly. 'The lotion won't help at all. The only thing it will do is attract the ants. Enjoy your last few minutes on this earth.'

In a panic, he kicked at the ants, but they kept at him, more and more coming under the door. He turned, saw the entrance to the next room, and dashed towards it, charging at it with his shoulder. It shuddered but didn't budge. He tried over and over until he was so exhausted he could barely hold his own weight, but the door wouldn't give way. Whoever had designed the rooms had done so with this in mind.

After wearing himself out and panting heavily, he fell to the floor, no longer able to stand. He could feel the mountain of ants covering his body but couldn't do a thing about it, instead, he tiredly closed his eyes and passed out from the pain.

CHAPTER 39

Chorlton High School
Twenty-seven years ago

Mrs Andrews was doing her best, but the rowdy class wasn't listening. She was losing her patience with them, although she understood they were excited about the upcoming camping trip. It happened only once in their five years at Chorlton, the opportunity to go away with the school for a few days.

'Please,' the teacher begged, 'can everyone just take a seat and listen?'

The talking continued, so she waited for the rest of the class to quieten down. She smiled sadly at the patient ones, the ones on course to get good grades, the ones whose futures looked, if she was being honest, brighter than the others.

'Right!' she screamed, slamming a hand down on her desk. The noise echoed out into the hallway. The talkative ones suddenly became silent, watching her with wide eyes from the back of the room, awed by her sudden outburst. In her eight months of teaching them, it was the first time they'd seen any flash of anger or emotion from the normally very quiet and reserved Mrs Andrews. 'Sit down and be quiet, now!'

The faces of the disruptive pupils warmed in embarrassment, and they returned to their seats, saying nothing further.

'Good.' She left her desk and wandered around the class, tapping a ruler on her palm. She was in her early twenties, with long dark hair tied back into a ponytail. She wore thick glasses but was slim, nervous yet attractive to the other male teachers around the school because of her shy, innocent personality. 'It's important as students that you listen to your teacher. Our job here isn't an easy one, and I must say, normally, this class is a treat, but enough is enough. Okay?'

She specifically stared at Debbie and Patricia, who were sitting at the back. 'Okay, you two?'

'Yes, Miss,' replied Debbie, breaking her eye contact, looking down at her table. Patricia shyly nodded.

'Thank you.' She returned to the front and spoke about the upcoming camping trip to Middleton Campsite, informing them of what they would be getting up to and what activities they would be undertaking.

One of the students — a thin girl with ginger hair — raised a hand. Mrs Andrews nodded at her. 'Miss, I hate making fires.'

'I hate many things, but sometimes you need to just get on with it.' Mrs Andrews smiled, then added, 'Why not think of it as learning something new? Just imagine you're out with your family, trapped somewhere, but knowing how to make a fire and keep yourself warm. It sounds simple, but one day, it could save your life.'

A few of the more mature students nodded in agreement as if thinking the same.

She continued to tell them about some water activities, which piqued further interest and brought the more challenging students on board with the idea.

'Miss,' a voice said from the back.

Mrs Andrews looked up and noticed Debbie Johnson with her hand up. 'Yes, Debbie?'

'Where's Mason today?' she asked, pointing at the empty chair beside hers.

'Mason is busy this morning with someone. He'll be back soon.'

'Is he coming to the camping trip?' another student asked.

'He certainly is.'

There were a few boos around the room.

Mrs Andrews frowned, pointing down at her desk, leaning forward. 'Excuse me. Now, that isn't kind, is it? We all know Mason has challenges, and we need to support him, not make fun and mock him. We, as a class, are a team, and when you're in a team, you help your teammates. You encourage them and improve their lives here, not tease and make fun of them. I've noticed some of your attitudes towards Mason, and I'm saying this now and never repeating myself. If I see any of you with a negative attitude or saying anything nasty to him, I'll stop you from doing your test papers, and you will leave school without any qualifications. You'll also spend the rest of your time at school sitting outside on a single desk by the headmaster's office.' She paused, allowing her bold statement to sink in. 'Do I make myself crystal clear?'

A wave of silence swept the room, followed by a sea of quick nods. No one dared to speak.

There was a knock at the door.

'Come in,' replied the teacher.

The door opened, and in came Mason with a support worker. 'He's all yours.'

'Thank you, Sharon,' she replied, then snapped her neck towards the back after hearing laughter from some students. She focused back on Mason and watched him walk to the back of the room, feeling embarrassed he'd spent time with a support worker.

Mrs Andrews smiled sadly to herself, wishing he could fit in more.

At the back, Debbie watched him, smiling as he approached. She leaned over and pulled his chair out for him. 'There you go, Mason.'

'Erm, thanks.' He removed his bag, lowered it to the floor, and then sat on his chair. He immediately yelped in pain and bounced up, pressing his hands on his buttocks.

The students laughed and pointed.

'What on earth is going on back there?' Mrs Andrews stood up abruptly and made her way down the middle of the class. 'What's going on?'

With one hand on his face to cover his tears, the other was pressed over his buttocks. 'It hurts . . .'

Debbie and Patricia, the closest students to him, pushed their lips together and looked forward, not meeting her angry gaze or indicating what they'd done.

'What hurts, Mason?' She turned him around and moved his hand slowly, seeing a pin stuck to the rear of his thigh just below his buttock. It didn't take her long to realise that Debbie had placed it there on purpose so Mason would sit on it. She glared coldly at them. 'You two, stand up and go see Mr Close.'

'Miss, it wasn't us, we—'

She threw her arm towards the door and screamed, 'GET UP AND GO SEE THE HEADTEACHER NOW!'

The outburst shook the whole class, and without any reluctance, Debbie Johnson and Patricia Keeton immediately left the classroom with their heads bowed and tails between their legs.

CHAPTER 40

Present day

A knock at 8 a.m. the following day took Steve Adams by surprise.

'Was that the door?' his wife Lilly asked, standing a few feet from him, dressed in her pink gown and fluffy matching slippers, cooking bacon on the hob in the kitchen.

'At this time?' He frowned up at the green circular clock on the wall. 'Weird if it is. It's early. I'll go see.' He rose from his chair, leaving his half-full coffee and iPad which he was reading the daily news on. In the hallway, through the glass at the front door, he could see the outline of a man dressed all in black, holding something in his hand. He unlocked the door, and the sudden December cold gushed in, attacking his bare legs where the dressing gown didn't cover.

'Parcel for you,' said the man, who leaned forward and handed him a box roughly a foot wide, a foot long, and six inches deep.

He scowled. 'I haven't ordered anything?'

The man in black tilted the box to see the label on top of it. 'Are you Steve Adams?'

Adams nodded. 'I am, but . . .' He took it. 'The wife's probably ordered it. Thanks.'

The delivery man wasn't interested in what his wife had ordered or hadn't. His only job was to deliver it; he didn't have time for meaningless conversations, not when there were over a hundred parcels to get through by mid-afternoon.

Steve closed the door, wondering what it was, making his way back to the kitchen. It felt so light he was unsure if it contained anything.

'Who was it?' his wife asked as he entered the kitchen.

The bacon sizzled in the pan, tiny drops of fat landing on the top of the hob. The kitchen was warm from the heating they'd put on an hour ago. Adams suddenly felt hot after the brief encounter with the cold outside.

'A delivery man — you ordered anything?'

She frowned and dropped her shoulder in thought. 'Not that I can remember.'

He took the box to the table but remained standing, using a sharp nail to pierce the seal. He lifted the flaps, peered inside, then immediately closed them, feeling his cheeks warm. He stared at the box, his heart rate instantly rising, pumping blood around his body.

'What is it, honey?' she asked, lifting pieces of bacon with a pair of tongs and carefully putting them on slices of bread. 'You want sauce?' No reply. 'Honey?' She turned towards him, but he was gone. 'Steve?'

He left the kitchen quickly and went upstairs to the bathroom, shaking as he did so. Once inside, he locked the bathroom door to ensure no one could get in.

He placed the box on the floor, took a step back, and brought his hands to his mouth, just staring at the box.

'Shit . . .'

'Steve, you alright?' Lilly shouted up.

'Yeah. Just on the toilet.'

He sat on the closed toilet seat and stared at the box, thinking hard about what to do, then patted his leg for his phone, which he pulled out and found the only number he could think of ringing.

'Come on, pick up, for God's sake!'

'Hurry up, Steve,' Lilly shouted. 'Your breakfast is going cold.'

Ignoring his wife, he focused on the ringing phone, but it went to voicemail. He tried again.

* * *

Across town, in an abandoned factory, packed inside a black bin bag in the corner of a small room and other belongings, a phone started to ring. After the man sitting at the desk heard the sound, he stood up, went over, and grabbed it.

He noticed the caller: *Steve Adams.*

The man smiled widely. 'Don't worry, Steve. I'll be seeing you soon.'

CHAPTER 41

Despite Fisher being low on fuel, they decided to go in her Volvo instead of Phillips's car. To put it bluntly, Fisher didn't like being a passenger, but Phillips wondered if his driving made her feel uneasy. Either way, he suggested a stop-off nearby to fill up before they headed over, so several minutes later, they pulled into Morrisons less than half a mile from the station. Phillips went in to get two caramel lattes from the self-service coffee machine near the door while Fisher filled up and paid at the pump.

Fisher climbed in and waited for Phillips, who walked over with the two coffees. She leaned over to edge the door open for him, and he climbed inside, the smell of the sweet coffee escaping from the tiny sip holes.

'Caramel?'

He nodded, handing one of them over. 'Your favourite.'

'Thanks, Matthew.' She carefully lifted the lid off, blew across the top, had a long sip, then placed it back on, lowering it into the cup holder between the seats.

'He seems in a better mood this morning, don't you think?' said Phillips. Fisher had to admit, DI James had seemed more upbeat in the morning meeting. Quickly recapping yesterday's events, Fisher had told the team what she'd found out last night at home about Debbie Johnson and Mary Steadman attending Chorlton High School in their youth. DI James had nodded at the suggestion they visit the school and attempt to find out more information and the possible identity of the schoolboy in the photos tucked inside the heads of both victims.

'Good work,' DI James had said, winking at her before they left.

'Yeah, he seems better,' she agreed.

Phillips sipped his coffee, then lowered it to his lap, feeling the heat from the base of it. 'I think he likes you, you know.'

She screwed her face up. 'Who?'

'DI James.'

She burst into laughter. 'DI Thomas James! Get lost.'

He raised his brows and looked forward again. 'Well, I think he does. The way he looks at you. I've noticed it.'

Fisher smiled. 'Well, if that's true, which I don't think it is, I don't feel the same.'

'Really?' He turned her way. 'He's a good-looking man. Tanned skin, slicked-back hair.' He flamboyantly ran his palm through his hair to imitate their DI, and they both chuckled.

'He isn't for me.'

'Seriously though, you don't have anyone.' He smiled. 'I'm just saying, if you're looking for a guy, I think he'd be interested, that's all.'

She saw the long road ahead, then glanced at him. 'Has he put you up to this? Are you on commission or something?'

'He promised me a promotion if I persuaded you to go on a date with him.'

They laughed, and she playfully punched his leg. 'I'm okay on my own for now, Matty. Seriously. Men are nothing but trouble. No offense.'

He raised a hand. 'None taken.'

'How're Janice and Dominic doing?' she asked.

'Yeah, they're good. Jan has started a running club. Goes out every Tuesday and Thursday night. Been doing it for a few weeks now. I don't know, she's obsessed with her weight for some reason. I think she's looking for another man.'

Fisher scowled. 'Isn't she like a size eight?'

'Yeah.' He sighed. 'But if it makes her happy, then so be it. She has her running, and I have my football.'

'You don't actually think she's after another man, do you?'

He turned her way. 'I hope not.'

'It's good you're still doing the football.'

'Yeah, when I can, or should I rephrase that — when I'm allowed.'

'How's Dominic?'

'Just the usual delight . . .'

Due to the morning traffic, it took them just over thirty minutes to travel the eight miles to Chorlton High School. She slowed the Volvo and took a left, passing a sign on the fence with the words *Show You Care, Park Elsewhere* — the public must have used the car park while shopping or doing other things. Fisher followed the road until they reached the car park, pulling up behind a small black Renault Clio with pink stripes stuck to the rear bumper, and a sticker just above with the phrase *Go Faster* on it.

'You should get one of those,' commented Phillips, smiling. He drained the rest of his lukewarm coffee and put the empty container next to Fisher's, who'd finished hers a while ago. She'd always been able to drink her coffee faster than him, not that it was a race. They got out and looked around, noticing an old building known as Mauldeth House, which was now closed. It had most recently been used by the school but had been closed for a while. The company that owned it had it up for sale, but with it not being the most attractive building in the world, it remained unsold.

'Busy place, eh?' said Phillips, silently counting the cars. There must have been over sixty there, making him think everyone didn't fully acknowledge the banner they'd seen on their way in.

They made their way to the front of a modern-looking building with a sloping roof and rounded edges. It wasn't brand new but had clearly been redeveloped in the last couple of years. As the doors slid open, they went inside, feeling the warmth of the heating system. Towards the left was a low desk with a woman sitting behind it, the lower half of her face hidden by a computer screen. It was immediately clear to Fisher that Phillips felt uncomfortable in his long knee-length coat.

'Hello, can I help you?' the female said. She wore thin-framed glasses, had blonde hair in a short bob, and looked around the age of fifty.

'Hi, I'm Detective Sergeant April Fisher from Greater Manchester Police.' She kept her focus on the woman but pointed to Phillips, introducing him too. 'We were wondering if we could look at some old school photos that may assist us with an ongoing murder enquiry?'

The receptionist frowned, cocking her head back. 'A murder inquiry?'

'Yes, that's correct.'

'Erm . . . can I see some ID, please?'

'Of course.' Fisher plucked her badge from inside her suit jacket, opened it, and lowered it so the woman could get a better look. Phillips followed suit.

'Okay.' She paused, thinking for a second. 'I'll just ring someone. Hold on.'

The detectives nodded and moved away from the counter for a moment. Fisher wandered over to a noticeboard filled with drawings from all different age groups, ranging from eleven-year-olds to sixteen-year-olds. It was a nice, effective technique to fill the entrance with colour, displaying the talents of their pupils.

'The headmaster will be two minutes,' the woman behind the desk said.

Fisher smiled, strolling back to Phillips, who was busy looking down at his phone. 'Who's that?'

'Huh?'

'On your phone — what's got your face twisted?'

He snapped out of whatever trance he was in and apologised. 'Sorry, Janice is complaining how hard Dominic is being, saying she can't wait for him to go to nursery.'

Fisher smiled sympathetically, not understanding the struggles of a parent. In a way, that was all she had wished for when she was pregnant, embracing the days of motherhood and bringing a child up through the years, mentally visualising each step. But now, she realised that although she couldn't say the miscarriage was for the best, perhaps the time wasn't right.

They heard quick footsteps behind them, and they turned to see a tall man dressed in a black suit, a white shirt, and a blue tie approach them.

'Joseph Henry.'

Fisher shook his hand firmly. 'DS April Fisher.'

Although Phillips stood at six foot two, he had to look up at Mr Henry as he shook his hand. 'DS Matthew Phillips.'

'How can I help you?' He had dark, serious, focused eyes, and the look on his face indicated that he was a man with little time to spare. His shoulder was back, his chin up, making him appear even taller.

Fisher mentioned the recent murders and the victims found at the libraries over the past few days. Mr Henry said he was aware of them from the news reports. Fisher pulled a photo from her suit pocket to show him.

He studied the photo, but nothing on his face indicated he knew or recognised the boy.

'That's an old uniform. Before my time, definitely.'

'But the crest,' she said, pointing to the photo in his hand. 'That's Chorlton High School, right?'

'Yes, it does appear to be. Before it was modified anyway.' He smiled, then scowled towards Fisher. 'Sorry, I'm . . . I'm not sure what you want me to do?'

'If the boy doesn't look familiar to you, perhaps there's a long-serving teacher still working here, someone who might recognise him?'

'Is there a date on the back, any indication of when this was taken?'

Fisher shook her head, smiling thinly.

He sighed, thinking about his staff members. 'We do have a teacher that's reached her thirty-year mark. Lisa Andrews. If she doesn't recognise him, then no one will.'

'Is she working today?'

'She is.' He glanced down at his watch. 'She'll have just finished her lesson. Would you like to follow me?'

On the second floor, they walked down a corridor lined with posters of sporting activities. It seemed the school excelled in rugby and football, judging by the number of images dedicated to those particular sports. They took a right and continued, Fisher surprised at how big the school was. Mr Henry slowed, angled over to a door on his right.

'She's just in here,' he told them, then knocked twice. 'Mrs Andrews?'

'Yes, come in,' her timid voice replied.

He opened it and went inside, almost needing to duck under the top of the door frame. The tables were positioned in a large U-shape. There was an old wooden desk in the far corner that, based on the feel of the classroom, didn't belong there. Sitting on a chair behind it was a small-framed woman in her late fifties, wearing a black cardigan over black T-shirt and trousers. She had a kind, warm face, which lit up when she smiled.

'Hello, sir,' she said to the headteacher.

'Lisa, if you could spare a few minutes, I'd like you to help out these detectives for me.' He introduced them both, and they exchanged pleasantries.

DS Fisher explained the sensitivity of the recent cases, then handed over the photo of the boy.

Mrs Andrews studied it closely, then brought a hand to her mouth.

'You recognise him?'

She nodded several times. 'I remember him very well.'

CHAPTER 42

Just after he finished the pasta his wife prepared him, Gary Orden put the empty tub in the sink, rinsed it, then left the small canteen. He knew eating so early meant he'd be hungry later, but he was starving and couldn't help himself. He grabbed his thin jacket from the hook on the wall near the toilet and put it on, knowing he'd have to be back soon. His wife said he needed to wear something thicker for the walk to work, but he didn't feel the cold. He unlocked the back door, edged it open, and stepped out into the fresh air. Above, the sky had darkened. Huge, grey clouds hung over him, threatening to rain any minute. He pulled out a cigarette, lit it, and took a long drag, plumes of smoke swirling above his head before being whisked off by the gentle breeze.

Down by his feet, he noticed a box propped up against the wall.

'What's that?'

The top of the box was sealed with sellotape and had a label stuck to it saying, *Digital workshop material*. He frowned, bent down with the cigarette hanging from his mouth, and picked it up to test its weight. The digital workshop had started, and there was a good crowd inside. An opportunity for adults and teenagers to build their computer skills with

201

the library staff, who'd undergone plenty of training courses. The sessions were typically held on a Tuesday and included basic coding programs, IT skills, maths and English with various quizzes to see what they'd learned.

The material delivery had been earlier, but Karen — the other library assistant working today — must have forgotten it. The council distributed material to them weekly, usually supplying lanyards for the people attending, along with stationary, memory sticks, and complimentary tea and coffee, which was always a welcome comfort in the cold weather. There were also headphones, computer mice, keyboards, and so on, which helped when their current stock was damaged or broken or had mysteriously gone missing.

He finished his smoke, flicked it carelessly away from the door, and picked up the box before he went inside. The library had a low ceiling with dull lights in desperate need of upgrading. Unlike other libraries in Manchester, much of it had been left in the twentieth century, though the computers and digital workshop were more representative of the twenty-first.

Once through the door, he rounded the desk and went over to the computers, which were occupied by two men and three women. One woman looked over the age of sixty and seemed like she was struggling with something, judging by her searching gaze.

'You alright?' asked Gary, seeing the familiar confusion, and set the box down near his computer.

'I-I don't know how to get to this part.' The woman shrugged and pointed timidly at the screen. It was the fourth time Gary had aided her, which he didn't mind; it was his job.

'Let me see.' Gary used the mouse and navigated through a series of screens until she was where she needed to be. 'There you go.'

'Thank you, Gary.'

'Pleasure.'

'What's in here?' Karen stood next to the box, pointing at it with a scowl. The man at the closest computer looked up at them, probably hoping for another free lanyard or another pen.

'Found it outside when I went for a quick smoke,' he said. 'Assumed it had been missed.'

She tilted her head in thought. 'I'm sure I brought them all in.' She shook her head. 'Never mind.'

A chorus of laughter came from the children's group to their left, who were reading books and singing nursery rhymes in the play corner. Karen smiled at them, admiring the mothers and fathers who brought their children here and involved them in a group activity. It would be easier to plonk them in front of a television or put an iPad in their hands, so it was good to see people making an effort.

'Wonder what's inside?' Gary stared at the box.

'Only one way to find out,' said Karen, digging her nails into the seal and ripping it off. Lifting the flaps, she brought the box closer and peered inside.

She screamed, threw the flaps closed, leaned to the right, and was sick all over the carpet.

'Karen!' Gary placed a hand on her back. 'Are you okay — what's wrong?'

The men and women at the computers stopped what they were doing and stared at them, looking blank and concerned.

She couldn't speak; instead, she pointed to the box.

'The box?'

She nodded twice, then moved her head away to gag again.

Cautiously, Gary lifted the flaps and had a look. A human male head stared up at him with wide, still eyes. 'Sweet Jesus.'

One of the men sitting at the computers smiled at Gary.

CHAPTER 43

Mrs Andrews continued staring at the photo of the schoolboy.

'So, this photo was found with the library victims?'

Fisher nodded. 'How long ago was this photo taken?'

She exhaled and tipped her head back. 'God, years. Let me think.' She focused back on her desk as if it would help her concentrate. 'Twenty-five, twenty-six years maybe. God, it's been so long. It's hard to pinpoint the exact date.'

'Is there a way,' DS Phillips said, 'we could look back at the class photos from that time, maybe get a better idea?'

Fisher nodded his way, approving the idea.

'I've kept all my class photos through the years. There are dozens, but it should be there. I taught him in my early years, so I'll know where to look. Erm . . .' She brought a thin finger to her chin. 'I'm trying to think where they'd be. Oh!' She pointed at them. 'I know.'

The detectives watched her slowly move from behind her desk and go over to a cupboard a few feet away. It was several feet deep and the width of a door, with multiple shelves inside stacked with paperwork and boxes.

'Let me see.' She rummaged a little, then pulled out a long, wide box roughly A4 sized and six inches deep. She turned from the cupboard and placed it on her desk. Fisher and Phillips got closer but gave her enough space so she didn't feel like they were being invasive. She lifted the lid and placed it to one side, and at the top of the pile was the most recent class photo, taken the previous year. The detectives leaned in and peered at it. They saw the date and a section with dozens of names at the bottom.

It looked promising.

If Mrs Andrews still had the class photo that included the boy, they were in luck. She lifted a handful and studied one beneath. She continued further, stopping a few years further back, absorbing the faces focused on the camera to see if she could spot the boy. The photos were in excellent condition; she obviously took pride in her career, saving these as tokens of her hard work.

Fisher wondered if she'd had a favourite class during her time here.

'Maybe the next one.' She raised the photo and peered at the one below.

The class was separated into three rows. The boy was in the middle row, standing three from the end. She pointed. 'That's him.'

Fisher leaned to get a closer look at his face, then her eyes dropped to the names, which were in the same order as they were in the photo. Phillips brought out his phone and took a picture of the group for reference.

'Mason Scott,' said Fisher.

'Mason Scott,' repeated Mrs Andrews. 'He was a lovely boy, was Mason. It's a shame he was treated the way he was during his time here.'

'How do you mean?'

The teacher gave a tight-lipped smile. 'Mason struggled to interact with people. He, er, well . . . maybe in this day and age, with the awareness of autism and ADHD and other various conditions, you would consider him 'on the spectrum'. Still, of course, we weren't aware of anything like that back then.'

Fisher waited for her to continue and, when she remained silent, said, 'So what happened?'

'He didn't have many friends. He used to spend time alone. And to be honest, he didn't know anything different, so I don't think he minded it. I've seen hundreds of students come and go here over the years. All I wanted, being a teacher, was for our students to come here, learn, have fun, then leave equipped with hopefully the right tools to set them up in life.'

Fisher smiled. The ideal goal for any educational system.

Mrs Andrews went on. 'Although I didn't see much happiness from Mason, he did find joy in books.'

'Books?' asked Phillips.

She nodded. 'He spent his free time here reading. Anything he could get his hands on. The other students used to mock him for it, calling him sad and telling him to get a life. It was only a handful, just so you know. They weren't all like that.'

Both detectives smiled sadly.

'Hang on a second,' the teacher said. 'Is this something to do with what's been going on? I watched the news. Two people have died. Two of my . . . ex-students, I believe. Mary and Debbie.' She looked down, sadness shaping her face.

Fisher frowned at the teacher's words. 'They were students of yours?'

She nodded. 'In the same class as Mason, yes.'

Fisher couldn't believe it and gave Phillips a sideways glance. 'Surely not a coincidence, Matthew?'

Phillips pursed his lips and raised his eyebrows at the revelation.

Fisher focused on the teacher. 'Mason is a person of high interest and we need to know everything about him.'

The teacher gently lifted her head in understanding.

'Did you have a library?' asked Fisher, moving things on.

'Yeah, we still do, although it's been renovated several times.'

'So, apart from being mocked for his reading, what else can you tell us about him?'

'Well . . .' Mrs Andrews leaned back, once again bringing a finger to her chin. 'It wasn't just making fun of him for his reading; it was more.'

Fisher and Phillips listened.

'Some of the students used to hit him, leaving him with a bloody nose. One time they locked him in the caretaker's cupboard until a teacher came and put a stop to it. He was locked in and fell over, burning his arm on some chemicals. The light switch was on the outside, so it was dark. I heard the screaming from down the hall.' A tear fell from the corner of the teacher's eye. 'I'm sorry, I . . . it's hard sometimes.'

Fisher placed a caring hand on her shoulder. 'It's fine. I can imagine.'

Mrs Andrews stared at the photo of the class, scanning the faces staring back, her primary focus on Mason Scott.

'And then the camping trip happened,' she muttered.

The detectives frowned.

'Camping trip?' probed Fisher.

'It was a night I'll never forget. God knows how Mason felt.'

'What happened?'

CHAPTER 44

Chorlton High School
Twenty-seven years ago

Mrs Andrews thanked the class for their efforts and informed them it was home time. They stood up, packed their books and pencil cases away, and put them in their bags. Over the past few weeks, she'd noticed a decline in their focus. She'd spoken to the headmaster, who had told her it was her class and her responsibility to rectify it. She wasn't the most out-going person, let alone very good with human conflict. Still, she did know it was her job to guide her students in the right direction, and if that included being a little stricter, then that's what she'd have to do.

All the students had left, leaving Mason alone, still sitting at his desk in silence with his head down, reading a book.

She looked up at him. 'Are they coming? You did tell them?'

'Yes, Miss,' he replied quietly, not taking his eyes from the page.

'Mason, how did you find today?'

'It . . . it was better. Thank you.'

'Anyone upset you?'

He shook his head immediately. Even if they had, he wouldn't have said. It wasn't in his nature to get others in trouble. He was the kind of person to hold everything in and let it simmer inside.

There were several knocks on the door. Mrs Andrews looked over, seeing Mason's parents standing there.

'Sorry we're late. Traffic was worse than usual,' said his mother.

Mrs Andrews stood. 'Don't worry at all. You're not late.' She went over to shake their hands. Once the pleasantries and introductions were done, they sat down next to Mason.

'How you doing, son?' asked his father. 'Good day?'

When Mason nodded silently, his father focused on Mrs Andrews. 'You wanted to see us?'

'Yes, I, erm . . .' She coughed. 'I'm not sure if Mason passed the letter on, but we have a camping trip next month, and I'd really like Mason to go.'

Jackie frowned at her son, then focused back on Mrs Andrews. 'He hasn't passed that on. What . . . what are the arrangements?'

'Well, the whole class goes to a campsite for two nights, two students to a tent. During our time there, we'll do fun outdoor activities, like fire building and team bonding. Just something different from the usual school environment. There'll also be water activities like canoeing and kayaking.'

Charles Scott turned to his son with a wide grin. 'Hey, Mason, that sounds fun, eh?'

Mrs Andrews smiled sadly at Mason's silence. 'It does sound fun, indeed. But Mason here has told me he doesn't want to go. I'm trying to persuade him, but he says he would rather stay behind and sit in with the class above while his class is away.'

'Don't be silly.' Jackie placed a hand on Mason's back. 'Mason would love to go, I'm sure.' There was a pause. 'Right, Mason?'

'I guess,' he muttered.

'Good,' the teacher responded. 'I really think Mason will benefit from the trip. It'll give him a chance to bond with others.'

'I don't know . . .' Mason whispered.

'Listen, Mason,' Mrs Andrews said, leaning forward, 'I know your time in this school hasn't been the most enjoyable, but unfortunately, you have to move on and grow as a person. From your time in my class, I've seen you come on leaps and bounds, and this trip will only make you more confident in doing things you've never done before. I really think you'll enjoy it.'

'Who will I share a tent with?'

'Don't worry about that. I'll find someone suitable for you to share with.'

'Can I take my books?'

Jackie Scott sighed, looking away for a moment. Mrs Andrews felt his mother's disapproval of his constant reading.

'Mason, give the books a rest, please.'

Charles turned to her. 'Hang on, Jackie. If Mason wants to read books because he enjoys them, let him. It's his choice. But I do agree with Mrs Andrews that this trip will do him a world of good. Mason, would you agree?'

'I guess.'

'And, we can have marshmallows by the fire and tell ghost stories,' the teacher added.

There was a sparkle in Mason's eye. 'Really?'

'Absolutely.'

His father grinned widely. 'Mason will love it.'

CHAPTER 45

Present day

After Fisher and Phillips had thanked Mrs Andrews for her time, they headed back to the station, quickly stopping off at a Subway for something to eat. Even though she was driving, Phillips made more of a mess than Fisher, spilling sauce down his front.

'For God's sake,' he said. 'Sorry.'

'As long as it didn't reach the seats, you're safe.'

In less than two minutes of being at their desks in the warmth of the office, DI James turned up, clocking the take-out coffee cup by Phillips's keyboard.

Fisher studied his face but couldn't judge what mood he was in. 'Hey, boss.'

He got straight to the point. 'Any joy at the school?'

She nodded. 'Yeah. Managed to speak to the teacher who taught the boy. Turns out his name is Mason Scott. She told us that his time at school wasn't enjoyable, and he was bullied severely.'

DI James nodded. 'The names?'

'Debbie Johnson and Mary Steadman were both in his class; she'd seen the news about their deaths.'

His eyebrows went up. 'Well, there's our obvious link, then.'

'There's more.'

James frowned. 'Go on . . .'

'I noticed the name Callum McCauley too. Baan and Jackson went to his house to speak with his wife, Linda, who said he'd just vanished.'

DI James thought for a moment. 'Can't be a coincidence.'

Fisher shrugged, tilted her head. 'It's a place to start.'

He leaned over, placing a hand on Fisher's shoulder. 'Good job, April.'

She smiled but pointed towards Phillips. 'Matthew came too; it wasn't just me.'

'Good job, DS Phillips,' James said, winking at him.

Phillips gave him the thumbs up and stood, removing his coat, finally succumbing to the heat around them.

'So, we need to find Mason Scott, then, see what role he's playing in all this. I don't like to make assumptions, as we all know that's a dick move, but there's a huge chance he's involved in this, or at least knows who is.'

Fisher nodded in agreement. 'After speaking with the teacher, it's very likely he's involved somewhere. I'm on it.'

DI James looked down at his watch. 'Right, DCI Baker wants me in a meeting with him. The county bigwigs are coming in to find out where we are with our current cases. Probably to take most of the flack, I assume. Wish me luck.'

Fisher winced at the thought of it, watching him run a nervous palm through his long blonde hair. It wasn't often management came in. 'You've got this, Tom. Good luck.'

'Thanks.' He turned, then stopped. 'Let me know what you find. Sooner rather than later, okay? Let's get these arse-holes off our backs.'

'Got it, boss.'

DI James left the office, went into the corridor, and disappeared out of sight.

'Hey,' Phillips said. 'I've got something.'

'What?' Fisher wheeled herself over, focusing on his screen.

'An address for Mason Scott.' Phillips pulled his phone out and took a snap of the information on his monitor. 'Let's go, then.'

They stood, put their coats back on, and left their desks. They marched down the aisle, past the rows of computer desks, catching the eyes of other PCs, who smiled briefly at them, wondering where they were going. Before they reached the door, her phone rang. She answered it quickly, 'Yeah?' It was PC Baan.

'April, you might want to go over to Gorton Library ASAP. They've found something.'

Fisher stopped in her tracks and inhaled the warm, stuffy office air. Phillips stopped and frowned her way.

'This never bloody ends.' She shoved her phone into her pocket and exited the building into the freezing car park.

CHAPTER 46

By the time Fisher and Phillips had pulled into the small car park at the library, it was not only dark but the heavens had opened. The ground was already saturated from the downpour, the roadsides now flowing streams. Unlike the previous crime scenes, there were no crowds outside watching anxiously from the crime scene tape, because nothing had been set up yet. PC Baan had informed them that everyone inside had been asked to move away and kept quiet with tea and biscuits.

'Why — what's happening?' asked one of the women, holding a young child on her knee.

'Please, can everyone just move over to that side of the library,' advised Gary Orden, the man who had found the box.

'Why was she sick? What's inside the box?' another had said.

Once they had been ushered to one end, they had called the police.

Luckily — or unluckily — PC Baan was close by and had arrived first with PC Adam Jackson. They did their best to settle the crowd, knowing this was different from the previous two library incidents. The previous body parts had been discovered in a quiet library first thing in the morning, but this was while the library was open and there were people inside. It was different; anyone in the library could be responsible for the box being there.

'It's all we need,' Fisher sighed as she unbuckled her seat belt. 'DCI Baker will come down on us like a ton of bloody bricks if we don't get this bloody thing solved.' She turned off the engine, the headlights fading against one of the damp walls of Gorton Library. It was a single-storey building, resembling an old church in its bricked structure and style; Fisher wondered if it had been at one time.

They quickly got out and dashed towards the entrance door, finding an unfamiliar PC standing under an umbrella, the sound of the rain pounding the top of it. The PC nodded when they flashed their IDs and moved out of the way so they could slip by.

Inside they noticed PC Baan standing next to a desk straight ahead, speaking to a man, taking notes, and nodding as he spoke. To the right, they heard conversations filled with worry and frustration.

'Why can't we leave?' one woman said. 'My daughter needs to get home.' PC Jackson assured them it wouldn't be too much longer.

Fisher and Phillips moved further into the library, absorbing their surroundings. The interior somewhat matched the outside in the way it was dated and needed modernising. She spotted the box to the left, resting on a desk beside a row of computers.

'Hey,' Fisher said to Baan.

PC Baan stopped scribbling, looked her way, and motioned to the man standing with her. 'This is Gary. He works here. He's just explained he brought the box inside, assuming it was material delivered from the council.'

Fisher turned to him. 'I'm DS April Fisher.'

He extended a hand but didn't say anything. Fisher noticed his hand shaking a little.

'He was here when the box was opened,' added Baan.

His face was drained, leaving the colour somewhere between white and grey.

'Who else works here?' Fisher asked him.

He cleared his throat to find his voice. 'Just me and Karen today. She's out back, in the toilet. She opened the box and saw the head first.'

Fisher nodded. 'Okay. And you found the box outside?'

He explained that he had and added that usually the boxes came with printed stickers, unlike the handwritten label on this box. He hadn't thought much about it at the time.

Fisher looked at Phillips. 'Want to check it out?'

'Boone just texted me to say she's on her way. She's bringing the trainees with her too.'

They thanked Baan and moved over to the small row of computers, snapping on a pair of gloves they'd pulled from their coat pockets.

'Ladies first,' Phillips said, motioning her forward with a thin smile.

'How kind of you.' She lifted the flap and stared silently inside the box. 'Jesus.'

This time, the head belonged to a male. There was a distinctive smell of rotting flesh, similar to the previous ones. However, it didn't affect either detective as they studied the still eyes of the victim.

'Has to be Callum,' said Fisher, thinking about the list of names on the school photo.

Phillips considered it. 'Think there'll be more to find here?'

Leaving the box with the head inside, they ambled around the library, meticulously studying the dozens of shelves and boxes. By the time Boone had arrived, they were about finished and had discovered nothing additional to pass on to the forensics team.

They showed Boone the box. She set down her forensics kit and opened the lid. With her were Stacy Coors and Jasper Allen, both wearing white paper overalls, keen to see some action, however unfortunate the circumstances.

Pamela Boone pulled on her gloves and told the trainees to keep their distance as she inspected the box.

While Forensics were doing their thing, Fisher and Phillips left them to it. They went to the group of waiting people, where the library assistant stood with one of the men from the digital workshop. PC Baan had a pen and pad out, ready to take notes. The detectives listened in.

'I could tell the package was unusual,' the man started.

'How?' Baan pressed.

'Just the way they weren't expecting it. Karen — I think her name is Karen — said she was sure she'd brought them all in, but Gary had found it. Anyway, she opened it and was sick immediately. I don't know what's in the box but judging by their reactions and the fact that you're here, I'm assuming it isn't good.'

The detectives nodded.

'Is it linked to the other library incidents?' he asked, now focusing on Fisher, recognising her face from the recent press conference aired on TV.

'I'm not at liberty to discuss the details yet, Mr . . .'

'Oh, sorry.' He smiled. 'Gregson. Alan Gregson. Nice to meet you — well, it isn't in the circumstances, but . . .' He trailed off, looked away for a second. 'Well, if it is linked, I hope you find the person responsible for it.'

'I hope so too,' she said. 'Thanks for your time.'

He dissolved into the agitated crowd. Fisher turned to Baan and Phillips. 'We can't interview everyone here right now. We don't have the resources or the time. Take everyone's name and contact details. We'll carry out interviews as soon as possible.'

Phillips pondered her words and agreed with a nod. He looked up. 'There appear to be cameras here, so if there's anything to see, we'll see it on there.' He peered over at Gary. 'Excuse me?'

Gary left the desk near the front. 'Yeah?'

'Have you got contact details for everyone here?'

'We have their names and numbers. Most activities work on a booking arrangement, so we have their details.'

'Thanks.'

'Is . . . is there anything you need me to do?' He appeared distraught, but keen to help.

Fisher raised a thankful palm and smiled. 'No, it's okay. We'll speak to them and let them know they can go.'

After the crowd had dispersed, two PCs stood at the door to prevent anyone else from entering. They apologised to any approaching members of the public, informing them the library was closed until further notice.

An elderly gent, who didn't look happy, said, 'When's it opening, then?'

'We don't know. Sorry.'

Fisher, Phillips, and Baan joined the forensic team. Boone was just about to pull the head from the box to inspect it. Jasper and Stacy stood by with wide eyes, overseeing Boone manoeuvre the head, tilting it back to see where the cut had been made.

'April . . . here it is. Stacy, could you grab those tweezers and remove what's hanging from the underside of the head, please.'

Jasper looked disappointed he wasn't asked but watched on, seeing Stacy slightly wince before picking them up. With trembling hands, she moved towards the head. Fisher and Phillips observed her. The stench of the dead flesh caught at the back of everyone's throat. Talk about pressure. She pincered what they all assumed was the edge of the photo and pulled a little, the sound of the material scraping off the flesh causing a small gag reflex, but she kept it down and maintained a strong head.

Once the bloody, brown, pasty photo was in the open, Stacy froze, not knowing what to do with it.

'Just hold it there a second,' Boone told her, who'd already laid down a sheet of clear plastic behind them on the floor and slowly turned, lowering the head. Jasper stared at it, seemingly wanting to say something but unable to find the words. It looked as if he was beginning to seriously reconsider his career in forensics.

'Here, let me.' Boone carefully took hold of the tweezers, maintaining the pressure on them to keep the photo pinned between the tiny pincers. 'Thanks.'

Stacy backed away, glad for Boone to take over, and sighed heavily. The colour had noticeably drained from her face.

'You okay?'

She nodded twice at Jasper, clearly overcompensating for the fact that she wasn't, but Jasper didn't comment, instead he froze, watching Boone in fascination.

'Okay.' Boone carefully unfolded the photo and showed Fisher and Phillips. There he was, staring at them, his innocent, young smile. Mason Scott.

'Thanks,' Fisher said, then looked at Phillips. 'You got that list from the class photo?'

'You betting the head belongs to Callum McCauley?'

'I'd say there's a very good chance,' replied Fisher. She studied Boone, who still had the photo pinned with the tweezers. 'Pamela, can you get a DNA sample ASAP and get it tested. I feel that the way things are going, there's more to come.'

CHAPTER 47

Middleton Campsite
Twenty-seven years ago

It had taken much persuasion for Mason to agree to go on the trip with his class. Charles and Jackie Scott were starting to worry about his anxiety, his lack of confidence, and the way he spent much of his time on his own. Mason himself seemed happy and content being that way. But there's nothing worse as a parent than feeling your child isn't fitting in, and not being included in group activities, or worse, being left out on purpose.

They'd arrived at the campsite on Wednesday afternoon. The bus they travelled on wasn't full so there were plenty of spare seats. As usual, Mason sat by himself, subject to small balls of paper being thrown at the back of his head from the students behind. He ignored it, having built some resilience and sad acceptance about how they treated him.

Sitting at the front of the bus, Mrs Andrews frequently turned to keep an eye on the children's behaviour, hoping her talk with them several weeks earlier had registered. So far, during class time, it had, but when she clocked Steve Adams throwing paper at Mason, her cold stare made it clear that if he was to carry on doing it, he wouldn't want to find out the consequences. Another teacher, Mr Shorton, and one of the school assistants, Mrs Farmer, had come along too. It would be a big ask for Mrs Andrews to keep her eye on twenty-seven students alone.

Once they arrived, they all got off, collecting their bags from the storage area underneath, the driver helping them. Mason's bag was bright green and old-fashioned.

'Is that your mum's bag?' Steve Adams laughed, along with some others standing by.

Ignoring them, Mason went to Mrs Andrews and stood in line, waiting for further direction. They were met by one of the site's officers, a young man in his early twenties with skin covered in spots. He had a specific look you would associate with someone being really good at tying knots, setting up campfires, and laughing at jokes that weren't funny.

'Hello, hello.' He smiled, then threw his palms up flamboyantly. 'Welcome to Middleton Campsite.' Placing a hand on his chest, he said, 'My name is George.'

'Gay George,' muttered Steve Adams. Beside him, Callum McCauley sniggered.

Mrs Andrews glared their way, silencing them immediately.

George led them down a dried mud trail towards a single-storey cabin by the lake's edge. It looked like it had been built very recently, judging by the colour and condition of the wood. The felt on the roof was in one piece, all the same colour, not weathered by years of rain and wind. They were instructed to leave their bags and belongings on the grass while they went in for a briefing, where George went into detail about their time there and what it would consist of.

'Does that sound like fun?' Mrs Andrews asked cheerfully after the guide had finished.

Most of them smiled and nodded. The more popular ones didn't, maintaining their cool personas as if it didn't impress them.

Once the students had collected their stuff, George showed them where they'd be camping. It was a few minutes' walk from the cabin, taking a narrow path along the water's edge until they reached an open area with a fire pit in the middle surrounded by over a dozen two-berth tents, equally spaced, their openings pointing inwards towards the fire. In reality, they were probably only suitable for one adult at best.

'I'm not sleeping in those,' Steve told George.

George turned to him, smiled, then motioned to an area between the fire and the tents. 'If you want to risk it out here with the bears, be my guest.'

Steve's eyes widened.

'There are bears here?' asked Mason, gazing around in fear as if one could appear at any moment.

Mrs Andrews, closest to him, placed a gentle hand on his shoulder. 'No, Mason. I think you'll be safe from bears.'

After several activities, they sat at nearby picnic tables to eat. Although the food offered was corned beef stew with buttered bread, the hungry students enjoyed it without much complaining.

It was just after nine when the sun started to fall on the horizon, the area around the tents becoming dull and grey. George appeared with some firewood and some matches and went through the simple procedure of setting up a fire. They all seemed interested because it was getting cold, and they wanted the heat sooner rather than later. With the students' help, George had dragged out some thick logs from the woods to use as seats closer to the fire. After a long-winded conversation about how the fire was dangerous and under no circumstances should anyone go near it, they lit it and kept their distance. It was glorious. Hot orange flames danced and cracked, the wood settling in, moulding with the heat, giving off that particular smell that everyone loved, reminding them of a BBQ.

Mason sat close to Steve, Callum, Debbie, Mary, and Patricia. They whispered various things. Whatever they were, Mason assumed they were about him, but he stared silently at the fire, listening to it crackle. He studied his classmates' faces one by one, surrounding the warm light, engaged in light conversations about various topics, one being their excitement about canoeing the following morning.

He grinned.

'He's even smiling to himself. He's weird.'

Mason took a lungful of warm air and snapped his neck to the right. 'What's your problem, Steve?'

'Listen, boys,' said Mrs Andrews from the other side of the fire. 'None of this, please. This is a bonding trip for our class, a chance to build better friendships. If this continues, I'll send you home.'

Steve muttered something, then laughed.

'What was that?' She glowered at him.

'Nothing, Miss.'

Mason smiled thinly at her in appreciation before focusing back on the fire. Out of the corner of his eye, he noticed Steve stand up and disappear, telling the others he was going to the toilet — a small well-made hut less than fifty metres away, coupled with several showers.

'You okay, Mason?'

He turned to the left towards the soft voice of Polly Mirken, who smiled sadly at him.

'Yes thanks, Polly.'

Polly, one of the eldest in the class, always looked out for Mason. She recognised the bullying and despised it, but even after voicing her opinions, there wasn't much she could do apart from checking on him when he felt down.

She leaned over, patted his hand, then returned to her conversation.

Mason felt warm inside, grateful for her care, and continued to look into the fire, thinking about—

A sudden pain erupted in his ribs on both sides.

'Ahhh,' he shouted, jumping up and turning to see Steve Adams laughing at him with his hands over his mouth. He'd snuck up behind him and dug his knuckles into his back, scaring him.

'Look!' shouted Callum, pointing. 'Look at his wet patch!'

Mason felt his cheeks warming and knew what he'd done. His legs were warm and wet. He couldn't help it; it was a reaction. It was the first time he'd ever wet himself, let alone in front of anyone.

'Steve!' Mrs Andrews screamed.

Without any control and feeling hugely embarrassed, Mason darted for Steve, who still had his hands up to his face in laughter and was too slow to defend himself when Mason punched him in the face.

All conversations came to an abrupt halt. All eyes were wide, watching what had just happened.

Did someone hit Steve Adams?

'Oh my . . .' Mary Steadman whispered, cupping her mouth with a palm.

'You're going to pay for that!' Adams went for Mason, but George, the guide, stepped between them before reaching him.

'No, no, no!' He had a firm grip on him. 'We don't do that here.' He turned to stare at Mason, then back to Adams. 'Never.'

'I'll get you back for that one, Mason Scott,' whispered Steve Adams. 'You'll see . . .'

CHAPTER 48

Present day

When DI James and a few others arrived at the library, Fisher was happy there were now enough resources to man the library and assist Forensics. Hence, she told James about the address they'd found for Mason Scott, and that they had been heading to his house before being diverted to the library.

'Yeah, go. I'll stay here,' he encouraged them.

'I'm taking Phillips, Baan, and Jackson.'

Knowing he had enough people there, James nodded and told her to keep him updated. If it really was the same Mason Scott as in those class photos, they were surely onto something.

'You watch how you go. If you think something is off, call me first.'

She nodded at him, and they left, Baan and Jackson making up the rear. Outside, the rain was heavier than before, making it considerably darker for the time of day. It felt like the end of the world, judging by how soaked the ground was and the quick flowing streams at the sides of the roads. Phillips said something on his way to the car, but his voice was drowned out by the rain pounding off the ground and the Volvo. PC Baan and PC Jackson rushed to their Peugeot, which was unfortunately parked across the car park.

Once inside, Fisher ran fingers through her damp hair. 'What did you say?'

'Huh?'

'You said something out there?'

'I said this weather is *shit*! Cold and wet.'

Smiling in agreement, she turned the key, the headlights illuminating the side of the library again, this time the lights brighter. She reversed out of her space and joined the main road with PC Baan driving behind. It took them just over twenty minutes to arrive at the address for Mason Scott. It was a semi-detached property on Old Moat Lane with a front door located at the side of the house. Luckily, the rain had stopped, but dark skies still threatened. Baan parked directly behind Fisher, and they got out, joining the detectives at the end of the driveway. There was no car out front and the house seemed quiet, with no sign of any lights inside.

'Don't think anyone's in,' noted Phillips.

'Won't stop us trying.'

Fisher asked Baan and Jackson to wait at the end of the driveway while the detectives walked down the path to the front door, feeling the cold as they moved. Weeds and nettles sprouted from the base of the building and along the fence between the two properties. It was also clear, judging by the condition of the paintwork surrounding the windows and door, that Mason lacked a little pride in the appearance of the house.

Fisher knocked twice, then took a step back.

Phillips stood beside her, then observed Baan and Jackson focusing on the windows at the front of the house for any signs of movement.

She knocked again, then took a healthy step back. She was always cautious knocking on doors as it reminded her of the time she had knocked on a suspect's property that had been linked to a robbery. A second after knocking, the door had opened and a man had charged out attacking her. Ever since, she made sure to be out of arm's reach, just in case.

Without an answer, they looked to the left, noticing a path leading to a gate. Fisher wandered down and tried the handle. As it opened, she paused, turning to Phillips, who was still damp from the earlier downpour.

'You coming, or are you just going to stand there feeling sorry for yourself?'

Phillips smiled, joined her, and went through to the garden, which was long but narrow, not much wider than the width of the house, separated by a six-foot fence on either side. They turned right and noticed another door which, judging by what they could see through the glass, led to a small utility room containing a cupboard, a washing machine, and a boiler fixed to the wall.

Fisher moved along to the next window, slowly leaned in, then froze.

'Matthew.'

'Yeah?'

'See this?' He moved around her and peered in.

It was the kitchen. 'What?'

She pointed to the small circular wooden table in the middle of the room, containing a set of knives inside an open plastic holder that had been rolled out flat. They counted seven knives in total. To the right of the blades, there was a small pool of blood.

'See the blood?' Phillips asked.

'I do, I see it.' She then gasped when she saw the objects on the floor underneath the table. 'God . . .' She covered her mouth with a hand. 'Call Forensics now.'

CHAPTER 49

Pamela Boone had to tie up a few loose ends at the library before she left, heading to the address DS Phillips had provided. During the quick call, he'd told her the nature of the scene at Old Moat Lane. She sighed heavily, telling him she'd be over when she could.

'*Don't* bring Stacy and Jasper to this one,' he prompted.

'I didn't intend to. I'll see you soon.' She hung up, and Phillips joined Fisher at the window.

'Well, there goes our search warrant,' he said, picking up a plant pot a few feet away, intending to throw it through the window.

Fisher held a hand out. 'Wait.' She pulled on some latex gloves that she always kept as spares in her suit jacket, something that others found amusing, but had served her well on more than one occasion. She tried the handle and it opened.

'Well, I never,' Phillips said, shaking his head and putting the pot back where it was.

They went inside cautiously.

* * *

When Boone turned up in her white forensics van, parking just behind PC Baan's Peugeot, she first saw PC Jackson, who greeted her with a professional nod.

'You been inside?' she asked him before he had the chance to speak.

He nodded. 'That's why I'm out here.'

She smiled sadly, knowing what that meant. With his hand, he directed her down the side, through the gate, and around the back, where she came across PC Baan, standing at the back door, peering inside. Baan turned her way upon hearing her light footsteps.

'Hey, Pam,' she whispered. She pointed into the house. 'Just in here.'

'Are April and Matthew inside?'

Baan said they were and moved aside as Boone carefully stepped through the threshold into the kitchen, carrying her forensics kit. The house felt strangely colder than it did outside; perhaps it was the nature of the scene. To her right, standing near the sink, were Fisher and Phillips, both with arms folded, staring silently at the body parts under the table.

'You haven't brought Jasper and Stacy with you, have you?'

Boone theatrically shook her head at Fisher and grew closer, the scent of cigarette smoke that seemed to constantly cling to her clothes filling the space.

'Good. Just checking.' Fisher sighed, then looked back at the table.

One by one, Boone placed plastic overshoes on to go with her white coveralls and left her kit near the door. She wanted a feel of the scene first and good peek at the knives on the table.

'Those blades look sharp.' She returned to her kit and grabbed her camera. She then spent several minutes taking shots of the kitchen from multiple angles, then took out her phone to record a short video. It was always good when doing her report to use a reference when describing the scene.

Fisher and Phillips observed her work and the meticulous way she decided which angles were the best.

'How old do they look?' Phillips asked.

'As usual, it's hard to say,' Boone informed him. 'A more likely indication at the moment is the colour of the blood.' It had turned a darker colour, bordering on brown. And it had thickened, which she explained to them was something that happened when blood mixed with oxygen over a certain length of time.

'What do you think?'

'Over a day, I'd say, April.' Boone nodded, confirming her thoughts. 'Have you told DI James about this?'

Fisher said she had. 'He said he's on his way over.'

'Before I inspect further, I will check for fingerprints or any signs of DNA first. You checked the house?' Boone didn't want to find some random man upstairs hiding in a cupboard.

Phillips said they had and that there was no sign of any-one. 'Wherever Mason Scott is, he isn't here.'

'Do you think the head at the library belongs with this?' asked Fisher.

Boone tilted her head. 'Possibly. I won't be long. Would you mind waiting outside?'

The detectives nodded and backed away to the door.

'Did you touch the handle?' asked Boone, nodding towards the back door.

Fisher held up her gloved hand and smiled.

'Good girl.' She then disappeared into the middle of the house, taking fingerprints from door handles, bagging tooth-brushes, and so on. When she returned to the kitchen, Fisher popped her head in from outside. Boone placed the collected evidence into a large plastic bag and put it down by her kit.

'April, would you mind helping me lay out the plastic? Give us enough room to put the pieces on.'

Phillips and Fisher stepped inside, helped Boone lay out the thick plastic sheet, and then stood back, watching her work. Very carefully, Boone grabbed hold of one of the arms. It was heavy with muscle and weighed more than she thought. She carefully laid it out, then went back for the other arm, placing it down next to it. She then went back for the legs and finally the torso.

The only item missing that would make a full body was the head. It was safe to say that the most recent head they'd discovered at the library was the missing part, but the DNA would confirm it later. Boone extracted a sample from each body part and labelled it before packing it. The arms matched each other, as did the legs, both in size and appearance, but they had to be sure.

They heard something behind them, and standing at the back door was DI Thomas James along with DC Arnold Peterson. James raised a hand to his mouth after Fisher moved aside, showing him the full extent of the scene.

'Jesus . . .'

They couldn't shake the thought that this house was where Mason Scott brought his victims back and chopped them up.

'We need to find fucking Mason Scott right now!' shouted DI James.

CHAPTER 50

A few hours had passed. Boone had made a decision and invited Stacy and Jasper over to Mason Scott's house after all. If they were to make it as forensic techs, they'd need to experience a scene like this sooner or later. Using it as training, they collected evidence that she already had, such as toothbrushes and hairbrushes, and extracted prints from door handles. All the evidence was secure, but the training exercises would be helpful for them moving forward, to gain experience in their field of study.

'Is it true what was in the kitchen?' asked Jasper, appearing both excited and nervous. Boone nodded, continuing to explain how they extracted prints from various places.

Most of the team — bar PC Jackson and PC Baan, who were asked to stay at the house in case Mason Scott returned — were back at the station in the meeting room with their focus on DI James. It was progress finding the body parts in the house, knowing that Mason Scott was responsible.

The issue was they didn't know what Mason Scott looked like now, only that he'd be around forty-one. He had no social media or professional profiles, no up-to-date information online at all. They didn't even know what he did as a job. But it was apparent he was still in Manchester, judging by what they'd found at the house.

After DI James had informed them of what had happened so far in the day, DC Peterson asked, 'Are we assuming the remains match the head found at the library?'

'We can't assume anything, Arnold. But given the evidence and the situation, it's likely. Boone will confirm hopefully later today.'

Peterson nodded.

DI James focused on Fisher. 'April, can you fill everyone in on the latest news on Mason Scott?'

She informed everyone they had spoken to a teacher from Chorlton High School who'd taught Mason all those years ago. She told them that Mason Scott was in a class that included Mary Steadman and Debbie Johnson. Fisher also relayed what had happened on the camping trip from what Mrs Andrews had told them. The story itself was enough reason to want revenge.

'God, that's awful,' said PC Amy Legg, slowly shaking her head.

'So is killing people and chopping them up,' replied DI James.

That was true. No one could argue with the DI on that one.

'The problem is,' Fisher went on, 'we don't know what he looks like. We could walk past him in the street and not even know. But we sent the photo of him as a schoolboy to Digital Forensics to try and come up something.'

It was very clever technology, putting a photo of someone much younger and transforming their face by so many years to form an image of what they could look like now, obviously pending specific issues like scars or plastic surgery. It was, more often than not, fairly accurate.

'Has that photo come back yet?' DI James asked her, knowing it often took some time.

'It has. Harry handed it to me before.' Harry Spooner, the IT wizard, had received a photo from Digital Forensics the previous night after giving them the age they assumed Mason would be. She rose from the chair, opened the thin folder on the desk, picked it out, then moved to the front of the room and turned to face them. 'This . . . is what Mason Scott might look like now.'

The eyes in the room absorbed the man's face, trying to see if he was in any way familiar.

'Anyone?' When no one recognised him, she told them Digital Forensics would check to see if there was a hit on the database. After all, it might be the same man but using a different name, which was often the case.

'Right, guys,' DI James said, clapping his hands quickly. 'We have work to do. We'll see if Digitals get anywhere. Everyone, let's find Mason Scott. I don't care where he is, we have to find him. Get searching.' He looked at Fisher and said quietly, 'April, can you stay back? I need a word.'

She nodded and remained seated while the others stood and made their way to the door.

When the room was quiet, and they were alone, he said, 'April, you won't like it, but would you mind doing me a favour?'

CHAPTER 51

Fisher drained the remainder of her coffee and set her empty mug on her desk. She sighed heavily. Most of the team had gone home, but DS Phillips had said he'd stay for support. DI James had asked Fisher to do another press conference, adding that he didn't feel confident enough to stand before a group of eager reporters and flashing cameras. In a way, she felt sorry for him. After informing him she wouldn't do the next one, she reluctantly agreed and watched him leave.

DS Phillips returned from the toilet, noticing the office had become much quieter. 'Has everyone gone home?'

'Looks that way.' Her tone was vacant, quiet.

He tiredly slumped down in his seat and looked at her. 'How're you doing, April? Nervous yet?'

She looked his way, nodded, and managed a thin smile. 'I'll be okay. I managed last time.'

'You were brilliant last time. Fair play to you. I certainly wouldn't be putting my hand up to do it.'

'It's probably why DI James chooses me.'

They shared a short laugh before Phillips asked, 'What's going on with him at the moment? You know him better than I do.'

Fisher pressed her lips together. 'The DI is a strange one to fathom. He comes across as so confident and macho at times, but I know much of that is just a front. Maybe he feels the need, being our DI.'

Phillips bowed his head, understanding her.

'He's put on a little weight recently and, believe or not, hates the spotlight, especially these conferences in front of the reporters and cameras.'

He smiled and, seeing the dark circles around her eyes, was going to ask why she looked so tired but decided not to comment, because he too felt the same. If anything, he'd need to support and help her through another grilling from the local media circus. Recent public complaints stated the people of Manchester didn't feel safe and asked what the police were doing or intending to do to put a stop to it. PC Legg had passed this on to DI James, who handed the task onto Fisher, who had done a great job in the previous conference despite her own insecurities about speaking publicly.

'What time you heading down?'

She glanced down at her watch. 'Very soon. Starts at six.'

'You want me in there with you this time?'

Leaning over, she patted his hand in appreciation. 'Thank you, Matthew.' There was a shuffling sound at the other end of the office. Phillips glanced over, seeing a police constable sliding her chair in and putting on a duffle coat, readying herself for the cold, dark rain outside.

'Can't wait for summer, you know.' Phillips smiled. 'We're going away to Tenerife in May.'

'You taking that daft brown coat with you?'

He grinned, playfully thumping the top of her arm. 'Be too hot but might wear it on the plane.'

'First time for Dominic abroad?'

He nodded. 'Yeah. We were going to go this year but thought he'd be no good in the heat.'

'Makes sense. I don't like the heat really. Need factor fifty as soon as the sun shows up; I'd be no good somewhere like that.' She wiggled her mouse to awaken her screen and finished typing her report for the day. Based on the missing person's report from Linda McCauley about her husband and finding the head in the box at the library, along with McCauley's name being on the class photo, there was a fair chance the head belonged to him. Still, Boone would confirm that once she knew, which wouldn't be too long.

Once Fisher had finished the report, she closed her emails and signed out, then pushed herself up and grabbed her dark blue suit jacket from the back of her chair. The material felt cold on her skin but would soon warm up. Noticing Phillips was still at his desk, she said, 'You coming, or you just going to sit there?'

He laughed as he stood, grabbing his jacket and putting it on. 'Let's go.'

* * *

They used the same room as they had for the previous conference. A woman stood in the doorway leading to the large room, watching them approach. The bright light inside the room shone out into the corridor, illuminating the side of her kind but serious, professional face. She was dressed smartly in a pencil skirt and white blouse, with a black, nicely fitted suit jacket on top.

'Do we have the pleasure of you both this evening?'

Fisher shook her head. 'Just me, unfortunately, Laura.' As the event organiser for the police, Laura sorted the arrangements and the venue, making sure everything went as smoothly as possible. 'DS Phillips will be in the crowd, *hopefully* cheering me on.'

'I'll do my best, April.'

Laura smiled and stepped aside, motioning Fisher and Phillips inside. The drone of mixed conversations faded when they entered. Fisher's pupils dilated to the change in lighting as the room became silent, bar a few whispers. The seated reporters appeared eager, serious, and excited about what was going to happen, ready with their voice recorders and cameras in their hands.

Phillips whispered good luck and turned left to find a spare chair. There were roughly ten rows with ten seats in each row, and the room looked about half full. A couple of stares trailed him as he moved past, no doubt people wondering who he was, but they settled on Fisher as she walked across the front of the room, stopping at the wooden podium that hid everything from her chest downwards, and turned to face the crowd.

Fisher felt her heart pumping in her chest as she gazed around the room. Everyone was still, waiting for her to speak. Since her last conference, she'd been looking online and watching videos to improve her public speaking. Apparently, it was common for even the most confident speakers to feel a certain level of nervousness. She had come across several articles from these so-called experts on how to deal with anxiety when speaking, picking up a few points on how to position her body and trying to turn her nervous feelings into excitement. She had learned that when the body feels either scared or excited, it releases the same hormones, so it's up to the speaker to pretend it's excitement they're feeling rather than wanting to run out of the room and cry in the car in solitary embarrassment.

From her left, standing at the door, Laura gave her the thumbs up. '*Go for it*,' she mouthed.

Fisher took a deep breath, faced the front, raised her hands, and gently placed her palms on the podium's flat area on either side of the microphone base. She noticed her hands shaking slightly before lifting her focus to the waiting crowd.

'Hello, everyone. Thank you for being here. I'm Detective Sergeant April Fisher. The Greater Manchester Police have been asked to provide up-to-date information regarding the recent discoveries of human remains in two of our local libraries. We—'

'Make that three, Detective Fisher?'

She frowned in the direction of the voice. 'I'm sorry?'

The man was in his forties, dressed in a black duffle coat, a woolly hat, and sported a goatee popular several decades ago. 'I said, don't you mean three? You said two? There was another body found today. Or am I wrong?'

Fisher didn't reply straight away. It was clear whoever the guy was, he was well-informed and had contacts.

'That's true, sir. I apologise. I'm here to provide information on the latest discoveries of victims found at *three* local libraries. '

'Based on the current evidence, we're looking for a man. We have an address for him which we've visited, unfortunately finding some remains belonging to an unidentified victim.' A sweep of shocked sighs moved through the room, silencing any previous whispers. 'Forensics have attended the scene and have removed the evidence for testing. We will soon have a better idea of who it belongs to.'

The new information stunned the crowd for a few moments.

'We can confirm from our Forensics team the first two victims found at Chorlton Library and Newton Heath Library are Debbie Johnson and Mary Steadman. Earlier today we found a head of a male victim and are waiting on DNA analysis to provide confirmation of his identity.'

The room was silent.

'Are there any questions?'

A hand went up.

Fisher pointed. 'Ah, yes?'

It was a man in mid-twenties, eager to please whoever he worked for with a good question.

'Yes, Detective. I'm Sam from *News GO!*'

'Nice to meet you, Sam.'

News GO! was a small media company offering online news about Manchester and the surrounding area. They'd started small with a few employees but had expanded over the past year, providing stories to rival the more prominent media outlets.

He tilted his head to the side and spoke in an accent belonging further south, perhaps Bristol or somewhere around there. 'If you're looking for a male suspect, then that must mean he's still walking the streets. What are you personally doing about that?'

'My job isn't to wander the streets, Sam,' she countered. 'My job is to investigate and solve crimes that unfortunately come our way.'

'Would you say you're too important to wander the streets?' Before Fisher answered, he added, 'Is that job beneath you?'

She knew Sam was trying to wind her up, to say something he could use for his news team, but she was too wise to him, too savvy to be led down that dark path.

'I believe all members of our police force play their individual roles, which are no more and no less important than any other role. Each employee of our force does a great job and gives their best to keep this city as safe as it can be.'

'Yet there's a man still out there who you believe has killed three people — possibly more, who knows? Can you explain to us how that's doing a great job?'

Her cheeks pinked in frustration, but she took a breath, squeezing the sides of the podium to release it. 'Our job as police officers and detectives is to provide and serve this great city. Regrettably, we can't control the evil some individuals have inside them. All we can do is bring the suspect or suspects to justice, based on the evidence we gather and our strategic efforts.'

'Do you have a photo of the suspect?'

The question came from another woman speaking for the first time.

'His social media presence is almost non-existent. But we have a photo from when he was younger, which our digital media team have enhanced to show what he could look like now.'

Fisher turned to her left and nodded towards Laura, who smiled, raised her hand towards the small black box fixed to the ceiling above Fisher, and pressed a button. The blank wall beside Fisher was briefly illuminated with a blue screen before showing a photo of their interpretation of what the suspect could look like. All the eyes in the room focused on the man on the wall.

'If anyone here recognises the man in this photo, please get in touch. This is a matter of urgency.'

Another hand raised. Fisher glanced over at the woman towards the right and nodded.

'Have you found any links between the victims?'

Fisher then informed them about Mary and Debbie being in the same class back in school.

'You've identified the first two victims. Have you got an idea who the third victim is?'

'Based on what we know, we have a good idea, but I'm not willing to confirm the identity just yet without DNA testing.'

A wave of silence swept the room, and Fisher waited for the next question, searching the room with her gaze.

'How sure are you that this is the man responsible for the murders?' The question came from a man sitting in the middle at the back of the crowd.

'From the evidence we have collected, if he isn't the man responsible, he certainly is involved, and because of that, we need to urgently speak to him. If anyone does see this man, please get in touch. I must warn the public not to approach this man under any circumstances. Please, if you see him, contact the police as soon as possible. Thank you.'

'Well, good luck in your search,' the man replied with a nod.

There was a flurry of questions, but Fisher had had enough and stepped away from the stand.

'Detective Fisher!' she heard someone shout, but by that time, she'd reached the door, where DS Phillips was waiting for her.

'Let's go,' she told him. They left the room, went back down the corridor, and headed out of the station towards their cars. They'd had enough for one day.

CHAPTER 52

Victoria Thomson sat on the sofa in her living room, gob-smacked, with her hand over her mouth. Although she had the heating on low, the room suddenly became unbearably hot.

'What the actual fuck?' she said, staring at the television after the conference had finished and the news reporter went on with the next story.

She was frozen, unsure of what to do, her eyes darting around the room frantically. She started to feel dizzy. She needed to stand and get away to allow what she'd just seen to sink in. Rising, she dashed out into the hallway.

'Where you running to, Vic?' her husband asked, looking up from his phone, sitting on the other sofa.

'Just a second,' she replied, heading into the kitchen.

He looked back at his phone, continued scrolling through his social media news feed. It wasn't unusual for Vicky to overreact, so he didn't bat an eyelid. It was probably some American actress who had got a slot on an upcoming show, and she had to tell one of her friends.

Before she really knew where she was, she found herself in the kitchen, staring out the back door into the garden, the lights on the decking out of focus and blurry. She pulled her phone from her pocket and unlocked it, then found Patricia's number in her contacts. She couldn't remember the last time she'd spoken to Pat and was surprised the number was still there. She pressed CALL and put it to her ear, in the back of her mind hoping Patricia still had the same number.

It rang twice before it was answered.

'He-hello?' The voice was quiet, cautious.

'This you, Patricia?'

'Yeah, who's calling?'

'It's Vicky, Vicky Thomson.'

A brief silence on the other end.

'Vicky? How . . . why are you calling?'

'Yeah, I know, I . . .'

'What is it?'

'Have you seen the news just now on TV? A police press conference thing?'

'No, I've been out for a meal with my husband. Vicky, why are you calling?'

'You hear about the library murders? The body parts found in the libraries?'

'I think I heard someone mention it.'

'They're saying the first two were Debbie Johnson and Mary Steadman. You remember from—'

'You're kidding?'

'I wish I was, Patricia. I can't quite believe it.'

Pat's voice grew quieter for a moment. '*Yeah, hold on, Mick.* Sorry, just talking to my husband. Erm, I haven't seen those two in years.'

'Yeah, I know. Me neither, but we were talking online, weren't we, recently? Remember?'

'. . .'

'Do you rem—'

'Yes, yes, I remember, Vicky.'

'There's been another body found too, but no information yet about who it is.'

'Shit,' she replied.

'I know. Do you think it has something to do with what happened all those years ago with Mason?'

'The camping trip?' whispered Patricia.

'*What camping trip?*' her husband asked, sitting at the table with her.

'Just hold on, Mick,' she countered.

'Yeah, I think so.' Vicky started to shake, leaning on the worktop in the kitchen. 'I'm worried, that's all, Pat. I-I think we're in trouble.'

'Listen, I need to go. I'll contact you soon,' said Patricia.

'Wait, just—'

The line went dead. Vicky pulled the phone away from her head and sighed. She thought about who else was there that night and remembered Steve Adams. With no reason to have his number, she searched his name online and found his profile. She double-clicked on the photo and, once enlarged, knew it was him. She sent him a message with her number, asking him to ring her ASAP.

Less than two minutes later, her phone rang.

'Hey,' she answered.

'Vicky?'

'Yeah, it's me, Steve.'

'Long time, no speak. How . . . How've you been?'

'Good. Listen, I need to speak with you. Could you meet me somewhere today?'

Steve stayed silent for a few seconds. 'I-I'm married now, Vicky, I can—'

'No, Steve. It isn't like that. Don't worry, I'm married too. I need to speak to you about Mason Scott.'

'Mason Scott — the fat, weird lad from school?'

'Yes. It's important.'

'Meet me today in the Trafford Centre. Costa Coffee. I have something to tell you.'

* * *

Vicky arrived first and ordered a caramel latte at the counter before taking a seat near the back so she could sit and watch Steve walk in. It would also help Steve identify her by seeing her face staring in his direction. Although it had been over twenty-five years, she'd recognise him. He was odd-looking but attractive, with strange eyebrows sitting above dark brown eyes that seemed to suck you in. There was one time she'd felt attracted to him back in school, and she expected to feel a little something for him as she waited nervously.

Steve walked in with a bald head and smiled, spotting her immediately. He noticed the coffee in front of her and tipped his head towards the counter to indicate he'd get one before sitting down. She nervously watched him place his order.

A few minutes later, he came over, placing the tray on the table. As well as a coffee, he'd ordered a toffee doughnut.

'Would you like one?'

'No, I'm okay.' It was easy to see that, as well as losing his hair, he'd put on some weight since the last time they saw each other.

'You're looking well, Vicky,' he said, taking a sip of coffee.

She wanted to return the compliment but couldn't bring herself to lie. He didn't look well, not compared to when he was younger. Along with losing his hair, most of his looks had faded too, although the caring reflection in his eyes was still present.

'Thanks. I go to the gym a few times a week and watch what I eat.'

'I can see that.' He placed his coffee down on the wooden table. 'Your hair is different too. It was always darker in school.'

She smiled, raised a hand, and ran it through her short, blonde-dyed hair. 'Like it?'

He nodded. 'I do.' He took another sip. 'So, Mason Scott?'

They spoke about the police press conference for a short time, then she said, 'I'm worried. I'm worried he's out for revenge.'

Steve pondered that, tapping the side of his mug with his fingers. 'I received something in the post yesterday morning. I haven't told anyone about it.'

She frowned. 'What was it?'

'It was a small box.'

'What . . . was inside?' Her eyes narrowed in curiosity.

'There was a photo of a schoolboy.'

'Mason?'

He nodded. 'Yeah, it was Mason. There were hundreds of ants in there too.'

'Ants? Insect ants?'

'Yeah.'

She shivered at the thought of it. 'What did you do with them?'

'Emptied the box into the garden hoping they'll go away. I don't understand it really. At first I . . .' He fell silent, frowning as he looked away from her.

'What?'

'Remember what Callum did to him? With the ants?'

CHAPTER 53

Middleton Campsite
Twenty-seven years ago

It was getting late. The issue with Steve and Mason had been resolved. Mason had apologised for punching Steve in the face, and Steve had apologised for scaring him but pleaded that although he had been silly, he hadn't deserved to be attacked for it.

Mrs Andrews had serious words with everyone, reminding them that their actions represented not only themselves but the school as a whole. If anything happened again while they were there, they'd be sent home with a letter to their parents explaining why.

They were all in their tents now by orders from the teacher. As a result of their being an odd number, Mason was in a tent by himself, the one closest to the lake. The tent next to his was occupied by Neil and John, two pleasant students who didn't join in with the others when they bullied or made fun of him, so Mason was at ease. On the other side of Neil and John were Debbie and Mary, making immature noises towards his tent to wind him up, but he lay still with his eyes closed and hands over his ears.

'Just one more night,' he whispered to himself as he drowned out the sounds of Debbie and Mary, thinking about a holiday he'd previously been on with his parents in Spain. They hadn't been in several years, and he suddenly realised how much he had missed it.

He turned over, grabbed his torch from the tent's floor, and shone its light on his ancient, brown-strapped watch. It was almost 11 p.m. His eyes widened. He wasn't often awake at this time, not even at home. The immediate sounds around him seemed to fade away, and all that was left were the distant sounds of wildlife, including birds' wings flapping as they left trees nearby. Another sound he identified was from the lake, probably ducks or birds swooping down for a drink. He wasn't sure. His eyes began to feel heavy. Switching off the torch, he placed it down beside him so it was within reach if he needed it, and closed his eyes.

When he woke, it was dark, meaning it was still in the middle of the night. They had been told sunrise would be just before 6 a.m. and they were not to leave their tents before 7 a.m. unless they needed to use the toilet. Mrs Andrews made sure they all had means of telling the time; most of them had watches, so there was at least someone inside each tent who would know. Breakfast would be served at 8 a.m., and it was safe to say Mason was already looking forward to toast, butter, and jam by the fire.

Unsure why he woke, he leaned over and—

A sharp sound froze him still.

Coming from in front of him. At the opening of the tent.

He shuffled up and rested the weight of his upper body on his forearms. 'Hello?' he whispered, courteous of others and not wanting to wake them. No one answered. Had he dreamed it?

Then he frowned when he heard the sound of laughter follow. It wasn't directly outside his tent but close enough to be a class member. 'Hello?'

'Go to sleep, freak,' a distant voice told him, but he didn't hear it well enough to know who said it.

He picked up his torch and shone it down on his watch. It was nearly 3.30 a.m. The tent was freezing, as if cool air was somehow drifting inside, but he didn't know how that was possible as the zip was closed.

He sat up. 'H-hello?'

'Go to sleep . . .' the voice said again.

He lay back down and closed his eyes, struggling to sleep, but he couldn't hear the sounds of the others anymore. All the rustling birds were sleeping, and the lake was silent, with no footsteps of creeping animals.

As he was about to succumb to sleep, his feet started to itch. He frowned, using a toenail from one foot to itch the other, but the itching became worse, then he felt a sharp nip on the bottom of his foot. He wondered if a sharp twig or something similar had fallen into the tent as he entered earlier.

'What?' he mumbled, rubbing one foot off the other quicker.

Then he felt more nips, as if sharp pins were being inserted into his feet.

'God, what is that?'

The feeling grew up his legs quickly. He wriggled up and sat, picked up the torch from beside him, switched it on, and then aimed it inside his sleeping bag.

'What the hell?' he shouted, frantically squirming out from the confines of the sleeping bag. Hundreds of tiny black insects were at the bottom of the bag, where he noticed a small hole had been cut or torn, a way for them to get inside. He jumped to his feet, the beam of light dancing across the tent floor, shining on the countless number of insects.

'Ants?' he whispered, gobsmacked, realising they were responsible for the bites. A dizziness overcame him, and he didn't feel too stable on his feet.

Above his desperate panic and racing heartbeat, he heard the sounds of nearby laughter. And that's when he passed out.

When he woke up, he was outside, staring at the bright blue sky. He raised a tired hand to shield his eyes from the sun.

'You're awake, Mason,' a calm voice said, followed by footsteps. Above him, Mrs Andrews stood, blocking the sun. 'How are you doing, Mason?'

Mason stared wide-eyed, remembering the ants inside the tent, waving the torch around, and feeling the stinging in his legs, which had somehow gone.

'What? Did I pass out?'

'Yes, you did — are you okay?'

She leaned over him and stroked his face with the back of her hand. 'We heard shouting from your tent, and you weren't in your sleeping bag when we came in. You were on the ground with the torch in your hand.'

'The . . . the ants?'

'Yes, some ants had somehow got into your tent and left you nasty bites. We got the first aid kit out and put some bite cream on. How does it feel?'

Mason wanted to lift his head up and check the bites, but he still felt dizzy. 'The bites don't hurt so much, but I have a headache.'

'You just need to rest. The medic said the bites will go down soon.'

'I think someone put the ants in there. The bottom of my sleeping bag had a hole in.'

Mrs Andrews smiled thinly. 'Now Mason, why would anyone cut your sleeping bag and put ants inside?'

A few metres away, sitting on a log with Steve Adams, Callum McCauley was smiling to himself.

CHAPTER 54

Present day

It was the first time in days that Fisher had arrived home without it raining. The thought of making tea when she got home was a strong enough deterrent to swing by Subway and grab a sandwich and a coffee on her way back. She knew she'd have to warm it, but she wasn't bothered; it had been a while since she'd had a Subway.

After locking her door, she turned on the lamp in the hall, kicked off her shoes, and hung her coat on the hook near the door. She carried her food into the kitchen, warmed the sandwich, carried it over to the table, and sat down to eat it.

Regarding how the investigation was going, the only victory of the day was confirming the head found in the library yesterday belonged to Callum McCauley, which was what they'd expected.

So far, in terms of locating Mason Scott, the police had come up short. It was as if he didn't exist anymore.

Her phone rang. It was DI James.

'Hey, Tom.'

'April, I just want to thank you for the press conference tonight. I should have done it myself but I'm going through some things at the moment, so . . .' He trailed off for a moment. 'Thank you for stepping up.'

'No problem, boss. Is everything okay?'

'Yeah. Have a nice night. See you tomorrow.'

After she'd eaten, she went upstairs, stripped off, and got into the shower, allowing the stress of another day to run off her. She was never one for baths; it took too much time. She liked to get in, get out, and get on with other things. Life was too short to be getting all wrinkly in the bath.

A little while later, after speaking to Freya on the phone about the recent boyfriend issues and a brief call with her mother, she sat in front of the television in the living room. She wore loose grey jogging bottoms and a thick black long-sleeved top. She opted for coffee instead of wine because she knew wine wouldn't allow her to concentrate on what she needed to do. Her focus was on her laptop, searching through news articles of anything she could find on Chorlton High School and Mason Scott.

The city of Manchester wasn't safe until he was found and put behind bars.

Before clicking on the next link, her phone rang. She leaned over, picked it up. It was PC Baan.

'Ashleigh,' she answered.

'Hey, just checking in.' PC Baan had been asked to cover a late shift and sit at the property in case Mason Scott returned home. Another PC had done it earlier, and Baan would do it until midnight, when another PC would arrive.

'I'm assuming no sign yet?'

'Affirmative. No sign of anyone.'

'Okay. How long you got left?'

There was a brief pause when Fisher assumed Baan was checking the time. 'A few hours yet.'

'If anyone turns up, let me know, okay?'

'Of course. You'll be the first to know. What are you doing?'

'Laptop. Doing some digging.'

'You never heard the word *chill*?'

'There's no *chilling* in this game, you know that.'

They ended the call and Fisher placed her phone back beside the laptop. It wasn't long till she came across an article from a local newspaper about a mother who was outraged by what had happened on her son's school camping trip. As she read the article, she knew it was about what happened to Mason Scott at Middleton Camp Site. At the end of the article, it included her name.

Jackie Scott.

'Interesting.' They hadn't been able to find much on Mason Scott but finding his mother's name was a start.

Fisher logged onto the police database and searched Jackie Scott's name in the Police National Computer. There were two hits. A Jaqueline Scott living in Leeds, and another in Manchester.

'Bingo.' She clicked the Manchester one and waited for the profile to load. Any persons found on the PNC had previously committed some form of offense, making it easier for the police to find repeat offenders in the future. If Jackie Scott hadn't been in any trouble in the past and wasn't in the PNC, it would have been more difficult to find her.

The Jaqueline Scott based in Manchester had been done for speeding twice, once seven years prior and on another occasion three months ago. Within her profile, it contained an address.

She picked up her phone and rang DS Phillips, glancing at the clock on the wall. It was just past 10 p.m.

'April?' he answered, his tone hesitant, no doubt due to the lateness of the call.

'Sorry about the time, Matthew,' she said. 'I have an address for Jackie Scott, Mason's mother. We need to go see her immediately.'

'Give me the address, April.' He paused a moment. 'I'll meet you there.'

CHAPTER 55

Middleton Campsite
Twenty-seven years ago

Mason had spent most of the day resting by the lake, watching the others in the water in the canoes, splashing around and having fun. The guide, a young woman by the name of Angela, had told them numerous times that water could be very dangerous. Although they were there to enjoy themselves, they needed to take it seriously and listen to her instructions. All the teenagers looked to be having so much fun. It made Mason sad; he wished he could join in. Mrs Andrews had spent most of the time aiding him, ensuring he was hydrated and as comfortable as he could be. He was sitting in a deck chair they'd found in one of the cabins, and his legs were propped up on a thick log, cushioned by a folded blanket. A campsite medic had just applied more cream to his bites, which, compared to earlier that morning, seemed to be getting better, the colour less red and prominent.

The heat was in the thirties, and all the children had sun cream on, including Mason, who was starting to feel uncomfortable.

'Can I sit in the shade? It's too hot.'

The teacher nodded and helped him move to a spot under a nearby tree with thick overhanging leaves. 'This should be okay, Mason,' she assured him.

He thanked her and watched her return to the lake, where she cheered on the others.

Later that afternoon, once they had eaten a BBQ by the fire, Mason felt well enough to go on the nature walk, where they were led on a trail to find clues, leading to a cave where they'd find treasure. The treasure was a bag of chocolate. Some students thought it was silly, a task for kids, but most of them joined in, letting their inner youth run free and enjoying the treat at the end of it. Afterwards, they returned to the camp. Mason was chuffed he'd managed it but did well to ignore the comments about *ants only bite people who have things wrong with them* on the way around. He said he was happy to have his food and stay inside his tent to read. Mrs Andrews tried to persuade him to join in with the ghost stories around the fire, but he didn't want to. The time they got on the bus to go home tomorrow couldn't come fast enough for him; he wanted to go home.

When the fire was almost out, the students were told to return to their tents to sleep. Mason used his torch for reading and didn't yet feel tired, so he continued to do so until he was told to turn it off. He'd managed to get through half a book in only two hours, which wasn't unusual as he was a quick reader.

'Mason?'

He glanced up, looking at the side of the tent. It sounded like Mrs Andrews, standing close by.

'Mason, could you turn the torch off, please? It's sleep time.'

'Okay, Miss. Night.'

'Good night, Mason.'

Her footsteps faded, and the site was almost silent, apart from a few muffled conversations in other tents. He heard footsteps again somewhere in front of the tent.

'Hello?' said Mason.

'*Mason*,' someone said in a mocking voice. '*Mason, it's the lake monster.*'

'Go away.'

Whoever it was started making a ghost-like noise and scratching the outside of the tent's fabric. '*Maaaaason.*'

The zip at the front of the tent was quickly unzipped, and someone — Mason thought it was Steve Adams — leaned in and grabbed Mason's bag, the one containing his books and wash kit.

'Hey, that's mine!' he protested, shuffling up to his feet and going after him.

Outside, the fire was almost out, but Steve had taken three books from Mason's bag and held them above the fire, teasing him.

'No! Steve, no, please. Not the books.'

Steve smiled at him widely, then dropped the books into the fire.

'No!' screamed Mason, darting to the fire to rescue the books. On his way, he didn't see the log and tripped, falling into the fire face-first. The blood-curdling scream woke up everyone in the camp.

Mrs Andrews appeared. 'What on earth is going on?' That's when she saw Mason squirming in the fire. 'God, help him, someone!' She dashed over, grabbed his ankles, and pulled him free.

'Oh God, Mason.' She gasped, throwing her hands to her mouth, seeing the damage it had caused. His face was singed and burnt, the skin blotchy and bloody. In his hand were two burning books he'd managed to grab, but the third one was in the fire, blazing away, its pages curling and sizzling into ash.

CHAPTER 56

Present day

Phillips was closer to the address than Fisher so he arrived first, parking his Mondeo directly outside the house. While he waited, he scanned the property for any signs of life. The hallway light shone through the small square of glass above the door, and there was a dim light against the other side of the closed curtains in the living room.

'Yeah, it won't take long,' he told his fiancée Janice, who was on the car's hands-free system.

Ever since they'd got together, he'd always said that work would play a big role in his life. But knowing that didn't ease the pain of him putting it first over his own family.

Before she had hung up less than thirty minutes earlier, Fisher had mentioned that, as Mason hadn't shown up at his own house, there could be a chance he was hiding at his parents' place, so to wait until she arrived before knocking on the door.

Fisher had taken the ring road around the city centre and joined Bury New Road, until she took a right at Northumberland Street, then a left onto Cheltenham Crescent. A moment later, she pulled into Broom Lane, seeing Phillips's car parked on the left, facing away from her. She slowed, passed it, and pulled into a space outside the house next to it. She turned off the engine, opened the door, and climbed out, wishing she was still sitting in her living room, feeling the warmth from the radiator.

'Hey,' she said to Phillips, who'd got out and waited at the bonnet of his car.

They turned, stepped onto the path, and, side by side, went through the brick pillars onto the tarmacked driveway, which looked new and felt smooth underfoot. The house was a modern semi-detached property, with a pristine black front door with four small squares of glass in the centre, running from head to knee height. To the left of it was a frosted window, probably where a downstairs toilet was situated. The house extended to the left a few metres, but even without it, it would have been a decent size.

Phillips banged on the door, then took a step back. It was almost 10.30 p.m., but it didn't deter him from knocking loudly. The light through the door brightened as if another light had been switched on, then a figure appeared through the small glass squares.

Fisher noticed the peephole, assuming they were being watched through it.

'Who is it?' a cautious voice said from the other side.

'It's the police,' replied Fisher.

'Show me some ID.'

Fisher unzipped her coat, pulled her ID from the inside pocket, and then pressed it up against the highest square of glass so whoever was requesting it could see it clearly.

The door unlocked and was slowly opened to reveal the face of a man in his mid-sixties with thick grey eyebrows that sat above bright blue eyes, so blue they looked like contact lenses. His hair was half a head's worth and wispy, a little all over the place. He was thin, not having the usual paunchy middle like most men his age possessed. He studied both Fisher and Phillips, then frowned.

'Can . . . can I help you?'

'Mr Scott?'

'Yes?' He edged forward a fraction.

Fisher introduced them both, then added, 'Could we have a word — it's about your son.'

He thought about it for a moment. 'It's a bit late to knock on doors now, isn't it?'

'We apologise, but it's very important.'

Mr Scott considered her request and stepped aside. 'Suppose you best come in then, Detectives.'

In the doorway to the living room over to the right, a woman in a thick fluffy dressing gown stood with a scowl. 'Who the hell are you?'

'It's the police — they want to speak to us,' the man replied as he stepped further into the hallway. 'Please, come through to the kitchen. I'll get the kettle on.'

Fisher and Phillips followed him, smiling at Jackie Scott as they passed her.

'The police?' she said, trailing them.

'Please,' Mr Scott said, holding a hand towards the square table, 'have a seat.'

They did.

'What are your names?' Phillips asked.

'I'm Charles, my wife is called Jackie. What's this all about then?'

Fisher pulled a photo from her pocket, the picture of Mason when he was in school, the same one found on the library victims. She showed it to them. 'Is this your son, Mason Scott?'

Jackie Scott studied it, then nodded. 'It was when he was around thirteen or fourteen,' she informed them. 'Why do you have that?'

'I'm not sure if you've seen the recent news about the bodies found at three libraries around Manchester. This photo was found at all three crime scenes. We are confident that Mason is somehow involved.'

Jackie and Charles frowned, looking at each other for a moment before focusing on Fisher and Phillips.

'I don't understand,' said Jackie.

'We need to speak to Mason immediately. He's our prime suspect in the murders, unfortunately.'

'That'll be a tough task for you,' she countered.

'How so?' Fisher tilted her head.

'Mason's dead, Detectives. He committed suicide nearly two years ago.'

CHAPTER 57

It was after 11 p.m. when Steve Adams arrived at his dark empty home. He'd been for a meal with a prospective client who wanted to show him a portfolio of projects in the pipeline. He'd seen the tidiness and craftsmanship of his work and wanted Steve in on the action, informing him it would be three years' work. So when the multimillionaire asked him to go to dinner, although it wasn't really his thing, he couldn't really decline the offer.

His wife Lilly was out, sleeping over at a friend's house, helping her prep a hen do for next month in Spain.

Steve switched off the engine, opened the door, and stepped out in the evening frost. His driveway was covered in a thin layer of ice that glistened in the nearby streetlights.

'Jesus,' he gasped as he rubbed his hands and inserted the key into the door. Once inside, he turned on the light and removed his jacket. Although it was late, he decided to put the heating on for half an hour, give the house some warmth before going to bed, and dream about the upcoming project he'd been told about. He couldn't wait to tell Lilly about it, to say that for the next three years, he'd have a guaranteed income.

He went upstairs and jumped in the shower in his en suite to warm his bones before bed. He often did that; it was the easiest and quickest way to feel warm. As he got out, he smiled in the mirror, feeling good about the meal and the future. Maybe if he did a good job, this new millionaire friend would recommend him for more work.

Switching off the bathroom light, he hung his damp towel on the door and climbed into bed. He grabbed a book off the small table next to his bed and opened it where he'd left the bookmark. It was Duncan Bannatyne's autobiography. He read a part where Duncan, as a young boy, went into a paper shop, asking for a paper round. The shopkeeper had informed him that there was none available, but instead of giving up, young Duncan decided to go knocking on doors and made a list of people that didn't currently get a daily paper who wanted one, and returned to the shop, asking if he could have that round.

'Amazing,' muttered Steve, impressed at the man's business mind at such a young age.

It was after midnight when his eyes felt heavy. Knowing he had to be up at 7 a.m. for work, he dropped the bookmark into the page he was on and placed the book carefully on the table beside him. He looked at his phone for a few minutes, then double-checked his alarms were turned on, then, before switching off his bedside light, he glanced to the left where Lilly normally slept and realised he missed her. On the far wall, he noticed something out of place.

He tilted his head, noticing that one of her hardback books was missing off the shelf on the wall just right of the window. He assumed she must have taken it with her; she couldn't go anywhere without a book. He turned over, switched off the light, the room falling to almost darkness apart from the sliver of light coming in through the door open a few inches to the landing. Lilly always liked to have a light on, so if she had to go downstairs for any reason during the night, she didn't have to worry about falling down the stairs if it was dark. Even though Lilly wasn't there, Steve had become used to it too.

He closed his eyes, trying to drift off to sleep, but the image of the ants in the box entered his mind, along with the photo of Mason Scott from all those years ago. Mason's smile and innocent stare at the camera. He clamped his eyes shut, trying to block it out, wishing the growing feelings of guilt and sadness about what happened to Mason would go away.

Was he in danger?

Were Debbie Johnson and Mary Steadman murdered for revenge?

'A coincidence,' he whispered in hope. He turned onto his side and pulled the covers up to his chin, trapping his body heat inside.

'Shit.'

He jumped up, remembering he'd forgotten to turn the heating off. Sighing, he swung his legs out of the warm bed and went downstairs, recalling the thermostat control was in the kitchen near the microwave.

'Why don't you keep it upstairs next time?' he scolded himself.

He reached the base of the stairs and took a right, along the dark hall and into the kitchen, turned off the heating, then brought the thermostat with him so if he wanted to, he could turn it on when he woke in the morning. He rounded the base of the stairs and started to climb them, but stopped, hearing something behind him.

He slowly turned.

'Hello?' he whispered.

Silence.

'Hello?' This time louder.

Staring down into the darkness of the hallway, his eyes flittered around as he listened carefully. After half a minute, he smiled, surmising the house's structure was contracting in the winter cold. It was too late for ghost hunting, so he headed back to the bedroom, edged the door closed enough to let sufficient light in and climbed back into his warm bed.

It wasn't long before he succumbed to sleep, but a short while later, he opened his eyes and found himself staring at the ceiling. For some reason, the room seemed brighter. Frowning, he lifted his head a fraction, noticing the door was more open than he'd left it.

'What the fuck?' He rubbed his eyes, wondering if he had imagined it.

Maybe Lilly had come home early, and without waking, got into bed. He craned his neck to his right to the side she normally slept on, but the bed was empty.

It was then he noticed something in the background, something unusual that caught his eye. He gazed across the bedroom floor slowly, feeling his heartbeat rising, and noticed something standing in front of the window, a dim silhouette against the streetlights outside.

'God . . .'

The tall figure was dressed in dark clothing, but his head seemed weird as if not human. It was too big, too . . .

He didn't know. He couldn't describe it.

It wore a dark mask, the eyes prominent against the material.

'Jesus!'

He pushed himself up, his elbow joint cracking as he did so.

The figure stared silently at him and didn't move.

'Who are you?'

Whoever the person was remained silent.

Steve was desperate to turn on the light, but he didn't want to take his eyes off the mask, didn't want to be exposed and unprepared. He shuffled to his left while keeping his eyes on the figure, reaching with his left hand for the lamp switch, but he couldn't find it, instead feeling empty space.

'Fuck — who are you?' he screamed.

The figure didn't move.

He took a sharp breath, looked to the left to see where the lamp was, and flicked the switch.

His heart pumped through his chest.

When he focused back, the figure was on the bed with its arm outstretched towards him.

'Jesus!' he shouted, raising his arms to protect himself, but the figure was quick and strong, climbing onto the bed and mounting him, pinning his arms down with sheer strength.

'Get off me . . .' Steve wailed, flaying his arms. He felt something on his face, like a rough textured cloth being forced into his nose and mouth with so much force the pressure was against his bones. Whatever it was, it smelled horrific. He couldn't describe it; it was medicinal.

He tried to swat it away but quickly felt weak and lost consciousness a few seconds later.

* * *

The shape pushed the cloth into his pocket and sat back, watching Steve unconscious on the bed, his body distorted slightly, and smiled behind the mask. He climbed off the bed, then dragged Steve to the edge of it, bent down, and, taking a deep breath, grabbed one of his arms, placed it up over his neck, and lifted him up, so his soft stomach rested on his right shoulder.

He slowly carried Steve's body out to a small van, the weight of him draining his stamina. At the rear of the van, he managed to quietly open the rear door and lower Steve inside, his bare skin scraping on the cold, hard, boarded surface. Closing the door, he removed the mask and looked up to the sky, smiling, knowing the person he was doing it for would be watching down on him.

CHAPTER 58

Fisher and Phillips exchanged frowns, then focused on the words of Jackie Scott.

'He committed suicide two years ago?' repeated Fisher, her brows furrowing to a point at the top of her nose.

Jackie and Charles both nodded sadly.

'Unfortunately, yes,' said Charles, who rolled up his long sleeves to reveal a gold wristwatch. Fisher wasn't a watch expert but knew she hadn't seen one like it before. 'But I don't blame him,' he went on. 'It was awful what he went through.'

Fisher didn't know what was happening but had a stab in the dark. 'The camping trip?'

'That was part of it, but that was only a fraction. Yes, Mason had a shit time in school. God . . .' He looked away, shaking his head, his mind going back. 'School is tough for everyone, especially if you didn't fit in. Children can be horrible little twats.' The detectives could hear the tension in his voice, and he was physically tense too.

Fisher and Phillips nodded in understanding, waiting for more.

'It was the scars on his face. He couldn't deal with it. He . . .' Charles took a deep breath and looked at the ceiling.

'That boy wouldn't leave the house anymore. He wouldn't even step foot outside of his bedroom. What they did to him was monstrous.'

Fisher and Phillips stayed silent, weighing up Charles's body language as he stood and started making small circles, the topic of conversation obviously triggering anger inside of him. The kitchen was warm from the central heating, making him tired and agitated. At any moment, when dealing with the public, the detectives needed to determine any potential danger. A part of their training was to observe people's behaviour, and, if necessary, take action to reduce the danger as soon as possible. But they wanted to see how it played out, get to the bottom of what actually went on, and how Mason Scott had thought suicide was the only way out.

'After the incident at the campsite, we went to the paper to complain, saying how it should never have got to that point. The school knew he was being bullied. Jesus, every time he came home, I saw the sadness on his little face. We went in several times to complain, but nothing was done. I don't know if the teacher was too soft with the class, but they'd have been disciplined properly if I'd been the teacher. I can promise you that.'

Charles's colour reverted to pink instead of red, and he returned to the table and sat down calmly next to Jackie, who was watching him with teary eyes.

'It broke this family, what happened that night,' Jackie said, turning to Fisher and Phillips, exchanging glances between them. 'Like Charles said, since the fire burned Mason's face, he went in on himself even more and stayed in his room. He had a couple of weeks off school, giving the burns time to heal. But when he went back, it continued to happen, and no one did a fucking thing about it.'

There was a moment of angry silence.

'Even the goddamn police. They did nothing.'

Fisher focused on Charles, offering a thin-lipped smile. 'I can only apologise on behalf of the police, but I wasn't there to deal with the investigation.'

'Investigation?' Jackie opened her mouth wide. 'I wish there had been an investigation. The police weren't involved. When I realised nothing would be done about it, I contacted the police, who sent an officer to the school to have a chat with the headmaster. I don't think he wanted anything published in the paper, so we thought we'd go to the paper instead. We needed the world to know about what happened to Mason.'

Jackie fell silent. It was Charles's turn to speak.

'When he went into the last year at Chorlton, his isolation only worsened. Everyone stared at him in the corridor; even the teachers looked oddly at him. God, he felt so ugly.'

'What had the fire done to him?' asked Fisher.

Charles raised a finger, pointing to his left temple. 'There were burns from here—' he indicated across his face, towards the jawline, then ran a finger across his nose — 'to here. He looked a mess. His lips and nose were all bent and scarred. Out of place, misshaped. I felt so, so sorry for him. There's a picture somewhere, but I'm not getting it. Can't stand seeing it.'

Fisher couldn't blame him and didn't really want to see it herself. It was such a sad story.

'What did the school do about it at the time?'

Charles shrugged. 'Not enough.' He shook his head, going back in his mind. 'The headmaster investigated it at the time, spoke with Mrs Andrews, Mr Shorton, and the assistant — I can't remember her name, but nothing ever came from it. We were furious with it all. The headmaster said it was an accident, that Mason must have tripped into the fire by mistake. None of the teachers saw it . . . apparently.'

Fisher pursed her lips, knowing all too well how lies were covered up and justice wasn't always served.

'When he left school, he decided it was best not to go to college. He couldn't face being around people. We begged him to do something, told him he was special and the world needed him anywhere apart from the bloody bedroom, but all he would do was sit up there reading his books. In a way, I think the books kept him isolated, but if it hadn't been for them, he'd have been completely lost.'

'What did Mason do after that?'

'We hired a social worker to come to the house to speak with him, hopefully making him see that scars were only skin deep, and what mattered was inside. She was lovely, to be honest.' Jackie angled to Charles. 'Wasn't she?'

He nodded. 'She worked wonders with him. He was starting to feel good about himself again. He started to accept what had happened, that there were nasty people in life, and that life was tough, and staying indoors and feeling sorry for himself would only make things worse. Then he started going out again. He got in touch with a few friends from school and started going to the cinema, that type of thing. He enjoyed his books and films too. But it wasn't long until the name-calling started again, even in his late teens. So he became a recluse, bound to his bedroom again.'

'And that's when he bought the mask,' added Jackie, shaking her head.

'The mask?'

'I don't know where he got it from, but he got hold of an ant mask. Aww, it was awful. Had these big white eyes and a weird-shaped head. He used to sit in his room with it on, reading his books.'

'And that's when he became distant from us. Didn't come down for tea anymore, just ate in his room. Charles and I didn't know what to do with him. But eventually—' she paused a beat — 'the isolation must have got the better of him because he started going for walks to get some air. He waited for Halloween night and went out with the ant mask on. He felt safe doing it, but as the days passed, he continued to wear it. Everywhere he went, he got stares, no doubt people wondering why a grown man was wearing an ant mask. Then the name-calling became worse. And because he put on weight from being at home and not doing much exercise, he was known as the "Fat Ant Man" around the streets.'

'How long did this go on for?'

'As long as we can remember,' she said, tilting her gaze on Charles, who regretfully nodded in agreement.

'I'm sorry, I know this is hard to speak about,' Fisher said softly, 'but what made him take his own life?'

Charles dipped his head at the mere thought of it, and his silence told Jackie that he didn't want to talk about it.

'When he found the website about him.'

'What was that?'

'At this point, he'd got a job at a local DIY store, had been there for a couple of years. He used to wear the mask to travel to work and travel home, but he'd become comfortable enough with the owner, who was a lovely guy, to take off the mask and work the stock out the back, so he didn't see many customers. He managed to save up enough money to put a deposit down on a house not too far from here. He wanted his independence, he said, and we couldn't argue with that. Being stuck at home with his mam and dad wasn't healthy at his age. The owner, bless him, said he deserved a chance, and if Mason felt better doing the work out the back, then he still should be given the opportunity to work and earn money like anyone else. I went round to his house to check up on him. I made a conscious effort to do that most days. The place, as usual, wasn't very well maintained, but I let him make it his own and live how he wanted to. After all, it was his house. When I went in, I heard something from upstairs. I thought someone had died the way he was going on. Anyway, I went into his room, and he was sobbing, staring at himself in the mirror.' He paused a moment. 'And that's when I saw all the blood.'

CHAPTER 59

'The blood?' Phillips asked, frowning.

'He was holding a razor blade in his hand, scraping at his face to try and remove the scars. My God, it was a mess. His face was covered in blood, his clothes — it was all over his room.' Charles slapped the table with the palm of his hand. 'The ant mask was on the floor next to him.'

As Jackie's eyes welled, she raised a finger to wipe away her tears.

Charles went on. 'I managed to grab the razor off him and persuaded him to go to the hospital. The plastic surgeons did their best, but as you can imagine, he looked even worse. He couldn't face it anymore, not even with the ant mask on.'

'You mentioned a website?'

'That was the final straw. Some bastards created a website just to make fun of him, and he found it.'

Phillips sighed heavily and looked down at the table. 'That's awful,' he said quietly.

'It was for him, yes,' countered Charles, nodding at the detective.

'And that's when he decided to end his life,' Jackie told them. 'It's coming up to two years on 16 January, next month.'

Fisher and Phillips weren't interested in them going over the details of how it happened. It wasn't necessary. Fisher thought about today's date being 15 December, knowing it was only a month away.

'We went to the police about the website. Guess what?'

Fisher stared silently at Charles, waiting for the answer she already had in her head.

'They did nothing about it. It wasn't their concern, apparently. They didn't have enough resources to deal with it at the time. The online stuff was dealt by another department. The list of excuses was pitiful. So excuse me if I'm not warming to you two, because all the police have done in my experience is absolutely fucking nothing.' He slammed a palm down on the table again, but neither detective flinched. Fisher thought about apologising once more on behalf of the police, but it would do no good, only irritate him further, presumably.

'Can I ask why you're here again? It's past half ten. And based on what we've already told you, you won't be speaking to Mason any time soon,' Jackie said, turning to the clock on the wall.

'Based on evidence, his address is now a crime scene.'

'A crime scene?'

Fisher nodded at Charles.

'What's happened?'

'We discovered body parts in the kitchen, all cut up in a pool of blood under the table. On top of the table was a set of sharp kitchen knives. Forensics have been to the house, assessed the scene, and taken the remains back to the lab at the station to check for DNA.'

Jackie raised a hand to her open mouth. 'I-I don't understand.'

Before Phillips could reply, someone entered the room. They all turned to see a woman standing there staring at them. Fisher guessed her to be in her early thirties.

'What's going on?' she asked, frowning towards Fisher and Phillips at the table.

'The police are here about something,' Charles told her.

She folded her arms. 'About what?'

'It doesn't matter, Julie. You go back in there and watch some TV. We'll be in soon.' Jackie smiled at her, nodding in the direction of the living room. Julie slowly turned, disappearing into the hallway.

'Sorry about that,' said Jackie, still smiling.

'Who might that be?' Fisher asked.

'That's our daughter.' She kept her voice low. 'She's struggling with going outside and other things. She's a little depressed at the moment.'

When neither Charles nor Jackie expanded much on that, Phillips said, 'We don't understand about the body either, Mrs Scott. That's why we're here.'

Fisher went on. 'Forensics have taken prints from the house and are examining them as we speak. Is the house still in Mason's name?'

Charles nodded. 'Yes. We put it up for sale a year ago but didn't have much interest then, so we took it off. We'll sell it eventually. Perhaps local people knew it was Mason who lived there and it put them off.' He shrugged.

'When was the last time either of you went to the house?' asked Fisher.

Charles blew a puff of air in thought. 'God, I don't know. Maybe six months ago. I used to go frequently to check for mail, but as time passed, it's become less and less.'

'So, besides you two, does anyone else have access to the house? Because it's evident someone is living there.'

Both Charles and Jackie scowled.

'I don't think that's possible,' Jackie said.

'Unless he's come back,' said Charles.

Jackie turned his way. 'He would have said.'

'Who's come back?' pressed Fisher.

'His brother Richard,' Jackie explained. 'When Mason committed suicide, Richard couldn't handle it anymore and moved away as far as he could, fearing he would do something stupid to the people who'd done this to him. The last time we saw him was at Mason's funeral.'

'Where is he living?'

'We tried to contact him, but he ignored us, blaming us for the way Mason was. He said if we'd been better parents, Mason would still be alive.' Her tone suggested it was painful for her to say the words. 'He wrote us a letter once, left his address on there. Hold on.' She stood up, walked across the white-tiled floor, and opened one of the top cupboards, then rummaged for a few moments and picked out an envelope.

Returning to the table, she sat, opened the flap, and pulled a letter out. 'Here it is.'

The detectives read the letter, Fisher reading it twice. It mentioned how disappointed Richard was, blaming them for Mason, which ultimately led to his suicide. At the bottom, he'd left his new address and had signed it John Harper.

'John Harper?' Fisher said, with a frown. 'Who's John Harper?'

They both shrugged. 'The only thing I can think is that he changed his name. The thing is, it wasn't just Mason that was a challenge when they were growing up. If anything, Richard was worse. He had serious behavioural issues, to the point we had to remove him from school due to the constant trouble he was in. Disrupting the class, fighting, swearing at teachers — you name it. We did our best for him and Mason but we don't know what else we could have done.'

'Do you think Richard still has a key for Mason's house?'

'It's possible. He always went there to see Mason when he was alive.'

CHAPTER 60

Fisher and Phillips thanked Charles and Jackie for their time and apologised for it being so late. In turn, the couple wished the detectives good luck in getting to the bottom of whatever was going on and happily handed the address over for their son Richard, along with a mobile number they had last contacted him on.

'Thanks for coming, Matthew. Apologise to Janice for me. I bet she isn't happy about all this.'

Standing by his car, with the nearby streetlamp gently illuminating his face, he shrugged. 'She knows what the job entails, April.'

'Everything okay, Matthew?'

'I think she's getting sick of it,' he explained. 'Sick of all the hours I'm doing.' He looked away for a moment. 'I know she finds it hard at home with Dominic. God, when I'm looking after him, I'm pulling my hair out half the time, so I can imagine it would be hard almost doing it on your own.'

'You're there on weekends, though,' Fisher said, trying to lighten the situation.

'I am, but half the time, I'm thinking about the job, about what cases we have going on. I find it hard to switch off, April. But being that way, I guess I'm not giving them my full attention. Not being the father I could be. Or the husband, for that matter.' He nodded several times, mentally collecting himself. 'I'll try harder with them, make some changes.'

'You get yourself home, Matthew. Get a good night's sleep. If Dom wakes up, you make sure you wake up first, give her a rest.'

'I'll do my best.'

They shared a knowing, tired smile before Phillips unlocked his car and opened his door. Phillips watched her go. 'See you bright and early.'

She turned to him. 'Not sure about bright based on today's weather, but it will be early. Good night.' She waved, took a few steps to reach her Volvo, and climbed inside. It was interesting speaking with Mason's parents about what had happened and the unfortunate suicide. Also, to know he had a brother had thrown a spanner in the works, certainly opening up the possibilities of where the investigation was heading. If, in fact, Richard — or John Harper — still had a key, there was a good chance, based on what they had found at Mason's house, that he was living there. If that were true, he was the man behind the library murders — he had to be.

She found Baan's number, pressed CALL, and put the phone against her head.

'April,' she answered.

'Hey, Ash, how're you holding up?'

'No wonder the police in the American films sit and eat doughnuts. There's literally nothing to do.'

'No sign of anyone, I'm guessing?' Fisher smiled.

'Not a single soul has even walked past. What's happening anyway? You're phoning late.'

'We got an address for Jackie and Charles Scott — Mason's parents. Just found out that Mason committed suicide almost two years ago.'

'You're joking?'

'I'm not.' Fisher shuffled in her seat to get more comfortable and put her seat belt on with her left hand while she

276

held the phone in her right. 'Turns out he has a brother called Richard who goes by the name of John Harper now.'

'Okay, go on . . .'

'He used to have a key to the house you're watching, and as it stands, he's our number one suspect in this murder inquiry.'

'John Harper — never heard the name. You want me to check it out?'

'It's okay. I'll do it when I get home. You sit tight for—' Fisher went silent while she checked her watch — 'another hour or so and get yourself home.'

'Okay, I've made a note of all the cars near the house and checked them on the database. No matches for Mason Scott or anyone by that name. I'll run through them again while I wait, see if John Harper pops up.'

'See, Ashleigh, that's why you're there, thinking for yourself and being proactive.' Fisher smiled to herself, proud of her.

'Thanks, April.'

'I know it's a lot to ask, but do you think if I speak to Inspector Thorne, he'll let you come in for dayshift tomorrow?'

'Call him and ask. I'll be happy to if he agrees, April.'

'Good. Thanks for doing this tonight. You know I wouldn't have asked if we weren't desperate.'

'Thank Inspector Thorne, not me. He's my gaffer. I just do as he asks.'

'Thank you anyway. I'll see you tomorrow.'

* * *

Fisher got home around twenty minutes later. It was nearly 11.30 p.m. when she removed her coat and made a quick coffee before heading into the living room and opening her laptop. She searched the PNC firstly for Richard Scott, which came up with nothing, then typed the name into various social media accounts, which brought up plenty of results, but none based in Manchester. Then she tried a search on

Google. Among many others, there was a carpenter called Richard Scott who lived somewhere in California, and an electrician based in the town of Middlesbrough in the North East of England. She tried the Police National Database, a separate system to the PNC, and some information came up for Richard Scott, a man aged forty-two from Manchester. His address was the same as his parents'.

'Bastard,' she muttered to herself.

Moving on, she tried the name John Harper in the PNC and PND, but nothing came up from a policing perspective. She tried social media, and again, plenty of names and profiles appeared, but nothing Manchester-based or anyone within one hundred miles.

She sat back, picked up her phone, and listened to the conversation with Jackie and Charles Scott again, hearing the phrase 'Fat Ant Man', then sat up, typed that into Google, and hit send.

There was a web page dedicated to it.

'Bingo,' she said, clicking on the link. The page header was *The Fat Ant Man*, along with a photo taken of Mason Scott close to what looked like his parents' house from someone sitting inside a car.

The description of the page read:

The Fat Ant Man, Mason Scott. To all who knew him, this weirdo should have been dead a long time ago.

Fisher frowned, assuming the page had been updated once he'd taken his life.

Mason was a weirdo, and a downright waste of space. He didn't deserve to be here.

Further down, there was a post from two years ago from *AdamS*, which read, '*Hey guys, who's got some photos of the Fat Ant Man?*' Fisher assumed this to be Steve Adams.

Below the question, there were replies by multiple people, posting photos of Mason walking the streets, some walking into a shop, and another from behind as he left work. Fisher scrolled down the photos, studying the names.

AdamS.
Cal Mac.
Pat Keet.
VikkiT.
DJohn.
Msteeeed.

'God . . . that's awful.' She went down the list and phoned DS Phillips, who, by now, would be in bed.

'He-hello?' he said, his voice stuck in his throat.

Fisher knew she'd woken him up. 'Listen, Matthew, sorry—'

'*Who the fuck is that?*' a frustrated voice said nearby.

'Hold on, Jan. Give me a minute.'

There was a rustle, a door opening, and a few footsteps. 'Sorry, April. What is it?'

'I'm so sorry it's late, Matthew. Please apologise to Janice. I haven't woken Dominic, have I?'

'No, no, he's asleep. What is it?'

Fisher could hear him losing his patience.

'Can you send me the photo you took of Mason's class at Chorlton High School? I need to check the names, please.'

'Found anything?'

'Yeah, maybe. Send it over if you can. I'm so sorry it's late. If I find something, I'll let you know first thing tomorrow.'

They ended the call and she got the photo via WhatsApp within a minute. She used two fingers to enlarge the names on the three lines. She wrote down Steve Adams, Callum McCauley, Patricia Keeton, Victoria Thomson, Debbie Johnson, and Mary Steadman.

She sighed, studying the names, knowing that Debbie, Mary, and Callum had already been killed and displayed at three libraries. If this was all about revenge and someone had seen this page, it was safe to say that Steve, Victoria, and Patricia were in serious danger.

CHAPTER 61

Fisher couldn't sleep very well. At 4 a.m., she decided to get up, put on her dressing gown, and go downstairs to make herself a cup of tea. It was an unusual thing for her to do, but she was feeling in an unusual mood. While she sipped the hot liquid, sitting at the kitchen table, she scrolled through her emails in case she'd missed something the day before. Then she grabbed her laptop from the living room, brought it back into the kitchen, and researched Steve Adams, Victoria Thomson, and Patricia Keeton.

She managed to locate Steve Adams through an online directory. According to the site, he worked as a painter and decorator. He had his own limited company, trading under Adams Decor. She clicked on a social media page where he'd posted dozens of photos of his recent jobs, along with reviews from delighted customers. She made a note on her phone of his address and postcode.

Moving on to Victoria Thomson, the search engine brought up several profiles, the first showing photos of a woman doing various activities in Manchester. It was clear to Fisher, judging by the effort put into her pictures, she was either a photographer or a keen hobbyist. She searched her name through the PNC and PND, finding some information on the latter and an address to go with it. Again she made a note and moved on to the next name.

Patricia Keeton was more of a recluse than Victoria. It seemed she didn't have any social media accounts whatsoever, but there was a newspaper article dated five years ago about some community work she'd done in her street with some of the other neighbours. They had dug up a few trees, replanted them, and helped with a building project to serve vulnerable children.

'Nice touch,' Fisher said, scrolling down the article.

Again, the PNC didn't have a hit, but the PND brought up two results, one in Manchester, and the other in Birmingham. She thought it would be wise to note the Manchester address and go from there.

By the time she looked up at the clock, it was just after 6 a.m. — where had the time gone? With no point in going back to sleep, she went upstairs, took a quick shower, and got into a new selection of her usual work attire. In her wardrobe were four of the same sets she changed each day. She applied deodorant and sprayed some perfume on her neck.

Not wanting to disturb DI James too early, she waited till 7 a.m. to ring him, informing him about the Fat Ant Man website she'd seen late last night. She told him her intentions before going to the office would be to go to Steve Adams's house first to warn him he could be in danger.

'DS Phillips going with you?'

'Haven't spoken with him yet,' she replied. 'You were my first call.'

'Ring him,' he said. 'We'll get Baan and Jackson there with you too. I'll arrange that. Let me know what happens.'

Before Fisher could reply, informing him that PC Baan had been doing the late shift at Mason Scott's house, he hung up. If James phoned Inspector Thorne and requested Baan, she'd have no choice. But if Fisher was being honest, it would be nice to have Baan there, someone she knew would have her back if things went south.

After a brief chat with Phillips, she locked her door and left the house by 7.30 a.m. Luckily, it wasn't raining, nor was it cloudy. The sun was somewhere on the horizon and on its way up, the dim orangey glow to her right, which made her smile.

'Good morning, Detective,' said a voice so close it startled her, making her nearly drop her laptop bag.

'God . . .' She turned to her neighbour Raymond, standing there with a stupid smile, wearing a long coat that ran to his knees and looked more for rain than warmth. 'Morning, Raymond. What are you doing standing on the street scaring people at this time?'

His smile faded into something serious. 'It's a free country. I can stand where I want.'

She unlocked her car, opened her door, leaned in, and put her laptop bag over the gearstick onto the passenger seat. She turned back.

'That's true.'

He's so weird, she thought.

He raised a finger as if pointing directly above him. 'Can I ask a question?'

'Of course, it's a free country, like you said.'

'How are you getting on with your current investigation, Detective?'

Weighing up his question with caution, she decided to play dumb. 'Investigation?'

'You know, the library murders.'

There was an awkward silence between them until a car went by, the sound of the engine and tyres on the road filling the gap while they stared at each other.

'Have you got a television, Raymond?'

He nodded.

'Then you can watch the press conference I did on Wednesday night. That will give you all the information you need.' She climbed into her car, then faced him again. 'If you'll excuse me, I have work to do.'

'You won't catch him . . .'

She frowned, closing her door, but pushed it open again. 'Sorry?'

'You have a good day, DS Fisher.'

He grinned, turned slowly, and ambled back up the street whistling a familiar tune, but Fisher couldn't think of where it was from.

CHAPTER 62

Fisher arrived at Steve Adams's house in less than ten minutes, fortunate to miss the manic rush hour and pleased she had. She turned the engine off and checked in her rear-view mirror for any sign of Phillips, knowing he'd be coming from the same direction. The road was clear and bright, the moisture on the surface glistening off the low-rising sun.

Parked a few houses along from Adams's house, she watched for any sign of life. It was early enough for people to still have their lights on, but it sat in darkness. There was a small white van in the driveway, with modern, italic font saying 'Adams décor' on the side. A cartoonish logo of a paintbrush and a smiley face were cleverly woven into each other.

A few moments later, PC Baan and PC Jackson arrived, coming down the road she was facing. She gave Baan a small wave as they passed looking for a space beyond Fisher. The street was quite full; no doubt the majority of people hadn't left for work yet. Her phone rang. It was Phillips.

'Hi,' she answered.

'Be with you in two minutes. Had to deal with one of Dom's tantrums before I left.'

Ten minutes later, once they'd all arrived and parked, they met on the driveway of the exquisitely presented semi-detached house. As you would expect, the paintwork on the windows and doors was second to none. It was nice when people took pride in their homes, but after all, what professional painter and decorator would stand for having a house that looked below par?

Taking the lead, Fisher knocked on the door. Instead of the knock vibrating against the hardwood, the sound faded, and the door opened an inch.

Fisher frowned at Phillips, who looked back to Baan and nodded, holding his hand out. She understood what he was after, and grabbed her baton, handing it to him.

'Thanks,' he said, taking it in his right hand and focusing back on the door. He turned his body so his left side was leading and tensed his grip on the handle. 'I'll go first.' He edged the door open further and stepped inside the dark hallway.

'Hello?' he said loud and clear. 'Is there anyone in here?' He waited for a beat, then added, 'This is the police.' After a few seconds of silence, he continued into the house. PC Jackson stepped behind him with his baton extended too.

'You search in there,' he whispered to Jackson, who nodded and shifted to the left to investigate the living room. Phillips went straight ahead towards the kitchen and had a look around. No sign of Steve Adams or that anyone had been there recently. No empty coffee mugs out and no plates with crumbs on the worktop. Nothing in the washing-up bowl. To the left, a door led to another room — the dining room, judging by the table. The lack of furniture made the room feel almost clinical.

Fisher and Baan appeared in the kitchen doorway, observing the house carefully as they moved through it. Phillips backed into the kitchen and turned their way, their eyes meeting.

'All clear down here,' he informed them, then pointed up to the ceiling. 'We'll try up there.'

Fisher nodded, stepped aside to let him pass, then trailed Phillips to the base of the stairs, where he stood with Jackson.

This time, with a higher risk they might encounter someone now that downstairs was cleared, he let Jackson go upstairs first.

PC Jackson stopped to check the base of his shoes before stepping on the cream carpet.

'Come on, this isn't the Ritz,' blasted Phillips, winking at him in a way that suggested to get on with it. 'Let's go . . .'

After searching every room in the house, their conclusion was that only the bedroom appeared messy.

The question in their minds still remained: where was Steve Adams?

'Steve Adams, are you here?' Fisher asked on the landing of the tranquil house.

PC Baan was still in the bedroom.

'April?'

'Yeah?'

'In here.'

Fisher went to the bedroom, noticing Baan bent over by the side of the bed, looking at something that had piqued her interest. 'Found anything?'

'Yup.' She stood, snapped on some gloves Fisher had given her before they entered the house, and leaned over to grab something from under the bedside table. 'Looks like a phone.' She stood, showing Fisher. 'Unusual for anyone to leave without their phone.'

Fisher cocked her head to look around the room. 'Maybe he's gone for a run?' Considering what had happened recently, that seemed unlikely.

Baan pointed to her own arm. 'Most people run with their phones strapped to their arm nowadays.'

Fisher shrugged, then a thought came into her mind.

Baan knew the look. 'What is it?'

Fisher found a number for Adams Decor on her phone and rang it. If the phone Baan had found was a spare, there could be a chance he had his other phone on him. She clicked CALL but knew in her head the phone in Baan's hand would start ringing at any moment and sighed heavily when it did.

'To be honest, I think we're too late. I think he's already in trouble. We need to call it in.'

Baan nodded in agreement, suspecting the same. 'I think that's wise.'

CHAPTER 63

Steve Adams opened his eyes and blinked several times as they adjusted to the darkness. There was a small amount of natural light coming from somewhere but it was minimal. He was naked, on his side, staring at one of the walls of the studded room.

He shifted up quickly, remembering the last time he had been conscious; the figure in the bedroom on top of him. He snapped his neck around, searching the space, checking if anyone was there. Luckily there wasn't, but the fact he was somewhere he didn't recognise didn't ease his fear.

'Where am I?' he whispered, then wearily climbed to his feet. He looked down and realised his clothes were missing, even his underwear.

He saw the door in front of him, frowned as he went over to it, and tried the handle, but it was locked. Above him, the dark, metallic corrugated sheets that made up the roof hung over him like a prison, robbing him of daylight. Judging by the gloomy grey skylight, he assumed it was the following morning. Had he really been unconscious for that long?

'Hello?' he shouted, his voice echoing around the studded room, then around the warehouse. The echo that returned informed him how ample the space was.

'Where the—?'

To his right, high up, were the sounds of heavy footsteps. Frowning, he turned, subconsciously covering himself with cupped hands, watching four people appear on some kind of suspended walkway, the structure supported by beams coming from the roof.

'What the fuck is this?'

The moving figures didn't answer; they just continued walking straight until they were level with Adams. When the lights came on, he shielded his eyes, and refocused on the silent figures, scowling at their weird masks.

'Who are . . . who are you people?'

The faces behind the masks smiled, hearing his voice crack in fear.

'Hello, Steve. Welcome,' said the voice on the speaker to his right, the sound startling him as it crackled and hissed. 'We have an easy task for you.'

'I-I don't understand,' he replied so quietly no one heard it. 'Who is this? What's going on?'

'All you need to do is go to the box, open it, and follow the instructions. It's quite simple.'

He scanned the room and noticed the box in the corner, near the door.

'Well, go on, it won't open itself,' the voice encouraged him.

He stood still, unsure what was going on. 'Box?' Reluctantly, he padded over to it, his cold feet on the hard concrete, and bent down on one knee. He gingerly lifted the lid and looked inside, seeing the photo of Mason Scott as a schoolboy and a key beside it. He disregarded the photo, not seeing why it would help him, and picked up the key. He immediately dashed for the door, but hesitated, unsure about the electronic box attached to the handle. After some thought, he put the key in the lock, and turned it. He pushed down the handle and went to the next room.

The figures moved down the walkway with him.

In the next studded room, a wooden chair with wide armrests, the type you'd see in an overpriced garden centre, was located in the centre of the space.

'I'd like you to take a seat,' the voice on the speaker told him.

'Why?' he shouted.

'Because you'll die of exposure if you don't do as I say.'

He angled his gaze up to the figures. 'The fuck you wearing those stupid masks for anyway? Why are you hiding your faces?'

They remained silent, smiling to themselves.

With reluctance and out of ideas, he observed the chair and grabbed the back of it, trying to drag it over to one of the walls to climb, but it wouldn't move.

A laugh broke out on the speaker. 'Do you think we'd make it that easy for you? Sit down, Mr Adams.'

'What happens if I don't — why don't you come down here and make me?' He smiled thinly.

'I'm sorry that it's come to this.'

'To what?' He then felt a sharp prick in his chest, jolting him back a few inches.

He stared down.

It was a dart. The point of the object, roughly an inch long with a red flight, had pierced the skin on his chest.

Desperate to remove it, he threw a hand up and pulled it out quickly. Blood appeared where the dart's tip had punctured the layers of skin and seeped down his chest, onto his stomach, then onto his genital area.

'What th . . .'

Before he finished his sentence, he fell back into the chair, unconscious.

* * *

When he opened his eyes, he felt colder than before, shivering profusely. He scanned the room; something was different. In front of him, something metallic, built on some kind of stand, caught his eye.

Squinting, he tried to lean forward but realised he couldn't, and his wrists were tightly pinned to the arms of the chair with some kind of metal brace, roughly two inches thick. Whatever the dart was, it had put him to sleep. He attempted to move both arms and failed; they were stuck solid.

'Fuck!' he screamed, then wriggled and squirmed, immediately becoming angry. 'Let. Me. Out.'

He tried to move his legs, but they were also bound by something similar. He had no idea why this was happening and would do anything to get out. He started to feel claustrophobic. He attempted to lunge forward, but something sharp dug into his chest, a large version of the braces around his wrist, this time tight up against his ribcage.

'Shit. Shit!'

The masks on the walkway started to laugh hysterically, which began to piss him off. He glared up at them, but his head didn't fully turn because something was wrapped firmly around his throat too.

The laughter from up on the walkway continued, along with the huffing and puffing from Steve Adams, until he'd run out of energy, his body becoming flaccid and weak. He breathed heavily, inhaling the cold, stagnant warehouse air.

'Please . . .' he begged. 'Let me go.'

'Now you have finished trying to get out of the chair, Steve,' said the voice on the speaker, 'allow me to inform you of your challenge.' There was a pause. 'In front of you, you will see an arrow pointing in your direction. Down by your right hand, you'll see a button that you can reach with your fingertip. You need to press it.'

His tired eyes fell to his right hand, and there, just like the voice said, was a small black square with a red button.

'What, wh . . .' He could barely speak, exhausted from trying to wriggle free.

'What's that, Steve?'

'What . . . what will happen if I press the button?'

'The locks that are holding you will be released.'

Adams didn't respond. Instead, he frowned, knowing it wouldn't be so easy. 'I don't believe you.'

'But there's a catch . . .'

Steve scowled.

'I'll clarify it. As soon as you press the button, the locks that are holding you will release and you'll have exactly three seconds to move out of the way before the arrow is fired at you. Do you fancy your chances, Steve Adams?'

A glimmer of hope rose inside his mind.

He could do a lot in three seconds. If all the locks opened simultaneously, three seconds should give him enough time to get away from the arrow and the chair. He looked down to study the chair and the wires running through the structure, going to and from the mechanical locks. In front of the chair, a thicker wire ran across the floor and up the wooden frame that supported the arrow mechanism facing him. It looked like a professional setup, not that Steve Adams knew much about it.

'What's around my throat? I can feel something.'

'It's something to keep your head in place to make you realise how serious this is.'

As if the solid leg, wrist, and chest braces weren't enough to make him realise that.

'Well, Steve? Three seconds is a long time.'

Steve managed to calm himself down and think about it. 'Okay.'

'Whenever you're ready . . .'

He took a deep breath, stabbed at the button, anticipating the locks to open that exact second. He tensed, ready to break free, but despite the lock opening, he heard something mechanical near his head coming from directly behind him.

A ticking sound.

The metal cable tie wrapped around his throat became taught, nipping harder against his skin as the seconds ticked by. He gulped hard, fighting off the sudden feeling of claustrophobia taking over him, but the tighter it became, the more he fought it.

Tick, tick, tick.

He didn't know that the metal strap was fixed to a mechanical device on the back of the chair, just behind his head, and was slowly pulling the strap tighter.

He tried to gulp, but the metal started cutting his skin. He couldn't breathe now.

There was an attempt to say something, but it was a gargled mess. He started coughing, retching, and wriggling, though he could do nothing. His face changed colour.

The figures watched in awe as Steve's throat was crushed; every second was more entertaining than the last.

His face became a darker shade of purple, and the whites in his eyes started to fill with minuscule red blood veins. Blood appeared where the metal tie had broken the skin.

More blood came from the opening wound, oozing down onto his chest.

The mechanical device continued to tick and draw the strap tighter and tighter until it slowed when it hit a bone. By this point, Steve had passed out, and he couldn't feel any more pain.

The device possessed so much power it pulled through the bone and continued to shear the tendons, muscles, and skin until, twenty-two seconds later, the cable tie reached the rear of the headrest, and the ticking stopped. At this point, his head was totally detached from his body and slowly slid off his shoulders, falling onto the cold, hard ground with a thud before coming to rest. His still bloodshot eyes and purple face stared at the growing pool of blood underneath the chair supporting his headless body.

CHAPTER 64

Fisher and Phillips returned to the station in their own cars. By the time they got there, they'd missed the morning meeting with DI James, who'd informed everyone, including the forensic team, what was happening in the recent investigations. Although he was staying positive, it was clear he was showing signs of stress and needed to find the person responsible for the murders.

If it wasn't for James asking to see Fisher, she'd have gone straight to Patricia Keeton's house. After all, she wasn't only in Mason Scott's class, she was on the camping trip and was involved with the website, so if someone was seeking revenge, she was in grave danger.

They both walked in together after arriving at a similar time. Once through reception, they split up, Phillips heading down the corridor into the main workspace while Fisher took a right down another corridor towards James's office.

She slowed her walk and tilted her head to listen if he was on the phone. After hearing nothing, she rapped on his closed door. 'Boss?'

'Come in,' he said.

As she entered, she saw a neat pile of paperwork on the desk beside a mug of coffee, the scent lingering in the air as she got closer. Sitting behind the desk, he was frowning at a computer screen, focusing on something that Fisher couldn't see.

'Please,' he said, looking up with a smile. 'Have a seat.' He motioned to the chair on the other side of the desk and she sat down.

'Updates?'

'We went to Steve Adams's house. He wasn't there.'

'Go inside?'

She nodded. 'Yeah. Door was open.'

DI James frowned. 'Strange.'

'Checked the whole house. Found his phone there. Think it's too late.'

'Could he be at work?'

'Perhaps, if he doesn't take his van and his phone to work. But no, I don't think so.'

'What about Mason Scott's house?' he asked.

'His parents said he has a brother who has a key and used to visit Mason almost daily before he committed suicide. So, as it stands, Richard Scott is our number one suspect.'

'Any sign of him?'

She shook her head. 'Not that we know. PC Baan was watching the place up until midnight, and another constable was there on nights.'

He sighed but seemed happy. 'She's a good one, is PC Baan.'

'She certainly is.'

'I think we need—'

The conversation was interrupted when a trio of quick knocks came from the door. It opened before either Fisher or James had a chance to say anything. PC Baan entered, her face flushed, a thin film of sweat lining her forehead. She was out of breath.

'Sorry, I-I couldn't find you.'

Both frowning, they waited, anticipating what she was about to say.

'One of the vehicles I noted last night, a small blue Vauxhall Astra van — there's a match to an owner called

Richard Scott.' She dashed forward with a piece of paper. 'Look.'

Fisher peered over at the details of the small van, the owner, and the registration plate. 'Excellent work, Ash. Thank you.' She turned to James, who also was nodding with appreciation.

'So, we know the van.'

'Who's watching the house at the moment?' asked Baan, knowing it would be someone no doubt on day shift.

'One of the PCs assigned from Thorne. PC Legg maybe?' Fisher stood abruptly. 'Let me find out.' She grabbed her phone, found Legg's number, and pressed CALL. 'Come on, pick up . . .'

James and Baan watched her, waiting for someone to answer.

'Hey, Amy, it's DS Fisher. Are you watching the house?'

'Yeah, why?'

She asked her if the van was there.

'No, it's not here.'

'Shit. Okay, thank you.' She hung up. 'The van has gone,' she informed Baan and James. 'I need to get in touch with Liam Harper at the city control and see if he can get a location on it immediately.'

CHAPTER 65

At the end of the phone call with Liam Harper at City Hall, she thanked him and hung up. She'd made the call from the office with Phillips sitting on his office chair, leaning over, and listening in.

'What's happening?' he asked.

She turned to him, placing her phone on the desk beside her keyboard. 'Said he'll be in touch when there's a hit.'

He nodded. 'Right, let's go see Patricia Keeton and Victoria Thomson.'

Fisher smiled. 'Most definitely.' She picked up her phone from her desk, unlocked it, and checked her notes. 'It looks like—' she frowned — 'Patricia Keeton's house is closer, if my memory of Manchester serves me right.'

'What are we waiting for, then?' He stood and grabbed his coat from the back of his chair. It was warm in the office today. No need to work in his ridiculously long coat indoors, but he knew from being outside earlier that the temperature was a couple above zero at best. Not only had the heating been fixed, but they'd also managed to get hold of a small heater that they plugged in under their desks. They'd found it in one of the cleaner's cupboards and would use it until told otherwise.

'What's next?' a voice said to their left.

They swivelled on their chairs to see PC Baan, looking keen. 'It's warm around here.' She frowned, leaned over, and spotted the heater near Fisher's legs. 'Oh, that's crafty!'

'We've got the address for Patricia Keeton and Victoria Thomson. We'll head to Patricia's house first.'

'Why don't Adam and I go to one house, and you two go to the other?'

Fisher turned to Phillips, who nodded, agreeing with the idea.

'Two birds, one stone,' he said with a shrug.

'I want to thank you, Ashleigh,' said Fisher.

'For what?'

'Helping us with the case.'

'Inspector Thorne told us as long as the case is open, we're at your disposal.'

Fisher gave her a mild frown.

'Honestly,' Baan reassured, 'it's fine. I'd only be chasing sweary teenagers on pushbikes otherwise.'

Fisher stood, picked up her jacket from the back of her chair, and put it on. 'You and Jackson go to Victoria Thomson's house. We'll go and see Patricia Keeton.' She pressed several buttons on her phone, then looked up at Baan. 'I've just sent you her address. Go and get Adam. Let me know when you're there.'

* * *

It took roughly twenty minutes to arrive at Patricia Keeton's property, a small, terraced house in the southeast of Manchester on Kettering Road. They approached an awkwardly parked van, and as the road was long and narrow, it was difficult for Fisher to pass, so she slowed to ease through.

'Idiots,' Phillips muttered as Fisher carefully guided the Volvo through the slender gap.

Up on the right, they stopped and pulled into a space outside of the house they were looking for. Before they got out, they studied it: the bricks looked damp, the black pipe-work was battered and flaky, and the white PVC front door had weathered so much it had turned a shade of magnolia. The small, fenced garden was gravel-filled with dozens of dark, moist weeds growing from underneath. They opened the creaking gate and knocked on the door.

A thin, blonde-haired woman in her early forties answered with a cigarette pressed between her lips. There was a tattoo visible on her neck, and crow's feet lined the edges of her tired eyes, making her appear as if she could pass for mid-fifties no problem.

'Mrs Keeton?' Fisher asked with a smile.

Scowling, the woman removed the cigarette between her lips. 'Who's asking?' She took a deep drag, then tilted her head to blow the smoke upwards, the plumes circling for a second before vanishing into the air as if courteously avoiding Fisher and Phillips.

'I'm DS April Fisher of Greater Manchester CID. This is my partner DS Matthew Phillips. Are you Mrs Patricia Keeton?'

She stayed silent but nodded curiously, unsure what it was about.

'Would it be possible to come in for a moment?'

She considered the detective's request and stepped aside. 'Mind the mess.'

You should never judge a book by its cover, but Fisher did within three seconds. The way she sucked the smoke into her lungs, the way she stood, and what she wore. She dreaded to think what inside the house was going to be like.

Patricia Keeton led them into the hallway and told Phillips, the last one inside, to close the door.

'Like I said, mind the mess. I'm having a sort-out.'

As they moved through into the dining room, there was no evidence to suggest she was having a sort-out. Every little bit of mess seemed to have its own space, and they knew, as well as Patricia did, this was how she lived. A faint smell of lavender drifted from somewhere. Fisher noticed the candle on the small table, but the smell was overpowered by the stale, hanging smoke.

Fisher and Phillips slowly followed her into the kitchen, gazing around, absorbing the house's clutter. She stopped at the kettle.

'Coffee?'

Fisher eyed the stained mugs on the worktop near the kettle, cringing inside. 'I'm okay, thank you. Had one before.'

Phillips raised a declining hand.

She flicked the kettle on and leaned on the edge of the worktop with her arms folded. 'So, what can I do for you, Detectives?'

'We're here because we're concerned for your safety.'

She frowned Fisher's way, then switched her focus to Phillips before settling back on Fisher. 'Safety?'

Fisher nodded. 'Have you seen the recent news reports about the library murders?'

Keeton said she had, then Fisher explained about the victims being in the same class at Chorlton High School.

'I was in that class.'

'Which is why we're here,' explained Fisher. 'We're aware of what happened on the camping trip, and the unfortunate incident with Mason Scott.'

Patricia slowly raised a hand to her open mouth but said nothing.

'We also saw the web page about Mason,' added Phillips, implying he didn't think it was too clever or decent. 'And we think the recent murders are because of someone getting revenge.'

'Revenge for what? The camping thing?'

Fisher tilted her head. 'Maybe. But maybe he committed suicide because he couldn't take it anymore.' She raised a hand. 'Listen, we're not here to judge anyone. But based on what's been happening and what we know, we need to inform you that your life is in serious danger.'

Patricia mulled over the detective's words with a slow, considerate nod. 'Okay.'

'Now, we're looking for whoever's responsible for the murders. Do you know Richard Scott?'

'Mason's brother?'

'Yes. According to recent information, he could go by the name of John Harper now. That name familiar?'

She said it wasn't. 'And you think he's coming to, what, get me?' She rolled her eyes as if she didn't believe any of it, or was she putting on a brave face?

Fisher shrugged. 'We simply don't know. We can have a PC watch your house for a couple of days to ensure you're safe. You think that's a good idea?'

Shaking her head, she said it wouldn't be necessary.

'We have to insist, unfortunately.' Fisher knew they weren't exactly flooded with staff but had to put public safety first. And, not to mention, limiting the number of casualties would be a bonus if Patricia was going to be a potential victim.

'Fine, whatever.' Patricia waved it away with a hand, sighing. 'Don't be expecting cups of tea and doughnuts, though. Like I said, I'm busy sorting the house.'

CHAPTER 66

'Well, *she* was helpful.' Phillips sighed as he pushed his seat belt into the catch.

Fisher smiled, put her seat belt on, and grabbed her phone.

'Who are you calling?'

Fisher found Baan's number, pressed CALL, and put her phone to her ear. 'Ashleigh, to see if they've spoken with Victoria Thomson.'

Phillips looked away from her, studying the street they were parked in. The houses were close together and narrow, with broken drainpipes barely clinging to the brickwork and moss-covered pavements. There were a few exceptions, but most houses could have done with a good paint and a little TLC.

'Hey, Ash,' Fisher said into the phone. Phillips angled her way, watching her. 'You spoken to Victoria Thomson?'

'Unfortunately not. There was no one in at the address.'

'You try knocking on neighbours?'

'Yeah, knocked two doors on either side. One neighbour told us to piss off because she doesn't like Miss Thomson and doesn't want to get involved in "whatever mess that daft cow has got herself into". The one on the other side said she hadn't seen Vicky for a few days.'

'Charming,' replied Fisher.

'I can stay for a while to see if she comes home, if you'd like?'

'Stay there until I send someone else over, then head back to the station. We need you with us.'

Baan hung up, and Fisher placed her phone in the storage compartment between the front seats.

'No joy?'

She shook her head. 'We'll head back, arrange someone to watch Patricia, and take it from there.'

* * *

It had just gone 3 p.m. by the time Fisher and Phillips were back in the office. They'd grabbed a quick coffee, and Fisher stood, making small circles near her desk. Phillips was seated, focused on his computer screen, making a list of Manchester libraries. Baan and Jackson showed up around thirty minutes later.

'Sorry we're late. Had some trouble on the way over,' said Baan, then informed them about an argument that had broken out between two drivers, both male, both under the assumption they were in the right. The other had made a mistake when one of them pulled out when there wasn't enough room to do so. Baan had managed to calm the situation and suggested it would be in their best interests to let it go, unless they wanted to spend the night in a police cell. Both men stared each other out until they reluctantly went their separate ways without it becoming physical, to the relief of PC Jackson, who, judging by their size, hadn't wanted to take them on.

DI James was in the office, fishing for an update, something to feed back to DCI Baker by the end of the day.

Fisher was the only one who stood; the others sat on swivel chairs clustered between the four desks, facing her, sipping on coffee.

'What you thinking, April?' James asked her, seeing the cogs turning in her head. They knew that it was Friday, they needed something good to end the week, something positive for the weekend. The last thing they needed was another head found in a library in the morning.

'We've made a list of the libraries in Manchester,' she started. 'So far, three have been targeted.'

DI James expelled a ball of air from his mouth. Fisher frowned his way, waiting for an explanation.

'There are too many,' he said, his tone already beaten.

'My theory is that if it's too late for Steve Adams, the chances of the killer taking his head, or whatever fucking body part, to a library is highly likely.'

Phillips's eyebrows raised at the language that came from Fisher's mouth. It was obvious it was all getting to her.

'What do you propose, April?' asked DI James softly.

'What I propose, Tom,' Fisher stated, 'is using our limited manpower to watch the remaining libraries in the city to see if we can catch anyone dropping anything off. I don't care if there's only one PC watching each one. We need to take action now.'

It was James's turn to raise his eyebrows and curl his bottom lip out, impressed with her determination to move the investigation forward. Even if it was a stretch, he had to respect she was making a decision. Whether it turned into a bad decision or not, it was more effective than doing nothing. Something to feed back to DCI Baker, if anything.

'Okay,' James said, then turned to Phillips. 'Matthew, how many so far?'

Phillips finished jotting another library down, then placed his pen on the table before picking up the notepad. 'Judging from this, there are eighteen libraries in Manchester.'

Fisher sighed, her shoulder dipping a little, though she wouldn't let it faze her. 'Right, okay. Well, we need eyes on the remaining fifteen, then, don't we?' She addressed James, who was the right man for the task. 'Can we speak to the other stations and get extra manpower on this?'

He nodded and sat up straighter. 'Yeah, sure, that'll be fine.'

'Show me the list, Matthew.'

He gave her the pad. She scanned them slowly.

'I've put a star next to the ones we've already found a victim at,' he said, pointing.

'Okay.' She paused for a beat. 'I'll take Hulme High Street Library.' She looked at Baan. 'Could you take Beswick Library?'

Baan nodded. 'Of course.'

Then to PC Jackson: 'Adam, can you go to Burnage Library?'

'I'm on it.' He stood and turned.

'Adam.'

He stopped mid-turn.

'We'll send someone over in a few hours. We know you finish your shift soon.'

'I'll call if I see anything unusual.' He left the office.

Baan put her jacket back on and pulled up her zip.

'Be careful, Ashleigh.' Her tone was sincere. 'Any sign of anyone or anything funny, ring me straight away.'

Once Baan had gone, they made a note of the remaining unmanned libraries. With the people they had at their disposal, they'd need another five volunteers at least. James said he'd sort it and grabbed his phone to make some calls.

Fisher put on a coat over the top of her blue suit jacket. According to the weather report, it was going to reach minus temperatures. Her parents had wanted to see her this weekend, and so had Freya, but it was the last thing on her mind. How could she unwind and go drinking when there was a killer out there chopping people up?

Fisher put the car in first gear and edged her Volvo out of the space, then stopped at the road, waiting for a car to pass before pulling out to head southeast. Hulme High Street Library was only six miles from the station, but judging by the traffic, it would take her twenty minutes minimum.

As Fisher pulled up outside the library, she frowned. Judging by the shapes and curves, it wouldn't have made the list of Manchester's most historical buildings. But what made her frown was the lack of life inside. Through the closed sliding doors, she could see several dim lights at the rear of the ground floor — it was obvious to Fisher that the place was closed. The lights were there to either deter thieves or aid security guards who may be working there, not that she'd think there'd be any guards minding the books.

She got out, shut her door, and dashed over to the closed doors. A notice beside the door with the opening times informed her that the library was closed on Fridays.

'Shit,' she muttered, wishing she'd checked before wasting her time. 'For God's sake.' She checked her watch. It was approaching 4.30 p.m. She pulled her phone out, tapped Phillips's number, and pressed CALL.

'Hey,' he answered, 'just got here. What's happening on your end?'

'A big fat load of nothing. This one's closed. Did you not check this when jotting them down?'

'Shit, sorry, April.' Phillips sighed heavily.

'Ooh, hang on,' she said, her phone vibrating against the side of her head. She pulled it away and saw PC Baan was ringing. 'Matthew, I'll ring you back.' She hung up and answered. 'Hey.'

'April, I've just seen a small blue van drive away from Beswick Library car park. I didn't see the driver. I was about to get out when its lights came on and it drove away. I'm trailing it now. The registration is his.'

'Keep following that van, Ashleigh. But hang back. And . . . *be careful*. I'll head over in your direction and ring you soon. I'll call for backup.'

CHAPTER 67

Without a second thought, PC Baan pulled onto Grey Mare Lane to join the flow of moderate traffic. It wasn't the busiest part of the city, and the road wasn't too bad because it was well past school finishing time. The blue van had a little head start, but she kept it in her sights as it drifted to the left onto Sunny Lowry Road. The van slowed at the busy junction and flicked on a right indicator.

Baan, conscious of travelling in a marked Vauxhall Astra, didn't want to make it too obvious she was trailing him. But on the other hand, losing him was out of the question, so she needed to be clever and hang back, but ready if he spotted her.

When the traffic allowed, the van set off, joining the A6010 southbound, then turned right at Ashton Old Road, heading towards the city centre. Baan kept back by roughly fifty or sixty metres and prayed the darkness of winter would add a little camouflage to the police car she was driving.

She continued to trail and kept her eyes on the van's rear, but as she passed Storage World, she noticed traffic lights up ahead, currently on red. She winced, knowing she'd have to slow down but not make it too obvious she was targeting him. The idea of pulling over crossed her mind, but the lights might change, and he'd get away.

The van slowed and stopped at the lights. Baan reduced her speed until she came to a halt behind it. She tried shifting to the right to look at the side mirror to see if she could get a good look at the driver, but the nearby streetlights did nothing to aid that, the driver's window a black reflective sheet against the brilliant white beams above. The van edged forward when the lights turned green and worked its way up the gears.

Using the hands-free system, Baan phoned Fisher, who answered after one ring.

'Still on his tail?' asked Fisher.

'Yeah, I'm right behind him. There was no other way. Not sure if he's noticed me yet.'

'Location?'

'Ashton Old Road, heading into the city.'

'Okay, I'll—'

'Shit!' Baan said, then gasped.

'Ash, what?'

The small blue van accelerated quickly, then overtook the car in front, barely pulling back in before an oncoming bus nearly wiped it out.

'He's seen me. He's going for it!'

'Call for backup. Get the lights on!'

'Okay, okay.' Baan took a deep breath and blinked a few times to get into focus, knowing what was coming next would test her driving skills.

'I'll stay on the line,' Fisher reassured her.

Baan turned her lights on, immediately seeing the blue glare of the spinning lamps on the roof, and dropped the Astra into third gear, then planted her foot. The vehicle surged forward, and luckily the car in front pulled in, allowing her to pass safely. The van was picking up speed, the gap growing each second.

'Come on!' she encouraged the 1.7 diesel engine. She dipped her clutch, pulled the gear into fourth, now reaching seventy miles an hour. If her memory served her right, there was a very busy intersection coming up, but she was gaining on the van, now roughly sixty metres away. She put her foot down, the engine sending a surge of power to the wheels.

The van weaved dangerously, barely braking at all; one wrong move would cause something catastrophic. Baan turned left onto the A635. The traffic had come to a standstill to let her on.

The van was just ahead, bobbing left and right, the brake light flashing repeatedly until it disappeared when it reached the tunnel that ran under the railway bridge. Baan's eyes widened. 'Shit. Where's he gone?'

When she reached the bridge, she was fortunate the public had stopped, making her life easier as she powered through, the engine's sounds rebounding off the ancient brickwork of the tunnel. She couldn't see the van in her lane when she came out the other end.

'Shit,' she said again.

There was a loud beep to her right. She snapped her neck around, seeing the van on the other side. Before reaching the bridge, he must have crossed over the kerbed island between the lanes.

'Bastard!' she shouted, realising a two-foot-high barrier now separated the lanes. Thinking quickly, she decided to drive alongside him, praying the cars would see and hear her car approaching them.

She leaned forward and pressed a button on the central console.

'This is PC Ashleigh Baan of Swinton's Unit, in pursuit of a vehicle failing to stop. I'm on Trinity Way, westbound, chasing a blue Vauxhall Astra van. My immediate assessment of potential casualties due to the level of traffic and road users is very high. Proceed with caution. I'll update when I can.'

She took a deep breath, readjusted her hands on the steering wheel, and watched the van pick up speed.

'Come on,' she said, focusing on the traffic ahead.

'This is PC Hamble, location A5067,' a voice said on the radio. 'Can you tell me the exact location of the Vauxhall Astra van, please?'

It was another PC responding to the call.

'Still on A635, merging onto A57,' Baan replied, then added, 'This guy's a lunatic.'

'Roger that, we'll assist. ETA two minutes.'

Because the blue van was driving against the flow of traffic, Baan was in a good position to keep up and watch the van's movements, settling at a steady 50 mph to match his speed, which was impressive as he dodged and manoeuvred around the cluster of oncoming cars and vans.

'Are you close, April?' Baan shouted.

'Not really, maybe six or seven minutes out. Just stay on him, Ashleigh. You're doing great.'

The chase continued for a few moments when Baan blurted out, 'God!'

'Ash, what's wrong?'

'He's gone the wrong way down a slip road.' Baan slowed, her head snapping in all directions to try and work it out. She'd missed his intentions and passed the opposite slip road. 'Ahh, I'm going to lose him, April.'

'Just stay calm. Have a look around.'

Baan continued to drive but knew she was going away from him as long as she kept her foot on the pedal.

'This is PC Baan in pursuit of the blue Astra van. The driver has taken a slip road off the A57 — I've lost sight of him. If you're close, please assist. I'm . . .' She went quiet for a few seconds, looking up to her right to see if she could see anything. He was gone. Sighing, she felt a failure and said, 'I've lost him.'

CHAPTER 68

When Fisher reached the A57 there was no sign of the speeding van. Baan had told her she would keep driving around, but it was in the hands of the locals to join in with the search.

She picked up her phone and found Liam Harper's number.

'Hey, how—?'

'Liam, it's DS Fisher. I need you to find a vehicle.'

'When?'

'Like right now.'

'Err . . .' There was a shuffling sound. 'Yeah, go on.'

She informed him of the vehicle's make, model, and registration plate. 'I need you to see if you can find it on the CCTV system. Does that sound like something you can do?'

There was a hum of silence.

'Liam?'

'Yeah, sorry. I was just eating something. Yeah, I'll give it my best shot.'

'Thanks,' she replied, and hung up.

With no sign of the van, she headed to Beswick Library, where PC Baan had first spotted it. There must be a reason why the van had been there, and she had a pretty good idea of what it was. Because of rush-hour traffic, it took Fisher eighteen minutes to reach the library.

She informed several colleagues, including DS Phillips and DI James, where she was heading. Baan had decided to join her and pulled up several minutes after Fisher.

'I feel such a failure,' Baan said to Fisher as she opened her door. Fisher was waiting at the kerbside, knowing she was en route. When Baan got out, Fisher pulled her in close for a hug.

'Don't be stupid; you did your best. We'll get him. Don't worry.' She looked deep and sincerely into her eyes. 'Okay?'

Baan nodded twice, perking up a little.

'Right, let's go.' Side by side, they headed for the entrance to Beswick Library. The building was huge. The front part of the structure was mostly glass, with a small protruding box made from yellow panelling that reflected the bright lights inside. The doors slid open, and in they went, immediately stepping into a small, warm foyer with a large banner informing them the building had two levels. The customer service point was located on the ground floor, which seemed a good starting point. Through the next set of sliding doors was the main room. There were lengths of tinsel fixed to each bookshelf, and at the end of the first row, closest to the door, was a six-foot Christmas tree covered with baubles and tinsel, cool-white lights gently flashing.

Over to the right, near a rectangular desk with an array of neatly piled books, a small, thin man stood wearing tinsel around his neck like he would a scarf. He gave them a stupid grin as they approached.

'How can I help you?'

Fisher introduced herself quickly and told him they weren't here for books before he started giving them a tour. For some reason, without being too judgemental, he seemed the type to enjoy that sort of thing.

He frowned. 'What can I do for you, then?'

She asked if there'd been any deliveries in the last hour or so.

'Not that I know of.'

'Has anyone been here, other than the usual customers?'

He curled his lip. 'Define usual . . . we tend to get all sorts of—'

'Please, just answer the question. We're short on time. Has anyone been here or signed in with in the last hour?'

Without replying, he dashed over to a table that was pushed against the wall. Next to the nicely positioned leaflets, there was a clipboard, one they used to sign people in and out. He picked it up and scanned it for a moment.

'The maintenance man called in. That's all I know. Apart from him, there's been no one other than customers.'

'Maintenance man?' Fisher's eyes narrowed. 'Can I see, please?'

He offered the clipboard, and Fisher gratefully took it, then had a look.

'John Harper,' she whispered.

Baan nodded several times.

Fisher focused back on the man, who looked worried now, wondering what on earth was going on. 'Please can you show us where he was working?'

'He . . . said he was checking the lights in the staff room. I can show you?'

Fisher and Baan nodded and followed him through a door to the left, along a small corridor, and into another room.

'Just in here. The lights have been dodgy for months now.'

'Have you seen much of this John Harper?'

'Never in my life. He's new, apparently. Been going around all the libraries, doing odd jobs and whatnot. Strange guy, if you ask me.'

Fisher turned to him. 'Strange how?'

'He carried his tools in a cardboard box.'

'When he left, did he have the box with him?'

'I-I can't remember. I didn't see him leave.'

Fisher observed the staff room for a few moments, especially the lights above. 'Do you get book deliveries?'

'Of course. Drivers usually come every Monday with new stock, depending on the newest releases. We're updating our stock all the time.'

He obviously took some kind of pride in that.

'Show us where, please.'

'Err, yeah, okay. Follow me.' They left the staff room, and instead of taking a left to head back to the library, they went right then through a door on the left. 'All the stock is in here.' The room was dark until he turned the switch on.

Among a handful of boxes, there were two shelving units with various stock like paper and stationery. It was relatively tidy and was too big for its contents. On the floor to the left, the man frowned at something.

A box with a label on.

'Hmmmm?'

He bent down and—

'Wait!' said Fisher, stopping him. 'Is that the box he came in with?'

'It might be.'

'Please,' Baan said to him, 'could you take a step back and turn away?'

He scowled, unsure of what was happening. 'Okay . . .'

Fisher pulled out a pair of latex gloves from her pockets, snapped them on, then lowered to her knees, pulling the flaps of the box open.

'Oh, God . . .' whispered Baan as she peered over it, looking in.

CHAPTER 69

Fisher and Baan waited for Pamela Boone, Stacy, and Jasper to arrive at the library. She had apologised to Boone, knowing it was getting late in the day. Still, she knew, as well as everyone else who worked for the police, that this job was a twenty-four seven operation, and that crime didn't stop outside the usual working hours.

Fisher had decided to leave the box in the stockroom and let Boone have a good look before moving it. It was unlike the previous crime scenes in that there was no extravagant display, so it was on show for the world to see, but it was a human head, after all. And it likely belonged to Steve Adams, but Boone would take DNA and get samples when she returned to the lab. Similar to the previous heads, it was severed at the neck with something very sharp. The cut, if anything, had been cleaner, as if the killer had improved over time.

Jasper and Stacy were there, standing close to Boone but far enough away to give her space to work. Jasper was dressed in his usual flamboyant fashion, opting for a bright-green jumper and dark jeans under his white coveralls. Stacy was dressed in black, appearing smart and appropriate for what she was doing under her whites.

315

In Fisher's opinion, Stacy was the more likely candidate for the job as Jasper didn't appear to be taking it too seriously. Both trainee forensic techs wore overshoes and gloves too, but they knew Boone would be doing most of the handling.

Fisher and Baan stood back, watching Boone slowly lift the head from the box. She'd already laid out a plastic sheet and taken photos of the head inside the box. Her forensics kit was open to her left with various clear bags, unopened packs of sterile swabs, distilled water, and several rolls of tape. She lowered the likely head of Steve Adams onto the plastic sheeting and gently tipped it back, then looked at Jasper.

'Please pass me the tweezers.'

Carefully, she nipped the edge of the folded photo from the bottom of the head and meticulously pulled it out, handing it to Fisher, who already knew it would be a photo of Mason Scott and wasn't proved wrong when she carefully peeled it open.

'We're just grateful we got to this before anyone else did,' said Fisher.

Baan nodded. 'Now what's the plan?'

Fisher handed the photo to Stacy, who placed it into a small plastic bag, ran her finger and thumb across the seal, and lowered it into Boone's forensic kit.

'Well, I haven't heard anything from dispatch about the blue van, so I'm assuming he's got away for now.'

Baan sighed, and her shoulders physically dipped.

'We'll get him, Ash,' she reassured her. She pulled her phone out and called Phillips, who told her he'd returned to the station and would stay back and wait for her there. Before she left, she asked the library assistant if there were any cameras inside, so she could get a good look at what Richard Scott had been up to.

'Bingo!' she said, seeing the man dressed in blue overalls walking across the library with the box in his hand. He was tall, thin, and walked with purpose. She asked if she could take a copy of the footage, to which the man happily agreed, and when she'd saved it, she placed the memory stick back into her coat pocket.

'Thanks for your time.'

They returned to her Volvo while Boone and the forensics team carried the head to the van. 'Ash, you come with me, you can pick up your car later.' Fisher raised the phone to her ear again.

'Who are you calling?' said Baan.

'I arranged with Inspector Thorne for a PC to watch Patricia Keeton's house tonight. PC Kristie Layton. I don't know her very well. I feel Mrs Keeton could be next. I know she wasn't interested in us watching the house, but I have a bad feeling about something.'

'Kristie's okay,' said Baan. 'She's new. She has a lot to learn but has a good head on her shoulders for her age.'

The phone rang three times before it was picked up by PC Layton.

'PC Layton?'

'Yeah, who's calling?'

'Hey, it's DS April Fisher. I'm just checking in with you.'

'Oh, hi . . .'

'Is Patricia still safe? Has there been any sign of anyone going to or from the house?'

'Not that I've seen. I've parked three car spaces down from her house and have a good visual.'

'Can you see her front door?'

There was a pause.

'PC Layton?' Fisher's tone became sharper.

'Erm, yeah. I can see it.'

'Are there any lights still on?'

The next pause frustrated Fisher.

'PC Lay—'

'No, the house is in darkness.'

Fisher sighed, knowing that when she had left, the lights had been on. It was getting dark, so if Patricia was still at home, she would have assumed PC Layton would be able to see some light coming from one of the rooms.

'Can you knock on her door and check, please?'

'Yeah, right on it.'

'Be careful. Call back on this number.'

As Fisher hung up and set off, her phone rang through the car's speaker system when she reached the junction. She dragged her eyes from the front windscreen to the central console, assuming PC Layton was ringing back quicker than she'd anticipated. But it wasn't the PC. It was Liam Harper from the council.

'Liam?'

'DS Fisher, we have a good idea where your van is.'

CHAPTER 70

Liam Harper informed Fisher the van had been spotted on the A56/Chester Road westbound, driving at a leisurely speed with the other traffic, doing his best to not attract any attention, which had given Liam the time to pause the shot and get a good look at the registration plate from one of the traffic cams.

'Then we picked it up again, passing the Safestore self-storage facility further down the road.' Liam went silent for a minute. 'He turned right at White City Circle and proceeded westbound for a little until he joined Wharfside Way, then onto Trafford Park Road. But the next available camera on the same road didn't see him. So, there's a very good chance he's around that area.' Fisher nodded but stayed silent, listening carefully. 'I've had a look at the map,' Liam went on. 'It looks like there's a lot of industrial places around there.'

Fisher pulled out onto the road and slowly shifted through her gears. 'What's the location of the camera that last saw the van and the location of the one that didn't? It'll give us a better idea of the possibilities.'

Liam told them.

'Okay, thank you.'

They ended the call, and Fisher brought the car over to the side of the road, pulling in far enough not to disrupt traffic flow.

'Ash, get it up on your phone please.'

Baan typed the location Liam had given and pointed to her screen, showing Fisher the camera position that had a visual.

'Go further, to the camera that didn't.'

Fisher pointed. 'So this area is potentially where the van could be?'

Baan agreed. 'We'll head over and see what we can find.'

* * *

Eight minutes later, they pulled onto Trafford Park Road. Up on their left was the first of only two potential turns the blue van could have made. Fisher slowed, flicked her indicator on, and angled left onto Third Avenue, a narrow road that ran alongside a long building made up, judging by the signs outside, of several businesses. Fisher came to a stop.

'What are we doing?' Baan quizzed, throwing her a look.

'Type those businesses into your phone and see what comes up.'

As Baan typed the first name in, Fisher's phone rang again, briefly distracting Baan, who glanced up to see PC Layton calling, then focused back on her own phone screen.

'Kristie?' Fisher answered.

'DS Fisher?'

'Yes, Kristie. What is it?'

'I've been inside Patricia Keeton's house,' she said timidly. 'The door was open an inch, so I just went in.'

Baan and Fisher both physically sighed, knowing it could have been dangerous to do so on her own.

'I know I shouldn't have, but I had a funny feeling,' she explained as if reading their thoughts.

'Go on . . .'

'Mrs Keeton is nowhere to be seen. She's gone.'

Fisher sighed and pressed a palm against her forehead.

'Okay. Leave the house and come over to us. I'll text you our location.' She hung up.

Baan told her that the three businesses she'd checked out were all legitimate and still functioning. She sighed and looked through her windscreen at the junction ahead, which led onto a main road, meaning the van could be anywhere. But, she thought, if it had gone that way, Liam would have picked it up on the closest traffic cams, so decided to do a quick U-turn and go back to Trafford Park Road, this time taking a left.

'The only other option before that camera is the next right,' Baan informed her, studying her screen. 'It's just up here.'

They turned into a wide road that led to a vast industrial space with dozens of factories and what looked like commercial buildings. The only issue was the closed gate in front of them.

'God's sake . . .' Baan covered her mouth, as if she was already beaten.

'Just wait.'

There was a small gatehouse on the left, the lights on inside, with a man visible, facing the road. Fisher thought he was looking down, probably on his phone or reading a magazine.

'It's locked, though.'

'Doesn't mean he's not here,' Fisher replied, slowing her car at the gate.

The man inside the small booth frowned their way, then glanced up at a small clock beside his head, obviously not expecting anyone to turn up at this time. He leaned forward and tiredly dragged the window open. Baan lowered the window.

'Can I help you?' said the man in a deep, raspy voice.

'I'm hoping so,' Fisher said, leading the conversation. 'We're hoping you could tell us if a small blue van has come through here in the last thirty minutes or so?'

The man considered the question. 'And who's asking?' He couldn't see Baan's police uniform under her coat. Fisher pulled out her ID, showed it to him, and then explained who she was.

He scowled. 'A blue van?'

They both nodded. 'Any sign of one?' Baan asked.

The man, without answering, leaned back and, to his right, picked up an A4-sized clipboard. He scanned the list. 'Yeah, a blue Astra van pulled in around twenty minutes ago.'

'Can you tell us where it is now or what unit the van is at?'

The man sighed this time as if whatever this was, he wasn't interested, and it was wasting his time. Turning back in the chair, he focused on something to the left. Baan and Fisher watched him, unable to see the collection of eight small security screens covering the twenty-four cameras dot-ted around the place.

He leaned forward. 'Follow the road down—' he indicated with his hand — 'then take a right, keep going, and you'll see it on the right. It's parked next to Talking Direct Limited, our only empty building. God knows why he doesn't just sell it. He always comes here, bringing potential buyers with him, but no one seems to want it.'

'Can you let us through? It's police business.'

His arm moved a little, then a sharp, loud buzz echoed around them as the gates mechanically opened, the sound of the whirring motor powering them. Once fully open, they thanked him and went through. He closed the window and returned to whatever it was he was doing.

Just over a minute later, they slowed and spotted the van exactly where the man had said, parked next to two other cars. A red Vauxhall Insignia and a white Ford Focus.

'There it is,' Fisher said, pointing.

'I wonder who the other cars belong to?'

'Only one way to find out, Ash.' Fisher picked up her phone and called dispatch, informing everyone she needed assistance.

CHAPTER 71

Fisher and Baan waited in the Volvo, parked opposite the factory, watching the single entrance door with hawk eyes for anyone to appear from inside. Next to it was a large, silver roller garage door which was closed. Nearby, the dim street-lights gently illuminated the building, giving Fisher and Baan a great idea of the size of the place. It must have been fifty to sixty metres long, maybe more. It was a tall structure; the first ten feet from the ground was made up of aging bricks that had weathered over the years. The remainder of the structure was made from thin metallic panels that ran all the way to the roof, the cool December frost clinging to the smooth surface in a shiny film that reflected the nearby streetlights.

The single entrance and roller doors were the only access points on this side of the building, positioned roughly fif-teen metres from the end. They assumed Richard Scott had used this entrance because of where the blue van was parked. Whether there were alternative exits down the side or on the other side of the building had crossed Fisher's mind. Still, she wanted to focus on the cars and the closest exit just in case someone appeared and slipped out.

From behind them, Fisher noticed headlights approach-ing in her rear-view mirror. She frowned at the vehicle as it got closer, recognising DI James in his Range Rover.

He turned off his engine, climbed down, quietly closed his door, and wandered to Fisher's open window to speak with her.

'Hey,' he said, then cupped his hands and blew into them. 'Frosty one tonight.'

'No kidding.'

'Any sign?' He pulled his eyes away from her and focused on the van and the vehicles beside it.

She shook her head. 'Nothing yet.'

'Looks like we have company?'

She shrugged.

He looked beyond her and smiled at Baan. 'How you doing, Ashleigh? Appreciate you coming along.'

'I'm good, thanks, sir,' she said, nodding, expelling a short burst of air to battle against the cold. 'Wouldn't miss this for the world.'

They all smiled, knowing that to be a lie, but the nature of their professions.

'Phillips is coming soon. He's only five minutes away,' Fisher informed him.

'Good.' He took a step back to gauge the size of the building. 'I've called for backup. Should be here soon.'

It wasn't long before DS Phillips arrived in his blue Mondeo, parking behind James's Range Rover, and soon joined them by Fisher's window.

'Think it'll be wise to park in front of the van and the other cars?' suggested Fisher.

DI James agreed, and when two marked cars silently pulled up, he instructed the PCs to park the Astras on the road in a way that would block the van and both of the cars if they tried to get out.

Once they decided on a plan, they walked over to the small, closed door, Fisher and Phillips leading the way. Immediately behind them were PC Baan and PC Jackson, with batons tightly gripped in their palms, ready to use if necessary.

'You ready?'

Fisher nodded at Phillips. 'As much as I'll ever be.'

He cautiously took hold of the handle and pushed down. The door opened towards them an inch. He glanced at Fisher, who nodded, as did Baan and Jackson, who were a pace behind. DI James watched from the rear of the group, with the other PCs standing a few metres back, scanning the length of the factory for any movement.

He opened the door and gingerly peered in without knowing what he'd see. The place seemed colder than outside, and it was dark, with only a tiny amount of light coming from the middle of the space.

'What do you see?' Fisher whispered in his ear.

He cocked his head back a few inches. 'It's a big warehouse, with some kind of wooden structure in the middle.'

Fisher nodded. 'Okay. Safe to proceed?'

Phillips leaned in to have a second look. 'Yeah. Can't see or hear anyone.'

One by one, they tiptoed into the darkness. James instructed two local PCs to wait outside to keep an eye on things. There might be a possibility more people were coming, and the last thing they wanted was to be trapped inside with no idea what they were getting into. James edged the door closed but didn't shut it entirely to prevent attracting any attention.

'What the hell is that?' Phillips whispered to no one in particular, eyeing the studded structure. The area around it was dark, but a square of light illuminated the cold air above it.

'No idea,' replied Fisher. 'Come on.' She moved forward, her eyes darting around, taking the place in. With the limited light making it difficult to see what was in front of them, she was worried they might knock into something, causing an unwanted sound, but at the same time, the darkness would act as camouflage.

'Shhh . . .' Fisher grabbed Phillips's forearm. Baan knocked into her, unaware she'd come to a sudden halt. 'Hear that?' she asked Phillips.

He turned his head towards her, listening with his left ear, a voice coming from somewhere. They all froze to listen, turning their heads.

'*It's pretty simple. All you need to do is that, and you're through to the next room.*'

Fisher and Phillips shared a knowing look; whatever the voice was referring to wouldn't be anything good.

'It's coming from over there.' Fisher pointed to where the light was coming from.

'*Please . . . just let me go!*'

'*Come on, Patricia,*' the voice said again. They could hear the distortion as if it were coming from a speaker, the clarity of the voice interfered. '*You can do this . . .*'

A scream filled the factory, startling them.

'Whatever is going on in there, we need to stop it,' said Fisher.

Phillips nodded and edged forward to take the lead. They moved further into the factory, scanning left and right. On the left was a small room made up of breezeblocks; a door with a label pinned to it saying *toilet* was closed shut. Beyond that, running down the left-hand side, a walkway marked with white paint ran along the length of the factory, leading to a closed door at the end. Fisher wondered how many exits there were and paused a beat, reassessing their tactics.

'What's up?' said Baan.

Fisher turned to DI James. 'Tom, there's an exit down there.'

He scowled in the darkness, following her finger, seeing the door on the other side of the factory.

'Ask one of the PCs to cover.'

Nodding, he backed away a few paces and opened the door they'd come through.

'What do you think's going on?' Baan asked, her eyes fixed on the studded room.

'Come on.'

Fisher edged forward with Phillips. Baan and Jackson trailed them, scanning for any sign of movement. Fisher looked up, seeing how high the roof was, noticing the multiple plastic panels that would offer natural daylight during the day.

Behind her, Jackson shivered, the cold, icy air around him getting through his limited layers. 'It's freezing in here.'

Fisher heard him but kept focusing on what was happening around her.

'*JUST LET ME GO!*' screamed Patricia from the illuminated room.

They were around twenty metres away. As far as they could see, they had a clear path, their eyes adjusting to the darkness well.

To the right, they could just make out the metal staircase that ran up the side of another breezeblock structure at least two stories high. Probably an office of some sort. The stairs went up halfway, then turned the corner, obviously going higher to access whatever was up there.

Very slowly, they continued moving forward as quietly as they could. It wasn't long before they passed the blocked structure on the right and the light from the studded room lit a metal walkway above it.

'The hell is that?' asked Phillips.

Fisher spotted the four figures standing on the walkway, looking down on the room, the bright light illuminating up their strange masks.

'What on earth?' Fisher scowled up at them, unsure what she was seeing or if she imagined it. The figures were still, their gaze down on what they assumed was Patricia Keeton in the room below.

For the moment, they weighed the situation up. They could see four figures watching the room below but were there more in here? Others watching or hiding somewhere in the darkness? Suddenly Fisher felt uneasy, just waiting to be ambushed.

'We need to do something,' she demanded.

Nodding in agreement, Phillips said, 'One of us go up the stairs, another go to the left, another to the right?'

'Yes.' Fisher turned to PC Jackson, the baton ready in his hand. 'Adam, go up the stairs, check out what's up there.'

He shifted right over to the stairs. Fisher directed Baan to the left and Phillips turned right. Fisher moved forward a little, her focus still on the figures. In her periphery, she saw Phillips, Baan, and Jackson moving in separate directions. She hoped they kept as silent as they had been so far.

'*Go on, then, we're all waiting, Patricia,*' the voice said on the speaker.

Then to her right, PC Jackson misjudged one of the metal steps and slipped, his knee colliding with the metal, causing a sharp pinging sound to ring out.

Fisher gasped, snapping her neck to the right, seeing Jackson in physical pain, clutching his knee. She looked up at the masks, all looking towards the sound. By that point, she knew their cover had been blown.

'Police, police, police!' she shouted, darting forward.

CHAPTER 72

Without hesitation, Fisher dashed right towards the stairs. PC Jackson had found his feet and used the handrail to propel himself up. Fisher was just behind him.

Baan's eyes were wide, watching them, not knowing what to do for a moment. She darted to the left, towards the other end of the factory, matching the strangers' speed as they sprinted along the metal walkway that seemed to run the whole length.

Metal clinked and clunked.

Hurried, panicked voices filled the place.

Patricia Keeton let out another scream from inside the room, obviously unaware of what was happening.

'Hurry up, Adam,' Fisher protested, shoving Jackson in the back, his knee obviously hurting from his slip moments earlier.

'I've got them!' DS Phillips shouted from the other side to where Baan was, running parallel to her without knowing it. Now they all had their torches out, not needing to stay in stealth mode anymore.

Jackson reached the second floor with Fisher right behind him. There was an opening to the right leading to a small room, but they took a left onto the metal walkway, where they could see the figures running away from them, currently halfway along the factory. Jackson went first, his feet pounding the metal, adding to the chaotic sounds. The sturdiness of the structure was questionable as it vibrated under the excess weight.

'Keep going!' Fisher persisted.

'I'll get them!' he reassured her. Fisher had seen Jackson give chase before, and she'd never seen anyone as fast as he was, so if anyone caught them, it would be him.

'Still got eyes on them!' Baan shouted somewhere to the left.

As Fisher moved quickly, scanning the room below, she noticed Patricia Keeton tied naked to a chair, her head tucked into her chest, sobbing. There was blood on her breasts. Fisher wanted to stop and check her, but she knew she couldn't help from up on the walkway. Carrying on, she trailed Jackson, the gap growing because of how quick he was.

The suspects, not wanting to be seen, kept their masks on but still managed to get across the walkway fast enough to reach the door on the other side before Jackson caught them up. The first one pushed the handle down and barged it open with a shoulder, spilling out into the winter air, closely followed by the others. The last one stopped once they were outside, turned quickly, and slammed the door shut. PC Jackson pushed the handle. 'It's locked!' He barged into it with his shoulder. The door rattled, but didn't give way. Whatever was holding it was solid and doing too good a job to be compromised.

Fisher also banged the door once she reached it. She stepped back and eyed another way through, but the door was the only accessible thing from the walkway. 'Come on, let's go back.'

* * *

Once the two police officers had reached the top of the stairs and gone left onto the walkway, Richard Scott stood up from behind his desk, grabbed his phone, and darted for the door. For a brief moment, he could see a woman giving chase after a man and decided now was a good time to escape.

He shot left, down the stairs. When he reached the bottom, he scurried towards the open door on the right, the one the police must have entered through moments earlier. The door was half open as he went through it, out into the cold. DI James, who'd heard someone coming, had waited a few feet from the door, and when Richard flew through it, James threw an arm around his neck to tackle him to the icy ground.

'Got you, you bastard!' James shouted, wrestling with him, but Richard was tall and strong. James, although on top of him, struggled to get an arm up around his neck to keep him pinned down. 'You . . .' James grappled with him. Grabbing Richard's head, he bounced it hard onto the concrete, stunning him, giving him enough time to get an arm under his chin and roll onto his back before choking him. Once Richard Scott's body went limp, James rolled him off and climbed to his feet, panting hard to get his breath back.

Fisher and Jackson appeared, storming through the door, stopping when they saw James panting hard.

'Richard Scott?' Fisher asked, eyeing the unconscious figure on the cold ground.

'More than likely,' he replied, doubled over, still panting hard.

'You okay?' she asked.

'Been a while since I got physical.'

They shared a weary smile.

Baan and Phillips appeared a moment later, both tired and exasperated through frantic running.

'Where are they?' Fisher asked.

'The door was locked, and we couldn't reach the walkway from below.'

Fisher slapped her thigh in frustration.

DI James remembered the PCs he had sent around the other side and made a move in that direction. He turned to

Baan. 'You watch him!' Then Fisher and Phillips followed him down the length of the factory, careful on their feet, and when they rounded the corner, they saw the two male PCs down on the road, one unconscious, the other with his hand on the top of his head, groaning to himself in pain.

'Where are they?' Fisher screamed, her gaze darting around the road and nearby paths.

'They've . . . they've gone,' the injured PC said. 'They got away.'

CHAPTER 73

After searching the industrial estate for more than twenty minutes, covering every square inch of the place, they accepted that the suspects were gone. Behind a building that looked like some kind of metal fabrication workshop, they noticed a gap in the wire fence that must have aided their escape.

Fisher had phoned dispatch immediately upon discovering the two injured constables, asking for assistance. Dispatch advised that several cars had been sent to the area after Fisher had given her brief descriptions of the escapees, but she wasn't holding her breath.

She and Phillips returned to the factory, where more police cars and ambulances were parked. Richard Scott was handcuffed and placed in the back of an Astra with his hands behind his back. Fisher met his gaze as she passed by, giving him a small smile, then she nodded to PC Baan beside the car. Another PC sat in the driver's seat, waiting for instructions to take him back to the station.

Near the single door where they'd initially entered the factory, Fisher saw Inspector Thorne and DI James standing, discussing something between themselves. They strangely fell silent when they heard her footsteps lightly crunching on the icy ground and turned to her.

'Where are the paramedics?'

DI James nodded. 'They're inside, looking at Patricia.'

'The bastards are still out there, though,' Thorne stated, shaking his head in disbelief.

Fisher acknowledged Inspector Thorne with a bob of her head, but passed them, entering the threshold of the factory with Phillips. They made their way to the studded room where she'd spotted Patricia from the suspended metal walkway, accessed from the other side of the factory.

Making her way through the room, it appeared from the unfinished boarded walls that it was purpose-built for whatever had gone on here today.

Had all the other victims faced the same fate — being subjected to these games with a crowd watching? The thought filled her mind as she stepped through the open door into the second room. Up ahead, she could see another two open doors, through which she could see Patricia Keeton lying on the ground, assisted by two paramedics leaning over her. But her concentration switched to something else.

'What the hell is this, April?'

Fisher acknowledged Phillips's question but didn't reply, only frowning at the big box before them. It appeared to be glass but was opaque, so they couldn't see inside. On one side was a hole, the other three sides were solid.

'God knows,' she muttered, pulling out a torch from her inside jacket pocket and leaning towards the hole with her face. She switched on the thin but powerful flashlight and raised the beam to the small opening.

'Be careful, April,' Phillips advised her.

'Don't worry, I won't be putting my hand inside.'

Keeping a distance, she studied the contents.

'Jesus . . .'

Phillips frowned and edged closer. 'What? What is it?'

'Here, have a look.' Stepping away, making room for him to check it out, she handed him the light. He peered in curiously.

'God . . . if she'd have put her hand in there?'

The inside was covered in long-bladed razors fixed at all different angles. Whatever the device was, it would have caused unbearable pain for Patricia if she'd reached that particular room.

Phillips moved away from the box. 'Just glad we saved her, and he's been caught.' They both looked through the open doors to their right, seeing the paramedics again. 'Come on, we'll check on her, see how she is.'

In the room at the end, the detectives observed Patricia in the foetal position, covered in a thick blanket, atop a thin foil sheet laid out to keep her off the icy concrete surface.

One of the paramedics, a female with short dark hair in her early forties, turned to them on their slow, measured approach. 'Hey.' She had a small piercing just above her right eyebrow.

'Hey,' Fisher said, then formally introduced herself and Phillips. 'How is she doing?'

'She's cold. We need to get her to the hospital as soon as possible. There're no obvious broken bones, but we need to take her in to make sure.'

Fisher nodded in understanding.

'Whatever happened here,' the paramedic said, indicating the several rooms with her finger, 'I'm glad you stopped it.'

Fisher smiled thinly, thinking the same.

'Ahh, here he is,' she said, looking beyond Fisher and Phillips at the male paramedic carrying a portable stretcher by his side, gently laying it beside Patricia. The paramedics placed her on top, then cautiously stood, making their way out of the room.

The detectives watched them leave and Fisher made a mental note to check in with Ms Keeton in a few hours to make sure she was okay. They stared at the empty chair that Patricia was in when they first arrived. It seemed like the game's purpose was for the victim to make it to the first room, or from their perspective, the last, because they must have been carried or forced through the other rooms to get there. The walls were high, lined with thick plasterboard

— definitely too high to climb, even if the victim was tall, strong, and fit.

'You think all this happened to the others?'

Fisher silently considered his question, thinking something similar, but without physically being there, they'd only know for sure when they interrogate Richard Scott down at the station.

It wasn't long before Pamela Boone arrived and had taken multiple samples from blood patches found in the first three rooms. The chances of the DNA matching with the library victims were good and would be sent away immediately. The thought of finding blood that didn't belong to the library victims had crossed Fisher's mind, meaning there could be more victims waiting to be discovered.

They continued searching the factory over the next few hours. Because of its size, DI James had requested help from another department to search it. PC Baan was still there, along with PC Jackson, exploring the far end for anything that didn't belong. Fisher and Phillips were up in the room where Richard Scott had been, where they checked through a computer system linked up with several cameras and other audio and recording equipment.

'Whoever this guy is, he knows what he's doing.'

Fisher didn't reply to Phillips's comment and continued rifling through the desk drawers with gloved hands. They heard footsteps in the doorway, and looked up to see PC Baan standing with something in her hand. The object was metallic and caught the shine off the lights coming from the ceiling.

'April,' she said, then raised her hand to show her the object. 'Found something at the other end of the factory. Just under the walkway where the others escaped from. It could have fallen from one of them.'

Fisher wandered over and softly took hold of it. It didn't take her long to realise where she'd seen it before.

CHAPTER 74

By the time DS Fisher and DS Phillips returned to the station, it was almost 11 p.m. They went into the quiet, eerie office. The nightshift personnel were out and about, patrolling the streets and dealing with the weekend mayhem somewhere in the city, leaving only a couple of PCs sitting at random desks. Friday and Saturday evenings were the busiest nights by far. However, with so much going on in Manchester, it was safe to say there wasn't an easy shift in this busy city. The weekend just brought out the drunken side of some people, adding further challenges to those who chose to work in the police and emergency services.

They went through a door and sauntered down a corridor side by side, both looking tired, dark semi-circles lining their eyes. Phillips appeared noticeably worse, his skin dry and pasty looking. He slowed his pace, falling behind her step.

'You holding up okay?'

He nodded, but it lacked confidence. 'A little light-headed, that's all.'

'You had enough to drink?'

Another faint nod. 'Where are the others?'

'DI James sent them home, remember? They've been out all day and most of the night.'

He smiled as they approached the closed door at the end of the corridor, motioning with his hand to allow Fisher through first. They walked a few paces and then stopped at the door on the left.

'Hopefully, this won't take too long,' she said, taking a deep breath, fighting the exhaustion herself — it had certainly been a long, arduous day. She turned to Phillips. 'You spoke to Janice?'

'Sent her a text before.' He smiled thinly, assuming by now her patience was wearing thin.

Fisher knocked twice and opened the door. Inside was Richard Scott, sitting down with slouched shoulders and staring at the middle of the wooden table in front of him. Opposite him was PC Amy Legg, who was working nights. She turned to them, smiled, and stood to make way. Richard Scott glared at Fisher, who took the lead and sat directly opposite him, matching his cold stare. Phillips dropped into the seat next to her. They thanked PC Legg before she exited the room, closing the door behind her.

To their right was a recording device. Fisher nodded at Phillips, who then leaned over and pressed the record button.

'This is Detective Sergeant April Fisher with Detective Sergeant Matthew Phillips of the Greater Manchester Police. We are interviewing our suspect, Richard Scott, who's been arrested for multiple accounts of first-degree murder and grievous bodily harm. The time is 11.12 p.m., and the date is 16 December 2022. Mr Scott has chosen not to be represented by a solicitor. He has agreed to conduct this interview by himself. Mr Scott, are you still happy to proceed?'

He stayed silent.

'Mr Scott?' persisted Fisher, staying calm.

'I'm happy to proceed,' he replied, smiling.

'That's terrific.' Fisher faked a smile, then became serious again. 'So, quite an interesting little crusade you've been having?'

'Not interesting enough.'

'How so?'

'There were more to go . . .'

'Well, guess we're lucky we caught you just in time, then.'

'But you've let four people die,' he said, grinning again. '*Four people.*'

DS Phillips sighed heavily, battling his will to lean over and grab the man around the throat with his big, strong hands, and decided to let Fisher lead this one.

'Yes, that is unfortunate.' Fisher nodded, breaking eye contact for a moment. 'Never mind.'

Silence filled the room until Fisher moved the interview on. 'So, as you can guess, we have several questions for you. Questions I believe which are in your best interest to answer, that will hugely affect what happens to you.'

Richard Scott rolled his eyes. 'The usual speech, then? Whether I say nothing or tell you everything, there's not much chance I'll be walking the streets anytime soon.'

'That's true, Mr Scott,' agreed Fisher. 'But if there's any decency left in there, I'm sure you'll do your best to make this go as easy as possible.'

He considered her request, rocking back slightly, but didn't indicate if he was going to play ball.

Fisher proceeded. 'Mr Scott, can you explain why you murdered Debbie Johnson, Mary Steadman, Callum McCauley, and Steve Adams?'

'They deserved it.'

'Why?' Fisher titled her head.

'For what they did to my brother,' he told them. 'I know you've done your research. I know you're aware of my brother, Mason, that he committed suicide two years ago. And I know you're aware of what happened to him on that camping trip when he was back in school.'

Fisher and Phillips stayed silent, waiting patiently for more, but he didn't respond.

'And do you believe their actions were enough to warrant their murder? Enough reason for you to kill them?'

He nodded firmly. 'I do, yes. What happened to him that night, and even in the years before and after it, ruined

339

our family. The stupid, thoughtless, bullying bastards had no idea what it did to him. If there's one thing in this world I fucking hate, it's a bully, let alone a group of them — it's even worse!' He brought his cuffed hands up from his knee and banged the desk, then lowered them out of sight again.

Neither detective reacted to his anger.

'How did you do it? Please talk us through it.' Fisher nodded again, maintaining eye contact to encourage him and keep him talking.

'I never finished school like Mason did. I struggled, and because of my behaviour I was home-schooled. Apparently, I was unteachable in a classroom environment, always disrupting others and fighting with people. My parents were pissed off, but in the end, they knew it was for the best. I heard about the issues Mason was having at school. The constant bullying. The way I used to see him hiding in his room after school and what he was like in the mornings before he went. You see, Mason was different. He didn't mix very well; he preferred to cut out the bullshit of life and sit and read, get his entertainment that way. Our parents constantly worried and really tried to help him. He even went to a counsellor, which seemed to help for a little while at school, but after what happened on the camping trip, the way his face was because of the burns, things just went downhill. He didn't even leave his room, then when he did, it was with a stupid ant mask he'd got from somewhere. He put on weight, and people started calling him Fat Ant Man.'

He fell silent a moment to collect the depressing thoughts as if going back and reliving them in his own mind. Fisher and Phillips watched him unravel and waited for more.

'Later on he had a breakdown and cut himself up. Then he somehow ended up seeing the posts online and showed them to me. The bullying bastards had made a website to make fun of him. And that's when he committed suicide. I was so fucking angry at them for what they'd done.' His face became physically red. 'I couldn't let them live. Can I have a drink of water, please?'

Fisher nodded, plucked her phone from her pocket, and dialled PC Legg. 'It's coming now.'

'So, because Mason loved reading, I thought the best way to humiliate them was to kill them and showcase their heads in libraries around this great city.' He grinned, nodding at his words. 'I think Mason would have liked that.'

'Do you think in your heart Mason would have agreed with what you've done?' The question came from Phillips this time.

'Absolutely not, Detective Phillips.' He turned his body towards him. 'Mason was the most kind-hearted person in this world, and because of that, I couldn't let it go. I believe the world has its own checks and balances, and removing those horrible people was something I needed to do.'

'So you got a job as a maintenance man for the council?'

He nodded at Fisher. 'I did. There was an advert in the paper.' He shrugged. 'I thought it would be a good way to access the libraries. It turns out there were no requirements for maintenance men at the library, but I strongly suggested, "being the bookworm I am"—' he brought his cuffed hands up and used inverted commas with his fingers — 'that the libraries needed more care and I'd be willing to offer that. After a while, I was trusted with keeping them going, fixing issues like toilet seats and taps. It all fell into place, really.'

'So, what about the victims?'

'Well, that was even easier. Do you know how easy it is to find people nowadays?' His eyes widened at the statement. 'Just go online or type in any search engine. I found an old school photo of Mason and his class, obviously finding their surnames. Everything else fell into place. Once I knew who they were, I studied them one by one, found out where they worked, where they ate, what gym they went to, and when the time was right, I got them.'

'Then what happened — at the factory, there seemed to be a little game set up?'

He started to laugh, rocking his head back. 'Well, I couldn't let them go too easily, could I? That wouldn't be fair, would it?' His smile vanished as his eyes became darker. 'Yes, we had a little game with them. Each started in the first room, with a task to complete before moving on to the next one. Their only issue is that they'd never get to the fourth room. But they didn't know that.'

'By "we", you mean . . . ?'

'Their audience,' he replied. 'The figures you saw.'

'Who were they?'

He giggled a little. 'Now, come on, I can tell you what I've done, but I can't tell you everything.'

Before Fisher replied, the door opened and in stepped PC Amy Legg, who gave them a tight-lipped smile in an apology for interrupting the interview. She leaned into Fisher and whispered something.

'Thanks, Amy.' A moment after PC Legg left the room, Fisher stood. 'Interview terminated at 11.37 p.m.'

'Where are you going?' Scott asked her, frowning at the sudden interruption.

'We have other more important matters to deal with.' She turned, headed for the door. 'Enjoy your time in prison, Richard.'

CHAPTER 75

Fisher decided to drive herself and headed straight for the exit door. Before they reached it, Phillips said, 'What did Amy say?'

'Exactly what we thought earlier. I asked her to check the place out to see what came back.'

He nodded, said nothing further, and pushed the release button for the door and held it open for Fisher to walk through first. Once they were inside her Volvo XC90, glad to be out of the sub-zero temperatures, she turned to him.

'You need to let Janice know you'll be late.' Her tone was soft, caring.

He gave her a slow shake of the head. 'Whether I go home now or in two hours, she'll be asleep, so it makes no difference, really.'

She smiled sadly, concerned for her partner's relationship with his fiancée. It was a demanding job most of the time and, in one way, not having a man in her life often worked out better; she claimed she wouldn't have the time anyhow.

They set off in the direction of the address they were heading to, being trailed by a couple of marked cars. The time on the clock was just after 11.30 p.m., the city as busy as it usually was for that time of night. They passed a few police cars going in the opposite direction, no doubt dealing with some drunk causing a scene somewhere.

'I can't believe this,' he said quietly, reflecting on what PC Legg had whispered to her moments earlier in the interrogation room.

She turned briefly to him. 'Hmm?'

'I really didn't see this coming.'

'You and me both.'

Approximately seven minutes later, they pulled up outside the house, very slowly coming to a halt. Fisher parked the Volvo in one of the only remaining spots in the street, so the two marked cars drove to the end of the street and found a spot there. Fisher and Phillips waited for the four PCs to join them before getting out, stepping down onto the shimmering, icy path. They were fortunate the street was well lit, aiding their vision, but it would be a disadvantage if anyone looked out of their windows and noticed their approach.

The driveway, as they assumed, was empty, only confirming their suspicions about who was involved. There was no doubt in their minds they'd try and lay low for a while. There was a chance they wouldn't be at home, knowing their car was still parked at the factory, and they knew that going back to collect it would be suicide. The whole house sat in darkness, but a gentle glow through the glass in the front door indicated a light on at the rear of the house, possibly the kitchen.

'Hey,' said Fisher to one of the familiar PCs, who'd recently transferred from Brighton. He hadn't worked with either Fisher or Phillips yet, so they didn't feel they knew him well enough to call him by his first name. 'PC Aitken?'

He nodded, his face stern, his body ready, slightly turned. 'What's the plan?' He held the battering ram firmly in his hands, ready for whatever instruction the DSs were about to give him. They'd been told he was the best door breacher on the force, and possessed superb hand-to-hand combat ability, according to his old reports from the Brighton management team during his transfer.

'Feeling strong?'

Under the bright white lights of the streetlamps, Fisher saw a smile flash across his face before he nodded and moved past her with his chest out. She then turned to PC Amy Legg and the other PCs who were working nights. 'Get your batons and spray ready. We don't know what's in there.'

With the time approaching midnight, they quickly readied themselves with their weapons and Fisher directed two of them down the side of the house in case they tried to escape out the back. They understood their task and quietly trotted down the dark path out of sight. PC Legg and the detectives strolled down the driveway towards the white PVC door, where the strong-looking Aitken was standing close to the step, ready with the ram. He looked back at Fisher, who gave him a firm nod. PC Legg kept her distance while he drew back the heavy weapon and brought it forward with so much force, the door's structure crumbled and swung inward on the first go, bouncing into the wall with a loud thud that rattled the whole house.

'Go, go, go!' she told them, pointing into the hallway. PC Aitken dropped the ram and went in first, closely followed by Fisher, Phillips, and PC Legg.

'Police, police, police!' Aitken shouted, his voice projecting through the house. They followed him in, keeping close, watching for any movement as they shifted into the darkness. Once inside, they could see a door almost closed at the end of the hallway, giving just enough light through the small gap to enable them to see where they were going. They assumed it to be the kitchen.

'Police, is there anyone there?'

There was no reply in the house, other than the sound of their own footsteps.

Fisher took the lead, holding Aitken back, before opening the door into what she realised was the kitchen. Inside, standing near the worktop with a look of horror on their faces, were the people she expected to see. There was a suitcase on the floor, multiple folded items, a washbag, and a thin sheath of paperwork on the kitchen table.

'Going somewhere, are we?' Fisher asked, smiling at them.

CHAPTER 76

Charles, Jackie, and Julie Scott glared at Fisher, Phillips, and Aitken as they burst into the kitchen with batons clenched tightly in their fists.

'Going anywhere nice?' added Phillips, eyeing the half-filled suitcase and items on the table. 'Hope it's warmer than here.'

Jackie and Julie remained frozen to the spot, but Charles turned and darted to the left, grabbed a large kitchen knife, and pointed it at them. The detectives focused on him, seeing the long blade in his grasp.

Fisher raised a hand. 'Now, come on, Mr Scott. It doesn't have to be this way. Please just put down the knife.'

The kitchen was silent but for Charles's heavy breathing. Jackie turned to her husband, eyeing him carefully. Their daughter Julie had taken a step back and covered her mouth with trembling hands, watching the scene unfold.

Fisher took a breath. 'Listen . . . you know we're only doing our job here. We just want to talk with you down at the station. You answer some questions, then we'll take it from there.'

Charles smirked a little, then slowly shook his head. 'I won't be going to the station with you.'

'There's no other way this can go,' explained Fisher.

'I'll bet the mortgage on this house there is,' he panted, his shoulders rising and falling with his short, frantic breaths.

Fisher and Phillips had been trained in these situations. There was a good chance that he'd grab either his wife or his daughter and hold them at knifepoint. Obviously, that would only buy a little time before the heavy artillery arrived — who had been informed via the red button on PC Amy Legg's radio — and took matters into their own hands. Fisher was confident they'd have it handled long before that happened.

Charles Scott still had the knife pointed towards them, standing slightly forward with his knees bent, ready to defend or attack. Fisher noticed Julie and Jackie move away inch by inch while Charles was switching his focus between Fisher, Phillips, and PC Aitken.

Fisher turned to Aitken and whispered, 'Go into the hallway, inform the others. Tell them to use the back door.'

'Hey!' Charles stabbed the air with the tip of the knife. 'What are you saying? What the fuck are you whispering about?'

Aitken nodded while keeping his eyes on Charles and backed into the hallway. He turned slightly to shield his message over the radio, telling the other PCs who were coming to use the back door if they could.

'Mr Scott, there are no options for you here.'

He swung the knife wildly in several arcs to keep them at bay, but they were a safe distance away. 'I'm telling you now, I'm not going with you. You'll have to come and get me.'

Fisher considered her response while his wife and daughter created further space between them, making her wonder if they didn't trust him with a knife. Did he have anger issues? Were they scared of him? Julie and Jackie had moved closer to the back door, over to the left, and Fisher spotted the two PCs through the pane of glass, the black outlines of their clothing dimly illuminated by the faint streetlights shining down the driveway.

'Just put down the knife, Charles!' begged Jackie. 'What are you going to do?'

He swivelled towards her, pointing the knife in her direction. 'One more word out of you, and you'll get this!'

Jackie yelped in fear, clinging to her daughter Julie, who appeared just as frightened.

'Please, Charles,' said Fisher softly. 'Put down the knife and gently kick it over.'

Julie and Jackie suddenly charged through the back door, and the two PCs pulled them outside, away from danger. With the door open, the sound of multiple sirens drifted in with the cold Manchester air, indicating that more help was close.

'Julie! Jackie!' Charles screamed, as the PCs restrained them on the ground outside. He charged towards the open back door with the knife.

'Shit!' muttered Fisher. If he got to the door before they did, there was no telling what he might do. She lunged at Charles, who moved fast for his age.

'April!' screamed Phillips. 'Wait!'

But Fisher was too focused on keeping the PCs safe from harm. Closing the gap, she met him at the open door, raised her baton as high as she could, and brought it down quickly, aiming for the arm which held the knife. She felt the impact as it hit his forearm inches from his wrist, and knew by his cry it had stung, causing him to drop the knife and stumble back into the side of a tall cupboard. The knife bounced and landed near his feet. Although off balance from the collision, Fisher raised the baton again, but Charles turned and threw a punch straight into her chin, rattling her for a moment. She reeled backwards, seeing a flash of stars.

'April!' shouted Phillips, bringing his extended baton down hard into the side of the old man's left knee. He did it three times until Charles buckled under his own weight, but Charles managed to get hold of the knife again and brought his hand up towards Phillips, who didn't hesitate to kick him in the face with the sole of his shoe, knocking Charles out cold. He slumped against the cupboard and slid to the floor in a heap.

'Jesus Christ!' said Fisher, holding her chin, then going for him again. 'That mother—'

'Stop, stop, stop!' declared Phillips, grabbing her arm and pulling her close. 'He's out, he's out.'

Moments later, an army of police turned up wearing stab vests, ready with weapons in their hands.

Fisher smiled at them. 'Oh, and now you turn up?'

CHAPTER 77

By the time Charles, Julie, and Jackie Scott were arrested and placed in three separate police vans, DI James had told DS Fisher and DS Phillips to go home. They'd been working nearly sixteen hours, and one night in the holding cells wouldn't make a difference before the suspects were interviewed early the next day.

'Go home, see your families.'

The phrase was aimed at Phillips more so than Fisher, but she didn't fight it, happy to be relieved and given a chance to go home, shower, and fall into bed. It was almost 1.30 a.m. when she pulled up outside her house on St Nicholas Road. As expected, the street was dark, full of parked cars, and quiet. She stepped down onto the icy path, shivering at the sub-zero temperatures, the thought of a hot shower like a stairway to heaven. There was a hum of noise coming from the city centre — the bars, pubs, and nightclubs filled to capacity. She smiled as she opened her front door, the thought of being in the midst of all that chaos worse than a nightmare. She was so tired, she decided to skip the shower and go straight to bed.

* * *

It was just before 8 a.m. when she opened her eyes and checked her phone. She'd never slept in that late before.

She shuffled up into a sitting position and swung her legs off the bed. Turning on the shower and stepping in, she rushed her usual shower routine and got dressed quickly, cursing to herself.

Her phone displayed two text messages from DS Phillips when she picked it up.

One read: *Morning, you close by? We're waiting to interview them.*

The other said: *April?? Wakey wakey . . .*

She phoned Phillips, explaining she'd be there soon. He joked that DI James wouldn't be happy, but they both knew he wouldn't say anything. Because she'd set off a little later, it took longer, and she reached the office just after 9 a.m.

'Someone sleep in?'

The sarcasm came from the woman sitting behind the reception desk. Fortunately, they were on friendly terms; Fisher still felt exhausted and wasn't in the mood for jokes today. She had wanted to be there first to interview the Scotts, so in her mind, the day had got off to a bad start.

Reaching the interview room with a coffee in her hand a few minutes later, Fisher stepped inside. They planned to interview Charles, Jackie, and Julie individually to see if their stories matched or if there were any discrepancies. They had been separated overnight, so they couldn't collaborate on any strategy or say something planned.

Sitting at the table opposite DS Phillips was Julie Scott, the daughter of Charles and Jackie. Once Fisher sat, they spoke about what had been happening. Julie told them she was aware of the library killings.

'What about the games?'

'The games?' Julie frowned innocently.

'At the warehouse?' persisted Fisher. 'Where you watched the victims die. You know — Debbie Johnson, Mary Steadman, Steve Adams, and Callum McCauley. And almost Patricia Keeton, if you hadn't been stopped.'

Her frown deepened. 'I have absolutely no idea what you're referring to, Detective.'

Fisher pushed out her bottom lip for a second. 'You're sure?'

Julie shrugged. 'No idea at all.'

Fisher leaned in and opened her file. 'Interesting comment.' The first page was a photo of Julie Scott with some basic information. The next document consisted of images taken the night before by a security camera positioned outside a factory close to where they had found Patricia Keeton and Richard Scott. The photos had been sent in earlier that morning by email.

'And what are these meant to be?' said Julie.

Fisher rotated the document 180 degrees and pointed. 'You see her?'

She nodded. 'Yeah. Who's that?'

'That's you, running away with Mam and Dad.'

Julie's mouth opened like she'd been told something utterly ridiculous. 'Are you joking?'

'Please, Julie, save the act. We don't have much time here today, so let's just get to the end.' Fisher stabbed the photo again. 'This is you!'

'How can you prove that?'

Fisher smiled, expecting that comment, then picked up the sheet of paper and moved it to one side to reveal the next. 'Because two streets away, you removed the masks, and as you can see, it's clear as day. Unless you three all have twins.'

Julie knew she was busted.

'So, anything to add, Julie?'

'I want a lawyer.'

'Thought you might.'

* * *

A little while later, PC Baan brought Jackie in, holding her forearm, guiding her to the seat opposite the detectives.

'Thanks, Ash,' said Fisher.

Once Baan had left, she explained they'd spoken with Julie, and she'd confirmed everything they already knew, so they wouldn't tolerate any bullshit.

'I have nothing to say to you. I want a lawyer.'

* * *

Without wasting much time, Charles Scott was brought in with PC Jackson and PC Baan. He directed a cold stare at Fisher and Phillips as he rounded the table and was helped to his seat, Baan's hand pushing down on his shoulder.

Baan nodded at the PCs. 'Thanks, you two.'

'So, the mastermind behind the whole charade, eh?' said Phillips.

Charles frowned, switching his focus between them. '*Mastermind* — isn't that a TV show?'

Both detectives grinned.

'Mr Scott,' Fisher began, 'what can you tell us about what's been going on?' She raised a quick hand. 'And before you start, we know you were there last night at the factory because, one—' she held out her thumb — 'we have you, Jackie, and Julie on camera running away. Two—' she extended her index finger — 'we found your gold watch on the ground just near the exit. And three—' her middle finger extended to stress the final point — 'we know the factory belongs to you. You own the bloody place.'

Charles Scott's eyes widened as if in shock at what he'd been told, and for a moment, he was lost for words.

'Not to mention your car was parked there too.'

He smiled.

'Well?'

'I'm not saying anything further without a lawyer.'

'Same old hymn around here, that one.' Fisher stood.

'Where's my son?'

'Richard, unlike the rest of you, has been honest about everything. He's told us what he did, how he did it, and why — under his own strange justification, of course. Nevertheless, we'll get you a lawyer. Seems like you'll be here for a long time, just like your son.'

CHAPTER 78

After all the interviews were complete, they'd learned that each of them had played a part in watching the games and had fully supported Richard Scott in his quest to avenge Mason's suicide. They said they'd do it all again and didn't show a moment of remorse.

DI James, who'd watched the interviews through the one-way glass, commended both of them for their clever questions and for getting the right information, and ordered both Fisher and Phillips to go home. Phillips didn't take much convincing after the earful he'd got from Janice earlier that morning before he left to attend another weekend shift. Still, he promised it wouldn't take long, and for once, he was right and was home before lunchtime.

On the other hand, Fisher didn't have much on and told DI James she could stay a while, but he insisted she needed a break, informing her before she left that what happened would be on the news shortly, so the whole world would know.

Before she left his office, he said, 'April . . .'

She stopped at the open door and turned.

'You and Phillips have both done amazingly these last couple of weeks. I'm very proud at how you've conducted yourselves.'

'Thank you, sir,' she replied, then turned for the door.

* * *

Fisher spent her afternoon, like thousands of others, in the warmth of her own home, sitting in front of the television, watching and listening to the press conference. This time DI James had chosen to do it, telling the public about what had happened and the final victim count. He detailed the lucky escape for Patricia Keeton, who was still recovering in hospital. He informed the press about Richard Scott and the members of his family that were involved, adding that the courts would hand out the prison sentences they felt necessary for their crimes.

Once it had finished, Fisher sat in silence, her eyes feeling heavy, which was unusual for late afternoon. She couldn't even be bothered to pick up her phone from the coffee table and check her socials, but when it rang, she pushed herself up from her slouched position and saw who was calling. It was a number she didn't have saved.

'Hello?' she answered, frowning.

'DS April Fisher?'

'Speaking . . .'

'Hello, hello,' the voice said quickly. 'I'm very sorry to bother you, but it's Lisa Andrews from Chorlton High School. Do you remember you came to see me about Mason Scott?'

Fisher sat up straighter, her tired frown deepening. 'I do, yes. What can I do for you?'

'Well, you left your card and said to ring any time.'

'I did.' Fisher sighed. It was the last thing she wanted to do today. 'How can I help you?'

'I've just seen the news about what's been happening — oh my goodness, Detective, it's awful.'

'It is . . .'

'And is it true about poor Patricia — did you save her?'

'I shouldn't really be discussing this with you, Mrs Andrews, I—'

'Please, Detective, just tell me quickly — you saved her from those monsters?'

'Yes, we did. We saved her.'

'Thank you for doing that. I . . .' She sighed and fell quiet for a few moments. 'I was relieved to hear she wasn't a victim and is recovering in hospital. What they did to Mason didn't really involve her as much. She was in the wrong crowd, I think. God, I'll get her some flowers or something.'

'I'm sure she'll appreciate that, Mrs Andrews.'

'Well, sorry for ringing again, Detective. I just wanted to say thank you.'

'It's my job. You have a great day now.' Fisher hung up before the teacher could reply and tiredly threw her phone down. 'I need my bed.'

Just as she was getting up, her phone rang again. She sighed heavily and saw on the screen an incoming call from her best friend, Kim. Wanting to ignore it, she couldn't help herself answering.

'Hey, Kim.'

'April, where have you been? It's an age since we've spoken.' Fisher couldn't remember their last conversation. All she could think about was her bed.

'You know, just busy with work and things. We cracked the case.'

'Great, well done. Well, I have some news for you too.'

'You do? What's that?' Fisher stood and ambled in small circles in the living room, feeling a headache forming at the front of her skull.

Kim went on to mention a date she'd been on, but Fisher, at that moment, was too exhausted to care. 'And he's loaded too.'

'That's great, Kim. As long as he treats you right, that's all that matters.'

'So, I was thinking, you want to go out tonight? Been a little while. I'm going out with a couple of friends and would like you to meet them.'

Fisher pondered the question, but realising Kim was out regardless of her being there, she didn't feel bad saying no, but she promised next time.

'Okay, your loss,' replied Kim. 'Let me know if you change your mind.'

I definitely won't, thought Fisher as she left the living room and went upstairs to bed.

CHAPTER 79

'Who are *they* for?' the man asked, walking into the kitchen just before 5 p.m.

Lisa Andrews looked away from the food she was preparing and down at the flowers and chocolates she'd bought from the local supermarket. 'Oh, these?' He nodded. 'These are for an old student. You know the thing on the news earlier?' Another nod. 'Well, I used to teach her. She's recovering in hospital as we speak.'

'And you're going to see her? With flowers?'

'I am. She was a lovely student who was caught up in the wrong crowd. I'm glad she's okay.' She looked up at the red, oblong-shaped clock on the kitchen wall. 'I won't be long. The hospital's only ten minutes away. I'll get tea made and be back within the hour.'

Her husband slowly shook his head and left the kitchen, settling back into his chair in the living room to watch the roundup of the day's football results.

Lisa, with the flowers and chocolates in her hand, said bye to him and left the house, locking the door on her way out. They always locked the door, something they'd done since some random homeless man walked in just over ten years ago, asking for money. Opening her gate, she almost slipped on the black ice lining the path.

'Jesus!' she gasped, managing to grab the wall before falling.

She got into her car, placed the flowers and chocolates on the passenger seat, and set off in the direction of the hospital. With Christmas coming next week, the city would be busier than usual with the influx of people outside of Manchester visiting places like the Trafford Centre, a popular place even outside the festive period.

After parking in a street close to Manchester Royal Infirmary, she walked into reception and approached a young, twenty-something woman with long blonde hair and small square glasses.

The woman looked up at her. 'Hi, can I help you?' Her voice was gentle.

'Good afternoon.' Lisa smiled. 'I'm here to see Patricia Keeton.'

The receptionist looked back at the computer screen. A moment later, she gazed up. 'Can I ask who you are?'

'Yes, of course. I'm an old teacher of hers. I heard what happened on the news and spoke with Detective Fisher from the police. I'm just making sure she's okay.'

The receptionist smiled at the gesture. She told her the floor and room number where Patricia Keeton was and wished Mrs Andrews a nice day.

'Thank you,' she said, walking along the corridor towards the lifts.

Lisa stepped out of the lift on the fourth floor and took a right, approaching a set of double doors. She pressed a button on the wall, shortly followed by someone saying, 'Hello, can I help?'

'I'm here to see Patricia Keeton in room fourteen, please.'

A buzzing sound rang out, and Lisa went through, taking another right after reading the sign on the wall indicating rooms 8 to 16 were in that direction. The corridor was a hive of activity, with nurses walking back and forth, focusing on clipboards in their hands. She passed a desk on her right, where a nurse in her fifties with short grey hair and glasses that enhanced the blue in her eyes gazed up with a smile.

Room 14 was a single room. The only occupant was Patricia, who lay on a single adjustable bed in the corner, the length of the bed against the wall on the right. Next to her were a drip stand, with multiple wires and hoses, and a bedside shelf with a jug of water and a half-filled white plastic cup.

Patricia was sleeping, snoring lightly.

'Oh, Patricia. It's so very good to see you again.'

* * *

Fisher looked at Phillips and slowly nodded before he leaned in and opened the door. They both had their batons out, and behind them, PC Baan and PC Jackson stood at the ready. The factory was cold and dark, but the small amount of light from the centre caught their attention. Fisher had to make sure no one else was nearby, searching the area with her eyes and not her torch. The last thing they needed was to attract any attention.

'You go first,' she told Phillips, who stepped inside and approached the studded room where the light was coming from. Fisher trailed him, followed by Baan and Jackson. Above the room, standing on a metal suspended walkway, were four figures, all wearing masks.

Suddenly, Fisher woke in her bed, sweating profusely, her heart beating so hard she could feel it in her chest. Her hair and skin were saturated. She was glad to be in her own bed, realising the vivid scene in her mind was only a dream. She swung her legs around, her feet resting on the carpet, and sat in deep thought for a moment.

She leaned over to grab her phone from the bedside table and noticed the time was just before 6 p.m. She phoned DS Phillips.

He answered with a tired, 'Hey, April.'

'Hey, sorry to ring again. I know you're home and I shouldn't be calling about anything work-related.'

'It's fine, April, we've just finished our tea. What's up?'

'You know when we went to the factory last night?'

'Yeah?'

'Were there three suspects or four?'

Phillips remained silent, thinking about it. 'I'm not sure. Three people were running away on the camera footage we received.'

'I know, but who's to say the fourth one, if there was one, didn't go in another direction? Maybe none of the cameras picked that up?'

'I suppose that's possible. What you thinking?'

Fisher's eyes opened wide as the thought flooded her. 'Matthew, we need to head to the hospital ASAP. I think I know who the fourth figure was.'

CHAPTER 80

Almost a year ago

Charles Scott opened his front door, the cold of the winter chill seeping in. Standing on the step was a woman who appeared to be in her mid-fifties. She looked familiar.

'Can I help you?' he asked, frowning.

'You can. I'm Mrs Andrews. I used to teach your son Mason at Chorlton High School years ago.'

He smiled sadly. 'If you're looking for Mason, I'm sorry to tell you he isn't here. He's . . .'

'I know about Mason and what happened. That's why I'm here.'

His frown softened, and he stepped aside. 'Come on in.'

He led her to the kitchen and they sat at the table. Jackie Scott came down in a dressing gown, wondering who was at the door, and saw the back of Mrs Andrews's head.

'Who's this?'

'You remember Mrs Andrews from Chorlton High School?'

The teacher turned to her, smiling lightly.

'Oh, of course. Mrs Andrews. What . . . what are you doing here?'

'I found something you really need to see.'

Jackie and Charles Scott sat at the table while Mrs Andrews showed them the website about Mason Scott, about him being labelled as the Fat Ant Man. Tears streamed down Jackie's face, whereas Charles' face turned red in anger.

'I don't believe this . . .' he said, his words almost clogging his throat.

'Why? Why are you showing us this?' asked Jackie.

'Because something needs to be done,' explained the teacher. 'We can't let them get away with this.'

CHAPTER 81

Patricia Keeton opened her eyes and saw Mrs Andrews standing at her bedside, staring down on her.

'Hey, Patricia.'

She frowned at Mrs Andrews. 'Do . . . do I know you?'

'You used to.' She smiled. 'I was your teacher in Chorlton years ago. Mrs Andrews is my name.'

Patricia tiredly nodded, recognising her now. 'Oh, Miss. What are you doing here?'

'I saw what happened on the news and I'm here to make sure you're okay. It was an awful thing what they did to you, Patricia.' Andrews smiled thinly and grabbed her hand, giving it a tight squeeze. 'I've brought you flowers and chocolates.'

'Thank you. I'm not in the mood for eating just yet but thank you.'

There was an awkward silence between the two, the teacher staring into her eyes for a long time.

'Everything okay, Miss?'

'It used to be.'

Patricia scowled. 'I don't understand.'

'What you lot did to Mason Scott was awful, utterly unforgivable. I saw the website you made and commented on. You should be ashamed of yourselves.'

Patricia looked down in embarrassment, her cheeks warming.

'You do know your comments caused his suicide, don't you?'

She kept her gaze on the floor, away from the angry teacher.

* * *

Downstairs in reception, Fisher and Phillips burst through the sliding doors and ran over to the reception desk. 'We need to know where Patricia Keeton is right now.'

PC Baan and PC Jackson came through too, seeing them at the desk.

The woman looked at them with a scowl. 'I'm sorry?' Then focused on Baan and Jackson. 'What's going on?'

'Patricia Keeton. Floor and room number, ASAP. She could be in danger.' To move things on, Fisher flashed the receptionist her ID. 'Come on, I'm with the police. It's important.'

They were told the floor and room number. 'Should I be calling security?'

'Yes! Send them to that room immediately.'

'Take the stairs. The lift can be slow,' she advised.

Fisher, Phillips, Baan, and Jackson all left the desk and pounded down the corridor, their heavy, quick feet slapping on the linoleum floor. They went past the lifts, opting for the stairs, and raced up to the fourth floor. Phillips was struggling with the intensity of it, unlike Fisher, who was barely panting from the inclined dash. At the double doors at the end of the corridor, Fisher frantically pressed the wall button and asked to be let in, explaining who she was and why she was there.

The door buzzed open, and they ran inside.

* * *

'What do you have to say for yourself, Patricia?' Lisa asked, now scowling down at her. She frowned, hearing commotion out in the corridor.

'I-I don't know . . .' Patricia's voice cracked in her throat, and she gulped.

Lisa placed the flowers and chocolates on the stand beside her bed, reached into the thick bouquet of white lilies, and pulled out a knife.

Patricia's eyes widened as she caught the glare from the lights above on the small blade. 'God . . .' She tried moving but was in too much pain.

'I'm sorry, Patricia, but there's no way I can let you get away with this. You've done enough damage.'

The teacher took a heavy, settling breath, and leaned closer to Patricia, who tried to wriggle away, squirming and twisting as the knife slowly came closer to her face.

'Now, hold on there. It'll be over soon.'

Andrews placed her left hand on Patricia's forehead to keep her as still as possible and brought the blade closer. Smiling, she pushed the tip of the knife into her throat but suddenly felt something grab her from behind, her arm being pinned back, and her body lifted up and away. Something hit her wrist, causing her to drop the knife, which pinged onto the floor.

* * *

As Phillips and Baan restrained Mrs Andrews, Fisher moved past them to check on Patricia, seeing blood oozing from the small cut to her throat. She quickly sat her up and grabbed a nearby sheet, wrapping it around her throat to catch the blood. A few minutes later, the room was filled with doctors and nurses, appalled at what had happened.

Mrs Andrews was arrested and removed from the ward, taken back down the lift in handcuffs, and put in the back of a police car.

Fisher sighed heavily, then fell into Phillips, wrapping her arms around him, her hands barely clinging to the other because of exhaustion. They both knew if they'd turned up a minute later, Patricia Keeton would be dead.

'I'm fucking glad this is over, Matthew,' she mumbled into his shoulder. 'I really am.'

EPILOGUE

After Mrs Andrews was interviewed and admitted her involvement in the murders of Debbie Johnson, Mary Steadman, Steve Adams, and Callum McCauley, she was given a lengthy sentence, one that would see her spending the rest of her time behind bars. Though she hadn't killed any of the victims herself, she did admit to being one of the masked figures, looking down on the victims and enjoying the outcomes of the sick games. She also acknowledged the whole thing was her idea, that she had gone to the Scotts' house about the website and the comments. Then Charles and Jackie had brought their son Richard into it, who had taken charge and put a plan in place. Safe to say none of them would be seeing daylight anytime soon.

DS Phillips sat down with Janice, who wanted to talk about a few things, primarily the amount of time he was giving to his job rather than his family. She told him that their son Dominic was missing him dearly. He explained to her that being a detective for the Greater Manchester Police came with a price, and that price was a hefty one; it meant doing more hours than he'd ever be financially compensated for or would ever be acknowledged.

DCI Baker commended the team for catching the suspects behind the library killings and bought DI James the most expensive bottle of whisky money could buy. He told Baker it was because of his team that they were able to solve the case, especially Fisher and Phillips, who had worked diligently until the case was solved and the killers behind bars.

Fisher was exhausted in the coming weeks, feeling the effects of her job and the demanding nature of the role. The thought had, for a split second, crossed her mind to quit the force and find something else, something more manageable, less burdening and chaotic, but she asked herself the question: would she be bored? This was all she'd ever done, everything she'd trained for. She knew, as well as others, she was very good at her job, so decided to stay put for now. Like her partner Phillips, the long hours, the working at home on her laptop, and the non-stop thinking had brought her almost to breaking point. And like Phillips, she had decided to take her foot off the gas a little, take some time to reflect and get away. So, with her sister Freya, she booked a holiday to Tenerife for some sun and time to put her feet up, rest her mind, and unwind. On her return, DI James called her into his office and told her that DCI Baker was moving on. James had been told if things went as they had been, there was a high chance he'd get the job, meaning there'd be a position open for DI. James told her she really had what it took and would be the ideal candidate if she was interested in the opportunity. Thanking him, she said she'd mull it over.

So for now, Fisher promised to make more time for herself, go to the cinema, listen to more music, see her favourite singers in concert, and enjoy life. She pondered maybe even getting herself a fellow to enjoy these things with. Then she shook her head and laughed; she knew better than that.

THE END

THE JOFFE BOOKS STORY

We began in 2014 when Jasper agreed to publish his mum's much-rejected romance novel and it became a bestseller.

Since then we've grown into the largest independent publisher in the UK. We're extremely proud to publish some of the very best writers in the world, including Joy Ellis, Faith Martin, Caro Ramsay, Helen Forrester, Simon Brett and Robert Goddard. Everyone at Joffe Books loves reading and we never forget that it all begins with the magic of an author telling a story.

We are proud to publish talented first-time authors, as well as established writers whose books we love introducing to a new generation of readers.

We won Trade Publisher of the Year at the Independent Publishing Awards in 2023. We have been shortlisted for Independent Publisher of the Year at the British Book Awards for the last four years, and were shortlisted for the Diversity and Inclusivity Award at the 2022 Independent Publishing Awards. In 2023 we were shortlisted for Publisher of the Year at the RNA Industry Awards.

We built this company with your help, and we love to hear from you, so please email us about absolutely anything bookish at: feedback@joffebooks.com.

If you want to receive free books every Friday and hear about all our new releases, join our mailing list: www.joffebooks. com/contact

And when you tell your friends about us, just remember: it's pronounced Joffe as in coffee or toffee!

www.ingramcontent.com/pod-product-compliance
Lightning Source LLC
Chambersburg PA
CBHW051321250626
47155CB00007B/2406